UNEASY LIES THE HEAD . . .

"Your Majesty," the Foreign Minister was saying, "it is not true that foreign confidence in us has been shaken. First of all, of course, you have the largest navy on the planet. People fear you, Your Majesty. And secondly, we isolated Smolen when we captured her coastline."

The king looked at the minister next in line. "And you, Dorskell, what have you to—"

He bit the words off in mid-sentence, for the Lord Chancellor had entered the room to stand quietly by the door. "What is it, Gorman?" Engwar said testily.

"Your Majesty, word has just come that enemy infiltrators have attacked our headquarters and destroyed it with explosives. The general has been injured, and many officers are dead."

Engwar II Tarsteng stared at the man. Such an act was incredible! Civilized people did not attack persons at high levels! "Is my cousin's life endangered by his injury?"

"They did not say so, Your Majesty."

"Well go ask them, dolt! Did you think I wouldn't want to know?"

"At once, Your Majesty," the man said, and left the room, Engwar glaring after him. The cabinet sat frozen by the news, and by Engwar's anger. After a moment, Engwar took his attention from the door and looked at the men around the table.

Before he could speak again, an explosion boomed, startling most of them to their feet. The M' balcony door, s uld see. And fel onto the floor, a fell, they heard t

Baen Books By John Dalmas

THE REGIMENT'S WAR

JOHN DALMAS

THE REGIMENT'S WAR

This is a work of fiction. All the characters and events portrayed in this book are fictional, and any resemblance to real people or incidents is purely coincidental.

A Baen Books Original

Baen Publishing Enterprises
P.O. Box 1403
Riverdale, N.Y. 10471
ISBN: 0-671-72155-0

Cover art by C.W. Kelly
First printing, February 1993

Distributed by
SIMON & SCHUSTER
1230 Avenue of the Americas
New York, N.Y. 10020

Printed in the United States of America

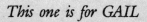
This one is for GAIL

Acknowledgments

I'd like to thank David Palter, Bill Bailie, and as always, Gail and Judy for reading and commenting on a preliminary draft of this manuscript.

I also want to thank Jack Jones, my black-belt son and eclectic martial artist, for reading the sections on hand-to-hand fighting.

Prologue

The audience room was richly fitted, its hangings dark, its light subdued. Centered in it, straight-backed before the throne, Ambassador Vilmur Klens didn't notice the buzz and click of cameras. His attention was totally on the king, who stood on the dais, reading the accusations in a loud, reedy voice. Klens had heard them before; they'd been read to him by a royal envoy on the day they'd been published. He'd then read and digested them himself before wiring them home. Now, a week later, he was hearing them from Engwar II Tarsteng himself.

Engwar's tone was merely petulant, but the malice in his glance turned Klens numb. When he'd finished reading the charges, he went on to read the appended ultimatum. An impossible ultimatum because the charges all were false: cynical and ruthless, lacking even a pretense of truth. Smolen had been given twenty-one days to deliver to Komarsi justice "those persons guilty of the outrages." Fifteen days now.

Engwar Tarsteng completed his reading, then rolled the parchment and slapped it against his plump palm, once, twice, a third time. If Engwar's reading had been loud and

1

reedy, his next words were almost purred. "I was generous," he said, "in giving your government twenty-one days. I should have realized that civilized deportment could not be expected from it. My sources assure me that it has made no slightest effort to comply. Instead you have mobilized your reserves, preparing to attack Komars."

Preparing to attack Komars! Did the vole attack the stoat? Vilmur Klens knew now what this meeting, this needless recitation was about, had to be about. Still emotionally numb, he felt the muscles of his chest and arms begin to twitch and tremble, and tried to control them.

The king put away his scowl. A smile curved his full lips, his remarkable cupid-bow mouth; he'd seen the trembling despite Klens's fashionably loose jacket. "Therefore," he went on, "I herewith declare that a state of war now exists between my country and yours, a war which shall not end until your evil, upstart republic has been prostrated, and its people properly punished!"

Engwar seemed to swell then. Two of his guards had stepped up beside Vilmur Klens. Now they grasped his arms roughly. Klens did not resist as they manacled him. The king continued, his voice rising further:

"You, as the representative of a vicious government, share its responsibility for this war, and for its costs-to-be in blood and treasure. Therefore I herewith arrest you in the name of the Crown of Komars, and of civilized states throughout the planet." For the first time, the Smoleni ambassador became aware of the busy cameras. Engwar shifted his attention to the officer who'd moved up beside one of the guards. "Lieutenant, I want this—criminal locked securely in the block. You know the cell."

He turned on his heel then, but as he left, he spoke to his lord chancellor, loudly enough for the room to hear: "Sixday would be nice for a public beheading, wouldn't you say?"

Part One

THE ASSIGNMENT

One

Colonel Artus Romlar lay listening behind a tree. There were many sounds. Just now, none seemed meaningful.

Insects buzzed and clicked and crawled. Sweat trickled. His shirt stuck to his back. He ignored them all. It was early spring in Oven's northern hemisphere, and the late morning temperature had risen well above a hundred. At least there was forest and shade, here in the Jubat Hills.

And the T'swa would be along soon. If he was wrong about that, he'd made a serious error.

Below him was a log landing on the Jubat Hills Railroad, a long strip of open ground used periodically for a rollway. The ground sloped downward at thirty to forty percent almost to the tracks, which here had been built along the bottom of a wide draw. Farther on, the draw became a steep-walled ravine; if the T'swa were going to detrain short of Tiiku Lod-Sei, this was the last good site.

The trick was to fool them into thinking he was somewhere else, hours away. Romlar considered he'd done that. The risk in *not* being at Junction 4 Village made it convincing. It was also the principal down side of his decision.

Regimental commanders don't customarily *lead* their

troops into firefights, but this fight would be pivotal, perhaps decisive. The situation had become increasingly critical, the overall odds poor. He'd long since consolidated the men he had left into two battalions. If he lost in this week's set of engagements, his regiment would be—not finished, perhaps, but so reduced as to lose much of its effectiveness. And the Condaros, the people who'd hired it, would be beaten beyond hope. On the other hand, winning here decisively could carry them a while longer, and give them some sort of chance.

Of course, the T'swa might not come. In that case, he'd left 2nd Battalion, along with his Condaro allies, in a precarious position to little avail. Though he still might be able to hit the Booly positions by surprise, and even the odds a bit. That was another reason he was leading 1st Battalion personally: Its commander, Coyn Carrmak was the best officer he had, but to Romlar's thinking, he had to be present at this action himself, to know the result promptly, and as fully as possible.

The T'swa would come though, reportedly a fresh regiment, full strength. All he had to do—*all he had to do!*—was beat it soundly, cut it up badly with relatively few casualties of his own.

Meanwhile the Booly 2nd Division was sure to hit Junction 4 and its village today, with its two regiments of Condaro defenders and his own 2nd Battalion. Might have hit them already. If he were there with 1st Battalion . . . But if the T'swa were allowed to intervene, there was no chance at all of pulling the fat from the fire.

There were many ways to lose this war. There might or might not be a way to win it.

Romlar didn't run all this through his mind now. It was there, had entered into his decisions, and that was enough. He had committed. Now he lay quietly relaxed, waiting and watching, alert without effort. He'd been through this before. It seemed his reason for being.

He heard the locomotive now, a laboring steam engine chuffing up the long grade. Assuming he'd judged right, and he felt ninety percent sure he had, the train would slow and stop just here below him, and the T'swa would start getting out of the open-sided wooden cars. He'd open fire when about half were still on the cars and half on the ground. If the engineer started the train moving again, he'd be abandoning the men already off, and besides, the terrain became difficult along the tracks ahead, even for T'swa.

No, they'd detrain here, then try to move back under fire, and that would spring the rest of his trap. They might well see it coming, but there'd be little they could do about it except fight furiously. Which in the case of the T'swa also meant intelligently and joyously. To them, too, fighting was fulfillment, the spice of life.

He could feel his troopers waiting. There was, of course, the danger that the T'swa would feel them too. But *he* felt them knowing they were there. They were relaxed, too imbued with the T'sel to be anxious. Thus the T'swa were unlikely to sense them. Except for the T'swa, there wasn't another fighting force in Confederation Space that could lie in wait like this and not be tense, not reek psychically. And except for the T'swa, he knew of no military force other than his that might detect that sort of thing.

The locomotive poked into sight, moving slowly, resinous woodsmoke issuing from the spark arrester on its stack. It wouldn't have to brake; the slope and the heavy gravity of Oven would stop it. With their typical energy and athleticism, T'swa began to pile out before the cars had totally stopped. Romlar leveled his bolt-action rifle and squeezed the trigger, and the ridge side to both his left and right erupted with fire—rifles, grenade launchers, and light machine guns all firing blanks.

Referees with the T'swa began to move up and down the line, shouting and pointing, and men "died"—lay down, rolled over. Others were returning fire, and the referees with Romlar's 1st Battalion went into action too. But Romlar's men had the advantages of position and cover. Some of the T'swa took cover behind the cars' steel trucks and chassis, while others backed down the slope toward the limited cover of the trees—backing toward the other jaw—two machine gun platoons.

The T'swa weren't really surprised to receive a new surge of fire from behind. The exchange continued noisy and intense; the referees continued busy. After a few minutes more their whistles blew, ending the action. Most of the "surviving" T'swa were free of the trap now, having overrun the machine guns, and the real harvest was finished. The referees needed to confer, to sort out the confusion and define the casualties on both sides. Meanwhile both troopers and T'swa stopped where they were and waited.

While the referees conferred, Romlar washed down a "sweat capsule" with a swallow of warm water, then got on the radio to Brossling, who'd kept comm silence till then because their frequency might be monitored. The Boolies had hit them, Brossling said, but the assault hadn't been as bad as expected. The referees there had agreed that 2nd Battalion and the Condaro had driven them off with fairly heavy Booly casualties and only modest casualties of their own. Modest because they were dug in, and because they hadn't let themselves be overrun.

Romlar's own casualties, the referees announced, had been relatively modest too, considering it was T'swa they'd ambushed, T'swa in their prefinal year of training, most of them seventeen years old. When the whistles blew again, the surviving T'swa would regroup and do whatever their commander decided. Romlar would move his men back to the abandoned logging camp at Junction 4, fifteen miles away. A camp that, in the never-never land of the training exercise, served as the nucleus of the mocked-up Condaro village at Junction 4, whose rough wagon road gave logistical access to the principal pass through this part of the Jubat Hills. The Condaros, like the Boolies, were mostly imaginary of course, represented by T'swa veterans, survivors of retired regiments, pretending to be non-T'swa. Veterans each of whom, for the purpose of the exercise, represented a Condaro or Booly platoon.

It was all as real as it could reasonably be made, but given the genuine and bloody fighting his regiment had been through on Terfreya, five years earlier, the difference had always been conspicuous to Romlar. Nonetheless, the regiment had learned a great deal in those five additional training years, learned much more than simply strategy, tactics, and fighting techniques.

Romlar had lost thirty-two percent of his command on Terfreya—real deaths by violence, not pretended deaths by referees' decisions—and like the T'swa, the "White T'swa" did not replace their casualties. But allowing for that short-handedness, he had no doubt that this regiment, under his leadership, was as good as any regiment in Confederation Space, whether at War Level One, Two, or Three. Which were all the levels the Confederation condoned.

True the T'swa were physically stronger than his men; they'd been born to this world's heavy gravity, as had their ancestors for a hundred generations. And his men would graduate with six years less training, though the Ostrak Procedures, and six years of work under T'swa cadres, had brought them close. Especially given the months of bloody combat on Terfreya. Perhaps more important, particularly in a Level Three War where night visors were prohibited, *Homo tyssiensis* had considerably better night vision than other humans.

But under his leadership ... Numerous T'swa officers were his equals in strategy and tactics, Romlar knew, and at spotting importances. But no one outguessed him, outpredicted him. That was his edge. Even in training it didn't always bring victory, but it was as good an edge as he could hope for.

The referees' whistles shrilled again, blowing the two forces back into action, and Romlar's buglers called a withdrawal. His major advantages here were gone now; it was time to get back to Junction 4.

The Game Master had declared the "war" over. The Condaros had broken, and with that the greatly outnumbered regiment had been chewed up. First Romlar, and later Carrmak and Brossling had been "killed" in T'swa night assaults, and Eldren Esenrok, still and always cocky, had led what was left of the troopers.

Now the entire regiment, survivors and casualties, sat together in the Great Hall to hear their efforts critiqued. Sat facing the Grand Master and the board of Masters. Tiers of wooden benches, dark and smooth, rose on three sides, holding other regiments in advanced training, those which were on base. The hall was well lit by T'swa standards, but the light was ruddy as a campfire. The timbered roof was high and dark, unpainted and with massive beams, its corners shadowed. All in all it felt primordial, despite the large viewscreen on the wall at one end.

Grand Master Kliss-Bahn was ancient, his frame still large but its covering shrunken. His naturally short hair, long-since white, had become thin and soft, and like himself no longer stood straight. He'd commanded the legendary Black Tiger Regiment in its time, survived its gradual shrinkage and final destruction, and had been overseeing training in one capacity and another for sixty-eight standard years.

His critique was direct, detailed, and generally favorable. When he'd finished, he turned his large, luminous black eyes on Romlar, who as regimental commander sat front and center facing him. "Now," said Kliss-Bahn, "let us hear from Colonel Romlar. Colonel, you may comment at any reasonable length on this exercise. And because it was your final exercise, feel free to address your training overall. Colonel?"

Romlar stood. He was rather tall, and massive for an Iryalan—as big as most T'swa. "Thank you, Master Kliss-Bahn. I'll keep it short. This exercise was a lesson in fighting for a losing cause of little merit, a lesson in dying with integrity." He grinned. "It was an interesting experience.

"As for our overall training—T'swa warriors have not only trained us; they've inspired us and been role models for us. And T'swa masters of wisdom have done much to expand us in the T'sel during the three years we've spent on your world. Basic to all that were the Ostrak Procedures, received from counselors of our own species in our first year of training. But even the Ostrak Procedures grew out of training in the T'sel, received by Iryalans here on Tyss six centuries ago. So it all comes down to Tyss, the T'swa, and the T'sel."

He looked around, scanning the black faces, the reflective eyes. "We are not truly T'swa," he went on. "Our scripting and imprinting have been different. The Ostrak Procedures, and our training by your lodge and by the Order of Ka-Shok, have made us close cousins to the T'swa; in most ways we have become closer to you than to our families, or to the friends of our childhood. But we remain Confederat-swa, and more specifically Iryalans.

"We will go somewhere to fight soon, taking with us what

we have learned from you. What we have learned not only about the art of war, but of the T'sel, of ethics, of integrity.

"As the T'swa well know and fully intended, the T'sel is infiltrating the Confederation, particularly at the top and most particularly on Iryala. In time, wars will cease; that is the direction the T'sel moves us, now that the hold of the Sacrament is beginning to crumble in the Confederation. In lives to come—perhaps not the next, or the one after that, but in some future life—we will do things beyond our present dreaming. But for this life we are warriors born and trained, and we will practice our profession as skillfully and ethically as we can, taking pleasure in its challenges and actions.

"Because we are Confederatswa, we will no doubt do some things differently than you would. But we will always act according to the T'sel. We thank you for all you have given us, and should it happen that we meet some of you in battle, we will not disappoint you."

As Romlar sat down, the T'swa regiments stood, clapping in the T'swa manner, strongly, rhythmically, large palms cupped, the sound resonant in the hall. A rush pebbled the young colonel's skin.[1]

---

[1] Background on the T'swa and the Confederation is provided in the appendix of this book.

Two

Elgo Valarton gazed out the broad window and uncon-
sciously added a sixth or eighth stick of gum to the wad in
his mouth. The building stood on a high rocky hill, giving
a marvelous view across Basalt Strait, its water a perfect
blue beneath a perfect sky, its whitecaps perfect white, the
sails of its pleasure sloops bright and vivid. It seemed to
Valarton that the view must be one of the loveliest on
Maragor.

Appropriately, for The Archipelago was one of Maragor's
wealthiest nations, and Azure Bay its richest and most
sophisticated city.

The receptionist looked up from her typing. "Mr. Helmiss
will see you now, Mr. Valarton."

Suddenly aware of the cud he chewed, Valarton dropped
it into a wastebasket before he walked to the office door.
The man who awaited him was standing behind his desk, and
leaned across it to shake hands. They sat down then.

"What can I do for you?" the man asked.

"Mr. Helmiss, let me say first that the matter I've come
to talk about is extremely confidential."

Klute Helmiss nodded slightly. "I treat every matter

brought to me as confidential, unless otherwise instructed. What may I do for you?"

Valarton found himself reluctant to begin; there was a certain risk to his country in this mission. "You're aware, of course, of the Komarsi invasion of Smolen, and how it's turning out. And of the broader political and human aspects of that war."

"Of course."

"Krentorf would like to see Smolen survive. And to see the war cost Komars enough blood and money that she won't be encouraged to assault her other neighbors."

Helmiss nodded.

Valarton paused another long moment. "The Crown of Krentorf would like to assist Smolen, but that assistance needs to be securely confidential."

"What do you have in mind, Mr. Valarton? Or what does your government have in mind?"

"This would not be an act of government. In a constitutional monarchy like Krentorf, if this were done by the government, it would soon be public knowledge. I am here as the personal agent of the queen. She will finance the project out of her own, personal resources, if the cost is one she can reasonably meet."

The Movrik Transportation Company's station chief on Maragor leaned back in his chair, folded his hands over his modest paunch, and waited.

"Her Highness has considered various possibilities, and it seems to her that—that to provide a regiment of T'swa mercenaries could have considerable impact on the war, while being essentially impossible to trace to her. Is she correct in that?"

On several trade worlds, Movrik Transportation served as the agent for the warrior lodge of Kootosh-Lan, of the planet Tyss, known also as "Oven." It was a hat that Helmiss hadn't actually worn in his four years on Maragor, but he knew the procedures. "That is correct, Mr. Valarton."

"What might the services of such a regiment cost?"

Helmiss turned, took a letter-size sheet from a file cabinet, and handed it to Valarton, who skimmed it rapidly, then handed it back. "I'm afraid Her Majesty's personal resources will not stretch so far."

When Helmiss did not reach to take the sheet back, Valarton laid it on the desk. Watchfully, for it seemed to him that Helmiss might offer some sort of terms.

"If the T'swa are too expensive, I have an alternative to offer. A regiment, a short regiment actually, of Iryalan mercenaries."

"Iryalans?"

"Trained by the T'swa. It should be graduating about now, and because it's not well known, I suspect it's more affordable. My company is not an agent for it, but I'd act as go-between if their, um, lodge would give Movrik the transportation contract."

Valarton pursed his lips. "Her Majesty didn't authorize me to hire non-T'swa. And newly graduated? They're inexperienced then."

"On the contrary. If you were hiring black T'swa, there'd be a fair chance you'd get a virgin regiment, unblooded albeit highly effective. These Iryalans, on the other hand"—he paused for effect—"it is they who drove the out-sector invaders off Terfreya, and that as a green regiment with only a year of training. Since then they've trained five years more. And it was their T'swa trainers who named their regiment 'the White T'swa.'"

Valarton wondered how Helmiss came to be so informed. "But you don't know how much they'd cost," he said.

"I'll find out for you." He touched a key on his commset. "Aron, I'm sending Mr. Valarton back out to you. Offer him refreshment. I'll be looking into a matter for him." He turned to the Krentorfi then, stood and indicated the door to reception. "I'll be no longer than I must."

There was something about this that seemed odd to Valarton, but he got up and went to the door. When he reached it, he turned his head . . . and saw Helmiss going through a door behind his desk. He got only a glimpse, but the room Helmiss was entering seemed small, with shelves and cabinets—an office supply room obviously. Then Helmiss closed the door behind him, and Valarton went on into reception.

The room that Valarton had glimpsed was somewhat wider than deep. When Helmiss had closed the door, he set the lock, and went to an apparatus at one side. It was a low platform with a tubular frame that looked like a doorway leading nowhere. There was a small console; he tapped certain keys on it, gazed at the monitor, then tapped some more. Faintly he could feel a power field develop, the generator subaudible. A green light came on beside the "gate." Looking through it, he no longer saw the wall a few feet on the other side; instead he looked into another room, seen vaguely. Without hesitating he walked through and disappeared. The green light winked out and the field died.

Splenn was the most sophisticated of the trade worlds, and one of only two with its own spaceships. Movrik Transportation owned most of them. The Movrik family was wealthy beyond any other on Splenn, though they did not flaunt it. They had more important purposes. Their influence, though mostly not apparent, was becoming ubiquitous on Splenn, while offworld they were covertly connected to the highest levels of Confederation government.

So closely connected as to have a teleport on the family's home estate, and one at most of their offworld offices. Something not known to anyone outside the loosely organized, secret society whose members called it "the Movement," and themselves "the Alumni."

A teleport needed only a transmitter, not a receiver, and gates could target far more accurately than a few years earlier. Though a matric attractor was necessary for fine precision. Movrik's various offworld gates opened into the middle of a room, on the family estate referred to as "headquarters." The same room held the gate used in returning.

This was the room into which Klute Helmiss stepped from his supply room nine hyperspace days away, with a lapsed time of zero. Except for him, it was empty. Rather than hunt through the house or disturb the domestic staff, he went to a commset on a desk, and keyed the personal communicator of Pitter Movrik himself. A moment later, Pitter's face appeared on the screen.

"Klute! What brings you to Splenn?"

"I have a potential job for the White T'swa. I need authorization, terms, a contract. . . ."

"Okay. I'm in Carris. I'm going to disconnect and call the

Confederation Ministry; the minister himself if he's in. I'll get back with you as quickly as possible. Can you wait there?"

"Can I have a prediction? I left a man in reception, back on Maragor, totally bewildered."

"Under fifteen minutes."

"I'll wait."

There were books in the room, the usual hard copies. Helmiss looked at their spines, and pulling one, began to browse. Within a few minutes the commset interrupted him.

"Klute, we're going to talk with Kristal on Iryala." He gave Helmiss a destination code to key into the gate controls. It would activate an algorithm to compute the constantly changing destination coordinates of the target. Klute followed his instructions, and stepped through the gate into a room on Iryala, in the office suite of Emry Wanslo, Lord Kristal. Within three minutes, the two Splennites were sitting at a table with Kristal himself, personal aide to Marcus XXVIII, King of Iryala and Administrator General of the Confederation of Worlds.

Elgo Valarton had waited less than thirty-five minutes when he was sent back to Helmiss's office. Helmiss had an authorization and a proposed contract. The cost was negotiable, though Helmiss didn't say so. Kristal wanted the regiment employed, and as described by Helmiss, the Smoleni cause appealed to him.

There was no dickering. Valarton had been selected for his discretion and reliability, not for any particular bargaining sense, and the price proposed was a bit less than he'd been authorized to meet. He was a bit spooked though by one of the signatures on the document: Emry Wanslo, Lord Kristal. There was also a delivery deadline. How had Helmiss gotten those? Surely he didn't have a stock of signed and dated contracts in his supply room!

The queen's emissary tried to avoid thinking about it. Somehow it gave him chills.

Three

It was late summer at the Blue Forest Military Reservation, the day a preview of fall. Colonel Carlis Voker had just returned to his office after lunch, and sat reading a report on his terminal. His commset chirped, and he reached to it. "What is it, Lemal?"

"Kelmer Faronya is here to see you, sir."

Voker glanced at the clock: 12:59. Young Faronya was prompt. "Send him in."

A moment later a young man entered, well built and rather tall, like his sister before him. He'd come to lunch from a training exercise, a four-hour run with a sandbag on a pack frame. The sweat had dried on his face, but his burcut hair was still awry from it, and his shirt stained.

He saluted, a trooper's casual hand flip. It wasn't necessary; he was in fact a civilian, not a trooper. On the other hand he'd trained with the 6th Iryalan Mercenary Regiment for just eight days short of a year. He'd done almost everything they'd done, although in part a helmet camera had substituted for a weapon.

Also he hadn't done the Ostrak Procedures. After the early training difficulties of the original Iryalan mercenaries,

17

the White T'swa, trainees had been run through the Ostrak Procedures *before* their training was begun. It had saved headaches of various sorts, as well as scheduling problems. But Kristal had decided that the "regimental historian"— actually an in-house journalist—should do without the procedures. That way he could write more nearly from a public point of view.

This did cause a complication, because without having been through the procedures, Faronya couldn't teleport without going psychotic. And die without quick and effective treatment. It had probably left him feeling a bit of an outsider, too, lacking a trooper's viewpoint, and major areas of a trooper's reality.

He wasn't even spiritually a warrior as they were. He *had* been born with the basic warrior under-pattern, but not in warrior phase, not for that lifetime. Thus he lacked a warrior's script, and a warrior's psychic and mental tool kits. He did have the metabolic attributes though; without them he would have washed out in training.

At a glance he looked like a warrior: A year's mercenary training, strenuous to the limits of endurance, had given him a physical hardness that, even in a baggy field uniform, was quite apparent.

"Faronya," Voker said, "I'm transfering you out of the regiment." The young man's eyes widened, and his lips parted as if to object. Voker went on. "You're familiar with the White T'swa, of course."

Faronya's objection stopped unspoken; he'd hear this out. He knew a lot about the White T'swa. His sister had been with it during part of its training, and when she'd come home had talked of little else to him. Then she'd ported with it to Terfreya as a stowaway, and ended missing in action, no doubt with her camera busy. Her loss had hurt him, but the war—the war had been so necessary, and the troopers so brave.

"Yessir, I know a lot about them. As you're well aware."

"I'm attaching you to them. They have a contract to fight a war on a trade world called Maragor. A Level Three War; nothing technical. You'll record and report on it.

"You can refuse, of course."

Kelmer Faronya's lips were parted again, not with

intended rejection now, but with surprise. "Refuse? No, sir! It's the sort of thing I wanted when I applied! I just hadn't expected it to happen so soon."

"Sooner than you think. A floater leaves here in an hour. That means you shower and pack and be at reception at 1:55, ready to leave. Someone will meet you when you arrive at Landfall. You'll leave there on a hyperspace courier later today, to join your new regiment on Splenn. Now jump!"

Kelmer Faronya sprinted to his barracks.

Four

Customarily, when a regiment had completed its training at the Lodge of Kootosh-Lan, graduation was at midmorning. For the comfort of unconditioned Iryalan guests, however, the ceremony for the White T'swa was held shortly before dawn, when the temperature was relatively cool—only 91 degrees on this morning in early spring.

Some of the guests from offworld were T'swa—the basic training cadre from Blue Forest, on Iryala. They'd ported in, more than four hundred of them, absent from their posts for a day. Their current cycle of trainees was almost at the end of their basic year and would get along very well under their student officers.

All through the ceremony, Romlar watched them from across the Great Hall, among them Bahn, his old squad sergeant; Dao, his old platoon sergeant; Lieutenant Dzo-Tar; Captain Gotasu; and his old regimental C.O., Colonel Dak-So. And Lord Kristal, representing the king; Colonel Voker, who administered the basic training program; and Varlik Lormagen, the first man to be called "the White T'swa," forty years ago on Kettle.

And Lotta Alsnor, who so far as he knew had been on

Tyss all along. In his three years there, he'd seen her just once and been alone with her not at all. She was shorter than average, and considerably less than half Romlar's mass, with a wiryness apparently more the result of genetics than of her early interest in gymnastics and dance. On Tyss she looked even slighter than before, as if the heat had dried her out, which didn't bother Romlar in the least.

Perhaps he'd have a chance to talk with her alone before she went back to Dys-Hualuun. It troubled him that he might not, and the feeling surprised him. To someone grounded in the T'sel, it was illogical. Their purposes in life, his and hers, were different, at least those purposes he knew of. This evening he would rebalance himself—enter a trance and regain neutrality on the subject. On Terfreya they'd had what they'd had together. If nothing more came of it, that would be fine.

On the other hand, perhaps something more would. Perhaps when the time came—when casualties had reduced the regiment below any effective level—perhaps then they would be together. Assuming he survived himself, which in a mercenary regiment in the T'swa tradition was unlikely, even for the commanding officer.

Mentally he shook his thoughts away and focused on Kliss-Bahn. The ancient veteran, owning humankind's most admired military mind, was worth his full attention, even making a graduation address.

Because of the offworld visitors, there was a reception after the ceremony, an opportunity to mix. Lieutenant Jerym Alsnor went straight to Lotta, his sister. "Hi, sib," he said. "I was hoping we'd have a chance to talk."

"Bet on it," she answered. "I don't have to leave when the others do."

"Good. What've you been doing lately?"

She grinned. "You mean have I been monitoring Tain."

He laughed. "You read my mind!"

"Not really. And, yes, I have been monitoring Tain."

Their eyes met and held. "How is she?"

"Happy."

"Really?" The last Lotta had told him, five years earlier

on Terfreya, Tain had been a prisoner on a warship from the empire. And amnesic.

"Really. She's married and has a child."

Jerym didn't answer for several seconds. "Does she—remember yet?"

"No. Not you, not me. Nothing."

Jerym thought of the out-sector marines he'd fought on Terfreya. Mostly they'd been small men, and hairier than anyone he'd ever seen before. They hadn't seemed entirely human to him. "What's her husband like?"

"He's a good person, Jerym. He's strong and considerate and loving."

"Remarkable." He wasn't referring to Tain's marriage, but to the welling in his eyes. He didn't feel sad at all, but there it was. "Anything more?"

"Yes. He's an ex-marine officer—and the emperor of eleven worlds. And he has a rare innate sense of how to treat the woman he loves." She didn't tell him the rest of it, and he didn't pick up on the omission.

His earlier reaction had receded. "Well. I'm glad, sib, I'm really really glad she's happy." A slow grin built. "I'll ask about her again in another five years. With an emperor for a husband, she shouldn't have any trouble getting authorization for all the kids she wants.

"Now. What have you heard from the folks?"

Jerym was already talking with Lotta, so Romlar sheered off. Dak-So, his old T'swa colonel, came over to him and asked questions about the fighting on Terfreya. Colonel Voker came over and stood listening. Dak-So's eyes seemed to gleam with a light of their own, and his white teeth were vivid in his black T'swa face. "You are changed, Artus," he said when Romlar had finished. "Beyond the changes generated by combat."

"As you expected. They've trained us well here, not only Kliss-Bahn's cadre, but the Ka-Shok adepts under Master Rinn. We're ready."

Dak-So laughed, a deep rich rumbling. "I believe you," he said. "Your higher center had already displayed itself during your basic training. Brigadier Shiller was sufficiently disheartened that he retired, beaten and embarrassed by a nineteen-year-old commander-in-training with less than a year's service."

Voker spoke then. "Speaking of ready, Lord Kristal wants to talk to you before he goes."

Romlar's pulse quickened. *A contract,* he thought, and wondered where for. Kristal wasn't letting grass grow under his feet or theirs. He looked around, but didn't spot him in the large crowded room. Who he did see was Lotta Alsnor coming toward him. *His lordship can talk to me later,* he told himself. "Excuse me," he said, and started toward her.

She grinned at him as they met, and her touch on his arm had an electric intimacy. Her gaze was direct but her words playful. "I had to tell Jerym it was nice talking to him, but that lovers outrank brothers."

Lovers. They'd never used the word before. It gave their feelings a certain standing. Lotta read his reaction and laughed. He gestured with his head in the direction of Voker and Dak-So. "Lovers outrank colonels, too. Shall we go outside and talk? There'll be some privacy there."

They wove their way toward the entry, among clusters of cadre and troopers renewing old bonds. Outside, there was enough dawnlight to extend visibility, and no one was in sight. Romlar felt an urgency now that took him by surprise.

"Colonels have private quarters," he murmured. "Would you like to see? It's been more than five years."

She purred. "A long five years. Let's go, before someone else comes out."

He took her hand then and they ran, his gait an easy lope. Her slender legs scissored quickly, feet scarcely seeming to touch the ground. The regimental officers' barracks were dark and silent. In his room, enough light came through the windows that they could see each other's eyes, if not their color. Their first kiss was cool, lingering, then they sat down on his narrow bed and kissed urgently, hotly, their hands busy. Within a couple of minutes they were naked.

When they were spent, they lay side by side holding hands. "I'm lucky," he said. "Lucky we found each other."

"It was an agreement we made, before this life."

"I've always thought so. That winter at Blue Forest, it seemed more like a renewal than a new friendship."

"It goes beyond this," she said, "beyond being together and making love."

"True." He lay thoughtful for a few seconds, then asked: "An agreement to do what?"

"I think we won't know until the time comes. Or it might simply be an agreement to love each other. I've developed a lot, training under Grand Master Ku; I can see more deeply than ever into other people. But not into myself, and when it comes to seeing my own script . . ." She shook her head and chuckled. "Ku says that's typical, almost invariable, even among masters. Otherwise it would remove much of the challenge and interest from life, and the lessons of experience." She turned her head to look at Romlar. "I'm done on Tyss, at least for the present. I'm a master now. Officially. I'm going back to Iryala at the end of the week."

He grinned. "You're *my* master, I know that."

She jabbed him with an elbow then, and they began to wrestle. He discovered he wasn't as spent as he'd thought.

Five

On Maragor the solstice was approaching, and the back-country village of Burnt Woods was in deep spring. The air smelled of forest in the flush of new growth. Birds sang, and—the flaw in the beauty—insects bit, Maragor's version of mosquitoes.

Burnt Woods was now the administrative capital of what was left of the republic of Smolen. The southern one-fourth—with ninety percent of the population and arable land—had been occupied by the Army of Komars. Except that it didn't have ninety percent of the population anymore. More like seventy-five percent. And in the north, throngs of refugees lived in scattered tent camps, while making communal shelters of logs against inevitable winter.

Burnt Woods' largest house had been turned over to the president for his quarters and offices. Not commandeered. Offered freely by the owner, the local fur broker, who lived now with his son's family in their home. The hotel *had* been commandeered—all twelve rooms of it—rented by the government for deferred rents that might never be collected. Would surely not be collected, unless some hard-to-envision military turnaround occurred. It held what was left of the president's staff. Officed them, that is, for they dwelt in tents like the refugees. And like the regiments stationed southward, prepared to meet as best they could any Komarsi strike.

A strike that might be made but seemed unneeded. There were nearly one hundred thousand people in the northland now, including troops. By next spring they'd be very hungry. There was neither arable land nor implements to grow anything like adequate crops.

The Smoleni had had a long history of oppressions, though none for more than four hundred years. And traditions had grown from those oppressions: notably doggedness, a refusal to give in. And a dedication to as little government as practical.

Most mornings, in the weeks they'd been in Burnt Woods, the president's War Council had met in his office, which for years had served as a family's dining room. His conference table had been their dinner table. President Heber Lanks was a very tall, rawboned man who'd gained weight in middle age and now was losing it. His arms were long, even for his height, their length accentuated by long, large hands. All in all, he was physically imposing, but his manner was mild.

He stood up to call the meeting to order, and on his feet studied briefly, soberly, the men he'd surrounded himself with. The night before, a floater had landed. A message had been delivered to his hand, and the floater had lifted again.

"Gentlemen," he said, "I have news from a source which I shall not identify. A couriered message. It seems we shall have some help." He paused, looking thoughtful, unexcited. "This is strictly confidential. I repeat that: this is strictly confidential. A regiment of mercenaries will be delivered to us. They . . ."

"*Mercenaries? Mercenaries?*" General Eskoth Belser had half gotten to his feet, his voice rising in anger. Vestur Marlim jerked on the general's sleeve and almost hissed the words: "Eskoth! For Tunis's sake shut your mouth! This is confidential! Have you no self-control?"

Belser's heavy features reddened and seemed to swell, but he settled slowly to his seat, jerking his arm free of

Marlim's grasp. The general was a thick slab of a man, while the War Minister was small and fine-boned.

President Lanks had looked briefly pained. "Not mercenaries from here on Maragor," he said. "These are civilized and highly trained professionals from offworld. T'swa trained."

Belser's clamped jaw relaxed slightly. "T'swa trained?"

Lanks told them what he knew.

"But only one regiment! We have twenty-six regiments of our own!"

"Not as many as we need."

"Of course not! Not by a long shot! But what good will a single additional regiment do us?"

"That remains to be seen. We know the impact the T'swa had in the Elstra-Tromfel War, and at Stemperos."

"But these mercenaries aren't T'swa. Correct? They're 'T'swa-trained,' you said."

"That's right. They're Iryalans."

Belser subsided into grumblings. "I've never even heard of Iryalan mercenaries."

Colonel Elyas Fossur looked across at him. Fossur was the president's intelligence chief and military mentor. "Actually, Eskoth, I think you have, but they weren't identified as mercenaries at the time." He turned to the president then. "I presume this is the regiment that drove the outsector invaders off Terfreya, several years ago."

"That's the information I have."

"Then they may not be T'swa, but they seem to be something quite like them. T'swa-trained indeed! The T'swa dubbed them the White T'swa."

The council sat digesting this, all but Lanks, who still stood. He'd digested it earlier, lying awake in his bed till the birds called the sun to the sky. Historically, the Smoleni experience with mercenaries had been as victims, not beneficiaries. He would make a point of welcoming this regiment as valuable friends, and hope its men behaved decently.

Belser was still disgruntled. "What we really need is for someone else to declare war on Komars," he said. "The Komarsi'd at least have to pull their troops south of the Eel then."

"There are various reasons that won't happen," Lanks said

drily. "And these Iryalan mercenaries may make a difference. Meanwhile they won't arrive for at least a week, and we'll need that much time to prepare a camp for them."

He handed a thin sheaf of papers to Belser. "This is not the contract," he said. "The party who hired them for us has that. But it does include all the operational clauses, and assigns responsibility to me. I'm turning that responsibility over to the army, specifically to you. It's important that we meet the clauses to the best of our ability; that was stressed to me."

Belser took the papers with his jaw clamped. It seemed to him that this would be more trouble than it was worth.

Six

At the Movrik family's large wildlife estate on Splenn, the weather was considerably different than at Burnt Woods. It was early winter there, and a cold rain fell steadily and thickly, drumming on the roof. The gray lake surface seemed to seethe with it.

Pitter Movrik loved that kind of weather; during the long rainy season he often visited the lodge just to experience it. But the decisive reason for being there this day was isolation. A teleport large enough to accommodate AG trucks, say, or floaters, was hard to camouflage in a populated area. Certainly it could be difficult to conceal the occasional traffic it received.

For example, 1,170 troopers plus their gear. They'd be impossible to hide or explain, even at the family's rural estate, where the sizeable domestic staff and farm crew would see them. Here, on the other hand, there were no neighbors at all, except wild animals. And the lodge staff of four, ported there as needed, were at least second generation employees of the family. They'd been educated in the family school with the family offspring, and received the

Ostrak Procedures as children. As their parents had before them. And finally, as adults, they'd chosen to stay.

The regiment had already arrived, and transferred to the HS *Maryam Burkitt*, which sat parked on a gravitic vector well above the weather. Just now, though, twenty-one regimental officers, including the company commanders and their execs, sat in the lodge's dining room, with old Pitter an interested observer. They were waiting for a situation briefing by Movrik's senior agent on Maragor, Klute Helmiss. The dining room opened onto a roofed deck which overlooked the lake, a view framed by rain forest. Water poured off the eaves onto rockwork below, except where a gable provided a gap in the cataract, a sort of window through which Movrik could see a shuttle parked close above the shore, waiting to take the officers up.

Helmiss finished writing instructions into the player, then turned to face his audience. He pressed a key, and the wallscreen lit up with a globe of Maragor. Slightly to the left of center, they saw a block of yellow and one of pink, together extending from about 45 degrees to nearly 53 degrees north latitude.

"All right, gentlemen," he said, "let's start." He spoke a bit loudly, to be heard above the rain and the splashing of the roof cataract. "We're looking at what by definition is the eastern hemisphere of Maragor. The country shown in yellow is Komars, and the one in pink is Smolen. And here . . ." The two countries filled the screen now, and briefly he described their demographics, Komars with its nine million people, Smolen to the north with three hundred and twenty thousand.

Graphs showed in windows on the map, replacing each other as he talked. In terms of area, the two countries weren't too different, but they differed greatly in the kinds of land they had. Komars was mostly a fertile plain, flat to rolling. The southernmost part of Smolen, "the Leas," was similar, if generally more hilly. The Leas, along with two northward extensions and a short strip of coastland in the southeast, made up twenty-five percent of Smolen, but contained almost all its farmland and manufacturing. The rest of the country was forest, lakes, and peat bogs, broken here and there by small farm settlements which became fewer as one went farther north. It was called "the Free Lands," because centuries earlier, the Smoleni peasants, suffering home-grown oppressors, would flee to its forests from time to time. There to starve and raid until coaxed back out by promises of justice.

"Normally," Helmiss said, "the Leas raise enough food to feed the nation, but without enough left for significant export. Smolen's on-planet exports are primarily lumber, paper, and furs. Its offworld exports are entirely furs, some ranch-grown but mostly trapped."

He went on to describe the events leading up to a Komarsi attack that had quickly occupied first the Leas, then the coast, and two valleys that extended northward. "Initially," he said, "the Smoleni policy seems to have been to cost the Komarsi enough in blood and material that they'd settle for limited objectives. It wasn't a promising policy, but it may well have been the best available to them. Obviously it didn't work. Now—" He shrugged. "Now I don't think they have a policy, unless hanging on and hoping qualifies. In fact, the Smoleni prospect seems nearly beyond hope. It appears that you'll find yourself in a no-win situation there. But you'll have marvelous opportunities to fight, and landscapes well suited to the operations of small, elite units.

"I've always found war intriguing, and I've read a great deal about it. Including Lormagen's video-studies of the T'swa, prepared before he got the Ostrak Procedures. I've also read about and watched the cubes on your training at Blue Forest, and your campaign in the Terfreyan jungles, and it seems to me you can find marvelous opportunities in this war. As the T'swa would."

Listening, Romlar chuckled to himself. With a little concentration, he could see auras, and Helmiss had a warrior underpattern manifesting strongly.

A few hours later, Romlar sat in the wardroom aboard the *Burkitt*, a cup of joma by his elbow, reading a book. Lieutenant Jerym Alsnor came in and sat down by him.

"What're you reading?"

Romlar held it up. "*Historical Strategies and Tactics in Level 3 Wars: Selected Case Histories.* Carlis wrote it just recently; he gave it to me on Oven, after graduation."

Marking his place with a napkin, Romlar put it down and went on. "The reason I sent for you is—" He paused for effect. "Tain has a brother. Kelmer."

Jerym cocked an eyebrow. "She mentioned that. He's quite a bit younger than her. And?"

"He's who we're waiting for here. He's following in his sister's footsteps; he's a journalist. Kristal's sending him with us to Maragor to record and describe the war, primarily our part in it. His official designation is 'regimental historian.'"

Jerym nodded. "And he hasn't been through the Ostrak Procedures, so he can't be ported. Right? Wouldn't it have been cheaper to gate us through to Maragor and have him follow in a courier?"

"He's not the reason we're shipping from here. Maragor's pretty conservative—the Sacrament's only been defused there for about twenty years—and the Movement doesn't want to draw attention there to the gates. Also, Splenn's only a nine-day jump from there, and because Movrik's agent on Maragor brokered the contract, Movrik had a fee coming from OSP. He was willing to take it in the form of a transportation contract."

"Um." Jerym repeated himself then: "And?"

"I'm assigning Kelmer Faronya to your platoon. Carlis tells me he was with the 6th Regiment through almost their full year of basic, so strength and endurance won't be a problem, and he should understand what you tell him without a lot of explanation. He trained with them as a combat journalist, not a fighting man, so on combat exercises his weapon was his camera. But he got a lot of basic weapons training, too, and the basics of jokanru.

"I want you to see he gets chances to do what he needs to do. And—" Romlar paused, frowning thoughtfully. "I was going to say I want you to keep him from taking reckless chances. But—" He shook his head. "I don't think he's the reckless type."

"Something Carlis said?"

"No. A feeling I have."

"Um. I suppose he thinks Tain's dead."

"Right. It's best that way."

"When's he coming aboard?"

"The courier arrived in-system last night. They should land him here before dark."

"I look forward to meeting him," Jerym said, and wondered if Kelmer Faronya looked at all like his sister.

Seven

The *Burkitt* was under way. On warp drive still; they'd jump to hyperdrive when they were far enough from the primary with its distorting gravity field.

Jerym shared a small cabin with another A Company platoon leader. They lay one above the other on shelflike, fold-down bunks, reading a manual on space warfare as it scrolled slowly up their wall screen. It was theoretical of course; there'd never been a space war in the Confederation Sector. But so far it was making sense.

The door signal beeped, and Jerym, having the bottom bunk, opened to a tall young man they'd never seen before. But dressed in regimental uniform, not the jumpsuit of a Movrik crewman. "Kelmer Faronya?" Jerym asked.

"That's right, sir. Colonel Romlar told me to report to Lieutenant Alsnor and get acquainted."

Jerym reached out a hand, and they shook. "I'm Jerym Alsnor," he said. "This is Furgis Klintok; he has First Platoon. Furgis, I'm going to leave you with Commander Fenner's good book, and take Mr. Faronya to the briefing room. Who knows? We might even find some privacy there."

The passageway wore a durable carpet for traction and

quiet, the same carpeting that spaceships had worn since before history. "My sister mentioned you," Kelmer said. "You were her—guide at Blue Forest. Were you her guide on Terfreya, too?"

"No. On Terfreya my platoon wore a particularly dangerous hat. We were attached to Headquarters Section and did special projects for Artus. Colonel Romlar. Till almost none of us were left."

Kelmer nodded. "And afterward, when the regiment got reorganized, I suppose you got a platoon again."

"Right. Actually my platoon got reconstituted on Terfreya, from remnants of a company that—pretty much had to be sacrificed, used as the bait for a trap. Then I lost most of that one in the big night raid that closed the book and won the war there."

Kelmer Faronya paled at that. He knew the history of that war in some detail and had watched the video cubes. The story had become part of the education of subsequent regiments. He'd felt intrigued but also uncomfortable with them, perhaps because Tain had died there. (So he believed. It's what he'd been told, and he had no reason to doubt it.)

He'd also felt discomfort at the other trainees' relaxed attitudes toward the casualties, and had blamed it on their youth. Most had been sixteen or seventeen years old when they'd begun training, while he'd been twenty-two, a worldly graduate in journalism. But Jerym Alsnor was older than he was, and had been there, had experienced it all. Had seen most of his men killed, and still seemed casual.

He wondered if he should ask him about it, then asked instead: "What's it like to be in combat for the first time?"

They came to the briefing room door, even as he asked. Jerym opened it, and they entered and sat down before he answered. "For us it was exciting. Exhilarating. I can't say what it'll be like for you."

"Exhilarating? Uniformly for all of you?"

Jerym smiled. "I haven't polled the others on it, but yes, I think all of us."

Like the T'swa, Kelmer thought. The black T'swa, the real T'swa. "I asked Sergeant Bahn the same question once, and that's pretty much what he said. He used the word *fulfilling,* but everything considered, he seemed to feel about the same as you." He paused then, looking at it, and decided he'd ask others when he had the chance. But it seemed to him that Jerym was right, that they'd all felt pretty much the same.

Jerym watched the other. Faronya was not a warrior, he told himself, and more, he no doubt believed that a person lives just once. You die and that's the end of you. "What do you expect your first combat will be like?" he asked.

Kelmer's strong young face turned very sober. "I used to think it would be exciting. But the more I trained . . . I think it was the cubes of combat. Old ones by Mr. Lormagen on Kettle, and Tain's from Terfreya. I saw men blown apart! Saw bodies lying with their faces shot off. Now I'm not sure. I'm pretty sure it won't be exhilarating though."

"I suppose you're familiar with the Matrix of T'sel."

"Yes. We were trained on that the first week, until I could diagram it from memory."

"Where do you suppose you're at on it?"

"I'm at *Jobs,* at the level of *Knowledge.* I asked Sergeant Dao, and he asked me some questions and told me that's where I was." Kelmer found that he was sweating.

"How did that seem to you?"

"Pretty good, I guess. It seemed accurate to me."

"Anything wrong with being at Jobs and Knowledge?"

"Well, when everyone else, my friends, the guys I trained with, were at War, at the level of—of Play! . . . Sometimes I felt a little out of place."

"You don't need to be at War, or at Play. You don't have a warrior's function; you're a journalist. How did your buddies treat you?"

"Okay. No one ever criticized or belittled me. Actually, training with them was the most consistently enjoyable time of my life. The most uncomplicated and active. I loved the training! Even running for hours with a sandbag, with sweat burning my eyes, or wading in a swamp full of mosquitoes. Even doing an all-night speed march on snowshoes after not eating since breakfast. I felt—I felt like hot stuff!"

Jerym was grinning broadly. "Yeah. It's a good feeling, isn't it? Kelmer, I'd say you'll fit in with us just fine." He cocked an eyebrow. "How long was the flight here from Iryala?"

"Fifteen days."

"Fifteen days on a courier boat? How'd you work out?"

Kelmer's answer was rueful. "Not very adequately. It had an exercise machine, and I did handstand pushups, but that's not like real training."

"They fitted out the *Burkitt* with a pretty good gym. Come on, I'll show it to you. You can use it on Second Platoon's shift tomorrow."

When Kelmer had returned to the cubby he occupied, Jerym went to the wardroom. Romlar was still there, watching two others play cards.

"Talk to you privately?" Jerym asked.

Romlar got up. "Sure." They went to his cabin, not much larger than Jerym's, but private. Its primary amenity was an electric joma maker. Romlar drew two cups and handed one to Jerym. "What did you think of him?" he asked.

"I like him. But I think he's got a problem."

Romlar raised an eyebrow.

"I've got a feeling he'll have problems under fire. First of all he's not a warrior." Jerym waved off a possible response. "I know. Some of our pilots on Terfreya, even gunship pilots, weren't warriors, but had no obvious difficulty under fire. As brave as you could ask for. But Kelmer— For one thing he worries about it. And for another—he threw a lot of *sirs* at me when we talked. I doubt he learned that at Blue Forest. I know there's been changes, but neither the T'swa nor Voker are strong on formalities. I assume it's him, the way he is. It came out as if he feels inferior to warriors. As if there's something in his case that makes him feel inadequate for combat."

Romlar took a thoughtful sip. "Hmm. Remind me to give you his interview analysis; it's in his folder. He has a warrior underpattern, so we can be sure he's been a warrior in some of his lives. But for this one he was definitely scripted as a non-warrior, and of course imprinted that way at home and in school. That's not much to override any past-life factors that might make him fearful and untrusting of himself.

"So we've got a guy who's strong and tough and weapons-skilled—even had basic jokanru—with a good education and a high intelligence score, yet who's afraid and a bit submissive.

With his psych profile, I'm really curious as to why Kristal chose him. It's got to have been intuitive."

They sat inhaling the aroma and sipping. "A warrior underpattern," Jerym said thoughtfully. "That explains his aura. And he says he loved the training; without at least some affinity with the guys, he wouldn't have. Maybe with combat getting close, his case is closing in on him."

Romlar shrugged. "We'll just have to wait and see. We've both read about guys who almost shit themselves waiting, they were so scared, and ended up decorated for bravery."

Jerym nodded. Time would tell.

Eight

There was an electricity among the troopers, a deep excitement. The world of their first contract was no longer a concept, no longer even a blaze against the blackness, or a beautiful blue, white, and tan ball. "Out there" had become "down there."

The *Burkitt* was a combination passenger and cargo ship, not built as a troop transport, let alone as a transport for egalitarian forces designed after the T'swa pattern. Thus the regiment's senior officers sat in the wardroom, watching on the large screen there. The platoon leaders and platoon sergeants watched on screens in the first-class dining room, and the lower ranks in their messhalls (they ate in shifts) and troop compartments.

On the screens, flashes of silver had become lakes, often in chains, and threadlike creeks could be made out where they flowed across open bogs and fens. Some of the fens in particular were large, showing pale greenish-tan, occasionally with islets of forest looking like black teardrops. Here and there, widely separated, were the lighter rectangles of farm fields, mostly in small clusters or strings. Romlar supposed they were along roads, but at first the roads couldn't be seen.

Most of it was dark forest though. As the *Burkitt* sank lower, the horizons drew in, the view became more oblique, and the forest appeared nearly unbroken. The terrain was gently undulating, approaching flat, with here and there low ridges crossing it, wrinkles on the plain. Then someone on the bridge changed the camera, and they were looking straight downward. In the local area shown below them now, fields were prominent. A couple of miles lower they became predominant, with scattered farm buildings visible. In the center, a village stood along the north side of a stream, with a mill pond and mill. On the south side of the stream, at a little distance, were the orderly tent rows of a military camp that would house, Romlar thought, a couple of regiments.

Their descent stopped and the intercom sounded. "Colonel Romlar to the bridge, please. Colonel Romlar to the bridge, please."

It was time. Romlar got up and left the wardroom, striding down the passageway to the bridge, a room not particularly large, resembling in size and shape the bridge on a surface ship. The central monitor showed the same picture he'd seen in the wardroom, but here it was flanked by an array of other views. The *Burkitt*'s captain motioned him over, and Romlar contacted the government below, to find out where to land.

As soon as Colonel Fossur's aide began to talk with the ship over the radio, the president rang General Belser's office and informed him. Then Lanks, his War Minister, his intelligence chief, and his daughter Weldi went outside. The ship hung motionless, something less than two miles above the village. It seemed very large. None had ever seen one before, and to Weldi especially, it was exciting. The four of them climbed into Fossur's open-topped army GPV, filling it, and trailing a long tail of dust, drove down the road to the landing site, to welcome the mercenary regiment.

When they got there, the ship still hovered above the village. The camp site had been prepared as agreed. Tent floors had been hammered together and stood in regularly placed stacks, with folded squad tents piled beside them.

Log footings had been set, and sills spiked on them. Mess tents had already been erected, along with the tents that would be regimental and battalion headquarters, and orderly rooms. Wells had been driven and hand pumps installed, the best the Smoleni could do under the circumstances. Latrine pits had been dug.

The ship was still parked above the village.

Another GPV sped down the gravel road, to pull up nearby. General Belser's aide got out and came over to them, trailed by a master sergeant. They saluted when they got there. "Mr. President," the aide said, "General Belser sent me as his representative."

Lanks nodded soberly. "Thank you, Major."

Vestur Marlim's lips thinned. Belser wasn't coming them. He was "making a statement," no doubt; he had "important" things to do, and the mercenaries weren't worth his attention. Actually, Belser hadn't initiated a single action since the Komarsi ended their advance. As if he was willing to sit here until the food ran out, making no effort. *If I were president*— The thought embarrassed the Minister of War, as if it were disloyal. He'd long admired Heber Lanks as a historian-philosopher and teacher, and admired him now as president for his patience, his humility—and yes, his judgment. Marlim was learning not to second-guess him; the man could be right with the most unlikely decisions.

But something needed to be done about that arrogant, surly, Yomal-punish-him Belser!

With the coming of the other GPV, the major's reporting, and his own thoughts about Belser, Marlim had lost track of the ship. Now he became aware that the others' attention had shifted upward, and he saw the ship lowering, even as it moved toward them. Within a few minutes it had parked only two or three feet above the ground. Massive jacks extruded, sought and found the earth, and the ship's AG generator gradually surrendered the *Burkitt's* tonnage to them.

Abruptly gangways opened and men poured out, boiled around the piles of floors and tents, and began to set up. As if they'd drilled it; no doubt they had. Others began to unload the ship's cargo holds, to set up prefabricated sheds and transfer goods to them. All this was under way before the mercenaries' commander had time to come over to the welcoming group.

President Heber Lanks watched him come, a man with thick shoulders and marked presence, flanked by what appeared to be two aides. Another man followed a bit behind them and to one side, wearing a helmet that seemed to be a camera as well; it had lenses, and a visor covered his upper face. It occurred to Lanks that he himself bore no insignia of office. Fossur was in uniform, and so was Major Oress, but Lanks wore comfortable yard clothes, with a heavy twill shirt to protect him somewhat from the bull flies, for fly-time had followed mosquito-time in the Free Lands. He looked, he supposed, more like a curious villager than an offworlder's concept of a president.

The mercenary colonel seemed to know him though. He stopped six feet in front of him, saluted casually, and spoke: "I'm Colonel Artus Romlar. This is my executive officer, Major Jorrie Renhaus, and my aide, Captain Fritek Kantros."

So young! "I'm Heber Lanks; I'm, uh, the president."

As Lanks had begun to speak, a bull fly had landed on Colonel Romlar's temple and dug in; clearly the young man had not applied a repellent. It distracted the president, and for a moment he'd faltered, then continued. "This is Vestur Marlim, my Minister of War; Colonel Elyas Fossur, my adviser and chief of intelligence; and Major Oress, aide to General Belser, who commands our armed forces. It seems I don't know Major Oress's first name. The young lady is my daughter and caretaker, Weldi."

The fly had continued to bite, and been joined by another at the angle of the jaw, but there'd been no indication at all that the mercenary commander noticed. Then Oress stepped forward and held out a folded paper to the young man.

"Colonel Romlar," he said, "these are General Belser's orders to you."

The young man took them, glanced at them, and handed them back. "Has the general read the contract of employment?"

Oress blinked. "I—don't know. I presume so."

Romlar smiled, his eyes steady on the major now, his

voice mild but utterly uncompromising. "It is quite explicit. First we are allowed two full weeks for reconditioning and to become familiar with the situation. I don't expect it will take that long, but it's ours if we need it. Furthermore, I am not subject to the general's orders: We are here to apply our military expertise, which includes my military judgment."

Oress had gone pale at this; the general would skin him for bringing such an answer. The young colonel continued. "I'll be happy to receive the general's briefing, and to coordinate my planning with his, or with whatever representative President Lanks may care to designate."

Both bull flies had gorged themselves and flown; another had settled on the colonel's other temple. President Lanks suspected that welts would arise at the sites. "I do urge, though," Romlar went on, "that whoever I work with be thoroughly conversant with the contract. Its language is straightforward and leaves little room for interpretation."

One of the president's long hands gestured as if dismissing the awkwardness. "Colonel Romlar," he said, "I appoint Colonel Fossur as liaison between you on the one hand and myself on the other. I am quite conversant with your contract, and I'll want to be kept aware of your plans and activities. I'm sure they'll be intelligent and potent, and I look forward to your results. If you're prepared to receive a briefing now, we will go to my office for it. I'm sure Colonel Fossur can deliver it without any special preparation."

He turned to Oress then. "Major, please radio for a vehicle for the colonel's use. There are too many of us for these two GPs."

"Of course, Mr. President."

Kelmer Faronya had kept his camera on the principals. He was more aware of the president's daughter, though, than of anything else, and he positioned himself to keep her in view. She couldn't be more than seventeen, he thought, tall and coltish and astonishingly pretty. In fact, it seemed to him she was the most appealing girl he'd ever seen. *Weldi.* It seemed to him the name was pretty, too.

Colonel Romlar hadn't said anything about the journalist attending any briefing, but when the extra GPV arrived,

Kelmer climbed into the back with Captain Kantros. Perhaps he'd have a chance to talk to her.

Lunch was brought to them in the president's office by his cook. Fossur kept finding more and more to tell, Romlar and the other two officers following on maps that Fossur gave them. It was late afternoon before he'd finished.

They'd taken a midafternoon break. Kelmer, going outside to move around a bit, had seen Weldi in the garden, and talked with her briefly. He'd learned that she was indeed seventeen, and that her father was a widower. She admitted to playing the piano, and invited him to visit them some evening, when she would play for him. He'd been in a state of bliss when he went back in the house.

Among the things that interested Romlar were: There had been no significant fighting for twenty days; the Komarsi seemed content to wait—starve them out. And General Belser, who'd earlier directed a dogged defense and hard-fighting withdrawal, had not suggested any further military actions, although the president had prodded him.

The boundary of Komarsi-occupied territory mostly ran east to west along the Eel River to Hawk Lake, where the Eel curved northward, continuing west from there to a monadnock named "the Straw Stack." This line was thinly manned by Komarsi forces, thinly because they correctly evaluated that any Smoleni breakout would be short-lived and very costly.

North of the Eel River, the Komarsi had no "held lines." However, they'd established a number of brigade bases in two major valleys whose streams flowed south into the Eel. Combined, these brigade bases held more troops than the entire Smoleni Army. The two valleys had some sizeable villages, most of whose families had fled. They also had substantial farmlands, and Komarsi occupation denied the Smoleni their crops and pastureage.

The Smoleni army had inflicted and taken heavy casualties in the south. The replacements were quite largely teen-aged recruits from the refugee camps, but there were also many Class B reservists from the northern districts, middle-aged backwoods farmers and villagers who logged in the winter as the markets allowed. The Smoleni Army had a leavening of trappers, many of them backwoods farmers who in winter worked so-called trapping "bounds" assigned to families. Also there was a tradition of solitary "wandrings"— often in winter—hiking or snowshoeing in the vast forests for days or even weeks at a time. The wanderer slept beneath the stars, or in a tiny lean-to set up where dusk found him, living largely off what he could snare or shoot or pull from the water. Most northern men, and more than a few towners and men of the Leas had done this, some only a few times in their youth, but many others repeatedly.

On occasion, squads of these backwoodsmen had gone AWOL, to bushwhack Komarsi patrols in the vicinity of brigade bases, with the tacit approval of their reservist officers. When Belser had learned of this, he'd forbidden it. To him it smacked of ill discipline.

Romlar was a very thoughtful young man as he rode to the regimental encampment. He'd already made certain working decisions, and shared them with Fossur on the condition that they not get to Belser till Romlar was ready.

Part Two

SUMMER WAR

Nine

A Smoleni reserve officer walked along one side of the mercenary camp, for no other reason than curiosity. He wore calf-high, laced moccasins instead of boots. That was one nonstandard thing Belser hadn't forbidden; boots were in short supply. His company was doing close-order drill, an activity he was required to order, though he thought poorly of it. His men had learned to walk in orderly ranks during their first couple of days in the army. To him it made no damn sense to spend hours at it now; He could think of lots more useful activities. But if he had to order it, he sure as shit didn't have to stand around and watch.

He heard voices ahead, more or less in unison, coming from what looked to be a mess tent. Curious, he walked toward it. A guard stepped out from behind a squad tent, an old Class C Smoleni reservist by his uniform and looks. He was a solid farmer pushing sixty, with graying hair and a rifle.

"Sorry, Cap'n. You need to go 'round. Ain't no one let to come through here."

The officer looked at him interestedly. "How come you to pull guard duty here?"

"Might's well. Belser got nothin' worthwhile for us to do. And seems there's an agreement that 'non-field personnel' will pull guard duty for the mercs."

"Hnh!" The officer gestured toward the mess tent. "What're they doin' in there? Sounds like they're chantin' Komarsi."

The guard looked troubled at the comment, and raising his rifle to port arms, made as if to push the officer back. "C'mon now, Cap'n. You ain't supposed to hear that. Move on back, or you'll get me in trouble."

"That's what they're doin', sure as winter. Must be learn-in' it." Except on the planets Oven and Kettle—formally Tyss and Orlantha—Standard was the language throughout the Confederation Sector. But the vernacular differed some-what from world to world, particularly on trade and resource worlds, where there would be different dialects even within countries. "I hear tell they learned to talk our lingo on the way here," the captain said. "That right?"

"Seems like. Good enough that a Komarsi couldn't tell the difference. I suppose it's in case they get took prisoner. They can say they're us."

The officer grunted. "Maybe they think if they learn Komarsi good enough, they can fool the real thing."

"The reason don't matter to me. I'm just supposed to keep folks away, so's they don't hear."

Grinning, the officer half turned as if to leave. "Best you don't let 'em get so close then."

The guard nodded ruefully. "Guess so. My wife's told me more'n once I don't hear so good no more. I never thought some'nd hear 'em from off here though."

The captain laughed. "Well, I won't tell nobody. They may be mercs, but they're our mercs, and I wish 'em well." He left then. He'd heard that one reason they were such a short regiment was, they'd done a lot of fighting somewhere else. He'd also heard that they weren't bound by Belser's orders. Another story was that most of them were going down to Shelf Falls, a lot closer to the Komarsi. He didn't entirely trust people who went off to fight in other people's wars, but help was help, and good help was something to be glad of. That old fart Belser had lost his appetite for fighting; maybe the mercs would go do some.

He left the camp at an easy trot. *There's them says the general knows what he's doin', that he'll move when the time's right. Shit! Time ain't likely to be any righter later than it is right now.*

He left the audience arguing the ethics of their insurrectionist intentions. What it came down to, it seemed to him, Soce of the High Court may as well be your judges when all is said and done . . .

*   *   *

Ten

It was near midnight. Kelmer Faronya lay on his belly on the side of a large stone pile, the boundary corner of four farms. Next to him lay Jerym Alsnor, and on Alsnor's other side a picked young captain, a Smoleni intelligence officer selected by Colonel Fossur. About half a mile ahead lay the village of Hearts Content, a large village, one-time seat of government for a large district. The Komarsi didn't call it Hearts Content. To them, according to the intelligence briefing, it was Brigade Base Four.

The least moon was near the zenith, and full. Another, a larger half disk, lay dusky gold on the treetops behind them in the west. Even in the light of just one, Kelmer felt dangerously exposed. Through his visor, he could see almost as well as by daylight, saw what his camera saw, and of course it adjusted to the available light. Specifically he saw Komarsi soldiers standing guard at the fence ahead of them. It had been decided by someone, perhaps Lord Kristal himself, that a journalist's video equipment, being non-military, need not meet Level 3 military restrictions. Colonel Voker had warned him not to tell the troopers what he saw through it though, said it as if he'd meant it. Kelmer wasn't sure what he'd do if Jerym asked him to.

Lieutenant Jerym Alsnor glanced back. It was time to move; the setting moon had half disappeared behind the treetops. The grass and weeds made better cover than he'd expected. The Komarsi had torn down the rail fences in the fields, presumably to prevent them being used for cover, then sent out crews with hay mowers to cut the grass and weeds. But they'd been allowed to grow up again. The responsible thing for them to have done, it seemed to him, was plow the fields, then harrow them every week or two.

Remarkable carelessness, born of overconfidence. *That'll change after tonight,* he told himself, *whether we pull this off or not.*

Scouting from a treetop at sundown, his binoculars had shown him the sentry posts around the ordnance dump, and at intervals around the rest of the camp. Now, with one hand he operated the signal scratcher he carried, heard it answered, then tucked it back into a shirt pocket. The sound they made was easily distinguished at some distance, but also easily dismissed as small night creatures. His men knew better. Then he flowed off the stone pile and began creeping toward the gate where the road entered the fenced compound.

The sentry stood with his rifle at order arms, as prescribed. His attention wasn't as prescribed though. He was thinking of the foreman's daughter back home. She'd never given him better than mild disdain, but in his imagination he enticed her into the hayloft, then grabbed and kissed her. Her eyes had widened, and she'd clutched him passionately. He'd slipped the skirt off her haunches, and . . .

An arm locked across his face, his mouth, and a heavy, razor-sharp knife drew firmly across his throat.

A moment later his killer stood in the sentry's place, the sentry's rifle at present arms. Seconds later he heard the wire cutters, kept hearing them. Now if the zone between the fences was clean, the way they'd been told . . .

* * *

At the truck-park office, only two soldiers were on duty, playing cards. There was no guard at the door. It opened. A man stepped in with a small crossbow, fired a bolt and dropped to his knees. Instantly the man behind him released another. The first Komarsi's forehead had hardly hit the table before the second was falling sideways.

Jerym walked openly down the street, followed by twelve troopers. They carried no packs, because in the village, Komarsi soldiers wouldn't ordinarily carry them. The weapons slung at their shoulders were submachine guns instead of rifles, providing heavier firepower for close range.

He'd know soon how good Colonel Fossur's informants were. At intervals he grunted a low "here," gesturing, and two men turned off to disappear into the shadow of some house. Finally there were only himself and two others. They continued to the inn, where Jerym stopped on the broad porch and sat down on a bench, as if for a chew of spice leaves before going in. The other two disappeared inside. One went on through to station himself in the back yard. The other, grenades dangling, sat down in the lobby, where he could watch the stairs and the hall beyond them.

At the ordnance dump, a man opened the gate, and a tarp-topped half-ton truck rolled out. He closed the gate behind it. So far, he thought, things seemed to be going perfectly. So far. At worst, now, they'd raise enough hell to make it worthwhile. He resumed his guard post, in case some Komarsi came while the others were stringing the det cord.

The half-ton rolled quietly, slowly down the street, headlights on but half-hooded, according to brigade policy as last known. It passed the inn, reached the village plaza, and followed the street around one side of it. The driver had thoroughly assimilated the intelligence they'd been given. He didn't review it now, didn't need to. He simply acted on it, on it and his warrior perceptions and reflexes.

At the far end of the plaza was the district government building and village hall combined, a large, two-story frame building that was now brigade headquarters and communication center. At least a skeleton crew would be on duty through the night there, and the brigadier and his immediate staff had their quarters in what had been the district magistrate's residence next door. There should be guards, but the slipshod way these Komarsi did things, he wouldn't bet on it.

The two guards at the headquarters entrance watched the half-ton approach. "Bloody strange," one of them said quietly. "The brigadier said headlights had to be full-hooded." He pursed his lips. "Somethin' mayn't be right. Get back inside the door and watch."

He moved quickly down the steps, submachine gun ready, and strode into the middle of the street, walking toward the oncoming half-ton. It slowed, stopped, and calling, he ordered the driver out. Instead of the driver, the man beside him got out and stepped toward the guard. He seemed to have no weapon. "What's the matter?" he asked, then abruptly dropped to one knee, drawing a pistol as he did so, and fired. The guard went backward, his weapon discharging into the air as he fell.

The truck jerked forward then, passing the kneeling trooper. At the same moment the other guard stepped onto the porch, firing a long burst through the windshield, hitting the driver. The half-ton rolled on, slowing, and the remaining trooper vaulted in over the tailgate.

Unsteered, it swerved, lurching to a stop a half-dozen yards from the building, and the remaining guard approached it crouching, ready to fire again. There was a tremendous explosion, a blinding flash as the truck erupted ...

Kelmer Faronya crouched by a tree near the base gate. The men who stood guard were men he knew. Earlier he'd almost died of nerves, waiting in the grass sixty yards away, his camera tracking one of them while they'd stalked the guards who'd stood where they stood now. Whose bodies they'd dragged into the shallow ditch beside the road. It had seemed impossible they wouldn't be seen, wouldn't be shot down, bringing the whole unlikely scenario falling with them. Nothing in the training at Blue Forest provided the necessary skills. He hadn't known there were such skills.

Simply by watching, he'd recorded it all. Now there was nothing to record, but from his tree-side vantage he recorded anyway, staring down the graveled main street into the village. It was difficult to breathe. Gunfire would surely break out any minute, and the sleeping village would erupt with armed and angry soldiers. A half-ton appeared, turned onto the main street, and he watched/recorded it recede toward the village center. He knew its roles: destruction and cue. It was almost time; perhaps they'd do it yet. It lost itself in the darkness, blocking the close fan of illumination from its hooded lights, and he waited some more. And waited.

Suddenly there was a shot, then another. A submachine gun belched. Seconds later the night was split by a powerful explosion. Almost at once there was more submachine-gun fire, continuing, and the dull roars of grenades. An alarm whooped needlessly, and he imagined soldiers pouring from the village houses, each of them a barracks of armed men. Then the ground shook, and again, and again, the explosions overlapping like a string of monstrous lady-fingers as ordnance bunkers blew.

His paralysis was gone. He wanted to slip back down the road, run through the grass, find the forest, but the two troopers stood watchfully at the guard posts, and he would not go till they did. They were his friends, and he feared their disdain even more than he feared the enemy.

Minutes passed with diminishing gunfire, then two of the troopers who'd marched up the street with Jerym appeared and stood beside Kelmer in the deep shadow beneath the tree. He felt safer with them there. Soon a GPV came, headlights unhooded, and together they hid from it, bunched behind the tree. A Komarsi officer got out and walked over to question the troopers by the gate. Their answers seemed to satisfy him, because he got back in the vehicle and it turned and drove back into the village.

Three more troopers arrived, one of them Jerym. "All right," he said, "let's get our asses out of here." Seen through the visor, he seemed exhilarated. They turned and trotted down the road a short distance till they were joined by men with light machine guns who'd been placed to cover them if they were pursued. They all left the road then, loping across the field, even the men carrying the machine guns running easily and swiftly. In eight or nine minutes they reached the forest edge. Jerym whistled shrilly, was answered, and soon others joined them; the men who'd blown the ordnance dump had gotten out earlier. But of the men who'd marched into town with the lieutenant, there were only the four.

The men that were with him, though, were grinning. Kelmer stood unbelieving. Then Jerym gave the order, and once more quiet, they headed into the woods along an old sleigh road.

The Regiment

Regiment.

Eleven

Half a mile back in the woods, the sleigh road petered
out. The major moon had topped the horizon behind them,
but even so, beneath the forest canopy it was so dark that
even on the narrow sleigh road, travel had been slow and
somewhat blundering. Without the road, it was too dark to
travel, short of dire emergency, so Jerym set sentries, and
the rest lay down to sleep.

They'd sweated off the insect repellent they'd worn, and
Kelmer applied more. They were all more or less inured to
mosquitoes, but it bothered him to have them biting when
he lay down to rest. He wondered if the troopers really
would sleep, they'd seemed so exuberant. He lay mentally
numb for a time, not really thinking, disconnected images
and fragmented thoughts passing through his mind. Once it
occurred to him that until tonight he'd thought of himself,
usually, as one of them, a trooper. Not always, but usually,
for here with the White T'swa, as with the 6th Regiment at
Blue Forest, the troopers were remarkably easy to be with,
get along with. But tonight it seemed to him that a gulf
had opened between himself and them, a gap that couldn't
possibly close. That he was no trooper, could never be. He

58

was an impostor. Finally he slept, dozing fitfully until dawn began to thin the darkness.

The sentries wakened them and they started on again, speeding to a trot when the forest became light enough. Apparently no one had followed them into the night. Kelmer wondered if indeed the Komarsi had any idea where they might be, or how many, or even what had happened at all.

After about two miles, they topped a low ridge, the highest in the vicinity, and ranged northward briefly along the crest to where they'd stashed their packs. Jerym called a halt there, and they opened their packs to eat before pushing on again.

At midday they stopped. Sentries were posted. They ate, and men lay down to nap for half an hour, Kelmer a little apart from the others. Jerym came over to him and sat down beside him. Kelmer avoided meeting his eyes.

"How did it go for you last night?" Jerym asked.

You know how it went for me, Kelmer thought. *You know exactly how it went for me.* "Not very well."

"Tell me about it."

There was no sympathy in the words, no consoling. But in spite of that, or perhaps because of it, Kelmer rose a bit from the mental quagmire he was in.

"I was scared. So scared, I felt like I couldn't move."

"Ah. Sounds like a bad night, all right. But you moved when you had to; moved up, moved back. And lots of people would have felt as bad." He paused. "Beyond being scared, how was it?"

The question struck some deep cord of dread in Kelmer. He put a cap on it, but it wasn't a tight seal. It seeped through. *Was it all the men they killed?* he wondered. That didn't indicate as part of it; a small part at most. No, what really bothered him was the troopers who hadn't come back. It had bothered him a bit when Jerym had talked that first night about a company being used as bait on Terfreya, bait in a trap, and getting shot to pieces. It had bothered him like a gentle prod at a ripe boil. But tonight had truly hit him, hit him hard.

Kelmer was able to look at Jerym now, at the calm face, the steady eyes. His voice was little more than a whisper when he answered. An intense whisper. "Where are Trimala and Fenwer, and Ekershaw?" It occurred to him that he hadn't sorted out who else was missing.

Jerym gazed thoughtfully at him, and to some detached part of Kelmer Faronya, it seemed that the trooper was looking for a way to put it. "Ekershaw's still alive, and so are Pelley and Kalbern. But BJ saw Kalbern go down, so I suppose he's wounded and a prisoner. The others are dead; Olkerfel died maybe an hour ago."

Kelmer's short hairs began to prickle. "How do you know?"

"When one of us dies, he joins us, lets the others know. That happened even on Terfreya sometimes. Last night it was strong. The training on Oven finished opening that channel for us."

Kelmer stared, then turned away. And began to shake, shake hard. He hadn't known any of the dead men closely, couldn't even place who Olkerfel was, but a deep grief welled up in him, a grief somehow too dry to find release in tears. He felt Jerym's hand on the back of his shoulder, a brief touch, then he was aware that the lieutenant had left.

Awhile later he heard Jerym whistle the nappers out of their sleep. Getting up, he put his pack on and joined the others. After a few minutes of hiking, he began to feel almost all right again.

Twelve

The Komarsi field hospital occupied what had been a
children's camp by a lake, and was busy for the first time
since they'd moved in. Sunlight streamed through screened
windows, floodlights for dancing dust motes. Men lay
sedated on the beds. At the foot of one of them stood
several officers. One was a surgeon in a pale blue gown,
monitoring what went on, prepared to step in, to demand
a halt if necessary. Not that he had the authority to stop it:
The subcolonel doing the questioning was General
Undsvin's intelligence chief. An aide stood behind the man,
pen poised over a secretarial pad.

"Tell me, Sergeant, what exactly happened?"

"I was in the first truck behind the escort, three gun
trucks. We was prob'ly goin' 'bout twenty-five per, not much
more than regulation. . . ."

The subcolonel interrupted. "What about spacing?"

"We—started out regs. But we'd closed up some at. Hard
to keep intervals on the road."

"All right. There'll be no action taken against you for
anything you say here. Continue."

"Well—all of a sudden there was a big explosion up

61

ahead. I think the lead truck got blowed up. Then other
trucks piled into the back of 'im. My driver braked so's I
got throwed into the windshield, but I had time to get my
arm up. Then some'n run into us from behind.

"My door'd flung open when we hit, but before I could
get out, there was a really big explosion from back t'the tail
of the convoy—an ammo truck must have blowed—and
pieces of truck come rainin' down. About the time they
started to hit, there was more explosions, just as bad. The
ammo trucks was all back in the back, per regs, and I reckon
they'd been keepin' intervals better. There was other explosions not as bad, mortar bombs I think, and when one of
'em hit an ammo truck, that's when it blew. You could feel
the ground jump!

"I knew that wouldn't be all of it, I knew that like I know
Yomal loves me, and that I needed to get out of there. But
I was too scared while pieces of truck was comin' down outa
the sky. Then it stopped, and I jumped out.

"I could see 'em then, runnin' cross the field shootin'! I
went for the ditch, but about the time I jumped, I felt
myself get hit. It slammed me in the back, and I landed in
the water. I just laid there then; 'tweren't deep enough to
drown in, less'n you passed out with your face down in it.
There was a lot of shootin' for a couple minutes. I was on
my side and I could see 'em runnin' round shootin' people.
I closed my eyes, hopin' they'd take me for dead, and finally
I couldn't hear 'em no more. After a few more minutes I
crawled out of the water. Then I donked out. I didn't know
whether I was the only one alive or not."

The subcolonel nodded curtly, then turned and walked
away without a "thank you," a major beside him, his aide
following. Outside, the subcolonel questioned the chief surgeon. "You said they killed all but three. Who are those
others in there?"

"I said fifty-six were killed and only three were wounded.
But there were six ambulances with twelve medics in the
convoy, going to Tekkeros to pick up overflow from the field
hospital there. Nine of the twelve were injured in the
pileup; none were shot by the raiders."

The subcolonel's interruption was testy. "Make sense,
man! You said only three were wounded!"

The surgeon's face tightened. "Their injuries were from collision, colonel. They were not shot; they wore blue medical corps jackets."

The subcolonel bit short what may have started as an oath, and turned away without acknowledging. *The damned hair-splitter!* The chief surgeon outranked him, was a full colonel, but he was also a commoner; you could smell it. Probably the son of a merchant family—the kind that tended to think they were better than their position in life.

He led his small party to the command car they'd come in. One was another subcolonel, chief of the general's planning staff. The planning chief walked beside him. "You say these raiders are offworld mercenaries. How can you be sure?"

"Our spies at Burnt Woods reported a regiment of foreigners were landed from a spaceship there. They saw the ship themselves, saw it come down. And before the day was out, they'd heard that a mercenary regiment had been landed from it. They then went to where they could see their encampment."

"I'm aware of that."

"They're the ones who attacked the brigade bases; that seems quite evident. The prisoners we took, and the bodies we recovered, were remarkably muscular. That and the way they operate are proof enough."

"And when the prisoners were questioned?"

"There were only a few, and none said anything. Unless you count howling."

"Perhaps further questioning will be fruitful?"

"There can be no further questioning."

"Dead?!"

"Dead."

The planning chief frowned and looked away. The intelligence chief said nothing. He'd erred, he recognized that now, in letting brigade G-2s do the questioning. They'd been traumatized by the devastation at their bases. Three weren't even intelligence-trained, had inherited the G-2 hat because brigade G-2s had been wiped out. He should have had the prisoners brought to Rumaros and questioned them himself.

No doubt General Undsvin would point that out to him quite forcefully.

Thirteen

The raids on Komarsi brigade bases were the major subject of conversation in the Smoleni army and in what was left of government. And the information that fueled those conversations came from more than the mercenaries involved. Each raiding team had been accompanied by a Smoleni intelligence officer, only one of whom failed to return safely.

"Belser's angry about it," Fossur said.

Romlar nodded, and sipped the "joma" Fossur's orderly had served. At Burnt Woods they called it, "war joma"; it was actually made from scorched grain. "He was angry from the start," Romlar said. "He's angry because we're here."

"True." The president had had to insist, when Romlar had wanted intelligence officers attached to the raiding parties, and Belser had left the meeting in a huff. "He'd have resisted harder if he'd thought you'd be so successful. Now he says you've stirred up a hornets' nest; he expects the Komarsi to mount punitive strikes."

"Mmm." Romlar sipped again. "It's to their advantage not to. They control the territory they need to win the war, win it by starving you out. But if they make punitive strikes,

64

they'll have to move on forest roads. In that case you can hit and run, hit and run. Bleed them badly.

"Meanwhile our raids tell your friends abroad that you're not just sitting in the backcountry waiting to run out of food. You're taking the war to the Komarsi. Consider the impact on public opinion in other countries when the cubes of the raid on Hearts Content get circulated around Maragor."

Fossur nodded. The Krentorfi ambassador had been delighted when they'd been played for him, and young Faronya had made copies for him to take back to the queen. Komars was not a well-liked kingdom, and Engwar a widely disliked monarch. Perhaps states besides Krentorf would be inclined now to provide aid. There'd already been a rumor that Oselbent and The Archipelago had discussed a mutual defense pact. If Selmark joined them, he had no doubt at all that Oselbent would provide an avenue for shipping in food and munitions. As it was, the Oselbenti feared Komarsi reprisals—the shelling of her ports.

"You haven't told me what you'll do next," he said. "You won't catch the Komarsi asleep like that again. They're already building gun towers, digging trenches, and hauling in a lot more barbed wire."

Romlar laughed. "We're working on several things. But they need to be kept absolutely secret from the Komarsi, and they almost certainly have agents here. Like you have there."

Fossur nodded; as an intelligence specialist, he took spies for granted. Romlar looked around, then got to his feet. "Let's take a walk."

They walked a meadow path along the bank of the Almar River. Romlar described his plans, most of them requiring cooperation, and they made some agreements. Fossur, who had friends and connections throughout the army and government, said he could provide the resources without going through Belser, for these were all small matters, small but crucial. "If necessary I'll ask the president for help."

He bent, picked up a short piece of branch left by floodwater, and threw it in the river. They watched it slide down the current to an eddy, where it spun around briefly, going nowhere, then emerged and floated on.

"I suppose you wonder why he leaves Eskoth in command."

"I've guessed because the general led a skilled and dogged defense in the south. And perhaps because of old friendship."

"Actually they didn't know one another until Heber was elected president, but there seems to be a certain affinity between them. You've noticed the president is invariably polite to him, regardless of how surly Eskoth might be. But when he says do such and such, Eskoth always shuts up and does it, however gracelessly. I have no doubt that if he ordered him to take his army and begin a suicide offensive on Rumaros, Eskoth would do it.

"Actually I think he might replace him, if he had someone he felt enough confidence in. I can think of several myself, and I've named them to him. But—" Fossur shrugged. "The president's a mild and patient man. Too patient, I'd say. Once he decides something though . . ." He glanced sideways at Romlar. "It helps that he's so big. And you've shaken hands with him; you know what his grip is like. He wasn't always an academic. As a boy and a youth he worked as a fuelwood cutter, felling and bucking trees, loading them on sleighs, and hauling them to his uncle's fuelyard at Collinsteth, where he'd help cut them up and split them. He's said to have been mild mannered even in those days, and usually with a book in his pocket."

When they parted, Romlar returned to regimental headquarters thinking how unusual a country Smolen was, and how unusual its president.

Kelmer sat in the president's parlor, showing the cube of the raid on Hearts Content. This was a command performance. Heber Lanks had seen it before, but his daughter hadn't, and she'd asked Kelmer to show it to her. So he'd brought the player from his tent. Initially Weldi Lanks had been more interested in seeing the rugged, good-looking young Iryalan than the video, but as he played it, she'd become fascinated.

When it was over, the president looked thoughtful and a little drawn. "War," he said, "is not an activity I greatly like."

"Me either, Daddy. But we didn't want the war! They invaded us! They forced it on us!"

"Yes, and sit safely in Linnasteth or on their estates, sending their serfs to die for them." He looked at Kelmer. "Bullets don't avoid journalists. What do you think of dying in battle, Mr. Faronya?"

"I—" Kelmer wanted to seem brave to Weldi, but he could not flagrantly lie, so he evaded the question with a half truth. "I haven't been exposed much to combat, Mr. President. But I don't find death comfortable to think about."

"And what do your comrades think of dying in battle? They've been exposed abundantly to it. Colonel Fossur studied their record on Terfreya, where they lost about a third of their number."

"On Confederation member worlds there are tests they give children," Kelmer said. "And make psychological profiles from them. Some people are born to be warriors; all of the regiment's troopers were. But I'm not, so I can't really know how they feel about things. I can only observe what they do and say."

Weldi looked interested. "What *do* you classify as, Kelmer?"

He thought of where he fitted in the Matrix of T'sel, but that was something else. "They don't tell you," he answered, "at least not ordinarily. You don't need to be a warrior to be a soldier, though; most soldiers aren't. As far as getting killed is concerned, troopers, the men of the regiment, don't seem to be afraid at all. But they're different than most warriors, too: they're T'swa-trained. And they believe implicitly that when they die, they'll be reborn as someone else."

"Really?" Weldi said. "They believe that?"

"Apparently."

"Umh," the president grunted. "How well does this belief hold up when they look down the barrel of a hostile machine gun?"

"You might ask Colonel Romlar, sir. Or maybe Lieutenant Alsnor; he led his platoon in repeated actions on Terfreya, and in time almost every man in it got killed. It was a special platoon that got especially dangerous missions."

"And does it still?"

"I'm not sure, but they made the Hearts Content raid. Company A is stationed at Shelf Falls now. I'm supposed to go there tomorrow, to rejoin him."

"You'll be gone then!" Weldi said.

Kelmer nodded. "That's right, Miss Lanks."

"Daddy, I've hardly had a chance to know Mr. Faronya, and now he'll be gone!"

The president smiled. "I have things to do in my office. Why don't you two stay here and talk."

He unfolded his long frame and left them. Weldi didn't give Kelmer time to feel uncomfortable; she began at once to talk. "Kelmer—may I call you Kelmer? You may call me Weldi. What is it like where you're from, Kelmer?"

Her gaze was intense, making him feel a little awkward. She was a very pretty girl. "I went to university in Landfall," he said. "It's a big city: more than a million people."

She nodded. "I've read about Landfall. It's thought to be the place where the first people landed in our sector. It must be wonderful to live there."

"It's nice, all right. But I grew up in a smallish town called Silver Lake. There are lots of lakes and wooded hills around there. Not wild forest, like you have here, but very lovely. Tended forest. And the trees are mostly leaf trees. One of the things I liked to do was hike and run along the roads. We use AG vehicles there, instead of surface vehicles; they run about eight inches above the ground. So the roads and highways are kept in grass, and there are beds of perennial flowers along the edges."

She put a hand on his. His collar grew suddenly tight. "It sounds wonderful. I'd like to visit there someday. In fact, I'd probably like to live there. What was it like at the university?"

They talked awhile longer, Weldi especially. Then the president came in and reminded her of her lessons; he acted as her study guide. Kelmer left bemused by her obvious interest in him. He'd never felt assured around girls, but neither was he inexperienced. And he found Weldi Lanks very stimulating. He fantasized about her all the way back to camp.

Fourteen

Lieutenant Rob Mesvik halted his platoon on a high, rocky bluff. They were in the rugged, mountainous western fringe of Smolen known as the High Wilds, fifty-five miles from the nearest village, and almost as far from the nearest farm. There wasn't a Komarsi soldier for a hundred miles.

Varky Graymar wiped sweat from his forehead, and looked across a gorge whose other side was in the Kingdom of Krentorf. This was the platoon's fourth day on the trail. With only brief breaks, it had been hiking since sunup, each trooper carrying a substantial pack despite the pack horses. Their packs held the gear each man would need on the mission. The horses carried what was needed on the trail and pulled the narrow two-wheeled boat carts that the troopers had occasionally needed to manhandle around switchbacks or up steep pitches. Occasionally their scouts, ranging ahead, had had to unsheath axes to clear windfalls from the trail.

The men all wore civilian clothes, rough work clothes that would look quite natural on country roads in Komars.

The river below was called the Raging River. From where Graymar stood, it appeared smooth and perhaps a hundred and fifty yards wide, flowing southward. He looked, than lay down by the trail, leaning back against his pack. Their packs weren't military either. They were of patterns that vagabond Komarsi laborers might carry.

They ate their midday ration and had time for a short nap. Then Mesvik whistled them up, and they started down a narrow crooked trail through patchy forest to the river. It was the worst stretch they'd hiked yet. Repeatedly they had to manhandle the boat carts around switchbacks, across slide-outs, and through narrow places. By the time they'd reached the boulder-littered shore, the sun had set behind the ridge on the other side of the river. The sky was clear, so they set up no tents. After supper they found the best spots they could to lie on, and slept for a time.

Their boats were a stable, durable design that had been known in a distant time and place as bateaux, used then and now on rough rivers, to carry rough men herding floating logs. The platoon and its boatmen-guides launched them by moonlight, hours before dawn. The troopers had trained briefly on smaller rough rivers, but this one was deadly in places, and the places wouldn't always be evident in advance. Thus they had river guides.

The country it flowed through was wild, but here and there were human habitations—cabins occupied mainly by trappers in winter. Occasionally, their guides told them, some would be occupied by sportsmen, but on the Smoleni side that had been in better times. So far as feasible, their guides timed the platoon's sleep so they'd pass such cabins by night. When they passed one by day, a close watch was kept for any sign of occupation, but they saw none.

Several times they'd bypassed dangerous rapids and cascades, struggling and sweating, manhandling the heavy, awkward boats around and over boulders and talus, and the wrecks of trees that had slid down from above.

For three days and nights they rode the current, speeding the trip by taking constant turns at the oars, three pairs plus a stern scull in every boat. Their guides, strong and enduring men, were impressed with the troopers' strength, efficiency, and seeming tirelessness, whether at the oars or on portage.

They'd tell stories about them in years to come, coming to believe their own exaggerations.

On the last day, the country became lower and less rugged, less wild. On the last night they crossed the border, though they didn't know just when. Twice, glimpses of lamplight marked Komarsi logging camps near the river.

The current that night was smooth, and they kept near midstream, with muffled tholes so their rowing couldn't be heard from shore. Here their guides weren't as familiar as they had been with what lay along the banks. Finally they heard a sound like distant thunder, a sound they'd been waiting for: Great Roaring Falls. They rowed to the Komarsi shore then, and the troopers got out, taking their packs. After that the four boatmen rowed away, one in each bateau, staying close together. In mid-river, all four transferred into one boat, and crossed to the Krentorfi side. The other three boats they let go, to ride the current and plunge over the falls. What remained of them wouldn't be distinguishable from any other bits of floating wood.

Fifteen

Some two hundred miles northeast, Jerym Alsnor crouched in the forest, waiting and listening. It was night. The mosquitoes swarmed in clouds; he didn't notice. He led two platoons on this mission: his own rifle platoon, and a mortar platoon. The rifle platoon carried no rifles this night; they carried light machine guns for reach and firepower, and submachine guns for close work.

They'd been moving slowly. The word was that since the night of the Great Raids, the Komarsi ran strong security patrols in the vicinity of their brigade bases. It was very doubtful that they moved in the forest at night, but they might well leave outposts at strategic locations—platoons or even companies—their guards listening nervously in the dark, with fingers on triggers.

It was difficult enough for *his* men in the forest at night. If they'd had the night vision of the T'swa, *Homo tyssiensis*, it would have been different. Or if it had been a Level 2 War, where they could use night visors. But at Level 3 they had to make do with their unaugmented human eyesight.

Three things made it feasible. *One*, under T'swa training, the troopers had developed the latent talent of "going without knowing." That is, if they knew a location, they could go there crosscountry without map or guide. Not easily perhaps, if there were obstacles for instance, but they could find it. It was difficult to disorient them, and nearly impossible to keep them disoriented. *Two*, the major moon was riding high. And *three*, their route took them through a tract logged selectively two years earlier, leaving the forest roof with enough openings to let significant moonlight through. That same logging, however, had left branches, tops, and cull logs lying on the ground, too often hidden in shadow, waiting for someone to trip on them.

What Jerym waited for now were the scouts he'd sent ahead. He'd come to the major skidway, a sleigh road through the woods, broad enough for sleighs eight feet wide. It was a logical place for the Komarsi to cover. If it was safe, it would take them to a preplanned firing position, a position from which they could fire for effect without first firing ranging rounds. He'd scaled it off precisely on a detailed forestry map before he'd left Shelf Falls.

There was a hiss ahead of him, a pattern of them, and dimly he made out a figure waving. He hissed back, then moved ahead, the others following: his two platoons plus a dozen Smoleni noncoms along for the experience. And Kelmer Faronya, wearing his helmet camera. Its visor made him the only one of them who could see decently. Each of them, in the mortar platoon and the rifle platoon, carried a .37 caliber pistol and a trench knife. The men in the mortar platoon also went burdened with a mortar tube or baseplate, or a packframe loaded with 66 mm mortar bombs, plus propellant horseshoes.

The way was clear, and on the skidway they made better speed. In less than an hour, the mortars were set up on the abandoned log landing where the skidway met the gravel road. On the other side of the road were fields and pastures. Beyond them lay a Komarsi brigade base, barely more than a mile from where they crouched. The village was on the forestry map, rows of tiny symbols for buildings. Added to this, Fossur's local agent had sketched in the QM dump, the ordnance dump, the motor pool, and other military additions. He'd even circled the more important buildings. At that range, even T'swa-trained mortar men couldn't expect to pinpoint buildings they couldn't see, but they should be able to do a lot of damage.

His machine gunners left then, each with his twenty-pound weapon ready, an ammunition belt in the metal box he carried. Jerym gave them time to take positions, beginning some two hundred yards up the road, counting off the necessary seconds in his mind. Meanwhile his mortar men had set up their weapons, set their phosphorescent sights, and snapped on the propellant horseshoes. He gave the low whistled signal to fire. If the map was accurate, things were about to get exciting in the brigade base. After that, things could get pretty exciting here, too, depending on the Komarsi response.

Kelmer listened to the thumps of mortar rounds being launched, a salvo of eight to begin with, targeted hopefully on the truck park. The next salvo was a bit ragged. After that the firing was non-synchronous. He stared; it was as if nothing had been fired, or as if the rounds had been swallowed into hyperspace. Surely, though, the Komarsi had seen the muzzle flashes. With the machine gun towers they'd built, they could hardly avoid it. And they'd have artillery.

Then he saw the flashes of the mortar rounds landing, and moments later heard the explosions. After that, the explosions were more or less continuous.

He didn't feel particularly fearful yet, it was all so far away. But he watched for possible flashes of artillery. If they saw any, the mortar crews were to disassemble the mortars at once—a business of short seconds—and run back up the skidway. Wait out the barrage and return to expend their mortar rounds. He, on the other hand, was to run along the road to the machine gunners, to record whatever developed there.

The mortar men had expended most of their rounds before they saw a response: A long row of muzzle flashes, virtually simultaneous, flared from the base. For a long moment Kelmer crouched transfixed, forgetting his order. Then the mortar crews were running past him onto the skidway. Remembering, he dashed onto the road, and along it northward. Now he saw something else alarming: a line of trucks moving out of the base, with headlights on unhooded! He heard the incoming rounds rumbling through the night air, and they began to fall in the field behind him, fifty or sixty yards short of the road. There were a lot of them, and their crashing roars lent speed to his feet.

Inside a minute he was with the machine gunners, who were spaced along the road, among the edge trees. His heart pounded wildly. When the trucks arrived, they'd be less than forty feet away. Kelmer realized he couldn't see well from where he crouched, and what he couldn't see, he couldn't record visually, so he crept out a few feet, to kneel on the back bank of the ditch.

Southward down the road, the next salvo of shells roared into the forest with terrific crashes, producing a long rain of branches and larger pieces of trees, invisible in the night. A third salvo landed still farther back, and the fourth mostly on and along the road. Clearly the Komarsi artillery observers didn't know whether they were long or short; they kept changing the range, plowing the pasture, the forest edge, the roadsides.

The lead truck turned onto the north-south road, and Kelmer scrambled back into the woods to avoid being caught in the headlights. A minute later, the machine guns began firing point-blank into the trucks, which were spaced much too closely. Some braked; some went into the ditches, some of these tipping onto their side; more crashed into trucks ahead of them. Tracers chewed canvas canopies, metal hoods, windows. Soldiers spilled out, spilled running. Many fell wounded or dead. More took shelter behind the trucks, or dispersed into the pasture. There was surprisingly little return fire at first, as if they were content to take cover.

Northward, a number of trucks had stopped short of the machine guns and unloaded their troops too. Some of these dispersed into the woods. With any leadership at all, they'd move to flank the machine gunners. Return fire began to increase, as the Komarsi recovered from their surprise and shock. Closer at hand, some began throwing grenades.

The troopers were heavily outnumbered, and the balance was shifting. Someone whistled a shrill retreat order, and the troopers rose almost as one, moving back into the woods. Kelmer got up too—and saw something land on the ground in front of him. *Grenade!* his mind shrieked, and with a hoarse cry he turned, starting into the forest, where he promptly stumbled and fell on some logging debris, not because he couldn't see—he could—but because he didn't see. His heart thuttered wildly, and he lay wide-eyed for a moment. The grenade had not exploded! At the same time, he realized that his rectum had spasmed, had sprayed his shorts.

Shaking, Kelmer got to his feet again. Then a row of shells exploded in the field not much short of the road, some in the farside ditch, on line with where he was, knocking him down again. As if some Komarsi officer had panicked, and radioed for artillery support, bringing the shells down on his own men. Kelmer and the others realized where the next salvo was likely to land, and despite the trees and shadow-hidden logging slash, they ran, hard. More crashes rent the night behind them, some of the shells bursting in the treetops, spraying the woods with steel and splintered wood. Kelmer, with his visor-given vision, outran the others until a fallen branch tripped him and he fell heavily, the breath knocked out of him.

A moment later, someone stopped beside him. "You all right?" the trooper asked.

"I think so."

"Good. Stay with me."

He recognized me, Kelmer thought. *He doesn't want me to get lost.* He followed gratefully.

They came to the skidway again and followed it. When they came to its end, they kept going, if more slowly. Soon afterward they reached the end of the cutting. The denser forest behind it was much darker. They groped their way into it perhaps twenty or thirty yards, then Jerym stopped them and posted sentries. The rest lay on the ground to sleep.

Hidden by darkness, Kelmer went a few yards apart, took out the packet of toilet paper he carried in a shirt pocket, lowered his pants and tidied up as best he could, then fastened them again. Lying beside a moss-grown log, he reviewed the experience. All in all, it seemed to him he'd done well. Or if not exactly well, he at least hadn't humiliated himself. He'd done what he was supposed to do, and had stood to the last.

If I just hadn't fouled my pants, he thought. It hadn't been too bad though—a spray—and he didn't stink. Perhaps no one would notice. He couldn't know till it got daylight again.

He was drifting off to sleep when it first occurred to him to wonder how many troopers had died. When he slept, he dreamed they had come to him, jollying him gently about his pants, and it didn't bother him at all.

When he woke up, he remembered the dream. He'd remember it as long as he lived.

Sixteen

Thunderstorms stalked the night over northwestern Komars, and wind lashed the forest. The civilian-clad troopers were soaked but not much chilled. They'd been alternately jogging and walking the forest road they followed, and the exertion warmed them. It was a good road, a major forest road, wide enough that, at night, light reached it from the sky. They could make out its edges and avoid the ditches on each side.

It was their second night on the march. They'd holed up during the day, laid low in a dense stand of young growth. They weren't ready to be seen yet. They'd already broken up into three groups, to find and follow three different roads east. This group was the larger, two squads, led by Lieutenant Mesvik.

Mesvik whistled a signal, and the men slowed to a brisk walk. Thunder rolled like some great bowling ball across the sky, to be answered by another, and another. Trees thrashed, genuflecting before the wind.

Varky Graymar paused for a moment on the shoulder to relieve his bladder; he could catch up easily enough. As he stood refastening his pants, lightning split the sky overhead, striking a tall tree, shattering it while thunder burst the night. The top snapped out. Pieces flew. The branchy top, hurled by the wind, crashed through other treetops and fell onto the roadside. A limb struck Varky, knocking him unconscious beneath it.

It had been no passing convection storm. An unseasonable cool air mass had moved in, undercutting muggy, unstable air, and the storm had continued for hours. Near dawn it blew over, and the lesser moon shone through the trees, though they still dripped. The jogging troopers looked forward to the sun and a chance to get dry. Dawn had paled the eastern sky when they came to the forest's edge, and Mesvik called a halt. In front of them was farmland, open and nearly level.

"This is where we split up," he said. "You know your partners, and your order of march. Urkwal and Graymar, when the sun comes up . . ." He paused. "Where's Graymar?" There was a looking about among the troopers. Mesvik looked back down the road and raised his voice. "Graymar?"

Nothing. "Anyone got a clue where Graymar is?" No one answered. "When's the last time anyone noticed him?"

It turned out that no one had since he and Urkwal had talked on a break before the storm began. In the storm and heavy darkness, the men had talked scarcely at all with each other, and mostly couldn't see who jogged or walked beside them.

"All right," Mesvik said. "Immeros, you and Smit will lead off instead. The rest of us will move off to the south a hundred yards or so and try to get some rest in the edge of the woods. Urkwal, go back up the road and find Graymar. If you haven't found him by ten o'clock, come back. If all of us have left when you get here, catch a nap and carry through with your orders. That's it. Go."

Urkwal acknowledged and jogged off. Mesvik watched him leave. *Not a promising start*, the lieutenant told himself. *Interesting but not promising.*

When the sun rose high enough, it aligned with the road and shone down it on Winn Urkwal's pack, and the back of his leathery neck. He hiked on, jogging enough to keep warm. A truck passed him headed east, loaded with logs, and after a while another. Later he heard a vehicle coming headed west, cut off from view by the brow of a low hill behind him. On an impulse he left the road, hurrying to cover behind a sapling thicket. It passed him, a sky-blue carryall with a decal on the front door. He returned to the road then and continued. Shortly a log truck passed empty, also headed west. Urkwal simply stepped off the road for it.

Minutes later he heard another vehicle coming, from ahead this time, and again he hid, now behind a convenient roadside deck of logs. It was the same carryall as before, traveling faster now. And he knew, knew as if he'd seen him, that Varky Graymar was inside, although the only visible occupants were strangers in the front seat.

He hiked on anyway, until just beyond a storm-felled treetop, he saw tire tracks where a vehicle had pulled off onto the saturated shoulder of the road. Turning, Urkwal examined the treetop. Some large branches had been chopped from it and thrown aside, their leaves only starting to wilt. Foot tracks told him that two men had carried something between them to the vehicle.

Winn Urkwal had no doubt what had happened: the treetop had struck Graymar, knocked him out and injured him. The two men had seen him beneath it as they'd passed, and had picked him up. And Varky's pack held incriminating contents: a submachine gun, broken down inside a waterproof bag; a holstered pistol; a roll of det cord; and half a dozen blocks of takite; all buried beneath a blanket, some food, spare socks.... If someone dug through it, an alarm would be raised.

Perhaps ... Urkwal knelt where the branches had been cut away, to scrabble beneath limbs and foliage. And here— here was the wrapped SMG, shoved back beneath some branches and weeds. And here the bagged explosive. And here the det cord! Varky'd managed to get his pack off, rummage through it, and at least somewhat conceal the dangerous stuff.

But where was the pistol? He crawled further, groping, and found it too, in its holster. But the magazine was missing. He hunted for it awhile longer, then gave up, put the other things into his own pack, and started back eastward down the road.

Before long he saw where a tree had been uprooted by the wind. He went to it, and with his hands dug in the soil where the root disk had been tipped up. Then he buried all but the det cord and takite. He had use for them later.

That done, he trotted back to the road, and eastward to his rendezvous.

Seventeen

The screened dining porch looked out over a neatly tended yard in the direction of large barns. In winter they housed registered livestock. It was a beautiful summer morning, fresh and cool after a hot and humid spell. A couple sat at a flower-decorated table, drinking midmorning joma that was not made of scorched grain. Physically the man was smaller than ordinary. His features, the gray eyes especially, suggested high intelligence and an even disposition. He was dressed in a gray riding suit of serviceable material, a white shirt and black ribbon tie. And boots suitable for both saddle and stable.

Their butler entered. "Sir, Mr. Chenly wishes to speak with you. When may I tell him you'll see him?"

Mild surprise registered. His chief forester had planned to check the thinning work on Compartment Four that morning. Fingas Marnsson Kelromak glanced at his wife, who nodded. "I'll speak with him now, Kinet."

The butler's nod was almost a bow, and he left. A minute later, Chenly stepped onto the porch. Kelromak sat back, his expression questioning.

"Good morning, sir. Bobbi and I were driving to

Compartment Four this morning, and we found a man lying by the road, unconscious. A drifter by the look of him. A tree had broken in the wind, and the top had fallen on him."

"Badly injured, I suppose?"

"When we got him here, he was able to take his weight on one foot. The other knee is pretty swollen, and something's wrong with a shoulder. And he's got a knot on his head like an egg."

"And?" Kelromak knew there was more to it than that, or Chenly wouldn't be troubling him with the matter.

"The storm went through in the middle of the night, and I wondered what he'd been doing on the road at that hour. Also he's a rather large man, sir, and hard, and—"

Kelromak interrupted. "Hard?"

"His body, sir. When Bobbi and I raised him up, I was surprised how hard and heavy he felt. And supporting him under the arms— He's got muscles like Big Farly, or maybe harder. A man like that could be dangerous, sir, if he's inclined to be lawless. So—" He held something up: the magazine from a pistol. "I took his pack off to lay him on the back seat, and threw it in front. And looked in it on our way back; I found this."

Kelromak pursed his lips. The forest country had always been a refuge for felons and runaways. They'd hide there till they got too hungry, or sometimes till the sheriff asked for a company or two of soldiers to sweep the forest for them.

It was Lady Kelromak who spoke then. "But no gun, Chenly?"

"No, ma'am. Just the magazine. He could have found it on the ground somewhere. I've had a magazine fall out of my pistol butt when the catch didn't latch like it ought to."

"What else did he carry?" Kelromak asked.

"A match safe, better than you'd expect, given the clothes he wore. And a horse blanket, half a loaf of cabin bread, a bag of dried *lumies*, most of a cheese, and some snare wire, as if he might take a *yansa* now and then. And thirty dronas."

Thirty dronas! A great deal of money for a drifter. Most, if they had that much, would be in town drinking it up.

"And a folding knife," Chenly went on, "bigger than usual

and razor sharp, but something anyone might carry, especially in the woods." He dug into a pocket, drew out the knife and opened it. The blade was nearly five inches long. "I took it and the matches, and left him with Frenis in the bachelors' quarters. He was pretty much in a daze yet."

Kelromak got to his feet. "I'll talk to this drifter, if that's what he is. See what I can find out."

"Well, that's another thing, sir. You see— I asked his name, even before I looked in his pack, and he said he didn't know! He could be faking, but that's quite a knot on his head. You can actually see it, what with his hair so short."

"Hmm. I'll see him anyway." He turned to his wife. "Excuse me, dear," he said, and left with Chenly. Kelromak limped, as if from some old injury grown used to, a limp sufficient to hamper him. "Have you called the outcamps to see if there's been thefts?"

"Bobbi's doing that, sir."

They crossed a broad lawn and went through a gate in a ten-foot privacy hedge. The bachelor's quarters were on the other side, a single-story frame dormitory, painted cream with white trim, and had a lawn of its own. Only two men were inside, one a burly middle-aged man with a fire-scarred face and vestigial right ear, seated in front of a window with a book open in his left hand. His curled right hand lay on a thigh, as if the elbow wouldn't bend far enough to help hold the book. The other man, young, lay on a bed with his eyes closed. His shirt had been removed, leaving a ragged undershirt, and his right arm had been immobilized—put in a sling and wrapped to his body with a bandage.

The older man lay his book on the sill and got stiffly to his feet. "Good morning, sir."

"Good morning, Frenis." Kelromak's attention went to the stranger; the young man's eyes had opened, but they didn't seem to focus. "How do you feel?" Kelromak asked.

The man looked at him blankly. "All right."

In the undershirt, his arms were large, and considering how relaxed they were, looked extremely muscular. Also, if he was feigning concussion, he did a convincing job of it. Kelromak knelt beside him, felt the lump on his head, then took the hand on the injured arm and examined the palm. "What have you been doing for a living?" he asked.

The man blinked. "Living? I don't rightly know, sir. Don't remember."

"Well." Kelromak straightened and turned. "Chenly, call Dr. Ammekor to come by and look at our visitor. He should check Dori-Ann, too, while he's here."

They left together then. "I'd judge he's no robber," Kelromak told the forester. "His hands are as callused as any I've ever seen. He's a laboring man, or I've missed my guess, probably come to the forest to find work. Now if he'd carried a gun— But as you said, he could well have found the magazine somewhere. And the money could have been earned; not every drifter drinks his up, I'm sure."

"You don't want me to call the sheriff to question him then?"

Kelromak grimaced. "No. Not unless Bobbi learns something suggestive from the out-camps. If Sheriff Geltro got hold of him, he might well try to beat some memory out of him. And possibly beat him to death in the process."

When the lord of the estate had left the dormitory, Varky Graymar closed his eyes again. His head ached and he didn't remember anything between the river and waking up by the road. But he knew who he was and why he was in Komars, and there was nothing seriously wrong with his thought processes. He'd functioned well enough to hide his stuff and even get his pack back on, damn difficult with a separated shoulder.

If they let me stay here, he thought, *I'll be functional in a week or two.*

Eighteen

The president's War Council was meeting in his office, and Romlar was there. He had a standing invitation, though he didn't regularly attend. General Belser's expression was stoney with suppressed anger, so instead of starting with Fossur's intelligence review, Heber Lanks opened the meeting with a question: "Does anyone have anything we need to get out of the way before Colonel Fossur brings us up to date?"

Belser heaved to his feet. "Yes, by Amber, I do! And I'm going to demand that something be done about it!"

Inwardly Lanks sighed; Eskoth was a difficult man. "Tell us about it," he said.

"*He* knows about it!" the general said, pointing at Romlar, "and so does he!" He pointed at Fossur. "And I suspect he does too!" he added, gesturing at Vestur Marlim. From the way he glared at his president, he suspected Lanks knew as well. He launched on. "Last night I learned that four—four!—enemy brigade bases were attacked by two batteries each of our pack artillery! That is eight batteries *committed to action without my permission or previous knowledge!*

Someone is covertly trying to take away my command! And if something like this happens again, I shall resign!"

By all means do, Fossur thought. The president turned to him.

"Do you know anything about this?" he asked.

"As liaison officer," Fossur said, "I've had your permission from the beginning to attach men to Colonel Romlar's units, so we and they would be closely familiar with how an elite force operates. I've been aware that the men assigned have accompanied the mercenaries into action as early as the Great Raids. I should comment also that I've questioned a number of these men, debriefed some of them in detail, and they and I all feel they learned a great deal from their experiences. In fact, they and their officers have been almost uniformly excited by what they've seen and observed."

He turned his gaze to Belser. "I do not try to keep a finger on everything that happens in operations that are established and going well. I did not know in advance about the artillery action you mentioned; I learned about it last evening, as you did. And I must admit surprise that such an operation was carried out under the guise of 'observing.' "

Fossur turned to Heber Lanks. "After the first raids, the Komarsi were forced to expend considerable effort and resources in strengthening their bases. This required different tactics on the mercenaries' part, and resulted in their mortar attacks on five bases. Since then the Komarsi have been forced to mount more, larger, and farther-ranging patrols, which the mercenaries have routinely attacked and really pretty much massacred. As I've reported to you previously. Now it seems that most of the patrols sent out, particularly those sent to patrol at larger distances, commonly go out and sit in some relatively secure position, hoping the mercenaries don't find them.

"My usual intelligence sources didn't learn this; mercenary reconnaissance patrols observed it. And decided to take advantage of it to shell the bases. Having no artillery of their own, they borrowed some—guns and gunners—from unit commanders they'd come to know. Nonetheless, most of the personnel involved were mercenaries. The guns, with mercenary escorts, were disassembled and packed to locations accurately identifiable on forestry maps, where they were reassembled. The mercenaries provided strong infantry protection for the batteries, and strong mercenary patrols ranged the vicinity. They had their own fire observers ahead to direct the fire. Bombardment was by daylight, when there were no visible muzzle flashes, and the Komarsi never located them. When our batteries had expended their ammunition, they disassembled the pieces and withdrew. They had no casualties. No equipment was lost. The enemy suffered painful losses of personnel and material.

"It seems to me that this was an excellent operation— one I recommend we repeat. My information is that the units involved are very enthused, and eager to do more of it. If the Komarsi increase their patrols, the mercenaries will eat them up. And if they don't, we can injure them at will."

As Fossur sat down, Vestur Marlim got up, a small, sharp-faced, and just now angry man. "Mr. President," he said, "I applaud this cooperation between Colonel Romlar's troops and our own. It's the sort of thing we should be doing. I applaud anything that punishes the Komarsi for their assault on our country and our people." He turned to Belser then, thrusting his face toward him. *"Of course you weren't asked or informed. If you had been, you'd have forbidden it!"*

His tone moderated then, for remarkably, Belser showed no anger, and this cooled his own. "In the south you were a lion," he said. "Since then—something has happened to you."

Normally Belser stood to speak. Now he stayed in his chair as if tired. "In the south I lost more than six thousand men, killed, captured, or disabled. And we lost all the resources we need to win this war. Our food supplies shrink daily, and we cannot replenish more than a small fraction of them. We cannot replace munitions expended. To fight with no prospect of winning is to waste lives."

The president spoke gently to him then. "What would you have us do, Eskoth? Surrender?"

Belser's voice was soft, hardly recognizable. "No. I do not know what to do." He looked away then, and Fossur stood, his voice quiet.

"Mr. President," Fossur said, "I have nothing I need to report." He looked around. "If no one else does, perhaps we should adjourn and meet again tomorrow."

"Not yet." Lanks stood and looked around the table. "We have not had an explicit, stated policy since we lost the south. That is my failure, and I'm going to remedy it now. But first let me say that I am president of the people. And the people, at least most of their soldiers, want us to fight. They'd like us to win, but that isn't the key issue; *they want us to fight.* And we are going to because they want us to, if for no other reason.

"And if we fight, we should do it in a way that grasps whatever chance we do have of winning. Using whatever works. We must show the rest of Maragor that we have heart, that we can hurt the Komarsi, that he is not the force they may have thought he was. We have already begun to do this, or Colonel Romlar has, and we must begin to take the larger role in it ourselves. We must define that role and play it to the hilt!

"Much of Maragor has seen the cube of the Great Raid, seen or at least heard of it. And much, perhaps most, of Maragor would love to see us win. Neither Engwar nor his father, nor his uncle during his regency, made many friends on this world.

"I will increase my efforts to gain their help. This will not be easy, given our geographic position, our lack of a coastline now, but I see possibilities. Ambassador Tisslor believes that, if the war becomes sufficiently troublesome for Komars, sufficiently unpleasant, Engwar will face sentiment to end it." The president paused, looking less than happy. "Perhaps not giving up all they have gained, but much of it. Enough that we can be a viable republic again, a nation that can feed its people."

Once more he paused, then went on quietly. "Who knows what may happen if we persist and strive.

"At any rate, there you have it. A policy: We will fight." He turned to Fossur then. "On your recommendation, I adjourn this meeting till tomorrow morning at eight. We will then discuss specifics."

The council got up and left without anything more being said.

Belser left the president's house and walked, rather than strode to his office. Sitting behind his desk, he looked tiredly at his in-basket. His door opened; his secretary stepped in and closed it behind him.

"General, Colonel Romlar would like to speak with you."

Belser looked up and said nothing for several long seconds, then answered. "Send him in."

The sergeant motioned Romlar in, then left them. Belser gathered a little of his old iron, though none of the fire. "What is it, Colonel? I'm a busy man."

Romlar moved a chair close to the general's desk, and sat down uninvited. "General," he said, "I have never led an army. I have never led a division, or even a brigade. Our specialty is small unit tactics against larger and more powerful opponents, tactics most efficient in circumstances like those we find here.

"In the north, the only effective way to hurt the Komarsi is with tactics of the sort I have used. But I have only one short regiment. You have in your army many backwoodsmen who can readily be trained to carry out the sort of actions we do. Readily trained because they already have the most important personal skills needed, and the necessary attitude. My regiment won on Terfreya when it had little more than begun its training, had finished just one year out of six! And we started training as unruly adolescents with none of those skills."

He paused, then leaned toward the general. "Let us select men from your regiments for their experience as woodsmen. Let us train those men, enough for a battalion to start with. And turn them loose on the Komarsi."

Belser said nothing, simply looked at him, seemingly without anger. After a long and silent half minute, Romlar got up. "Thank you, general. I appreciate your granting me the time for this talk. I hope to see you tomorrow morning."

Belser nodded acknowledgement. Romlar bowed slightly and left, Belser watching him out the door. Then the general noticed something on his desk, which Romlar must have left. He picked it up: a food bar, one of the merc's imported iron rations, honey-sweetened, rich with nuts and wrapped with chocolate. He examined the label, then unwrapped it and bit off a piece, chewing thoughtfully.

Nineteen

Rumaros was the farthest north of any sizeable town in Smolen, and the Rumar River was navigable there for sea-going ships. Thus the commander of Komarsi forces in Smolen, General Undsvin Tarsteng, had chosen it for his headquarters.

More specifically, he'd chosen its district courthouse for his headquarters, and the district administrator's office as his own. Its furnishings had been plain before the conquest, and remained so. Unlike his cousin Engwar, this soldier had no compulsion for the trappings and ornaments of power. For him, it was enough to have an army.

"Gentlemen," he was saying to his staff, "it is time to cut our losses. Given the recent aggressiveness of Smoleni forces, or more specifically the mercenary force they've employed, our advanced brigade bases are a needless and embarrassing expense to us. They were established to deny to the Smoleni the food-growing potentials of their districts. They've accomplished that; the summer is now too far advanced for anyone to plant and grow crops there.

"Accordingly, I am going to withdraw all military forces south of the Eel River-Strawstack line. We will burn the

91

villages as we leave them. It is not in our interest that the Smoleni reoccupy them, and we will not need them again. By next year at this time there will be no Smoleni government, no Smoleni army, and no war.

"This withdrawal will begin no later than a week from Twoday, and will be carried out in no more than three stages. Colonel Daggit will coordinate the planning, and will report to me each . . ."

He stopped at the sound of muffled gunfire within the building, and his very first reaction was not alarm but anger: *This was the last straw! Those drunken fools had gone too far this time; he'd send them all to the stockade!* Alarm followed though, for that first gunfire was answered at once by shouts and more shooting. There was an outburst of it from the end of the corridor outside the chamber, an intense flurry of it somewhere on the ground floor, terminated by a grenade. And then, more from nearby in the headquarters billeting district. All this in less than five seconds. Undsvin drew the large pistol holstered at his side and moved toward the door despite the gunshots in the corridor. He hadn't yet reached it when a massive explosion shook the building, followed almost instantly by two others. Behind him a section of wall fell, and the floor collapsed beneath his feet. . . .

Even in the larger towns of the south, enough people had left ahead of the invaders that there were numerous empty houses. In one of them were six men in Komarsi uniform shirts. They were all more or less large and physically powerful. None of them wore trousers or shorts, for they were in the process of raping twin girls of perhaps fifteen years. By then the girls were in shock, and the soldiers resorted to occasional knife jabs to elicit movement from them.

In the distance they heard gunfire, but ignored it, were scarcely aware of it. They were off duty, drinking, and occupied. Then there was a large multiple explosion, and they paused. One of them went to his trousers and picked them up. "That's from over 'round headquarters," he said, and began to pull them on. "Get yer pants on and let's go." All but one moved to obey; he was building to a climax. The man who'd given the order strode to him, one hand still holding up his pants, and kicked the man powerfully in the buttocks, dislodging him. "Now!" he bellowed.

Drunk or not, in half a minute they were ready to leave. With a thumb, the leader gestured at the girls still lying on the bare floor. "Kill 'em," he said. "If they get home, they may tell what we look like, and it could get to the general."

One man laughed and moved toward them. He didn't need to draw his knife. His boots would do.

Twenty

It was twilight. In a working-class section of Linnasteth, the capital of Komars, two drifters carrying rucksacks turned into a weedy yard and walked up a broken sidewalk to a house. One of them knocked. A large middle-aged woman opened. "What do you want?" she asked.

"We been told this's a place that'll rent a flop to an old soldier."

She cocked an eye. "You ayn't soldiers, and you ayn't old. Whadya got for me?"

"Good news and bad."

The formula completed, she stepped back. "Come in," she said, and when they had, she closed the door behind them. "We've been worried about you. Day after tomorrow's the day, and the others have checked in." Her speech had lost the twang of the shanty towns outside the city. An old man had entered the room from a hall, and she turned to him. "Mogi, fix something to eat for them." She looked the two up and down. "Damn! They picked you people for strong! I've got uniforms for you, but they're not going to fit worth a damn. I'll have to do some altering tonight." She turned, gesturing. "Come on. I want you to clean up while

94

Mogi's heating something in the kitchen. Then I'll show you what we've got."

She shook her head. "You people have really stretched our resources. But at least for you two we don't need to make passes with photographs."

Twenty-one

The main gate into the walled government district accommodated two wide lanes of traffic, with a sidewalk on either side. The midmorning traffic was considerable, and the gate guards busy. The workman with a tool chest stopped for one of them.

"Your pass."

The man put down his chest, took out a wallet, and displayed the pass in it. The guard waved him through without looking in the chest. The man had been told it would be that way, but his chest had a tray in the top, with tools, just in case. He picked it up and went through, glancing at his watch as he walked. The better part of an hour yet. Inside, someone hailed him, and he recognized his partner. They met and shook hands, as if they hadn't seen each other for some time.

"Security is as poor as Jenni said it would be," the first commented quietly.

"I'll take all the breaks they'll give me," the other answered. "Barrek and Norri have already gone ahead."

They moved on then, noting the names on the buildings,

following the route they'd memorized on a map nearly four hundred miles away.

A van bearing the name and logo of a well-known delivery firm stopped in the horseshoe drive that curved to the front entrance of the War Ministry. Two men in coveralls got out, went to the back, and slid out a sizeable chest with carrying handles jutting out at both ends. Two uniformed armed guards followed the chest out. The two who took it were strong-looking, but even so, it was obviously heavy. The van then pulled out of the drive and stopped at the curb across the street.

They carried the chest laboriously up the steps, then set it down as one of the entrance guards came over to them. He barely glanced at the courier guards; his attention was on the men with the chest. "Whadya got there?" he asked.

"Reports from archives. For the adjutant general's office."

The entrance guard looked at it for several long seconds, as if x-raying it with his eyes, then nodded. "All right, go on in. They'll tell you in reception where his office is."

The two picked up the chest and lugged it inside. The armed guards followed them without challenge. If the door guard had looked inside it, all he'd have seen was report binders held shut with rubber bands. Unless, of course, he'd dug beneath them.

The morning was already hot. A fan on the windowsill drew in more humid air, mixing and stirring. Colonel Torey Eltrimor wished he hadn't been given a rear office. At the War Ministry, rear was south, and hot. Although it could have been worse, for this was the second floor. The top floor, the fifth, became unbearable on days like this.

Eltrimor made most of the Commissary Department's meat purchases. He bought livestock on the hoof, and was known for driving hard bargains. He liked Fingas Marnsson Kelromak, as much as he allowed himself to like anyone he did business with, but he would not bend when it came to prices.

"I don't doubt your word," Eltrimor was saying, "but the department's overbought on grade B just now. It's only used in officers' mess, you understand. I can pay what you asked for for one car of it, but everything else I'll have to buy as C, regardless of the actual grade."

Fingas nodded. It was cheaper to market to the War Ministry—it was the easy way, so to speak—but with a modest effort, he could sell all the grade B he wanted to commercial buyers, for B prices. He raised very few cattle that graded C or lower—culled dairy cows, mainly, and an occasional sausage bull.

"Fine. One car of B then, and I'll ship the rest to Brisslo. Will someone come out? Or can your man check them on arrival?"

"In your case, arrival will be fine. You've never sent me anything yet that didn't meet . . ."

He stopped in mid-sentence. From some other part of the building came the sound of shooting, muffled by distance and walls. "What is it?" asked Fingas, alarmed.

"Damned if I know. Gunfire, but . . ." A muffled boom followed, spelling "grenade" to the colonel. "Fingas," he said, heading for the door, "we'd better get out of here!"

Others were entering the hall as they did, but Eltrimor's office was nearest the back stairs. On the level, Fingas could move quickly when he had to, but on the stairs his bad leg slowed him. Eltrimor reached the first floor well ahead of him. Others passed him, jostling him as they hurried down. Sporadic shots continued, three- or four-round bursts from an automatic weapon, and he could hear shouting.

Fingas had expected to find the first floor corridor full of people, but there were relatively few. *Of course,* he thought. *There's a side exit.* The rear door was something of a bottleneck, but the press of bodies was not severe. He was carried out the door with the flow, then lost his footing on the outside steps. As he fell, there was gunfire ahead of him— a submachine gun, and screams. People in front of him fell. Someone stomped hard on his chest, the pain making him gasp; someone else trod on his hand. Someone else fell on him then, and someone else. Behind him, inside the ministry, a great explosion roared, jarring the massive stone building.

In front of him the shooting continued.

The fuses were short. It wouldn't do to have them noticed. And radio detonators that would have allowed blowing the charges from a distance weren't permitted in a Level 3 War.

The Linnos Ordnance Depot was temporary, had been set up for this particular war. And instead of storing explosives in massive bunkers, as in permanent depots, the Komarsi War Ministry had elected to rely on distance to protect the surroundings from possible accident. It saved the cost of construction, and made access far easier and quicker. They'd set it up in a poor, sandy, grazing area, four miles downstream from Linnasteth. For simplicity in handling and transshipping, materials were segregated by class. High explosives, tons of them, were held in the southeast quadrant.

Of course the area was well secured. A heavy chain link fence surrounded it, eight feet high and topped with barbed wire. Outside lay a double barrier of accordion wire, while beyond the accordion wire was sandy pasture, still picked over by leggy cattle, and providing no cover. Inside the fence, armed sentries walked their posts, and guards watched the surroundings from corner towers.

Loading of munitions was done by dock crews, who entered with the trucks. Invariably they brought their mid-shift lunches, day or night, and no one ever thought of checking their boxes or pails to see what sort of sandwiches they held.

Casual labor was provided by drafts of new recruits, looking awkward in unfamiliar fatigue uniforms. That was how Chelli Morss got in.

The depot mission was the iffiest and most challenging part of Operation Scorpion. It involved the most uncertain preliminary steps, required the most on-site decisions and innovations. For example, Chelli couldn't know in what part of the HE quadrant the charges had been set.

He'd hardly arrived when he'd been given a bucket of paint and a brush, and detailed with several others to paint a shed. A corporal had been with them, and Chelli'd had no chance to slip away. So he'd painted fast, if somewhat sloppily, to finish the job as soon as possible. They'd just finished washing out their brushes when he heard a distant boom. The War Ministry; he knew it by the sound, and the timing was right. It had been scheduled first.

No one else seemed to notice. They'd started handing out sickles to cut grass with, inside the fence and between the piles. Chelli had seen his opportunity and crowded in to get one. They'd hardly started when they heard a much greater explosion, a great thunderous roar that he knew was at the harbor facilities some three miles away. He'd felt it through the ground! Surely someone in command would think of the depot now, and take quick action to increase security.

As soon as he dared, he separated himself from the others, slipping into one of the traffic aisles between piles of boxes. Once alone, he began to scout the piles, chopping at grass now and then in case some noncom looked down an aisle and saw him. Actually he was looking for the red crayon streaks that should mark the fuse locations. Any one charge would do. He saw a red streak on the end of a box, went to it and looked around for the fuse. There! He reached into a pocket and found the small lighter buried beneath his handkerchief.

"*Hey, you!*"

He turned. "Yessir?"

A sergeant was striding down the aisle toward him, with another man. The sergeant wore a holster at his hip; the other carried a rifle.

"*Get your ass back to the trucks,*" the sergeant called. "*Now!*"

"Just a minute, boss. I dropped something." He bent, and lit the fuse.

"Yomal *damn* you Amber-damned recruits!" The sergeant came up to him and punched him. "Don't you 'just a minute' me, you son of a bitch! When I say *jump*, you better damned well jump! Now let's go!"

"Sergeant," said the private with the rifle. He was staring at the fuse. "What's that? Looks like a . . ."

Chelly hit the sergeant in the throat with a spear-hand, felt the trachea crush and saw the eyes glaze. Before the man could fall, he'd pulled the sergeant's pistol from its holster, thumbing the hammer back as he drew it. The rifleman was good. Quick. He swung his rifle around and pulled the trigger at the same moment Chelli pulled his own.

The difference was that the rifle had a cartridge in the

chamber and the pistol didn't. The shock of the bullet knocked Chelli down, then the man dropped his rifle and went for the fuse. Even as Chelli hit the ground, lung-shot, he jacked a cartridge into the chamber, rolled onto his side and pulled the trigger again. The .37 caliber slug took the soldier behind the ear, killing him instantly.

Chelli raised up enough to shoot the sergeant too, just in case, then fell back.

There were shouts now. Men drawn by the shooting were running up the aisle from the other direction. The trooper grinned; they'd never make it. It was a short fuse.

Twenty-two

The Royal Council sat around a polished table of some dark wood, the king at one end. The table was raised there, stepped up to accommodate his throne, which was on a small dais.

"Your Majesty," the Foreign Minister was saying, "it is not true that foreign confidence in us has been shaken. They were inevitably surprised by the recent Smoleni efforts, even impressed by them, especially since the widespread theater distribution of certain cubes. But I know of no foreign government which imagines that it was other than the effort of a dying state."

Engwar looked past the man, lips pinched, still unhappy. The Foreign Minister went on. "What is true is that there have been from the start—from before the start—certain factions in those countries that wish us ill. But even these do not imagine that the Smoleni might win. They'd simply like to see the war go on, see the Smoleni persist as long as possible and fight as long as possible, embarrassing us and costing us lives and money. It is these who make much of the recent Smoleni successes, small though they are. They—"

Engwar interrupted. "They were intolerable! Insolent! I'll see they pay for them, a hundredfold."

"I have no doubt of it, Your Majesty."

The king glared at him for a moment, then subsided. "You were saying."

"Yes, Your Majesty. These factions are agitating their governments to provide aid to the Smoleni, and of course most of those governments must at least pretend to listen. But I predict that nothing will come of it. First of all, of course, you have the largest navy on the planet, both in tonnage and firepower. People fear you, Your Majesty. And secondly, we isolated Smolen when we captured her coastline. Supplying her—"

Again Engwar interrupted angrily. "Someone supplied her with those mercenaries!"

"True, Your Majesty. But it is generally agreed that they are from offworld, that they were landed from a spaceship. No one is going to supply Smolen with food and munitions by spaceship. First, there is no precedent for it in practice or in law. And secondly, the cost would be prohibitive."

With that, the Foreign Minister stood silent. Engwar glowered. "Is that your entire report then?"

The man inclined his head. "It is, Your Majesty."

The king looked at the minister next in line. "And you, Dorskell, what have you to—"

He bit the words off in mid-sentence, for the Lord Chancellor had entered the room to stand quietly by the door. Such an intrusion must signify something important. "What is it, Gorman?" Engwar said testily.

"Your Majesty, word has just come from Rumaros that enemy infiltrators have attacked General Undsvin's headquarters there and destroyed it with explosives. The general has been injured, and many officers are dead. The infiltrators have all been killed or captured."

Engwar II Tarsteng stared at the man. Such an act was incredible! Intolerable! Civilized people did not do such things! They did not attack persons at high levels! "When did this happen?"

"I'm told it was at 1110 hours."

"Is my cousin's life endangered by his injury?"

"They did not say so, Your Majesty."

"Well go ask them, Dolt! Did you think I wouldn't want to know?"

"At once, Your Majesty," the man said, and left the room, Engwar glaring after him. The cabinet sat frozen by the news, and by Engwar's anger, for Gorman was his right hand. After a moment, Engwar took his attention from the door and looked at the men around the table.

Before he could speak again, an explosion boomed from somewhere inside the government district, startling most of them to their feet. The Minister of War, who'd already risen to give his report, hurried to the balcony door, stepping out to see what he could see. And fell backward into the room and onto the floor, a hole in his forehead. As he fell, they heard the shot that killed him.

Engwar stared wide-eyed, not angry yet but shocked. *His palace had been violated! It could have been himself who lay dead there!*

Twenty-three

"Fingas, it's really good to see you getting around so soon. And a relief as well. Would you care to enumerate your injuries?"

Fingas Kelromak smiled slightly. "Those you can see are a broken hand and cheekbone. The more severe are less visible: cracked ribs, a broken rib, and a punctured lung. They're what kept me in the hospital." His smile turned wry. "Our country has had some remarkable experiences lately."

Lord Jorn Nufkarm grunted. "Indeed. I suppose you read of them or had them read to you; those you didn't experience personally."

The War Ministry had been evacuated for major reconstruction; eighty-four had died there, not including raiders. And of course there was the sniper killing of Lord Dorskell, in the cabinet room itself. The ship *Pride of Komars*, with a cargo of munitions, had been blown up at the dock, surely also by raiders. The explosion had considerably damaged the harbor facilities, with a reported additional 107 dead or missing. While the ordnance depot ... "I've visited what used to be the Linnos Depot. The hole in the ground is some hundred yards long, and said to be thirty feet deep. I can't vouch for the depth; there's a small lake in the bottom."

"I understand they caught none of the raiders alive."

"That's right. There are rumors that two or more escaped from the government district, and I suppose it's possible. As for the escape or death of those responsible for the other disasters—there aren't even rumors."

Nufkarm pulled a bell rope. "I suppose you've read that they blew up three of the four bridges across the Komar, too."

Fingas nodded. "They mined the fourth, but something went wrong and only one charge exploded. It's already back in operation."

A servant entered. "You rang, m'lord?"

"Yes. Would you bring joma please, Varel. With honey and cream for Lord Fingas." He turned again to his visitor. "My physician insists I lose weight, a great deal of it. Thus I now take my joma innocent of flavorings.

"As for the problems of war—the greater problems are rather like the injuries to your ribs and lung; they're not readily visible. Nor are they discussed in the papers. They're not as impressive, and Engwar doesn't want them written about. I speak of inflation, fiscal deficits, proposed new taxes—and of course the labor shortage. Which will grow noticeably worse when harvest comes, as you know better than I. And when manpower is short, field crews can become unruly, or at least insubordinate, for only then do they have any power at all. At the very least they don't work as hard as they normally do, and at the exact time they're most needed.

"And when it's over and the army is disbanded, we'll have one hundred and forty thousand ex-serfs who've gained their freedom by enlisting. There'll be little work for them, of course, and they'll expand and overflow the shantytowns, giving rise to an increase in hooliganism. All because of one man's irrational greed."

Fingas Kelromak didn't reply, didn't nod, simply held the older man's eyes for a long moment. "And how do our peers view all this?" he asked at last.

Nufkarm grunted. "Many of them are heedlessly and self-righteously loyal to our good sovereign's ambitions, of course. To be expected. On the other hand, there are people of influence who did not like this war since before it began. More than a few of them, including"—he gestured theatrically—"you and I. But went along with it because there seemed nothing we could do to stop it, and because the war's result seemed a foregone conclusion. And of course because we were afraid of our good king."

Fingas exhaled audibly through pursed lips. "And what seems to be known of the raiders? I've read that they're supposed to be offworld mercenaries. Does there seem to be anything to that?"

"I have no doubt of it. A few prisoners were taken, wounded prisoners, in the raids on brigade bases in Smolen. But they didn't survive interrogation." He grimaced. "They're said to be T'swa-like, but white. Very muscular, quite fearless, and extremely crafty. I have no doubt at all that they're from offworld."

"And the effect on foreign opinion—what's that been? Have you heard? The papers have avoided that, too."

"I haven't heard, but I expect to have supper with The Archipelago's consul this evening. I may learn something there. Logic says they must be impressed with what Smolen's accomplished, but it's questionable whether that will translate into actual assistance to President Lanks's unfortunate people. Token assistance at most; token assistance covertly delivered. Now if the Smoleni could maintain this sort of activity— But that's scarcely imaginable. These various raids aren't likely to be repeated; they were successful only because they were unexpected, and security, apparently, was terribly lax."

Varel returned with a tray, set it between the two, and while they waited, poured for them. He left then, and after Fingas had stirred in cream and honey, so did his host.

"So," Nufkarm went on, "given the circumstances of distance and accessibility, any aid the Smoleni might receive will be ineffective. The rational thing for Engwar to do would be to ignore it."

Fingas nodded. "And of course, he won't do the rational thing."

"He might. Cairswin's advice carries weight with him. But he also might send out fleet units to harass foreign shipping, perhaps even search for contraband. Which could result in some form of concerted counteraction."

Fingas nodded thoughtfully. "So certain persons are worried."

"But will do nothing."

"Unless someone else starts it."

"I hope you're not thinking of it. You've already offended Engwar with your proposed reforms of the serf laws. And Engwar is doubtlessly inclined, just now, to take harsh action against anyone who treads on his toes. With trumped up charges, if need be.

"And really, Fingas, we need you for better things. You are one person the party might be willing to rally round, when the time comes."

"It might be worth the risk."

"Umm. Well—" Nufkarm appeared to consider something, then went on. "I have heard a rumor," he said. "One I tend to credit. And if it's true, broad support will surely fail to materialize. It will probably even weaken support from those you'd count on most."

"And that is?"

"That Engwar has decided to hire a regiment of T'swa. If he does, everyone will wait to see what happens."

That closed the subject, and they spoke of other things. Eventually they rode Nufkarm's elevator to his roof garden and had lunch there. After lunch, Nufkarm accompanied Fingas to the foyer, and they shook hands.

"You will keep me informed, I trust," Nufkarm said.

Fingas raised his eyebrows. "Informed? About what?"

Nufkarm smiled. "Why, whatever there is, young Kelromak. Whatever you feel I should know about. Or whatever you feel I might help you with."

The cab Fingas had called for was waiting. He went carefully down the steps, and gingerly entered it, meanwhile thinking of certain possibilities.

He was also thinking of the "drifter" he'd left behind at his estate.

Twenty-four

General Undsvin Tarsteng entered his new headquarters building, the four-story Hotel Rumaros. One of his arms was in a cast, and he rode in a wheelchair, pushed by a corporal and accompanied by two large and formidable armed guards. As he rolled into the lobby, someone shouted "at ease," and the room went silent. Hands slapped shirt pockets in salute. He acknowledged them collectively with a scowl and a single curt nod. The general was clearly in a vile mood; no one moved, outside his small entourage, until the elevator doors had closed behind him.

A man was waiting in the reception room to the general's office. He was Captain Gulthar Kro, a rather large man, though not so large as the two guards with the general. His shoulders were conspicuous in their width and thickness; the rest of him seemed almost slim by comparison. His face was scarred as if by assault with a blunt instrument, which in fact it had been several years earlier. He'd risen when the general entered.

"You asked for me, sir."

"Damn right!" The general turned. "The rest of you OUT!" They jumped, then started for the door. He added

then, more moderately, "Lersett, you stay, damn it! How
am I supposed to get around?" The corporal stopped,
shaken, and when the two guards had closed the door
behind them, Undsvin continued, grim again. "Captain,
what, precisely, is your post?"

Kro alone, among the people who'd met or accompanied
the general, seemed at ease with him this morning. "I'm
the commander of your personal unit, sir."

"*And isn't one of its central responsibilities to protect my
person?!*"

"Yessir."

"THEN WHERE IN AMBER'S NAME WERE THEY
WHEN I NEEDED THEM?"

"Two of 'em were in the corridor outside your office door.
They ran to the head of the stairs when they heard the
shootin' below, and got killed there. Of the rest, a third was
trainin' by your orders, and—"

"*And the other two thirds were drunk!*" The general
shouted this too, but it lacked the fire of his earlier outburst.

"No, sir. Not more than one third was drunk: the ones
that had passes to be off base. They knew better'n to take
liberties with me."

Undsvin's lips drew in, leaving a slit. "Captain, your unit
is a disgrace."

"Sir, they're your unit, not mine."

The corporal behind the wheelchair blanched at the
impertinence, but Kro went on. "You had 'em recruited
from stockades and jails. You wanted the toughest sons of
bitches you could get. Then you asked me to tame 'em for
you. I done the best I could with what you gave me." He
might have added that if the general thought he could get
someone better, he should try. But he didn't; Kro had integrity, not insanity.

Undsvin Tarsteng examined him long. He'd put out word
that he needed someone self-disciplined and extremely
tough, someone who could command respect from and control the toughest, most undisciplined men. He'd had half a
dozen prospects brought to his attention, and Kro had
ended up with the job. Undsvin had no doubt the man had
a hidden history, an interesting one, but all he knew of
him was that he'd made sergeant first class within a year of

enlistment. Which was truly remarkable even then, when the army was beginning to expand rapidly.

When Undsvin spoke again, it was calmly and quietly. "I haven't paid much attention to their training. What are they good for? What can they do?"

Kro's expression didn't change. "They're strong and they're tough; that's what you picked 'em for. But most of 'em got no judgment 'cept what I beat into 'em. They're mean; they'd rather cut a man up than kill 'im, and rather kill 'im than talk to 'im. You dint have that in mind, but it's what you got.

"Physically I've got 'em hard and kept 'em that way. "They hate long runs, but they don't mind speed work. I run 'em hard down one side of the track, and let 'em walk the rest of it to rest, then make 'em do it some more. They can run down just about anyone you want, up to a quarter mile; then they're used up. They'll lift weights all I tell 'em to, 'cause they like to be strong, and they beat the heavy bags bloody. I got to replace a busted leather bag near every day. And they love to rassle each other. They'd rather beat one another bloody, but I've forbid it; I'm the only one supposed to beat on 'em. And they've been happier since I had posts set in their exercise yard. They thraw knives at 'em by the hour. They don't knife each other though. You prob'ly remember I flogged one of 'em to death for that. The lesson took.

"Before the war, when we were at Long Ridge, I took 'em in the woods and tried teachin' 'em to track and sneak. Most of 'em dint learn to track much at all, but they learnt sneakin' pretty smart. Plus they did good at just about all their infantry trainin', includin' drill. They hated drill, but I told 'em when they learned it good enough, I wunt make 'em do it no more.

"Most of 'em I wouldn't trust around the corner; they're like to do anything they think they can get away with. Those what're different, more reliable, are the ones I made squad leaders and platoon leaders."

He shrugged. "And that's it."

Undsvin regarded the fingernails on his good hand, then glanced back at the man behind his wheelchair. "Corporal," he said, "wait outside the door." When the man was gone, he turned to Kro again.

"Captain, these raids have humiliated me, and more to the point, they've humiliated the king. To make matters worse, the military situation dictates a withdrawal to the Eel River. At this point in the war, such a withdrawal does the enemy no good, and it greatly reduces his opportunities to harass us. But the appearance is of a victory for him, and a loss for us.

"So I want to hurt him. Punish him. Remind him of reality." The general looked quizzically at Gulthar Kro. "Surely your men are as tough as the mercenaries the Smoleni have hired. What might they do to accomplish that?"

Kro read Undsvin Tarsteng's face, his eyes, his attitude: the general truly wanted something of him, but didn't really expect anything. "My men are at least as tough," Kro answered, and believed it. "But from what I heard, those mercs have a hundred times more discipline. They have to, to do what they did. My men only cooperate when you tell 'em just what to do, and you watch 'em. And if they figure you might beat 'em up or flog 'em for screwin' off. There's no way they could bring off the sort of things the mercs done.

"What they mawt *could* do, though, is assassinate Lanks and Belser, like the mercs tried to kill you and the king. Mawt be they could kill the merc commander, too."

Undsvin stared, and a slow smile formed on his face. "Remarkable, Captain! That's exactly what I had in mind, right down to the mercenary commander! You impress me! Now, tell me how you might carry out this intention."

Twenty-five

Fingas Kelromak was almost always glad to get back from the capital. For one thing, his estate was home, and for another, his wife seldom went with him to Linnasteth. And of course, things invariably had come up which wanted his personal attention. Things he could actually do something about.

The evening he got home was invariably given to being a husband and father; he was not to be approached with any matters of the farm, except perhaps a screaming emergency. He did have a note placed on Chenly's desk though, to see him in the morning, in his office.

Chenly was there when Fingas walked in after breakfast. "Good morning, your lordship."

Fingas's face was still discolored, and his left hand still in a cast. The face in particular held Chenly's eyes, and his own showed dismay.

Fingas smiled wryly. "Rather colorful, isn't it."

"I read about what happened, in the paper, but . . ."

"Well. I was one of the lucky ones. I wanted to ask you how our—guest is. The drifter you found beside the road. Does he remember anything yet?"

113

"Seemingly not, sir."

"What did Ammekor say about him?"

"The knee was pretty badly sprained. That seemed to be all of that. Also his shoulder was separated, the collarbone torn partly loose from the shoulder blade. And he said a knock on the head like his was could lose a man his memory. But that it should come back to him sooner or later; probably sooner. That's how he put it, sir."

"And how is his recovery coming?"

"He uses both hands now, and helps around the workshop, but nothing heavy yet. As for the knee—I had him show it to me yesterday; I assumed you'd ask. It's still swollen a bit, and he limps, but he walks on it."

"Um. I suppose someone's cleaned up the broken tree by now."

"Oh, yes, sir."

"Did they, ah, find anything there?"

"Sir?"

"Like a pistol that might go with that magazine you found in his rucksack."

Chenly shook his head. "Not that I know of, sir. And I'm sure they'd have told me if they had."

"I want you to take me there this morning, Chenly. We'll go in your utility vehicle."

"Yes, sir. I'll call camp and tell them I'll look at the slow-bear damage with them tomorrow."

"Good. I'll see you at the front entrance at—" He glanced at his watch. "At 8:20. Just the two of us."

The lightning-shattered snag was conspicuous beside the ditch. They searched the grass and weeds thoroughly, and with the broken treetop gone, found something Winn Urkwal had missed: a thick roll of plastic tape, suitable for all kinds of things. For example, mending tool handles until they could be replaced. But the cardboard spool had the name of a Smoleni manufacturer printed on it, and the color was Smoleni army green. And it could also be used to tape blocks of explosive together.

Fingas looked long at it, lip between his teeth, then handed it to Chenly. Chenly examined it, then looked worriedly at his employer, saying nothing.

"Let's go back," said Fingas. "I need to speak with the man, see how he explains this. Say nothing about it to anyone. Nothing at all to anyone at all."

The forester nodded. They got into the utility vehicle and started back down the road. "Chenly," Fingas said, "there are things we need to talk about, you and I, and we need to be completely frank." He paused. "Tell me what you think of this war we're in."

Varky Graymar's remaining limp was feigned. The examination by Fingas's physician had been superficial—it hadn't seemed to warrant anything more. The actual degree of healing would have surprised him; Ka-Shok meditation had very definite medical applications.

His pack still held most of the 30 dronas cash, and over the last several days he'd stashed hard crackers filched from the table, and candy and dried fruit purchased from the estate commissary. On Sixday evening, most of the bachelors would ride in a crew bus to a dance in the nearby town. Others would visit friends. If he wasn't in his bunk when they got back, no one would pay much attention.

He had no doubt whatever that he could find his way several hundred miles cross-country to Burnt Woods.

This morning he sat cleaning the beginnings of rust from shovels, sharpening them with a mill file, and rubbing them with an oily rag. It was the sort of work a man could do who didn't get around well and was thought to lack proper mobility in his left shoulder.

Fingas Kelromak came into the tool shed, his forester with him. The forester held a pistol, and stationed himself to one side of the door. Varky put the shovel down and looked at Fingas questioningly. "It seems," said Fingas, "that you are not the only injured man about the place."

Varky nodded, completely calm. "I heard folks tell what happened to you."

Fingas's eyes latched onto his. "I suppose you've heard too of the great damage done. It's thought to be by mercenaries from Smolen. The generally accepted theory is that they were smuggled into the country on a freighter, perhaps from Oselbent. But they could have gotten here cross-country, through what the Smoleni call the High Wild."

"Yessir, I heard that too."

"I have another theory."

Varky said nothing.

"They could have come down the Raging River in small boats. I'm sure there are Smoleni who know the river well enough. Then separated and hiked to Linnasteth, to regather there." Varky's gaze never wavered. "If they had," Fingas added, "they'd probably come through here."

Still there was no reaction.

"Our government failed to capture any of the raiders. If they had one, they'd question him at length. Undoubtedly a horrible experience."

It was Fingas's eyes that turned away; he reached into a pocket and held up the magazine. Varky knew at once where it had come from. "You see what this is," Fingas said. "It was found in your rucksack while you were being brought here, and given to me. I decided then that it was simply something you'd found."

"Could be. I don't recall."

Fingas looked long at him again. Finally he said, "I need you to do something for me: I need you to tell me the truth. And when you have told me the truth, I'll need you to do something else for me: an errand." He paused to let his words sink in. It wasn't necessary. "But first the truth—two questions. Number one, how did your hands get so heavily, and really rather peculiarly callused?"

Varky waited for three or four seconds before answering. Not making up his mind; his reaction to the situation was as quick as his reactions to physical confrontations. He simply knew without computation that Fingas Kelromak expected a lag, and it would be better to meet his expectation. He held up his hands as if examining them—and answered with a typical Iryalan accent. "They result mainly from a form of training, but partly also from the temperatures in which the training was done."

"Ah!" Fingas's face twisted, as if with some inner adjustment. "My second question is, are you able to travel cross-country now, with your injured knee and shoulder?"

"I can travel."

"Good. Now for the errand: I want you to convey for me a message to your commander."

Varky nodded. Fingas drew a thick envelope from inside his jacket, and handed it to him. "You may read it if you'd like. In fact I recommend it."

It was open at one end. Varky shook out the contents and scanned them; there were several pages.

"You can see it wouldn't do to be caught with it. If at some point you seem to be in danger, I want you to burn it. Are you sure you're willing to do all this?"

The risk this Komarsi nobleman was taking was remarkable, Varky realized, even astonishing, given what he had to lose. Romlar and the president would very much want to see this letter. He folded it, put it back in the envelope, and tucked it in his own shirt. "More than willing," he said.

"Do you think you can find your way?"

Varky let himself grin. "Like a migrating bird," he answered.

Twenty minutes later they were in the carryall, Varky in the back out of sight, traveling up the road first north, then west. Food had been provided for Varky's rucksack—cheese, bread, honey in a can—and insect repellent, which he could have done without but was happy to have.

Several miles within the forest, Chenly pulled off on a spur road and drove to near its end, where they got out. Now Fingas drew his own pistol, extending it to the trooper. "Best you take this. And—" Reaching in a pocket, he took out the magazine. "See if it fits. The design is standard, but the make is undoubtedly different."

This, Varky thought, *is a real man!* He removed the magazine already in the butt and tried the other. Standard didn't mean as much on the trade worlds as on Confederation member worlds, but he wasn't surprised to find it fitted. He slid the action back, and a cartridge seated nicely.

"Thank you, sir. Much appreciated."

He slung his pack, being only a little careful with his shoulder, then turned and jogged off easily toward the north without a limp.

Twenty-six

Gulthar Kro was the grandson of freed serfs—freed for having served in the last war with Selmar. His childhood was spent in a shantytown outside Wheatland, a provincial seat. At age twelve he'd gotten into trouble with the authorities for excessive fighting in one of the poor, ill-taught schools provided for freedmen. He'd hit the road, working at whatever he could, stealing as necessary.

At age sixteen he'd been sentenced to life in prison. He'd waylaid and beaten a notoriously brutal undersheriff, would no doubt have killed him if two constables hadn't interrupted. He was already man-sized and more than man-strong, with a reputation among the drifters for ferocity in fights.

In prison he was assigned to quarrying rock. Because he was so strong, he was alternately a hammer man, whaling away with a twelve-pound sledge, and a prizer, using a crowbar to move blocks of granite. This work, imposed on an exceptional genotype, developed extremely powerful back, arms, and shoulders. The sledgehammer work in particular developed ferocious strength in his hands and forearms.

In the prison camp, fights were frequent. He soon became respected by the toughest inmates, and feared by the rest. He wasn't sadistic, but he could be ruthless, even brutal when it served his purpose.

At age twenty-two he was part of an escape that left three guards dead. Once out, he left the others, mistrusting their judgment. The camp had been in the hills that farther north became the "High Wild" of western Smolen. The others had determined to move eastward out of the forest, planning to sleep in haystacks and rob farms. Kro, on the other hand, had moved northward through the forest, stealthy and swift, disciplining his hunger, sleeping on the ground. Two days later he found a woodsmen's shack, where he stole a can of beans and two cold pancakes, but nothing else. With three men living there, so little might never be missed.

The next morning he ambushed a timber cruiser and killed him. First he ate the man's lunch, then took his belt with its knife and pistol, and hid the body in a ravine.

The next day he was across the border. Already he was becoming woodswise; it seemed natural to him. Eventually he found work as a log cutter, and got the feel of the Smoleni speech. When fall came, he'd joined with two Smoleni brothers who trapped in the High Wild.

By spring he was tired of the quiet, the lack of excitement. However, for the first time in his life he'd lived among men who were reasonable and cheerful—neither violent nor contentious—and he'd been affected by it. He traveled south again, by bus now, returning to Komars where he joined the army. The law required identification cards, but these were not ordinarily asked for, and their lack was disregarded in men volunteering for the expanding army. He was a natural warrior, his mind was quick, and he was self-disciplined. He was also a natural leader, and advanced quickly.

After being selected for the Commander's Personal Unit, he was promoted to warrant officer and made a platoon leader. Within two weeks the unit commander was removed as ineffectual, and Kro was made acting commander. Two weeks after that, having beaten several men severely for insubordination, his appointment was made "permanent" by the general, who rammed through a jump to captain for him.

The post remained his for more than a year.

Twenty-seven

A submachine gun resting on his lap, Gulthar Kro rode in a commandeered Smoleni bus, sitting next to the driver, where he could see out. He'd selected twenty two-man teams, men who might at least attempt to carry out their mission, while leaving the unit most of its officers and sergeants.

For ten days he'd worked the selected teams in the forest, making sure they could use a compass and read and follow maps. He'd made competitions of it, and before the ten days were over, the men were competent and confident. Each man wore a captured Smoleni uniform; each team had a book of forest maps taken from the captured headquarters of the Smoleni Forest Survey, maps showing the major variations in forest types, every creek and pond, and every open fen larger than perhaps twenty acres, which gave them many reference points to guide on.

Finding Burnt Woods was entirely feasible with them. The question was, how many would do it. Because it was also feasible to desert now, hike westward to the Raging River and cross it on a raft or stolen boat, or even travel eastward to the border with Oselbent. He guessed that

121

perhaps half would try for Burnt Woods. They'd been shown a sketch map of the village, with the president's house marked, and the general's, and each team had been assigned a primary target. When they got there, they'd have to play it by ear.

They'd been shown where, on the appropriate forest map, the merc headquarters was, too, but he hadn't assigned its commander to anyone. No one knew what he looked like or what tent was his, and anyway it seemed to Kro that it would simply waste a team to try for him.

The bus had taken them west along a graveled east-west connecting road, and he'd dropped off team after team at intervals marked on the maps. The first stage of the troop pull-back had been completed, and tomorrow this road would be left to the Smoleni, too. Not that they'd get any good of it; every farmstead along the road would be burned, as well as the sole village.

Now Kro was the only man left on the bus besides the driver, who'd turned it around on an old roadside log landing and was driving back eastward. Kro watched through the windshield for a landmark, and when he saw it, told the driver to stop.

He turned to the man before stepping out the door. "When you get back," he said, "tell your commander I gave you a message for the general—an important message that he's gawta get." He stopped, waiting for the man to digest that, then went on. "Tell him I'm gawn north too. And with enough luck, I'll be back.

"You got that?"

When the man had repeated it to him, Kro nodded, stepped off the bus, and disappeared into the forest. The merc commander was his target, his alone.

Twenty-eight

Kelmer Faronya had been having nightmares. He'd felt better about himself after the night of the mortar attacks. He'd done his job in the face of heavy fire, and stayed as long as the others. But on several nights since then, he'd had recurring dreams in which the grenade once again landed in front of him. In one of them, Jerym had thrown himself on it to save him, and it had exploded. Then Jerym's corpse had followed him everywhere in the dream, mangled and bloody and grim. He'd get in front of Kelmer, stand in his way, take Kelmer's seat at the table. There was no escaping him. The dead mouth moved, but no words came out. The dreaming Kelmer was sure that the message it mouthed was horrifying, that if he ever heard it, he too would die. Meanwhile the corpse decayed. Pieces sloughed off. He could even smell it! Finally, with a horrid resonance, the words would start: "Kelmer . . ." And he'd waken sweating—with the smell of putrefaction seemingly still in his nostrils! It seemed to Kelmer that odor had never been a part of his dreams before.

More terrifying, though, was the one in which the grenade landed and Kelmer ran. And running looked back—to

123

see it rolling and bouncing after him! He would run and run, but always it followed him, getting nearer. And implicit in the dream was the certain knowledge that if it caught him—*when* it caught him—it would explode. He tired. Actually it was as if the air thickened, making running almost impossible, and his legs grew heavier, harder to move. Then, looking back, the grenade would be closer, almost at his heels. Sparks flew from it! He *knew* with dead certainty it was about to explode.

That's when he'd waken, sweating and panting, a wakening that was like a reprieve.

It was twelve days after the action, and he'd just dreamed of the rolling grenade for the third time. He lay on his cot at Shelf Falls, wide-eyed and gasping, when the thought struck him. *The dream, it seemed to him, was a warning, a premonition. In the next action, or the one after that, or perhaps one later, a grenade would kill him. And somehow—somehow he would cause Jerym's death!* There was no doubt in his mind that this was so.

So when, on the next day, a message came from Romlar that he was to come to Burnt Woods, he felt like a prisoner pardoned. For Burnt Woods was far away from combat, and Jerym wouldn't be there.

Romlar had a different kind of assignment for him. The repeated successful strikes at Komarsi brigade bases, followed by the raid on Komarsi army headquarters at Rumaros and the destruction at Linnasteth, had rejuvenated the Smoleni. Even Belser had come around to an activist position. He'd approved the training of Smoleni ranger units, men selected for their wilderness skills, their marksmanship, and their warrior auras. Troopers would be their cadre.

Kelmer was to record some of their training on video cubes as part of regimental history. Selected parts would be distributed to other countries on Maragor, as public relations for Smolen.

Beyond that, he was to record civilian survival activities. These had been underway earlier at backcountry villages, but now the refugees had joined in. He took cubeage showing trees of certain species being felled, the bark stripped from them and carried in pack baskets to village houses and refugee camps. There the inner bark, the phloem, was scraped off and pestled into pulp that would be added to flour for baking. Centuries earlier, "bark bread" had kept their ancestors alive when they'd hidden in the forest, and the process had been passed down in stories and history books.

That wasn't all. Crews with scythes hiked to wet meadows in the forest, where they cut hay and stacked it to dry on racks made of poles, so the horses herded up from the Leas could be fed that winter.

There was even a pair of crews sawing *roivan* trees into five-foot logs, splitting staves from them, and cross-stacking the staves to dry. They could be shaved and carved into bows, against the time when ammunition might run out. Still others cut and peeled osiers from stream banks and fen margins, and straightened them, to be made into arrows if the need arose.

Concussion grenades were thrown into lakes, stunning and killing fish. These floated to the surface, and were gathered in baskets for drying or smoking.

More important, it seemed to Kelmer, were activities near Smolen's northernmost village, a tiny place named Jump-Off.[2] The border lay only forty miles north, forty miles of true wilderness. The Granite River flowed out of it, south through Jump-Off; the river was the only road there. In summer the village was reached by boat, in winter by skis, snowshoes, or sleigh.

Tiny as it was, and more than two hundred miles north of Rumaros, Jump-Off nonetheless had strategic importance. Smoleni diplomats outside the country were negotiating secretly with the governments of Oselbent, The Archipelago, and Selmar for food and munitions. Oselbent was a long and mostly narrow country, mountainous and incised by fjords, living largely by its fishing boats, merchant marine,

---

[2] North of the border was "The Great Wild," a wilderness reserve established by the Confederation, which made modest annual payment to the three bordering nations on the south. Controlled fur harvest was allowed, and Jump-Off was the base from which licensed Smoleni trappers left in autumn for their territories.

and mines. It feared Komar's army and fleet, and would like to see her militarism broken. Especially since, with the Smoleni coast occupied, Oselbent had Komarsi forces at her southern border. And it seemed to the Oselbenti that once the Smoleni surrendered, the Komarsi would be tempted to conquer Oselbent, or make a tributary of her. Besides, Oselbent, like Smolen, was a republic, of which there weren't many on Maragor.

But to antagonize Komars could be fatal.

The Archipelago was another republic. And more important, from the Smoleni and Oselbenti point of view, she had a strong fleet. If she could be gotten to sign a mutual defense pact with Oselbent . . . But she had her own vulnerabilities.

Selmar was the kingdom to the south of Komars, and a considerably more limited monarchy. No friend of her northern neighbor, she'd lost the last war they'd fought, along with some of the planet's diminishing iron mines. Potentially she was as strong as Komars, but suffered serious political and economic problems that a new constitution and king had only recently begun to ease. If The Archipelago were to sign a favorable trade agreement with her, the Selmari economy and morale would substantially improve, and Komars would find a revitalized old adversary on the south. One worrisome enough that Komars might be reluctant to extend her northern war to Oselbent.

If a mutual defense pact could be engineered between Oselbent and The Archipelago, and a trade pact signed between Selmar and The Archipelago, then surely, covert assistance agreements could be worked out for Smolen, with The Archipelago as the main supply source.

To Kelmer Faronya, a young man of the Confederation, all this seemed very very foreign—something out of a novel—and beyond photography.

The other problem of foreign supplies was getting them into Smolen, now that her coast was occupied. This was one the Smoleni could do more about, and one readily recorded on cube. Jump-Off was fifty-four miles from the border with Oselbent, and seventy-five miles from the town of Deep Fjord, which was a busy, even somewhat congested, harbor. The Falls River, which emptied into the fjord, was the site of a large hydroelectric development, which supplied the power for a large plant that manufactured nitrogen compounds, notably nitrate fertilizers. (Ironically, it was also a major supplier of nitrocellulose for the Komarsi munitions industry.) On the plateau above the fjord, and near the border with Smolen, were mines producing iron and magnesium. Thus a railroad climbed its way up from the fjord almost to the border.

Ships of many nations came to Deep Fjord, including ships from The Archipelago. It was the logical transshipment point for supplies to Smolen, if an agreement could be reached.

The problem of getting such supplies to the Smoleni army might seem to be worsened by the nature of the terrain, for that part of Smolen was largely peatlands—fens, moss bogs, and muskegs—but to the Smoleni, that provided not difficulty but opportunity.

An army engineering officer and a logging operator took Kelmer to photograph part of the supply road they were "building" to Oselbent. Actually they were building nothing, nor did they need to. What they were doing amounted mainly to staking the route, marking it with tall flagged rods. So far as possible without adding much length, the route was marked across open fens and moss bogs. Where these were absent, it mostly passed through muskegs—forested swamps. In much of the muskeg, the trees were sparse and stunted, and little obstacle. Sometimes, though, it was necessary to flag the route through heavier muskeg, where crews had begun to clear the right-of-way with saw and axe.

Over the years, trains of large sleighs, drawn by giant steam tractors, had been used in Smolen to haul logs on frozen rivers. Now, if the diplomats succeeded, similar trains would be used in winter to haul supplies from Oselbent across vast roadless swamps to Jump-Off.

Here and there, non-swamp intervened—mostly glacial till and outwash, and rarely low outcrops of the underlying rock. Kelmer visited one of these, a neck about a hundred yards wide, fifteen miles east of Jump-Off. A small crew was camped there, with axes and saws to fell trees; picks and shovels to dig with; dynamite to blow rock and stumps; and small, horse-drawn drag scoops to move earth and broken rock. They were cutting a narrow roadway almost to swamp level, so the sleigh trains wouldn't have to climb. On hard-packed snow, one great steam-powered crawler tractor could pull a whole train of large, heavily-loaded sleighs, if the road was level.

There already were steam tractors at Jump-Off, barged up the Granite. More could be brought as needed. A large crew of men was converting logging sleighs into cargo sleighs, building 20- by 8-foot cargo boxes of planks on the heavy skids and cross-bunks, which were hewn or sawn from tree trunks. The only metal in the sleighs were spikes and bolts, nuts and washers, stout chain-and-ring couplings, and stake pockets.

The only road maintenance equipment was drags made of logs split or sawn in half lengthwise, and bolted together with braces into a V-shape twelve feet wide at the tail. Dragged along the route in winter, by either horses or teams of native *erog*, they would pack the snow. Beneath soft snow, the swamps froze, but the frost was often honeycomb frost that would not bear weight. By contrast, where the snow was packed, the peat would freeze six- to eight-feet deep, and hard as concrete.

Kelmer left impressed, more by the resourcefulness and matter-of-fact attitude of the people undertaking all this than by what they were doing. He'd discovered a backwoods mentality, and hoped that the diplomats, in their way, could match it.

Twenty-nine

Artus Romlar awoke with something on his mind. He didn't know what inspired it. It simply arose from his "warrior kit," the set of talents and potentials he'd been born with as a warrior, freed up by the Ostrak Procedures and through meditation, and sharpened by training and experience.

He considered it while he dressed. It was important but not terribly urgent: certainly it could wait a few hours.

Normally he awoke earlier than his men; in mid-Sixdek[3] the sun didn't rise as early as it had when they'd first arrived, but at 0540 it was already well up in the northeast, high enough and warm enough to bring the morning's first bull flies buzzing sluggishly around him as he stepped out of his tent. His aide was waiting for him, and without speaking, they jogged together the two hundred yards to the exercise area, where they stretched and did light calisthenics to warm up. After a few minutes they did some easy work on

---

[3] In the Confederation Sector, the year on each world is divided into ten "deks" of equal or nearly equal length. These are numbered in order from the winter solstice, however slight it may be.

the high bars and parallel bars—in field uniform with boots!—increasing the intensity until they were sweating freely. That done, they did some mild tumbling runs—nothing very difficult for them—and went to the jokanru area. There they did some forms, then sparred for a while.

By 0645 he saw and heard the troopers of Headquarters Camp starting out on their morning run.

So far, he and Kantros hadn't spoken yet. In the wash area, bathing out of wooden buckets by a pump, he broke the comfortable silence, thick hard muscles bunching as he soaped himself. "Why was Komarsi security so lax?" he asked.

Kantros grunted; the question seemed rhetorical. "Because they felt secure. They didn't imagine anyone could get at them."

"What do you think of security around here?"

Kantros's lips pursed. They had a few guards around the borders of camp—limited-service Smoleni reservists—but that was all. They depended on distance and wild country to protect them here at Burnt Woods. "According to Smoleni intelligence," Kantros said, "the Komarsi T.O. doesn't include units that could operate through country like this. We've assumed the only way they could get here would be by an offensive over ninety-five miles of roads from Brigade Base Seven. Which they've abandoned; now they'd have one hundred and eighty miles up Road Forty from the Eel. If they had suitable personnel for a small strike force, they could try to penetrate without being seen, but it's very doubtful they could do it."

Blowing and sputtering, Romlar poured a bucket of cold well water over his head, then pumped another.

"Do you think they'd try?" Kantros asked.

"Not really. It seems more practical for them to select and train half a dozen infiltrators, dress them in Smoleni uniforms and send them north to wipe out Heber and his government. March up to the president's house as if they belonged there, maybe during a War Council meeting, then rush in with grenades and submachine guns. I don't doubt they have the necessary intelligence sources."

He began to dry himself. "But that could be tricky; uncertain. There'd be opportunities for mistakes, for being recognized as foreign, for blowing their cover in advance. And War Council meetings aren't on any real schedule; some days they hold one, while on others, like today, they don't.

"Suppose, though, you sent up half a dozen picked men, singly or in pairs. They might even infiltrate cross-country; they must have some who are woodswise. Brief them on what was the president's house, perhaps even what bedroom was his. And Belser's, say. They might even know what tent was mine. They could strike at night."

Fritek Kantros nodded thoughtfully. It wasn't the sort of thing one expected of the Komarsi, but it was conceivable. And Heber Lanks, it seemed to him, was the leader Smolen needed—the right personality, the right character with the right touch. He'd also become the symbol of Smoleni persistence, at home and abroad.

If Lanks was killed, whatever chance Smolen might have seemed as good as gone.

In midmorning, Romlar ran into town. Afoot, at an easy lope. He hadn't been running lately, and knew he'd lost some endurance, but he was surprised at how much. He completed the two miles leg-weary and sweating heavily, with the decision to start running regularly. He spoke first with Fossur, describing his thoughts about infiltrators, then went to Belser's headquarters.

Belser still was not cordial; cordiality was foreign to him. But he listened and nodded, and thanked the mercenary commander gruffly when he'd finished.

Romlar had no doubt at all that Belser and Fossur would establish some sort of security system for the village. He, in turn, would assign a company for security at camp.

Fossur and Belser consulted, and two-man lookout shifts were posted round the clock, in the bell-tower of the village hall. It gave a good view of the approaches to "the Cottage," a humorous term for the president's house. Guards would also be posted at each door. Perimeter guards were posted outside the village edge. The general's house and the Headquarters Company officers' billet would also have guards around the clock, and the occupants would sleep with weapons handy in their rooms.

They weren't really concerned, but it made sense to take precautions.

Thirty

Oska Niemar knelt to examine the dung beside the trail. It was small and felted with hairs, but there were also tiny seeds of stinkberry. A female with a litter, then; nothing else than nursing female marets and some birds would have anything to do with stinkberries.

He straightened, and scanned the treetops. The nests built by marets to raise their young could be hard to spot. Usually they chose a high fork in some *roivan*, a leaf-tree, but in summer, the leaves obscured them.

He'd been seeing lots of signs. He'd left this part of his bounds untrapped the last two years, letting populations recover. The last two winters had been relatively mild, the snow less deep than usual. The deaths of furbearers from starvation and freezing should have been few; such years always built up populations.

He resumed his watchful walk then, his calf-length moccasins leaving little sign. His eyes noted saplings bark-stripped by *herva*. Fawns of the year, by the height and tooth marks. *Herva* numbers were high, too, after two mild winters, and jackwolves would have produced litters the last two springs to take advantage of it. There was always a good market for jackwolf pelts, soft and silver-gray in winter.

The problem would be marketing the furs, with the Komarsi blocking exports. But you could always stockpile them. The animals, on the other hand, you couldn't stockpile; come a hard winter, losses were always heavy. Trapped or not, many would die. And they were due for a hard winter.

A game trail circled a small bog pond, or rather, it circled the band of bog osier that girdled it, and despite his sixty-five years, the trapper speeded to a smooth trot. Off to his right an *oroval*, a small furbearer, trilled indignantly at him from a branch till he passed out of its territory. Now the game trail curved upward, crossing a low rounded ridge, and Oska slowed to a walk. Near the top, the sparse under-brush was burgeoning where a great old *kren* had been overthrown by wind, letting sunlight reach the ground. Had been overthrown that very summer, for its needles were still yellow-green, not tan. And wind had not acted alone; numerous pale stalks of *flute*, growing on the uptilted root disk, had curved to adjust to the new vertical. Obviously the old tree's roots had been badly rotted with flute in advance; the wind had defeated a giant already failing.

And something else—animal, not plant—had died nearby. Recently by the smell. And been mostly eaten, for the stench, though putrid, was not strong. He stopped, wet a finger at his mouth and held it up. West. He moved toward it. Nearby, behind an old, mossgrown blowdown, were the remains of a *herva* fawn. The jackwolves hadn't left much—bones, hooves, head, and scraps of hide. The pack shouldn't be far. It would surely have a litter this year, likely within a mile or so and probably somewhat closer, for they ranged no farther than necessary from the den-bound pups and mother.

He'd barely started off again when he heard the *nut-yammer*. At first scold he guessed it was screeching at a *maret* or *oroval*—some threat to its nest. But the scolding persisted without intensifying, and that told him it was likely a man. On what business? This was *his* bounds, and folks weren't likely doing wandrings with the war on.

He moved in that direction, and now his mode had changed: He trotted in somewhat of a crouch, soft-footed

and smooth, more alert even than before. Not that he
expected danger, but he wanted to observe unnoticed. He
came to a tangle of old blowdowns, mostly broken instead
of uprooted, as if a whirlwind had touched down there. The
gap had grown up thick with saplings, head high and more,
and he slid along its edge. The indignant *nut-yammer* was
on the other side.

"I hate them little sonsabitches screechin' like that!"

The words startled Oska. People didn't often talk needlessly in the woods. Nor so loudly; the speaker seemed
someone loud by nature.

"Goddamn it," said another voice, "dawn't shoot! Someone could hear!"

"Shit! Who's to hear?"

"I dawnt know and you dawnt neither. Now I'm tellin'
you—"

The first man laughed. "Don't get your ass all bloody,
Kodi. I wasn't gawnta shoot. The little bastard dawnt hold
still long enough."

A third voice spoke then, a growl not loud enough that
he caught the words. On all fours, Oska crept to where he
could see them, some forty yards away. They wore uniforms,
Smoleni by the look, but that dialect! He'd never heard
Komarsi talk, but these strangers surely weren't from anywhere in Smolen. And they carried submachine guns!

He watched them pass out of sight, then got to his feet.
He'd track them, and see where they were going.

Kro had sent Scrap Iron Nagel and Kodi Furn out as a
team. Kodi was a corporal, so he'd been put in charge. The
day before, they'd run into Chesty Inkermun by himself,
and Chesty had joined them. His partner, Chesty said, had
cut out for Krentorf.

The cramp hit Scrap Iron just as they crossed the low
rock ridge and saw the creek ahead. The day was hot, and
they were sweaty, and needed to refill their canteens, so the
other two went on while Scrap Iron squatted down by a
clump of evergreen shrubs to shit. Thus he was low, quiet,
and holding still, when he glimpsed someone following
them, a civilian slinking along with a rifle. The shrubs were
between them, and Scrap Iron's head, with its green field

cap, was just high enough to see over them. Slowly, slowly
the Komarsi reached, picked up his submachine gun, and
silently slipped off the safety. His pants were around his
ankles; he left them there.

At about sixty feet he stood up, and the civilian, an old
man, found himself staring into the muzzle of a .37 caliber
SMG. It was kind of comical how surprised the old guy
looked. "Drop your rifle, old man!" Scrap Iron called.
Loudly, so the others would hear.

For once Chesty didn't talk. He came running, half a step
ahead of Kodi. The old man had dropped his rifle, of course,
and stood big-eyed and worried looking. Chesty laughed.
"Well I'll be damned! What's that you got, Scrap Iron?
Caught you with your pants down, dint he."

"I caught him. He was followin' us. He must have heard
that loud mouth of yours."

Chesty laughed again, unpleasantly now, and walked up
to the old man. "Now that you caught us, what you gawnta
do, eh?" Without warning, he struck the old man in the
face, getting leverage into it, knocking him flat, and while
Kodi Furn stood watching, kicked him heavily and repeatedly in the body. Scrap Iron, meanwhile, wiped himself and
pulled up his pants.

"Ayn't that about enough?" Kodi asked mildly.

Chesty turned, angry at the suggestion. "The old fart was
gawnta bushwhack us!" Then he turned to his victim again.
The old man was doubled up, his arms wrapped around his
ribs, his neck corded with pain and the effort of silence.
His face was a smear of blood. Chesty drew the trench knife
from his belt and dropped to one knee. Before the others
realized what he was doing, with a powerful stroke he severed the old man's left Achilles tendon.

"Yomal, Chesty! Cut his throat and have done!"

Chesty snarled, literally, all pretense of wit gone now.
"Don't watch if you ayn't got the belly for it. I'm gawnta
give 'im somethin' to remember." And turned again to the
old man.

Thirty-one

It was early evening at the Lake Loreen Institute on Iryala. Early evening but dark, for it was autumn there. A brisk
wind blew, rattling the purple-bronze autumn leaves on the
peiocks, throwing an occasional handful of them against her
windows.

Lotta Alsnor didn't notice. She sat in trance, on a mat in
her room. She'd spent the day coaching five selected students in advanced meditation. All were in their mid-teens,
had been students at the institute since age six, give or take
a few months. They'd grown up in the T'sel, and done the
Ostrak procedures through Level 8. They'd learned early to
meditate, but only to the level of stilling the mind. The goal
had not been to produce seers or psychics, simply highly
stable, highly rational, highly ethical people for the Movement. And gradually to transform the Confederation. Psychic
incidents occurred, but except for a very few persons, they
were not regular events.

Lotta had been one of the exceptions, and among exceptions
she'd been *the* exception. That, with her strong interest and
intention, had gotten her sent to Tyss to study under

Ka-Shok Masters there, and eventually under Grand Master Ku.

She'd become a recognized Master herself, but her progress had slowed, perhaps ceased. Ku had said she might or might not continue to expand, but if she did, it would be on her own; guidance could help her no further. She was welcome to continue at Dys-Hualuun, but she might do as well somewhere else.

The trance she was in was not meditative. She was checking on people for whom she felt interest and concern. It was in her power to help them, at times, even at a distance. But at a distance, such help was limited; mostly it amounted to "scripting" therapeutic dreams or opening exploratory dreams, and helping the dreamer through them. This evening she'd looked in on Tain Faronya, three hyperspace years away but getting nearer. Now she reached elsewhere.

Since undergoing the Ostrak Procedures, Artus Romlar didn't move around a lot in his sleep. Just now, however, he slept restlessly, his hard 234 pounds forcing an occasional squeak from the wooden joints of his Smoleni army cot.

He dreamed, a dream more coherent than most. In it he commanded a spaceship, an enormous warship accompanied by a fleet of lesser, subordinated vessels. They seemed not to be in hyperspace, because he could look around him and see the other ships, not as symbols generated by his ship's computer, but as if he were looking through the ship-metal sides of his flagship in a spherical 360 degrees.

He was not the giant ship's commander. He was admiral. The ships all were his, and somehow that admiralcy inspired a despair that enclosed and saturated him. The reason wasn't part of the dream.

It was a slow dream, almost like suspended animation. Things happened slowly, with long dark pauses, as if he were trying to hold something off, prevent or delay it. Men came to him with questions and reports, and to dream-Romlar they seemed unreal, insubstantial. Then another man entered the bridge, and with his entry, the dream accelerated to an apparent rate of something like normal. The man rode a wheelchair, and sat wrapped in an old-fashioned blanket as if the ship were cold. Attendants accompanied him. The hands folded on his lap were thin, showing sharp tendons and blue-gray, wormlike veins. Only his face was blurred, as if too terrible to see, but dream-Romlar knew it well, and knew he knew it.

"Are you prepared, Admiral?"

It seemed to Romlar he couldn't breathe, yet from somewhere he found the breath to speak. "I am ready, Your Imperial Majesty." He could see the eyes now, kind, loving. Implacable. Mad.

"Excellent. Give the command."

The dream slowed again. Dream-Romlar felt his lips part, his tongue poise. His vocal cords vibrated with the beginning of a word—

Romlar jerked bolt upright on his cot, sweat cold on his face, staring into the semidarkness of a moonlit night. There was no ship's bridge, no bridge watch intent on their monitors. Only a squad tent, shared with his aide and his executive officer. For a moment he sat breathing heavily, feeling enormous relief. The dream was fading, mere impressions, then they too were gone. But the feeling remained that it had been terrible, the sort of dream no one should have after the Ostrak Procedures, and certainly not after the spiritual training of the Masters of Ka-Shok.

He untucked the mosquito bar from beneath the edge of his narrow mattress, swung his feet out, got up and dressed. He needed activity, to walk, perhaps to think.

For awakening, he felt a concern that hadn't been there when he'd laid down. A concern that this war would waste his regiment, eat it up, that he would need it somewhere else but only a remnant would remain, too few to do what was necessary. True they were occupied largely with training Smoleni rangers just now, but that was temporary. It was also true that the Komarsi units they'd fought so far were neither well trained nor well led; casualties had been light.

But bold new actions were necessary. The status quo— even the new, adjusted status quo—seemed to lead ultimately to defeat for Smolen. And if the Komarsi brought in T'swa . . . The thought took Romlar by surprise, but once looked at, it seemed to him very possible.

*　　　*　　　*

Lotta had monitored the entire dream without impinging. Three hyperdrive years away, the kalif's invasion fleet had left Varatos, and at a very deep level, Romlar had become aware of it. It had touched, had stirred, a very powerful sequence of incidents in his remote past—many, many life-times past. In a vague and general way, Lotta had known it existed—Wellem Bosler did too—and what it was about. Both of them, in processing Romlar, had glimpsed it. Now she knew more, knew certain specifics.

She thought of communicating to him, then didn't. Troubled as he was just now, and introverted, he might not receive her anyway—not consciously. And at Artus's Ostrak level, to dream script for him might do more harm than good.

Besides, it would settle out by itself, for the most part, unless it was further restimulated.

She decided to look in on him from time to time though.

Thirty-two

Kro preferred water from a wild creek to that in his canteen, even when the creek was amber brown tea, flavored with tannic acid, steeped with dead bog moss, fallen needles, and last year's leaves. His knees were wet from kneeling beside it, and a pair of bull flies bit his neck, but he swigged deep, his face to the water, drinking noisily uphill like a horse.

While he drank, a sound reached him, a yapping of jack-wolves. When he'd finished, he listened, and though his knowledge of them was limited, it seemed to him they must have something treed or at bay.

He'd started this mission feeling a certain urgency, but four days in the forest had eased it. And he was curious. So instead of continuing due north, he angled off easterly toward the yapping. He found them less than a quarter mile off; they had something backed into the hollow base of a large old, fire-scarred *roivan*. They were so intent, they didn't notice him, and he edged around for a look at their victim.

It was a man!

Kro stepped forward then with a sharp shout, and the

small wolves parted, startled, saw him coming toward them, and after a moment's hesitation fled silently.

The man stayed in the hollow base. He had a knife in his hand, its blade bloody, otherwise they'd have had him: dragged him out and torn him up. Kro was sure all the blood on the man's clothes wasn't wolf blood. And the man, he saw now, was elderly, his face blood-smeared.

"You gonna be all right?" Kro asked.

The old man laughed with irony. "I can't walk and they cut my nuts out," he said. "They cut my heel tendons and busted some ribs, too. Other'n that, I'm fine." He crawled from the hollow, gasping and sweating at the pain of it, then collapsed on the side where no ribs were cracked. After a long moment, he opened his eyes again and looked up at the newcomer. Realizing he'd confused the man, he explained. "My problem weren't jackwolves; it's human wolves done this to me." He eyed Kro critically. "Dressed like soldiers, same as you, but they talked like Komarsi."

Kro realized then that he'd spoken with the Smoleni accent he'd cultivated as a logger and trapper. He'd intended to, of course, when he got to Burnt Woods, but hadn't consciously thought to just now. His dialect wasn't perfect, but good enough to pass for someone from another district.

He knew damned well who'd done this—not specific individuals, but they'd been his men, no doubt of it. He knew them, to a large degree understood them, and had tolerated their aberrations, not happily but of necessity. He exhaled gustily. "Well shit! How far to the nearest folks?"

" 'Bout six mile." The old man gestured eastward with his head. "There's a hand-plus of farms over there. I got a shack at my daughter's. Her man got called up with the reserves, and killed in the fight at Island Cove. I help her farm." As quickly as he'd said that, his voice changed, as if he'd just seen for the first time the long-term consequences of his mutilation. "Leastwise I used to help her."

Kro made a decision then, and took off his rucksack. "This is gonna hurt like fire," he said, holding the pack up. "But I want you to wear this. Then I'm gonna hoist you on my back and carry you. You'll have to tell me the way."

Oska Niemar eyed him, then nodded stoically. He'd had the notion that this man might be of a piece with the others, in spite of his speech. A submachine gun out in the bush like this, and a big, scar-faced man . . . But he weren't the same. "Put it on me," he said.

Just stretching his arms back while the stranger put the pack on him hurt badly, and when the man rose with him on his back, Oska nearly passed out. Then the stranger started walking. Every step sent pain stabbing through the old man's chest.

It was when he came to a pond surrounded by floating bog, that Kro realized the old man had passed out. He'd asked which way was best to go around, and got no answer. So he chose a way and slogged on, guided by intuition. Things got worse when he came to an old burn, littered with the crisscrossed bones of fire-killed trees, and choked with brush and saplings. He chose a direction and skirted around it. The sun was down when finally he stumbled into a hay field, grown knee-deep again since the first cutting. At the far end of the clearing was a log house and log outbuildings. Kro strode more strongly, now that an end was in sight.

The farmer and his family were eating, but forgot their food when Kro put down his burden at their door. Kro had begun to wonder if he was carrying a corpse, but there still was breath in the unconscious man, and a discernible pulse. The farmer made a stretcher out of two pitchforks and a blanket, and they carried Oska Niemar to his daughter's, a quarter mile away, while the farm wife followed.

The two women stripped and washed the old man. There wasn't much more they could do for him. Then, while the daughter put her two round-eyed children to bed, the farmer took a bottle of turpentine and splashed some on Niemar's wounded crotch as an antiseptic. When they'd put the old man to bed, the farmer and his wife went home again.

Niemar's daughter wiped her hands on her apron. "My name's Seidra. I guess you heard them call me that."

"Mine's Gull. Gull Kro." He looked at her straight. She was a handsome woman, strong, with strong hands and forearms.

"You must be hungry," she said.

Kro chuckled. "More like starved. I've been totin' your dad since midday. I was lost—don't know my way around here—and when he passed out, I got all tangled up with burns and blowdowns. Seemed I best not put him down, otherwise I'd a had to carry him over my shoulder like a sack of grain. And if his ribs are busted, like he thought, that mighta killed him."

She'd already eaten, she and her two children, but she fried up salt pork and boiled two potatoes, sliced some bread, and got butter and buttermilk from the well-house. For gravy, she heated some cold stew. He ate ravenously, and she kept him company with a slice of bread.

"Your dad said your man got killed."

Seidra nodded.

"How you gonna manage?"

"I got cousins here at Wolf Creek, and a nephew that's thirteen. And my husband's uncle will help when he can. And Tissy is nine now, old enough to take on more of the housework."

The talk dwindled then, as if she was sorting out the situation. When Kro had finished eating, she got up. "I'll show you Dad's cabin; you can sleep there. You'll prob'ly want to start for Burnt Woods tomorrow."

Kro nodded. They walked through the twilight, she with an unlit candle. At the door, she lit the candle with a waxed match. The cabin was a single room, with a small, sheet-iron stove. It was orderly, the old man's clothes hanging from wooden pegs. He told himself that if he learned who cut the old man, he'd show him what suffering was all about.

"This is it," she said. "There's *roivan* bark for kindling, if you want a fire. You got matches?"

"A fire starter," he said.

She nodded, still standing in the middle of the floor. "You been long from home?"

He nodded. She closed the door and began to unbutton her blouse.

"It's been a long time for me, too."

Thirty-three

"Umm, Kelmer? I think we should go in the house."

He hated to stop. Weldi Lanks kissed very nicely, her lips full and moist and exciting, and his hand had begun to stroke the back of her thigh. But this was not a good place for further developments.

"I suppose you're right," he answered, and got reluctantly up from the narrow wooden bench in the rose arbor. It was dark, really dark, with a thick cloud layer cutting off the stars. The house was a vague something to their left, barely discernible. At least, he thought, the darkness had given them privacy, the most they'd had yet. Even the lookouts in the bell-tower of the village hall, assigned to watch the approaches to the president's house, couldn't see them crossing the lawn, he was sure.

The house was unlit, from this side at least. Maybe they could sit together in the parlor for a while, he thought hopefully; her father was a man who went early to bed and was up with the birds.

They went to the side porch. No uniformed guard was visible by the door but that didn't register with Kelmer. His mind was on Weldi. She wondered though, and looking around, her foot bumped something lying by the stairs, something heavy but yielding. Kelmer heard her gasp.

"What's wrong?" he murmured.

She hissed him silent, then whispered. "I think it's the guard!"

He knelt and groped. It was a man, and *his shirt was sticky with blood!* "He's dead!" Kelmer whispered.

He found the gun still holstered, and removed it. Then he stood, and setting the safety, shoved the pistol in the back of his belt. "Darling," he whispered, "go around to the front and tell the guard there. If he's—like this one, go to the rose arbor. I'm going inside."

He thought she nodded. At any rate she turned and started round the wraparound porch. He went to the door, then changed his mind. Whoever the intruder was, he was there to kill the president, and he'd have to find his bedroom. Kelmer decided to be there waiting for him. It was a corner room upstairs, with large windows opening onto the roof; Weldi'd given him the tour.

Getting onto the porch railing, Kelmer climbed a scrolled corner post and pulled himself onto the roof as quietly as possible, then began creeping along it toward the president's room. The roof sloped enough to give him nervous stomach, even without the tension inherent in the situation.

When he'd rounded the corner, he could see a faint paleness at the president's window; there was a night light on inside. The window was open but screened. He recalled that the screens downstairs were held at the bottom by a hook. Even the villages were primitive here! With the pistol barrel he poked a hole in the screen, large enough for his finger. Then, disengaging the hook, he opened the screen, and looked in.

There were two windows in the west wall and two in the south. The bed was near the southwest corner, to take advantage of breezes from either direction. The president lay on his side beneath the sheet. Kelmer couldn't hear a thing. Silently he let himself in. His right foot had barely touched the floor when he saw the bedroom door start to open, and froze.

A man stood in the door with a submachine gun. He seemed not to see Kelmer, as if his eyes had found the bed and stopped there. Kelmer stood paralyzed, his pistol untouched in his belt, as the man raised his weapon. There was a boom from the hallway behind him, and the man spun, firing a burst down the hall. For a long frozen second, Kelmer stared, then another boom shocked him out of his momentary paralysis. The would-be assassin pitched forward on his face, and the president, in a nightshirt, was moving to the door with a large pistol in his hand.

It was all over.

Weldi had found the front door unguarded too, but instead of returning to the rose arbor, had slipped inside. She had the advantage of close familiarity with the house, and moved with certainty. In the parlor was a gun cabinet. Groping, she'd found it and taken out the first gun her hands met with, a double-barreled shotgun of about ten gauge. Without even checking to see if it was loaded, she'd crossed the living room to the stairs, and started up. Like Kelmer, she was sure her father was the target of assassins.

It seemed to her she could sense someone in the hall above. She counted the carpeted steps, skipping the one that always squeaked. When she got to the top, she was unsure what to do. Then, at the far end of the hall, her father's door opened, letting faint light out, and not twenty feet in front of her she saw the back of a man who was not her father. She raised the shotgun and pressed on the trigger. Nothing happened. Then she thought, drew a hammer back with an audible click, and pulled again.

The weapon boomed. The man in front of her was the second of two, and the hammer she'd cocked was to the full-choke barrel. A concentrated load of number three shot drove into his chest from behind, killing him instantly. At the same moment, the shotgun's powerful recoil, taking her by surprise, knocked her onto her back.

The man in her father's doorway had turned and fired a burst down the hall, the slugs going above her where she lay. The president had started from his sleep with the sound of the shotgun, and with a single movement snatched up the pistol that lay on his bed table. He'd shot the remaining gunman in the back, through the heart.

There'd been just the two. Weldi had killed one, her

father the other. No one had even noticed Kelmer still seated on the windowsill.

He followed the president to the door, where Heber Lanks switched on a light. The corpses lay in the hall, and Weldi was just getting to her feet. The shotgun lay on the floor. Kelmer crowded past the president and threw his arms around the girl, who clung to him shaking.

Downstairs voices were shouting, and lights were turning on. "It's all right," called Heber Lanks. "Everything is all right."

Half an hour later, Kelmer Faronya was trotting down the road toward camp. He had mixed feelings, mostly not good. He'd frozen at the climactic moment. Yet if he hadn't, the gunman would quite possibly have seen him and fired. He'd be dead now. As it was, everything had turned out well.

On the other hand, it seemed to him, his courage had failed utterly.

Thirty-four

Gulthar Kro hiked the last sixteen miles to Burnt Woods on roads, the last five being on the main road from the south, ditched, graveled, and graded. The farm families in the Halvess settlement had accepted him as Smoleni; he'd continue as one.

He'd burned the incriminating mapbook; he didn't need it now.

The road passed through intermittent farmlands the last few miles, emerging finally from a short stretch of swamp forest to enter continuous fields. Across them he could see Burnt Woods, more than a mile away. A formation of uniformed men came toward him down the road, double-timing, and he stepped aside onto the shoulder to watch them pass. He knew them at once, though he'd never seen any before—mercenaries; a company of them. They wore a uniform like none he'd ever seen; the cut was standard, but the color was mottled green and brown and yellow. The rationale behind it was obvious. And they weren't double-timing after all; their pace was considerably faster, a brisk trot. They wore packs, too; not combat packs or field packs, but pack frames with what appeared to be sandbags.

148

What impressed Kro most about them was their sense of presence. He felt it as they passed; these were warriors, all the way. These were the men that had given Undsvin fits. To kill their commander might be even more difficult than he'd thought. As for escaping afterward—that, he judged, would be the real challenge.

The road he was on ended at a junction, and instead of turning east into the village, he turned west toward the merc camp, to have a look at it. Nearing it, it seemed to him much the same as any regimental camp might be. Near its near side, he saw activity, and went to watch. He'd never seen gymnastics before. The difficulties would not have impressed the judges at a meet, but the exercises they did there were powerful and demanding, and they impressed Gulthar Kro deeply. He'd never seen anyone do giant swings before. And while he'd learned as a boy to stand on his hands, and even walk on them, the mercs kipped up and planched into handstands on horizontal and parallel bars. Beyond that they did tumbling runs, boots flying, shirttails flapping.

He would have missed the close combat drills, because the jokanru ground was on the far side of camp. But an off-duty Smoleni had strolled up beside him, and the two of them carried on an intermittent conversation while they watched the gymnastics.

"Somethin', ain't it?" the Smoleni said.

"Yup. Sure is."

"You ever watch 'em practice fightin'?"

"What d'ya mean?"

"You know." The man stepped around as if in some dance, moving his arms. "Hand to hand."

Kro frowned at the exhibition. "Nope, never did. Where do they do that?"

The man pointed. "Round t' the far side." So after another three or four minutes, Kro trotted over there. Several pre-teen Smoleni boys were already watching. These drills were even more interesting to Kro than the gymnastics had been, and he began to grasp a concept he'd never known before; the concept of personal development technologies. The platoon he watched was sparring, the men matched off in pairs. One played the role of a man who had

a knife but lacked jokanru. He'd attack using some technique, and his "victim" would counter and "destroy" him.
Then they changed roles. These encounters were brief, over
in a moment, but Kro's warrior eye, evaluating, saw how
truly powerful the techniques were. Then they faced off as
two jokanru opponents. Some of these bouts lasted as long
as fifteen seconds, and were even more impressive. He saw
the techniques here as for use between men who were more
or less equals. Then the troopers grouped in threes, two as
canny fighters lacking jokanru; the one would subdue the
two. Kro recognized that such skills could only have grown
from true talent drilled at length.

Finally that platoon moved on to other activities, another
platoon replacing them. They started with stretching, even
though they'd just come from the gymnastics area. Men
stood on one booted foot, with the other leg out straight,
foot at shoulder height, reaching out with their hands to
pull back on their toes, stretching the Achilles tendon. After
two or three minutes of stretching, they began their forms,
as flowing and rhythmic and graceful as ballet, but moving
ever faster. Watching them almost hypnotized Kro; this, he
realized, was the basis of the fighting skills he'd just seen.

He watched the platoon through a full twenty-minute
cycle, then hiked thoughtfully back toward Burnt Woods. *If
they develop such skill in hand-to-hand fighting,* he told
himself, *they no doubt do as well with their weapons.* To
kill their commander, it seemed to him now, might best
take an indirect approach. Perhaps he needed to get hold
of a rifle, and a sniper scope if the Smoleni had them. Make
his strike from a distance, then disappear into the forest. It
was not an approach he cared for.

Meanwhile he needed to find a home, a unit to live with.
After getting directions, he went to the Smoleni army camp
south of the village, and presented himself to the personnel
officer. The captain there frowned at Kro's coarse-stubbled
face, and at the dirt ingrained in clothes and skin. The captured Smoleni uniform Kro wore had sergeant's insignia on
the sleeves, and the unit emblem of a regiment from the
Eel River-Welvarn District.

"Where have you been, Sergeant?"

Kro had had days to concoct a story, should he ever need one, and he knew enough about the fighting in the south, that spring, to make the story sound real. He'd been in the Eagle Regiment, he said, an outfit that had fought long and hard to hold the coast, and been pretty much shot to pieces. When his company was overrun, he'd hidden in a culvert. After that he'd picked his way west and north through occupied territory, traveling by night and hiding by day. Civilians had given him food, and at times had hidden him. Finally he'd reached the Free Lands, and made better time. Now he was here, reporting for assignment.

The captain bought it all. And looking beneath the unsoldierly appearance, he recognized Kro's strength and presence. There'd been an attempted assassination of President Lanks, two nights earlier, he said. Since then, 3rd Battalion had been scouring the woods for Komarsi infiltrators, and lost several men in shoot-outs. They'd be glad to have a seasoned replacement.

Gulthar Kro had a home.

Thirty-five

Varky Graymar was trotting. He'd had hard country to cross, mountainous part of the time, and been living off the land, so when the terrain permitted, he went for speed. The sooner he delivered the letter he carried, the better.

He knew he was near settlement. Not only had the forest been logged through; the unmerchantable tops of fallen trees had been hauled away for fuelwood. Just now he ran along a narrow sleigh road.

He heard a gunshot some distance off, followed immediately by screams, almost certainly by women. He veered off, moving quietly. Shortly he heard men laughing. Ugly laughter. He slowed to a walk, his senses turned full on, Fingas Kelromak's pistol in his hand.

One thing he would not do was endanger the mission Kelromak had given him—to deliver the letter to Romlar. But he'd take a look.

He glimpsed movement ahead through the trees and undergrowth, lowered himself to hands and knees and crept to where he could see. Several *happa* trees lay freshly felled, and large baskets stood near. There were two men there. And two—three women. Two they'd bound, and seemed to have gagged. One of the men was holding the third, while

152

the other raped her. He saw two army packs with guns lying on them, submachine guns.

Varky scanned the vicinity and saw no sign of any other men. It seemed highly unlikely that there were any; they'd be with the two. He crept forward on his elbows, pistol in his right hand, belly on the needle mat, pushing with knees and feet. The rapists seemed to be soldiers, perhaps Smoleni. He'd give them a chance to surrender.

At eighty feet he rose, pistol leveled with both hands. "On your feet," he shouted, "hands in the air."

He didn't expect compliance, and wasn't surprised at what happened. The man doing the holding half rose and dove for a gun. Varky's shot burst into the soldier's temple and blew half his forehead away. The other man pushed away and turned in a crouch.

"Hands in the air!" Varky repeated, and this one too dove for a gun. A bullet burst his upper mandible from the front, and destroyed the second and third cervical vertabrae. The woman who'd been on her back sat up staring, her face a smear of blood from someone's fist. Varky had crouched again, following the second shot, and scanned around, listening intently. He spied a fourth woman then, surely dead. After a moment he trotted over to the women who were tied, and with his knife cut them free. The cords they'd been bound with had cut deeply. They too were bloody-faced, and more or less in shock. One had lost her front teeth; the other, luckier, had had her nose broken. It took a moment before either got up. Then the one with the bloody mouth rolled to her knees, got up, and with a cry ran to the one who'd been raped. They clasped each other and wept. They were young, Varky realized, hardly more than girls.

He went to the two army packs and scouted the contents, found the mapbooks and suspected what they meant.

Then he waited, letting the women help each other, not questioning them. For whatever reason, they'd been peeling the bark from *happa* trees. Apparently the two men, seemingly Komarsi infiltrators, had heard them.

He relaxed, and undertook to commune with the spirits of the three dead. He could sense them in the vicinity of their bodies, but at first none of the three acknowledged him. They were too deeply in shock.

Then the spirit of the woman responded, and he perceived through her what had happened. They'd been collecting bark for bark flour, only a mile or so from home, when they'd been attacked. She was older, an aunt. When she'd tried to stand the two men off with an axe, they'd gut-shot her. She might have lived, but the bullet had cut a major artery, and she'd bled to death internally.

She gave her attention to the surviving women then, but they weren't aware of her, and after another minute she left. Varky didn't notice when the spirits of the two men left. They'd been there, then were gone.

The girl with the broken teeth helped the naked girl put on her cut and torn clothing, and when they were done, they all started home. None of them said a word to Varky till they stopped at a creek to wash the blood off. Then the girl with the broken nose came over to him. The blow had caused her eyes to swell; she peered through slits now. She told him essentially what the dead woman had shown him. She also said that the men weren't Smoleni, she'd known that at once from their speech. "Komarsi," she said. "They'd got to be Komarsi."

They passed the first farm, going on to the one the two sisters were from. The people there had heard the shots, but occasional gunshots weren't alarming in the backcountry.

At the farm the girls were from, Varky was an instant hero, the man who, with a pistol, had shot two Komarsi soldiers armed with submachine guns. And saved the girls' lives, there was little doubt.

They questioned him more from curiosity than any demand to know. He sounded Smoleni, but his work clothes weren't those of a woodsman, and his accent wasn't quite what they were used to. He told them a version of the truth: that he was one of the Iryalan mercenaries, "the white T'swa." He'd been spying in Komars, and was returning to Burnt Woods when he heard the shot and investigated.

Varky would not have to run the last thirty-four miles to Burnt Woods. After they fed him, they put him on a horse, and two men rode with him, rifles across their horses' withers, in case they ran into any more infiltrators.

Thirty-six

The Smoleni platoon sergeant dismissed his men to wash up for supper, and went to his lieutenant. "Lieutenant, you know the new man? Kro? I had 'em all to the range, shootin' at jump-up targets, and that son of a gun shot a perfect score. Tough-lookin' cuss, too, but he seems to get along all right. Just don't talk much. And gettin' here like he did, all those miles through Komarsi territory . . ."

"So?"

"Him already havin' sergeant's stripes, I heard the cap'n say he was gonna, make a squad leader out of him, if he worked in all right. But seems to me he might better be transferred to one of the ranger units the mercs are trainin'. They're trainin' up officers from scratch, in the ways they do things, and from the way Kro acts, and what little he says, seems like he'd make a good one. Appears to be smart, and he's the kind that, if he told me somethin', I'd pay attention. A born leader's what he is."

The lieutenant shook his head. "If he's that good, I'd hate to lose him. And we're short now; two men killed moppin' up infiltrators, and already seven gone to the mercs for trainin'."

The sergeant nodded. "But we're gonna lose him anyways. We don't need a squad leader. He'll get assigned to some other platoon; maybe even some other company."

The lieutenant looked at that for a few seconds, turning it over in his mind. "Mm-m. I'll talk to the captain about it. If he's willin', I suppose that might be best. If this Kro is that good, that's prob'ly where he oughta be."

Thirty-seven

Romlar had read Fingas Kelromak's letter and carried it personally to President Lanks. Lanks had read it, gone over it with Elyas Fossur, then radioed Romlar's headquarters: He wanted him to attend a War Council meeting in the morning, and he wanted Corporal Graymar there to describe personally what had happened.

Scrubbed, shaved, and wearing a clean field uniform, Varky described his experience briefly to the council. Then the president spoke. "I'll read the letter to you," he said, and adjusting his half-moon spectacles, he began. After brief self-identification, Kelromak had written that a large part of the Komarsi public—perhaps a majority—were badly disillusioned with the war, and that numerous persons of economic and political influence even said as much. But not publicly; their discontent was not strong enough to make them so bold.

And if the wealthy were unhappy with the war, the laboring classes would be at least equally unhappy, for they were particularly hurt by the shortages and currency inflation of war time. Thus there seemed to be a potential for

civil disorders that could well bring agitation by the nobility
and merchants to end the war.

After that, the letter included pages cut from a Reform
Party journal, reviewing the class of freedmen. Serfs were
bound by law to the estate they were born on, and under
ordinary circumstances were not accepted by the armed
forces. But commonly during war and the preparations for
war, they were, and satisfactory completion of their military
service gained for them the status of freedmen.

Some newly freed serfs found employment quickly
enough, and became part of the general commons, more or
less, though there tended to be a lingering prejudice against
them. Most however, gathered in shanty settlements at the
edges of the larger towns, where they provided a body of
casual labor, and made a more or less precarious living. The
movement of shanty-towners into the population of general
commoners was slow, and in general they were chronically
discontented.

The freedmen also provided most of the subclass called
"drifters," men who drifted about the country doing casual
labor wherever they could find it. Shanty-towners and drifters contributed much, and probably most, of the crime in
Komars.

Following the cutout pages, Kelromak suggested an
action; the raiders who'd struck targets in and around Linnasteth had proven themselves resourceful men who could
pass for Komarsi. Judging by the courier, they were also
bold, physically impressive, and had presence—the sort of
men who could become dominant in harvest crews, which
consisted mostly of drifters. And Kelromak believed that,
properly incited and led, the freedmen could be brought to
disorders, even insurrections here and there. Which might
be as effective as an army in bringing the war to an end
with Smolen surviving.

His final item was quite different. And troublesome. It
was rumored, he said, that Engwar had sent an agent to
The Archipelago to contract for a pair of T'swa regiments.
He considered the source reliable.

When the president had finished reading, the room was
quiet for long seconds. Then Vestur Marlim had a question

for Varky Graymar: "What do you think of this Lord Kelromak?"

"I trust him. And the people who work for him like and respect him. Also, he was injured during our hit on the War Ministry, so apparently he has business with them."

Fossur spoke then. "Kelromak's a leader of the Reform Party. His father was Marn Kelromak, who led the party till he got so radical he frightened them—worried them at least—and they elected someone else to the job. The family has a history of reformist causes."

The president looked thoughtfully at the tabletop, then across at Varky. "And he gave you his pistol. Did you have the slightest urge to shoot him?"

Varky looked surprised at the question. "None whatever, Mr. President."

"Any discomfort at being given the gun?"

"No, sir. I wasn't even surprised at it, though I hadn't foreseen the possibility."

Lanks looked at his council. "It is my observation that our mercenaries are unusually perceptive. I give Corporal Graymar's impressions more than a little weight."

Belser looked at Fossur and spoke. "Elyas, have your agents picked up anything about a T'swa contract?"

Fossur shook his head. "Not a hint of it. All we have is this letter."

"Perhaps it's not true then."

"Possibly not. But given Komarsi wealth and Engwar's pride, and their recent embarrassments, I rather suspect it is."

Heber Lanks spoke then: "Colonel Romlar, do you have any comments?"

"Yes. Regarding the T'swa: They won't send him two regiments, unless they're greatly reduced regiments, somewhat smaller than mine. It's lodge policy. And considering scheduled graduations, they're very unlikely to get a new and unreduced regiment. In fact, they may very well have to wait a bit for any at all. What they can expect is a short regiment—at least somewhat short."

Belser interrupted. "Colonel," he said slowly, "could you defeat a T'swa regiment?"

Romlar leaned back and folded thick arms over a thick

chest. "One not much larger than mine—maybe. Note that I didn't say probably. I also consider the reverse to be true: they could quite possibly defeat us. But I don't consider that the key issue here. They can play a more important role by attacking you, and I have little doubt they'll tell Engwar that. Just as I can make the greatest difference by attacking the Komarsi.

"Regarding their importance to this war: They are *very* good, very dangerous. But their advantage over you is less than our advantage over the Komarsi." Romlar paused, looking the room over, and repeated himself before elaborating. "You have many troops well suited to traveling and maneuvering in the forest, troops who respond quickly to situations. They're not likely to panic or freeze if surprised. All in all, they're a lot better suited to fighting the T'swa than the Komarsi are to fighting my men. This is particularly true of the units we're training now, the ranger units. They're not equal to the T'swa, not at all. But the T'swa will find them dangerous opponents, opponents to tell stories about in their old age—those few who live to old age.

"The T'swa can't destroy you by fighting us. They can only destroy you by fighting you. And we cannot defeat Komars by fighting the T'swa, but we can strike the Komarsi and hurt them deeply."

It was Belser again who questioned. "Then you don't expect to fight the T'swa?"

"I don't expect to seek out the T'swa. Nor do I expect them to seek us out. But will we fight each other? I have no doubt of it. Circumstances will see to that. We'll meet; sooner or later we'll meet. And then we'll fight."

He leaned forward now, resting his elbows on the table. "We haven't talked about Kelromak's suggestions yet. If Colonel Fossur thinks they might be worthwhile, we need to act, to get agitators into Komars before harvest."

The meeting went on to other matters then. When it ended, Heber Lanks watched thoughtfully as the others left. His mind was on the comment he'd made after listening to Corporal Graymar: that the mercenaries seemed exceptionally perceptive.

No doubt it was that perceptivity, as much as their fighting

skills, that made them so effective—enabled them to do
what they had. It would be useful in battle and in planning.
And Colonel Romlar—so often when he thought of him, it
was with the shadow label "the boy colonel"—Colonel
Romlar undoubtedly brought that perceptivity to the War
Council.

He'd make a point of asking him to attend more often.

Romlar didn't leave at once. Instead he went with Fossur
to the intelligence chief's office, where they discussed how
to insert troopers into Komars as agitators. Fossur seemed
to have sources of information everywhere, and remarkable
recall for details. His orderly brought lunch for both of
them, and when Romlar finally left, it was with a written
plan.

Carrmak would lead the infiltrators. Esenrok would take
over Carrmak's battalion.

Driving himself back to camp, something else surfaced in
Romlar's mind. The T'swa would come, he had no doubt.
His men were able, and as a commander he'd shown himself
equal to the T'swa. At least equal. But the prospect of fighting them troubled him.

Well. Every T'swa regiment got used up sooner or later;
it was the other side of being warriors. It hadn't bothered
him on Terfreya, when he'd lost so many, and he'd seen no
sign that it troubled his troopers. Not even Jerym, who'd
been sent repeatedly to lead men into no-return situations.

And his old cadre—Sergeant Dao, Sergeant Banh, Captain Gotasu—they'd all been through it. Found fulfillment
in it. After four wars on four worlds, Colonel Dak-So had
lifted from Marengabar with fewer than two hundred men
of what had been the Shangkano Regiment.

Was there something that different about losing men on
Maragor?

If Lotta were here they'd sort it out, he had no doubt.

Thirty-eight

Council meetings in Linnasteth were quite different from those in Burnt Woods. Different as the personnel were different, especially the central figures, Engwar II Tarsteng and Heber Lanks.

General Undsvin Tarsteng had never attended one before. His role in the war had been limited entirely to carrying out the king's edicts, and that was the way he preferred it. As a first cousin of Engwar, they'd been childhood playmates periodically, and sometime associates in adolescent mischiefs. It had been Undsvin, two years the elder, who'd introduced Engwar to the pleasures of having serving girls available, an activity not unusual in many noble households.

But he'd never been an adviser—hadn't even seen his cousin since the war began—and wondered what this "invitation" meant.

He arrived by floater and was escorted limping to the council chamber by a sychophant he would willingly have done without. He found Engwar's entire council waiting, and waited with them. They were expected to be early, and to wait without conversation; it was a foible of Engwar's.

Eventually a marshal entered, and announced, "His Majesty the King!" Everyone got to their feet, and Engwar entered, well guarded. He was pale, his expression strained; Undsvin wondered if his cousin had been ill.

The king said nothing as he walked to the head of the table. He took his seat stiffly, and without even calling the meeting to order, made an announcement that stunned all of them.

"I am going to end the war," he said. "I am going to requisition every floater in my realm and drop bombs on the Smoleni government, every Smoleni supply depot, and on the mercenary camps!" When he'd finished, his expression dared anyone to disagree.

Undsvin stared. He couldn't believe what his cousin had said. Currently the war in Smolen was the only war on Maragor, which meant that all three Confederation monitor platforms would be parked over this part of the continent. And the Confederation Ministry in Azure Bay reportedly had more than its share of agents planetwide, their ears everywhere.

It was the Foreign Minister, Lord Cairswin, who broke the silence, after first rising, as protocol required. "Indeed, Your Majesty, that would certainly break the Smoleni ability to resist, and no doubt weaken their will. How did you plan to keep this action secret from the Confederation?"

"The Confederation be damned! They cannot dictate to me!"

"Of course not, Your Majesty. But after the deed is done . . . do you have a plan for that?"

Engwar didn't answer, but his eyes seemed to bulge with anger. Undsvin eyed the Foreign Minister, a man tall and lean and calm. He had guts; he was taking his life in his hands. "They'll probably let you choose your successor," Cairswin went on, "but whoever you select, it would be best if he has a plan of government when the Confederation task force . . ."

"SHUT YOUR MOUTH!"

Cairswin bowed and sat down. Again no one spoke. It occurred to Undsvin that if Engwar insisted on this—and he was nothing if not obstinate—it could well bring on a coup before he could carry it out. And the coup would be justified. For aerial bombardment—even aerial reconnaissance—was banned in Level 3 wars. And a Confederation takeover would ruin every family involved in top government levels; it had happened before, elsewhere.

Undsvin found himself on his feet then. "I've heard, Your Majesty, that you're bringing in T'swa. Two regiments in fact."

"They'll only let me have one! And it won't be here for deks!"

"Ah! But bombing—Heber Lanks would hardly live to crow, but later, when the Confederation marines arrived, the remaining Smoleni would be enjoying victory, while we'd be eating ashes and drinking gall. Komars would be stripped to pay reparations and penalties. A shame, when there are alternative means of breaking Smoleni insolence. Of burning their hopes and costing them blood and supplies."

He bowed to his cousin then. "You are the king, of course; your will be done. But truly, Your Majesty, I hope that in your wisdom you'll reconsider."

Engwar stared narrow-eyed at his cousin. "Indeed! And what is this alternative means of breaking Smoleni insolence?"

"I've given it careful thought," Undsvin lied. "I propose a destruction strike deep into Smoleni territory, with mounted infantry and mobile artillery. Not to capture more territory, but to strike and destroy Smoleni supply depots. Their supply situation is desperate, as you know, and they'll have to defend them with everything they can bring to bear."

The ideas had begun to flow for Undsvin as he spoke, and his assurance infected the others, even Engwar. "We succeeded early in the war, when we forced them to defend fixed locations. We could bring our strength to bear on them then. More recently, facing the vast Smoleni forests, we ceased to attack, and they brought what force they had against fixed positions of ours. I'm simply proposing to reverse this again. We can bloody and rout their defending forces and capture their supplies. Next winter will be hungry for them at best. This move will leave them truly desperate, while the capture of their munitions will make them less able and less willing to fight."

All that was left of Engwar's earlier rage was a jutted jaw. *He's given in,* Undsvin thought. *But he'll want to save face with these others.* "Indeed!" Engwar said. "You should have told me in advance."

"I'd thought to use the T'swa in this, as well as forces of our own."

"Umh! When will you start?"

"It will take some preparations, Your Majesty, notably logistical." Engwar's brow pulled down. "But four weeks should do it."

He'd prefer more time, but better to say four weeks and strive for it. After four weeks, Engwar's attention would have gone to something else, perhaps the approaching arrival of the T'swa. A request then for two or three more weeks wouldn't seem like much.

"Very well." Engwar looked around the table. "All right. Arlswed, give us your intelligence report."

The room seemed almost to lift with relief.

On the flight back to Rumaros, Undsvin examined possible resources and tactics. And possible uses for his personal unit. He knew where he'd gone wrong there. Strength and fighting qualities (among which he included arrogance) were more easily recognized in hooligans, but most hooligans lacked other necessary qualities.

He wondered how many Gulthar Kros there were unrecognized in the army, men deadly yet disciplined. Very few, he suspected. But surely there was a sizeable number who more or less approached Kro in soldierly qualities. Perhaps when the war was over, he'd make a project of finding them, perhaps even enough for a battalion.

Thirty-nine

The train rolled through a shallow valley whose sides curved mildly up. Sheep grazed its grasses. Beside the tracks, a considerable river surged and roiled, the color of clear tea.

The train was mostly ore cars, full of reddish earth and stone, but behind the engine was a single coach, such as might take bachelor miners to town for the weekend. This, however, was Threeday.

There was no long plume of coal smoke trailing behind, snowing acid soot, for this train rode an electrified track. Thus the coach wore a pair of cupolas, with seats for those who wished to watch. Coyn Carrmak sat absorbing the scenery. Behind the train, the late sun lowered in the rounded notch that was the valley. Ahead, the ground disappeared into a much sharper, deeper notch—the fjord.

They rolled into it, and the grade steepened. To the side, the valley walls had become emerald green scraps, with dark wedges and strips of trees. The stream no longer flowed. It leaped, foamed, plunged toward the hydroelectric plant, dropping far more steeply than the tracks. Afternoon was left behind, replaced by false evening born of shadow, the shadow of the walls themselves.

A few miles ahead and a thousand feet lower, Carrmak could see larger water, Deep Fjord, with its harbor and nitrates plant.

And unless something had gone wrong, a ship from The Archipelago that would carry him and his forty troopers to Linnasteth, unarmed. Their weapons there would be their minds and tongues.

Forty

They left Deep Fjord in moderately rough seas, the wind out of the southeast at first, shifting round to the east, then to the north of east. Thus the SS *Agate Cliffs* took the seas more or less broadside. She rolled heavily, and in their hidden compartment, the troopers were crowded. Most of them were seasick, too, a condition contributed to by the sickness and stink of those who got sick first, and by the honey pots.

For there was no fresh sea air where they were. Their narrow compartment had been built into the starboard trim-tank, hurriedly and specifically to accommodate them. At the dock in Deep Fjord, in a single night, by the chief engineer, no less, with the help of his first assistant and four Oselbenti. Most of the crew had been ashore or asleep.

The idea was that no one, especially no crewmen, should know who didn't have to. Light was provided by two drop cords. Sanitary facilities were three steel drums, each cut off at about twenty-two inches, with a top welded on, and baffles, and a seat and hinged lid. Handles of steel rod had been welded to the sides for carrying. Drinking water came from pails with dippers. Holes had been cut in a bulkhead, opening into the portside fuel bunker, thus what air they got smelled of coal dust.

It hadn't been feasible to bring mattresses aboard, not secretly. So for beds they had folded tarpaulins—old, worn hatch tarps stored overhead in the boiler room to supply tarp patches, and hand rags for the firemen. They were softer than the bare steel plates.

Their only heat was body heat. When they'd first slipped aboard, about three o'clock one morning, the night had been chill. The seawater was cold too, and the ship. But after a time their compartment warmed up, from their bodies and the poor ventilation.

Food, for those who could eat, and water was passed to them through a hatch by the four A.M. to eight A.M. deck-watch. Twice a day: once before dawn, just after he came on his morning watch, and once after dark, not long after he got off his evening watch. At first, he was the only one aboard who had any contact with them, and one of only five who knew they were there. For obvious reasons, the food required no preparation. It was loaves of sliced bread, cans of jelly, a pot of beans, and fruit. On his own, the deckwatch passed them an unofficial jug of whiskey, too. He was also the ship's medic, and the whiskey was part of the closely guarded medicinal supply. They ate little, even those who weren't sick, and drank almost none of the whiskey. Mostly they slept and meditated, waiting.

Coyn Carrmak was one of those who hadn't gotten sea-sick. What he had gotten was a chest cold, one of several, before the ship had ever left the dock. Faintly the deck watch heard their coughing as he crossed overhead, and passed a warning message to them later. From that point the coughers huddled under a piece of tarp and did their coughing there. They still could be heard, but the sound was faint, and not easily identified.

What worried the *Agate Cliffs'* captain was Komarsi paranoia from the Day of Destruction. In Komars, the authorities didn't even allow ship's crew ashore, not even to handle lines on the dock! Longshoremen were assigned to that. He'd been warned to expect ship inspectors aboard as soon as the *Cliffs* tied up, hunting for possible infiltrators. If they heard the coughing, they'd surely investigate.

The chief engineer provided a possible solution. He personally strung a cable over the grating close above the boilers, tightened it with a turnbuckle, and hung a tarpaulin over it to form a sort of tent. There were two boxes to sit on. In the dark of night, the coughers were led from their hideout two at a time, and hustled to the makeshift sauna to spend an hour baking. It was hotter than a summer afternoon on Tyss, and weakened them temporarily, but their coughing lessened.

This project required that two more crewmen become privy to the secret: the stoker on the twelve-to-four watch, and his coal trimmer. It was unavoidable. They were told only that these were four Smoleni spies, and were sworn to secrecy. *No one else must know, not their messmates, no one. Not now, not later. Their grandchildren perhaps, if they ever had any.* Like Archipelagons in general, the crew didn't like Komars, and liked even less their assault on Smolen, so the two swore willingly, and their oath was readily accepted. They didn't know about the other thirty-six troopers.

On the third day, the rolling ceased. Carrmak was awake, and noticed it at once. The ship still rose and fell, but the seas were from the stern now, and he realized they'd turned, were headed west into the Komar Gulf. To the southwest would lie Komars, to the northwest what had been the Smolen coast. A few hours later, all wave motion was gone; they'd entered the Komar River. Occasionally, through the deck plates, he heard the ship's whistle as they met outbound ships in the river. Then he slept.

The trimmer, on break from his wheelbarrow, came to take them again to the dark boiler room. On deck, Carrmak saw sparse lights on both sides of the river, but mostly on the south where Komars lay. They moved silently to the boiler room door, heat flowing sluggishly from it as from the entrance to hell. Inside was scarcely less dark than night. They entered, and descended a ladder to the grating and their sauna tent.

Inside the tent, Carrmak relaxed, became semicomatose. Soaking up the heat, breathing the dry hot air, he lost track of time. From the other side of the bulkhead, the dull booming of pistons lulled him. From the boiler room itself came little more than the sound of the shovel ringing on the deadplates, as the stoker fed the fires, and the sound of coal being dumped from a wheelbarrow.

At one point he heard bells jangle. The ship slowed, stabilizing at half speed. He'd almost dozed again when the jangling repeated. The speed slacked even more, and he became aware of another change in sound: the great induction fan had ceased turning, ceased sucking air through the boiler fires. Close at hand, a chuffing sound began, somehow alarming.

Abruptly the safety valves blew, first on the starboard boiler, a second later on the port. The sound was stupendous, overwhelming, driving both troopers to their knees, hands over their ears. Seconds later the deckwatch was crouching in the opening of their tent, face a twisted grimace at the sound, beckoning them to come.

They followed him quickly, down another ladder into the stoke-hole. Usually it was semidark, lit only by two small tubes. Now the four big fire boxes added to the light, their doors open to cool the backheads and help draw down the steam pressure. The stoker stood alone, eyes squinched, jaw set against the sound, frowning questioningly at them. Speech was hopeless in the thunder of the safety valves. In response, the deckwatch gestured and shook his head, then hurried the two troopers to the far bulkhead and into the bunker alley. There a single tube gave light enough to work by. At the far end, the sinewy coaltrimmer stood by his big-bellied wheelbarrow. Speech was possible there by shouting.

A Komarsi guard boat had pulled alongside, the deck watch told them. They were going to put inspectors aboard now; that's why the ship had slowed to slow-ahead. Unexpectedly, which had caused the valves to blow. The two troopers would pretend to be trimmers. "Get in the stoke-hole," he told the trimmer. "Grab a shovel and pretend to be a stoker." The trimmer, a teenage boy, grinned, nodded, and hurried out.

"You!" the deckwatch said, gesturing at Carrmak, "take the shovel!"

Then he left the alley, shooing the other trooper ahead of him. The trimmer had been filthy with coal dust, so Carrmak buried his hands in slack, then rubbed them on his face, his shirt, his thighs. Behind him the safety valves cut off, the sudden silence a lifting of oppression. He heard clashing then, as the stoker and trimmer closed the heavy furnace doors. After a couple of minutes he heard voices, one interrogating, the others answering. With his shovel he began to load the wheelbarrow, tossing the coal to make a maximum of dust. It billowed 'round him. He became aware of someone blocking the door to the bunker alley, and looked up. A strong flashlight caught him in its glare. He grimaced, and raised a hand to shield his eyes. Then the light was gone. He finished filling the barrow and stood for a long two or three minutes. The trimmer came back in, still grinning.

"They've gone," he murmured. "Stupid fookin' Komarsi lubbers! They think it takes two to fire a watch on this bucket!" He shook his head at such ignorance. "Stay here awhile, till we go to half speed. That'll mean they've left the ship."

He grinned again, and thrust out a filthy hand. They gripped and shook.

Ten minutes later, the deckwatch led the two troopers back to their covert, and came inside long enough to talk. "They took us by surprise," he told them. "It's occurred to them that a ship could send someone ashore by boat or raft, so now they check when you first enter the Linna.

"Be ready. I 'spect the skipper'll want to unload you before too long. In case there's more surprises ahead."

Actually they didn't leave till near dawn. The freighter slowed briefly to slow ahead, and put a life raft into the water through the fantail gangway. Half a dozen troopers got onto it, and the deck watch let go with the boat hook. The ship was passing only fifty feet from the channel's edge, so they didn't have to row. They were on a rope end, which gave them velocity, and used the steering oar to slant them ashore. Then the raft was pulled back to the gangway for another load.

It was the right side of the river, too. Linnasteth was upstream on the far side, and that's where security would be strongest.

They were spread along a mile of riverbank, of course. But they didn't need to rendezvous; in fact, to do so would be unwise. And they all knew what they were supposed to do.

They'd most spoken about a night at Weildiland, of course,
but that she'd good to make sense and I'd so the so could
he sounds, and they'd have what they were supposed to
you.

Forty-one

Kelmer Faronya had spent six days recording the trooper-
directed training of a ranger company. The emphasis was on
small-unit tactics in T'swa-type actions. The trainees learned
quickly. And enthusiastically, for this was the kind of tactics
that felt right and natural to them.

They'd been six good days for Kelmer. Days and nights,
for there'd been night exercises too. But through it all he'd
had a piece of his attention on Weldi Lanks.

Seemingly neither father nor daughter had realized his
funk that night; hadn't been aware that he'd stood unable
to move when the Komarsi infiltrator had pushed the door
open, prepared to gun the president down. Weldi had even
regarded him as a hero, for having been there. Particularly
for having gotten there as he had, climbing a pole and working his way along the sloping roof.

He'd said nothing to disillusion her. Inwardly he even
agreed that she had a point; he'd made the effort, and put
himself at serious risk. He wasn't even sure that he might
not have acted, tried to shoot the gunman, if the circumstances had been slightly different. And as it stood, he'd
done the right thing. But he remembered the fear and

174

paralysis he'd felt when the Komarsi had pushed the door open. Thus he found little solace in that rightness.

Despite his self-invalidation, he had sense enough to realize that in life as a whole he was competent: intelligent, diligent, and generally ethical. And when the war was over, his production here would make him a celebrity video-journalist at home on Iryala. His income would be quite good.

Weldi clearly dreamed of living on Iryala someday. A dream very difficult to realize for a citizen of a trade planet, even the daughter of a president, because immigration visas to Confederation member worlds were few and hard to get. Except for spouses of Confederation citizens.

He told himself that when he'd finished his week with the ranger trainees, he'd visit Weldi. And if the time seemed right, he'd ask her to marry him.

Weldi had observed some training that week too. With Colonel Fossur's wife, she'd gone to the mercenary camp and watched their morning workouts in gymnastics and jokanru. And been very impressed. Could Kelmer do those things? she wondered.

When he came to call, the next evening, they'd walked together along the millpond. She'd left the house without saying anything; otherwise her father would have sent armed guards with them. It seemed to her that if any assassins had survived the sweeps, they'd have shown themselves by then or fled the district. Besides, Kelmer carried a pistol on his belt now.

He told her what he'd seen, while he'd been away, and she told him of seeing the troopers train. "Can you do those things?" she asked, and having asked, wondered if she should have. For if he couldn't, it might embarrass him.

He grinned and nodded. "Not as well as they do, though. They trained for six years; I trained for one. In the first year you only learn the basics of jokanru—of hand-to-hand combat. But—" He stopped, stripped off his shirt, and crouching, planched into a handstand, then walked on his hands for her on the uneven ground, ending with a dozen handstand pushups. In a tanktop, his muscles were quite impressive. She watched delighted. When he was back on his feet once more, she asked to feel his bicep. He flexed his arm and she squeezed it, first with fingertips, then with a whole-handed squeeze.

"Oh!" she said. "It's so hard! And so *big*!" Then blushed delicately.

Kelmer blushed more vividly. And somehow, that evening, couldn't bring himself to propose. It hadn't been fear, he insisted inwardly on his way back to camp. After her comment, it just hadn't been the right time for it.

Weldi watched between the curtains as Kelmer trotted off up the graveled street. He'd been so sweet, blushing as he had. She guessed he'd be good in bed; he had a wonderful body. He'd be surprised how good she'd be. Not that she'd had experience, but she'd daydreamed of making love often enough. She'd even done some heavy petting with a younger cousin, a couple of times. She'd been fifteen then.

She wouldn't go that far with Kelmer though. He wasn't thirteen, and she wasn't stronger than he was. Besides, if they made love before they were engaged, he might not propose.

Forty-two

They were an entire brigade, the 3rd Mounted Infantry.
And they'd arrived, they thought, to take part in maneuvers.
Five miles west was another brigade, the 6th, with the same
idea, prepared to be their opposition. The mounted infantry
were proud units, proud and privileged—*ride* to battle, then
fight on foot—and the 3rd and 6th were judged the two best
brigades in the Komarsi army. Their troops were the sons of
yeoman farmers, sturdy, self-reliant young men who considered themselves much better than units manned by serfs
and freedmen, and willing to prove it if asked.

Maneuvers were to begin the next morning, and surprisingly they'd been allowed to lay around camp all day; no
drill, no fatigue duty. And like all soldiers, they knew what
to do with slack time: sleep. So that day, napping was the
principle activity of two brigades, some twelve thousand
Komarsi soldiers.

Only a few hundred had pulled duty, loading caissons and
light but rugged campaign wagons. The brigades' packs and
saddlebags were already packed, ready for the next morning.

They were three miles south of the Eel River, the boundary

177

between Komarsi-occupied south Smolen and the Free Lands.

Autumn was pending, the nights much longer than they'd been. It was twilight when bugles blew, calling the men from the tents they'd occupied. Within the hour they'd struck camp and were riding north toward the Eel through moonless night.

The 3rd Brigade stopped a mile from Mile 40 Bridge, and were told that this was no exercise. The same was happening to the 6th, near Mile 45 Bridge. They were going to strike deeply into Smoleni territory. Very deeply. A thrill passed through the young soldiers, spiced with a tinge of fear. This promised to be a different kind of action than the drive to the sea that spring: more venturesome, less predictable.

They were to wait till *Eliera* rose, then ride most of the night. With luck, the Smoleni wouldn't know they were there till after daylight.

Forty-three

The squad of young Smoleni soldiers had made their hidden out-camp as comfortable as they could. They were recon cavalry, an outpost with radio, set to watch Mile 40 Bridge over the Eel. There was a similar squad watching every other bridge. It was isolated duty, but included no drill or make-work. Nor was there any commissioned officer, just Sergeant Murty, though Lieutenant Hoos checked on them every day or two.

They had a small lookout platform in the top of a tall, clean-boled *jall*, with a rope ladder to climb it. A pair of side branches had been removed in its top, giving a clear view of the bridge, but the platform itself would be hard to spot. The tree stood on the riverbank two hundred feet downstream of the bridge, and it seemed unlikely that the Komarsi knew it was there, or that they were.

Private Tani Berklos had stood a number of lookout watches so far—he'd lost track of how many. You stood watch one hour in eight, theoretically so you wouldn't get bored and careless. By day, watching was easy. By night, if it was cloudy enough or there was no moon, you listened and imagined. Of course, by night, two other men watched from a thicket near the base of the bridge, too. He'd pulled that duty, they all had, and preferred the platform.

Just now there was no moon, and clouds dimmed the starlight. He could sort of make out the bridge, but he couldn't have seen anyone crossing it.

Off watch they were allowed to sleep as much as they wanted, on the assumption that they wouldn't then get sleepy on watch. And there was some truth to that. But just now, Private Berklos was fighting sleep. There weren't even many mosquitoes to help; their numbers had dwindled greatly through the drier than normal summer.

Even standing he'd dozed, and stand you must, for there was no place to sit. Unless you sat on the small platform itself, which was strictly against orders. There was a safety line around it, about waist high, so you wouldn't fall off, but Tani didn't trust it. He feared that if he fell asleep standing, he might fall and be killed. So in spite of orders, he sat down with his back to the trunk and his knees drawn up. He had no doubt at all that he'd fall asleep, so he draped one wrist over a ladder step. If Sergeant Murty came to check, or his relief started up, he'd feel the ladder jerk, and waken.

To his credit, he tried hard to stay awake. He pinched himself, rubbed his bur-cut with his knuckles, and thought about girls. It wasn't enough. His lids closed without his realizing it.

It was the ladder that woke him, and he jerked to his feet. Enough time had passed that *Eliera* had risen, and he could see the bridge plainly despite the clouds. Nothing was there but the timbers and planking. Meanwhile his relief climbed faster than he'd expected, and when the man stepped onto the platform, Tani turned to say something. And realized, even in the cloud-dimmed moonlight, that the grinning face before him was one he'd never seen before.

A trench knife struck deeply into Tani's abdomen and thrust upward into the heart. He didn't even have time to scream. But then, none of his squad were alive to hear him if he had.

Forty-four

Third Brigade had ridden till after daylight before they met opposition. Till then there'd been no evidence that it had been detected. The lead battalion was crossing an open field when a Smoleni force estimated at two companies of infantry opened fire from the cover of forest, with rifles, machine guns, and light mortars. The Komarsi dismounted and advanced. Fighting was heavy but brief; the Smoleni were flanked and routed. Two miles up the road, another small Smoleni force repeated the performance.

The apparency was that they were trying to gain time, to bring more forces and no doubt prepare some sort of defensive positions.

Private Marky Felkor knelt behind a fallen tree, one of many felled across the road, more or less crisscross, their tops pointing generally south, toward the enemy. And not just across the road; the barrier stretched on each side of the road for two to three hundred feet, though it was deepest in the road. It would be hard to flank, too. One flank of the barrier was guarded by fen, the other by moss bog, in either of which a horse would sink to its knees.

The Komarsi were coming, supposedly a whole division of them, and 2nd Battalion, 5th Regiment, was supposed to hold them here as long as they could.

Fifth Regiment had taken heavy losses defending the coast that Fourdek, and many of its replacements were like Marky, less than eighteen years old, without combat experience, and short on training. But Marky was from the backcountry; his ax had felled a number of the trees in the barrier, and he was at least as good with the rifle as the ax.

Ahead he heard a rattle of rifle fire, as Komarsi scouts met Smoleni skirmishers. Gradually the noise grew, coming nearer. On the flanks, along the open fen and bog, mortars thumped, preregistered on the road ahead. *That'll slow 'em,* Marky thought. Moments later he heard the crashes of mortar bombs landing, hopefully among the Komarsi. Ahead, the rifle fire slacked. Either the skirmishers were being overrun, or the Komarsi had backed away.

Another sound overrode the spatter of rifle fire then, a thundering sound not too far ahead. A muted rumbling followed, like nothing Marky had ever heard before. But he'd heard it described, and fear spasmed in his guts.

Then the earth shook with explosions. Dirt flew, and branches, and sections of tree trunks. Marky was raised from the ground and thrown down again. The crashing continued, though not as concentrated as the synchronous opening salvo, but nothing more hit as close as the shell that had lifted and dropped him. Eyes bulging, rifle still clutched tightly, he no longer knelt. He hugged the ground, as low and flat as he could make himself.

After about two minutes the shelling stopped. Though Marky didn't know it, the Komarsi batteries were well ahead of the brigade's supply column, and were being frugal with their shells. Ahead, the rifle fire picked up again. The lieutenant shouted, and Sergeant Torn called: "Steady, boys. They're comin'. Don't rush now. It's *aimed* fire we want! *Aimed* fire!"

Clover Meadows was a considerable village at the meeting place of Road 40 and a major east-west road, which was why the army had located a major supply dump there. There were also two large tent camps, one military, the other of refugees.

It was a beehive now, with soldiers and civilians, more women than men, loading boxes and barrels onto wagons, all the wagons they'd been able to scrounge, to send it north up Road 40. They'd even started loading boxes into crude slings across the backs of horses and cattle.

Because the Komarsi were coming. During the preceding four days they'd moved eighty-four miles north from the Eel. The people loading wagons could hear distant gunfire—artillery. The fighting was too far away yet to hear the rifles and machine guns.

The last of the wagons moved off, and people flopped down on the ground to rest. More wagons were supposed to be coming from both west and east. There'd better be; there were still a lot of supplies stacked there, and supplies were life, and the means of resistance.

After six days of fighting, the brigade had stopped. It had stopped before, briefly but repeatedly, to fight and to clear the road of fallen trees. The entire thrust of the offensive had been speed. They'd even pushed ahead by night, when the Smoleni fire was not so damnably accurate. They'd slept in snatches, mainly while they waited for the artillery to catch up, and the supplies.

This time, however, they were to stop for the night, and Rumaros be damned. The men desperately needed sleep.

B Company, 9th Regiment, had drawn picket duty, and Captain Jorn Vilabo had posted his company in five-man fire teams, with orders that at least two in each team should be awake at all times; most would manage that, he thought. He had no illusions that they'd stay alert though. The solution, such as it was, was to post *lots* of pickets, and the brigadier had assigned several companies to the duty.

Hopefully things would get easier from here on. Maybe they'd even capture a supply dump, which they'd been told was the main purpose of this operation. So far the Smoleni had left little for them. It seemed to him that had been the hole in the plan: The advance hadn't gone badly, although the big brass in Rumaros were probably dissatisfied. They hadn't expected the Smoleni to muster the wagons and labor and energy to move the dumps the way they had.

Trooper Karly Nelkrim lay in the shadow beside a stone pile. Low shrubs grew around its base, where the hay mower had failed to reach. It was night, but moonlit, and he was looking at Komarsi soldiers sleeping no more than twenty yards in front of him.

The tricky thing had been getting through the pickets unobserved. It had taken more than an hour of careful movement.

The Komarsi hadn't pitched tents. There had been no rain during the offensive, and this was the first night with appreciable cloudiness. The clouds helped. Here in the open you moved when the moons were hidden, lay still and plotted your next move when they weren't. Fortunately the two moons up were only six or eight degrees apart; when one was hidden, usually both were.

They were shining now. The Komarsi were dark oblong lumps in separate small groups, probably squads. He'd have preferred they weren't lying so close together. He hadn't spotted a sentry yet, but surely there were some.

Another slow cloud hid the moons, and Karly moved forward smoothly but quickly till he came to the nearest Komarsi. Reaching down, he drew the knife strapped to his leg and cut the man's throat. The body spasmed once. Then he moved to the next, wondering how many he could kill before an alarm was raised. And whether any of the others had reached the sleepers yet.

Sergeant Pitter Pross was unhappy: The paddock guards fell asleep faster than he could circle the paddock and wake them up. He hoped the pickets were doing better, and wondered how he'd been able to stay awake himself. Or for how much longer. His eyes felt gritty, and he'd caught them sliding shut a couple of times, even as he walked.

He felt ill at ease about this night. He'd overheard the C.O. telling the lieutenant that they should have made a stop like this one two nights earlier, when everyone wasn't unconscious on their feet. That the decision to keep pushing had come from Rumaros, from some sonofabitch who slept between sheets eight hours a night, plus a nap after lunch. Men so short on sleep not only had trouble staying awake, Pross told himself. Their judgment went bad. They fell asleep on their feet or in the saddle, dreaming they were awake. They were short on rations, too, and on grain for the horses. Thank Yomal! The brigadier had passed the word that they'd wait here till the supply train caught up.

Somewhere a man screamed. The sound stiffened Pross for a moment. Then it was quiet again. Nightmare, he told himself. And it would take more than a single scream to wake most of them.

Abruptly a machine gun began to fire, and another, and another, firing into the horse herd from close up. Abruptly Pross was wide awake and swearing, looking around for the muzzle flashes. He couldn't see any; they seemed to be on the far side of the horses, which were milling wildly now, crowhopping with their hobbles on, some of them screaming. Abruptly randomness became direction, away from the machine guns and toward him. Horses charged through the rope fence, the whole herd coming his way with an up-and-down, hobbled-horse gait.

There was no chance to run. Pross crouched till the first one was virtually on him, hoping to clutch its mane and pull himself onto its back, but its clumsy gait foiled him. It struck him with a shoulder, knocking him down, and the horses behind it trampled him to rags.

Kelmer Faronya listened to the staccato of machine guns, the rumbling of hooves, and felt a distancing, a separation of himself from the event. Looking out from the forest's edge, he could see the oncoming horse herd. They were nearing, but also, hobbled as they were, slowing. At a hundred yards, Jerym's hand clapped his shoulder.

"This offensive's been running on borrowed time and borrowed energy," he murmured. "Now it's time to foreclose the mortgage."

Tired, and confronting the dark forest, the foremost horses slowed to a hobbled walk, the momentum and energy of those behind insufficient to force them. At about thirty yards, Jerym whistled a command, and A Company trotted out in a line, armed for this mission with grenades and submachine guns. They began a butchering, while Kelmer, neither frightened nor excited, recorded it all. Tired as they were, it took time for the horses to turn around and flee again. There was a great squealing and dying before those behind got turned around. Then slowly, heavily, the survivors began to run again, back the way they'd come.

It seemed to Kelmer that they should not show this cubeage.

Forty-five

It had been raining for a day and a half, and rivulets of cold water trickled down Colonel Renvil's slicker as he watched his brigade straggle by. He wore no insignia of rank. He'd cut them off after a sniper had killed Brigadier Lord Willing, leaving him in charge.

Commanding officer! He grunted. Spectator was the word. The brigade had been misused, the men overspent. Willing had known it, and had argued on the radio with Rumaros, to no avail. Now the mortgage had been foreclosed. (If he'd known that a mercenary officer had used the same metaphor, two nights ago, he'd have thought it a fitting irony.)

At the beginning, Willing had tried to make it a fighting retreat, though mostly the men had lacked the energy for it. Then the downpour had begun, no transient summer convection storm, but a slow-moving, pre-autumnal cold front undercutting warm moist air. All fighting response had dissolved in it, and the men rode soddenly southward, hoping the snipers would sight on someone else.

Where the land was suitable, stretches of the road were flanked by narrow fields, mostly no more than two hundred yards wide. The fields were glacial till. Generations of farm boys had picked rocks in them, and each year frost heaving provided a new crop, to be piled as fences along the edges of the field, especially along the back edge, the forest margin. It was there that sniping was the worst, especially when the rain thinned a bit, for the Smoleni could shoot in safety.

More often, though, the forest came up to the ditches, and the sniping was much less heavy there.

The men were desperate for sleep, and if they'd been on foot, it would have been worse. Many more would have lain down beside the road, rain or not.

As it was, they still had to walk from time to time to rest the horses. Rather often, in fact, for they were short on horses. They'd lost enough, that first night, that they'd started back with many carrying two men. And some of the snipers seemed to target horses; even indifferent marksmen could easily hit them. (It never occurred to Renvil that the Smoleni looked at his horses as food, to be smoked and stored for winter.) Doubling up became more common, almost the rule. Men had broken discipline, cutting artillery horses free to ride them, leaving the caissons and guns in the ditches for the Smoleni. In the rain, the caissons wouldn't even burn readily.

Troops afoot sometimes took cover in the shelter of a roadside fence, mostly not to shoot back, but for a reprieve and a nap. Willing had forbidden it. The column had to keep moving, and once a man fell asleep, even on that cold wet ground, it was nearly impossible to wake him. Sometimes, enticed beyond resistance by the shelter of a roadside stone fence, they lay down despite orders and threats. At one stretch, the Smoleni had violated such a shelter with mortar fire, throwing the column into confusion, and causing more concentrated casualties than sniping did.

Men slept on horseback, but that wasn't really effective. Occasionally one fell out of the saddle without being shot; some didn't even wake up when they hit the ground. Some who'd lain down and refused to get up, Willing had had shot, and the problem had abated somewhat till nightfall. When daylight came, they were hundreds of men short. Much of this was certainly due to night ambushes by submachine gunners, who struck, then quickly withdrew, but as certainly, many had simply gone back in the woods a bit and lain down to sleep.

He had no doubt that the Smoleni had made that sleep permanent; they had no facilities for prisoners.

The night before, they'd passed the remains of the supply column—corpses and broken wagons. With the heavy cloud cover, it had been necessary to use battle lamps to stay out of the ditch, and by their light, it seemed the fighting had been heavy there. That might have been the Smoleni's major effort, with supplies the incentive and prize. He hoped they'd paid heavily for them.

He'd never believed in Yomal; educated people didn't. But just in case, he prayed they'd meet a relief column before night fell again.

Forty-six

Major Jillard Brossling commanded the White T'swa's 2nd Battalion, his office a squad tent shared with his E.O. and Master Sergeant Hors. Hors, once a platoon sergeant, had had a knee smashed on Terfreya by a shell fragment. Even after repairs it hampered him, and he'd been given an administrative job. His desk faced the entrance.

Brossling was not long back from "the south"; 2nd Battalion and its ranger trainees had been part of the gauntlet along Road 45, and the scourging of the Komarsi 6th Mounted Infantry Brigade.

A large man in Smoleni uniform looked in. "Sergeant Gull Kro reporting," the man said. "At the major's request."

Hors motioned him in. Brossling had looked up at Kro's words, and gestured toward a folding chair across from his own. There was no salute. Kro had learned that the mercs had no rules about saluting. They saluted when they felt like it, and most often as an acknowledgement and conclusion, seldom as a greeting. Even in form it was different: They touched their cap instead of clapping hand to heart.

"Kro," said the major, "your cadre keeps saying good things about you: how quickly and how well you learn, about

your talents as a ranger and your abilities as a platoon leader
. . . and how well you operated down south last week." He
paused, examining Kro's aura. It showed little reaction; the
man handled praise easily. "They've also told me you tended
at first to be overbearing toward your men, and learned to
tone it down. Anything you'd care to say about that?"

These last several weeks, Kro, still young himself, had
grown used to officers above him who were little or no
older. "Yessir," he said. "My old outfit was mostly from
towns. They needed pushin' sometimes, and some would try
to get away with things. These rangers are different; got
different attitudes. They need to be handled different. And
I seen how you people operate."

The major grinned. Kro still wasn't entirely used to how
often the mercs grinned, or at what. "Good," said Brossling.
"The reason I called you in is to give you a conditional
promotion. I'm trying you out as trainee company commander, starting tomorrow. If at some point I decide to
give someone else a chance at it, it won't mean you're not
measuring up. We might just want to see how he does. If
one of us thinks you're fucking up, we'll tell you about it."

He stood, and the two shook hands. Then Kro saluted
and left, thinking again what hard damned hands the mercs
all had. Brossling, he thought, was as strong as he was,
pound for pound.

Forty-seven

It was not the usual War Council meeting. There were guests: the ambassadors from Krentorf and Oselbent, and an envoy from The Archipelago. They'd come for a summary report of the Komarsi offensive, its accomplishments and defeat, and for a status report. Meanwhile, quiet orderlies entered at intervals, replenishing their cups of "war joma," and the cookies deliberately made with "bark flour"—actually three parts wheat flour mixed with one part bark flour. The refreshments were almost the only purely PR act, to demonstrate the make-do resourcefulness of their hosts.

The battle summary began with a map showing the launch points of the two Komarsi strike forces, the location of Smoleni supply depots, the rates of Komarsi advances, and the sites of major fights.

Video cubeage was shown of people, mostly women, old men, and adolescents, laboring furiously to transfer a supply depot. It gave the diplomats the sense of an entire people united in resistance to an invader. They saw the night assault on the Road 40 spearhead, the decimation of its horse herd, and the hundred-mile gauntlet the 3rd Brigade had suffered

192

through. For the two brigades combined, the count of dead Komarsi was 5,437, almost half their total strength! It was hard to imagine.

They also saw the butchering, the wholesale cutting up of dead Komarsi horses; the smoking of horse meat on hundreds of improvised racks; the salvaging of Komarsi supplies, of ammunition from the belts of dead Komarsi soldiers, and the boots from their feet. Little was wasted.

Kelmer Faronya hadn't gotten a whole lot more sleep than the Komarsi soldiers.

The diplomats weren't shown Komarsi prisoners. There were only a few hundred of them. The Smoleni troops were inclined to shoot anyone wearing Komarsi brown, especially the severely wounded, because facilities and medical personnel, like supplies and food, were seriously short. The prisoners who were taken were stripped of clothes, all but their boots, and a shallow x was cut on their foreheads to leave a scar. An oath was required that they not again serve against Smolen. With the understanding that if they broke it and were captured, the scar on their forehead would be a death sentence. Then they were herded south on foot.

The overall strategy and battle plan had been Belser's. The tactic of attacking the horse herds had been Romlar's.

There was no exultation, least of all by President Lanks, whose face was grave. Belser had a satisfied look, which was new to him, but that was all. Romlar was calm and matter-of-fact as always.

Vestur Marlim summarized the overall military situation, which actually hadn't changed much. The Komarsi still had far more power, but an all-out Komarsi offensive would be risky. The north was too big, too wild, and the Smoleni could not be pinned down. While on Komars's southern and western borders, Selmar and Krentorf remembered old wrongs. At the same time, however, the Komarsi could not be driven from the Leas or the coast, where their army could see and target the enemy, and manuever its large forces more or less freely.

And the Smoleni supply situation, while eased a bit now, was still poor. By winter's end, unless supplies were brought in, there'd be serious hunger among the people, and next summer would see it worsen despite some limited acreage of crops. Unless events intervened, a second winter would bring wholesale deaths from the combination of hunger and sickness.

Elyas Fossur gave an intelligence summary then. His new material was more political than military. There was widespread, if generally subdued, discontent in Komars with the war. People of every class were unhappy with one or more aspects of it: cost, taxes, shortages including labor shortages, overwork, and the increased disobedience, even insolence, of the laboring classes, which went with the labor shortage. If the discontent was to worsen substantially, pressure by the nobility and merchants might well result in a Komarsi offer of terms.

"What terms would Smolen consider?" asked the envoy from The Archipelago.

Fossur turned to the president, who answered. "During this emergency, I rule Smolen, subject to impeachment by popular referendum. But I would not sign a peace without its approval by my Council of Ministers. I can say this much unequivocally, however: All Komarsi forces would have to withdraw south of the legal boundary—the Komar River. We would not, I think, demand reparations, but I would probably want a trade agreement as well as a treaty of peace."

The ambassadors from Krentorf and Oselbent contemplated the president's strong words. Only the Archipelagon seemed to take them without discomfort. After a moment the Oselbenti said, "Mr. President, Engwar would never accept that. He is too proud."

Heber Lanks answered mildly. "Proud? I would have said 'arrogant.' But if his nobles and merchants are sufficiently unhappy with the war, his power may be diluted against his will. There are few kings on Maragor with power as nearly absolute as his. Yet almost every kingdom whose people enjoy a decent constitution, was once as his is. And until the time came, it no doubt seemed inconceivable that they would change.

"Indeed, it may be that in attacking Smolen, Engwar has set in motion the downfall of his power. His merchants and nobles may trim his wings, or even depose him."

The president paused, his expression not entirely clear.

To the envoy from The Archipelago it seemed somewhere between reflective and glum, but with an underlying doggedness. He would listen closely to this Heber Lanks. Even if his own government decided not to involve itself as Smolen's covert supplier, there'd be food for thought in this man's words.

"For that to happen, though," Lanks went on, "we here in Smolen must survive and fight on. Many of us will never surrender. We will eat what we can find, and fight with bows if need be. But we cannot be effective eating bark and fighting with sticks. If it comes to that, and we die, it will stand as a reproach to the rest of Maragor."

He sat back then. It would have been an effective note to close with, but the ambassador from Oselbent cleared his throat and spoke almost apologetically. "Mr. President, have you heard that Engwar has contracted for a regiment of T'swa?"

"I've heard he was trying to."

"Our ambassador to Komars was recently invited to meet with Engwar's Minister of War, who showed him a signed contract with the Lodge of Kootosh-Lan. A regiment will arrive in—" He frowned, calculating mentally. "In about six weeks."

Lanks knew the mystique of the T'swa. These diplomats and their governments might well consider that with T'swa in the equation, Smolen could not last long. And that to help a hopeless cause was both dangerous and wasteful. "Colonel Romlar knows the T'swa intimately," he said. "For six years, he and his regiment were trained by them. He's engaged in maneuvers with them. Colonel, what effect do you think a regiment of T'swa will have in this war?"

Romlar stood to speak. "Less than you might suppose. They're as good as you've heard, but there will be only between about eight hundred and seventeen hundred of them. And they will fight only soldiers, not civilians, unless the civilians take arms against them.

"Against the Komarsi or any usual army, they would be a major element. But here they will not dominate as they usually do. The Smoleni are much better suited than most to fight them, especially the Smoleni ranger battalions we've been training. Many of the Smoleni troops are woodsmen and sharpshooters, self-reliant and self-assured. All of the rangers are. And the tactics the rangers are being trained in are well-suited to fighting either Komarsi or T'swa in the wild country. You'll hear more of these rangers. They do not hesitate to act, do not fear to act, and they act skillfully. And like the T'swa, and like ourselves, they hit what they shoot at."

He shook his head. "The T'swa are better; you need to know them to know how good they are. But the Smoleni, especially the rangers, will make them pay in blood. When the T'swa survivors return to Tyss, they will tell stories about the Smoleni and their fighting skills."

He sat down then, and when he was seated, the envoy from The Archipelago spoke. "And you, Colonel, you and your men—how do you compare with the T'swa?"

"Ask again a year from now. We've never fought them. We've beaten them in maneuvers, but those were maneuvers, however realistic. We're as good as they could make us, as good as we can be. They're the ones who named us the 'White T'swa.'

"I guarantee, though, that here in the north, in these forests, our advantage over Komarsi troops is much greater than the T'swa advantage over Smoleni troops."

The president followed Romlar's commentary by having Kelmer show cubeage of the mercenaries' own training routines, and of rangers in training. He then ended the meeting by reminding the diplomats of the cubeage they'd seen at the start of the meeting, of the devastation along Road 40. He didn't want them to leave with the T'swa on their minds.

With his training and the Ostrak Procedures, anxiety had become foreign to Romlar, but he'd felt a pang of it when the T'swa were mentioned, and it was still there, a deep psychic bruise. And with it a thought: *He was in danger of wasting his regiment!* But a regiment of warriors lost in battle wasn't wasted; not if seen from a neutral viewpoint. Not if winning or losing was unimportant, and warplay itself the purpose.

Yet it seemed to him he *was* basically neutral regarding the outcome of this war. He would use his skills to the utmost for the Smoleni not because of his liking for them, but because it was part of the T'sel. He did like the Smoleni, liked and admired them and wished them well, but if they lost, he would not grieve. The past was past. The spirit ensouled a body to experience, to learn. When the spirit was released and the body left behind, soon enough it would ensoul another.

So why the anxiety? He hadn't felt it on Terfreya. He hadn't felt it the first weeks here. The T'swa seemed the key. When T'swa regiments fought on opposing sides, sooner or later they'd fight each other. It wasn't so uncommon. And when they did, their casualties were often heavy: over several engagements they could chew each other up.

Of course, it was customary for warriors to be chewed up sooner or later, if they were fulfilling their warrior nature. And the prospect of death—his or others—didn't feel like the key to his problem.

No. The problem was, it felt to him that he'd need his regiment for some other purpose. Then was there some purpose, waiting in the future, about which he did not feel neutral? He examined the thought, consulted his feelings, and decided that that wasn't it either.

He snorted. *Enough of this wallowing,* he told himself. When the time came, he'd know. Meanwhile he had a war here to fight, and probably a regiment of T'swa before long.

And with that, the anxiety faded. Though its root was still there; he could feel it.

That afternoon, after the diplomats had left in their separate floaters, Heber Lanks sat down with Marlim and Fossur. And concluded they'd probably get the level of supplies, that winter, that they'd earlier felt encouraged to hope for. Not as much as they needed—the limitations of wilderness transportation alone prohibited that—but enough to make a difference. It would extend their efforts, and allow more time for something truly favorable to develop.

Forty-eight

On the great estates of Komars, two kinds of men worked the harvests. One was serfs, part of the real estate, legally bound to the farms they were born on. The other, the crews brought in, consisted of "casuals"—mostly freedmen: shanty-towners and drifters. Many worked the grain harvest in midsummer, picked fruit in late summer, and in autumn harvested potatoes and sugar beets.

The Iryalan infiltraters had dispersed, placing themselves with different labor brokers so they'd be with different crews, working different estates. They wanted to agitate as widely as possible.

On the first farm he'd worked at, Major Coyn Carrmak, alias Coyn Makoor, hadn't said a lot. Certainly nothing contentious. He'd learned the ways, the thinking, and the temper of the casuals; absorbed the situations; and learned the work of the potato harvest—all things he needed to know. Besides, on the first estate the conditions were relatively good, and the men didn't complain among themselves. They even commented that the cots and pads were better than at most places, that the barracks windows were screened, that there were even bathing facilities and brooms.

198

And that the food was better than they usually were given. They had fried potatoes and pork for breakfast, with bread, butter, and jam, and an apple. For the midmorning and midafternoon lunches, bread and butter, boiled eggs, and apples. And after work, wheat and beans boiled with beef, boiled greens in broth, and pickled beets, again with bread and butter. All you wanted of them.

The work was simple enough, but hard. There were men who wielded spading forks, digging up the potatoes, and more men who bagged them. And there was an elite who were paid a bit more: the men who followed the rows of sacks, accompanied by horse-drawn wagons. They'd pick up the heavy bags and throw them aboard. It was the hardest labor, and the foremen assigned the stronger-looking men to it. Carrmak was made a loader on the first morning, and was an immediate success. For where the other loaders on his crew hunkered down and lifted the sacks in their arms, Carrmak simply half squatted, gripped a sack with a pinch-grip, and with an easy-seeming swing, threw it on the wagon.

Some of the others tried it then. It looked easier, and it was, for those with exceptional hand strength, because it wasn't necessary to squat as deeply or bend as low. Most who tried it gave it up though. Either their grip wasn't strong enough to do it at all, or after a bit their strength gave out.

Meanwhile it made Carrmak an instant special figure on the crew. It also drew the quick attention of the foreman, because the technique was faster. He made Carrmak, alias Makoor, the strawboss—a man who worked like the others but had authority over them to see they neither loafed, nor interfered with the work of others. It also earned him an additional half drona a day, and provided status.

He was careful not to exercise his authority beyond necessity. Actually he didn't need to; men tended not to cross him. And during the lunch break, and after work, he made a point of being one of them, a quiet, unobtrusive one of them. Only one man challenged him, a large aggressive drifter named Kusmar. Carrmak threw him heavily to the ground, so quickly and decisively that everyone stood astonished by it. Then he helped the man up, clapped his shoulder, and said he wasn't half bad, not at all.

* * *

The next estate was something else; the men began to grumble at once, about the barracks, the food, the foreman. Almost everything about the job was substandard. After the first job, the broker had hired Carrmak out as strawboss. It would be his job unless the foreman demoted or fired him.

On the second day, word of the grumbling reached the foreman's ears. Their mid-afternoon lunch had been a baked potato each, and they'd shouted their complaints. One of the estate's teamsters told him about it. He went over to check it out, and rode up to Carrmak. "You're the strawboss, right?" he said.

"That's right," Carrmak answered. The foreman knew at once he'd erred in riding up to this man, because Carrmak had gripped the bridle, taking control of the horse.

The foreman looked at him and decided a mild approach would be best. "I like the way you work, Makoor, but you gotta keep your crew in line. They're wastin' time and energy complainin'. We can't have that."

The entire bucking crew, the strongest men on the whole harvest crew, paused in their work to watch. Carrmak looked the foreman in the eye and drawled: "Well, tell the fuckin' manager to get his head out his arse then, and give us decent food. That'll cut the yawpin' by at least half."

The foreman blanched. He was a large, thick-bodied man himself, physically powerful though somewhat porky. But Makoor, he realized, was dangerous. As foreman, he wore a truncheon on his belt and carried a bullwhip coiled on his saddle, but it seemed to him he'd have little chance to wield them against this man.

Yet he couldn't let the challenge pass. He jerked the reins, trying to cause the horse to rear, to jerk free. It danced but didn't rear. Then one of the other workmen was there, grabbing at him. Cursing, the foreman drew his truncheon to strike at him, but another man ran up to him on the other side, grabbed his stirruped boot and heaved upward. He lost his seat and fell to the ground, where workmen's stout brogans kicked him into huddled submission.

The crew looked to Carrmak then, excited but scared. They'd gone too far to stop, and wanted to be told what to do. He still held the bridle. The horse had quieted.

"Well shit," Carrmak said, "the fat's in the fire now. Let's bust this place up. Who's with me? Kusmar?"

It was Kusmar who'd dumped the foreman from his horse. He was grinning from ear to ear now. "All the way, Makoor."

"Good. Let's go!" Carrmak swung into the saddle then and led them to headquarters. They trashed the barracks, throwing stools out the windows and smashing benches. They were stacking the sleeping pads in the middle of the floor, prior to setting fire to them, when they heard someone bellow.

"Come out of there or we start shootin'."

Inside, the crew stopped, looking around at each other, suddenly sober. They recognized the voice: it was the overseer, a bull of a man known for the beatings he'd delivered. With him he'd have his three enforcers, large dangerous men also known for their fists. Their gaze stopped at Carrmak, who stepped to the window for a brief look, then turned to the others. "He's got a shotgun," he said. "The others only got billies."

He turned back to the window then. "All right. We'll come out." He was grinning when he looked at the others again. "I'll take his gun from him," he murmured. "You follow me, with stools and that like. We'll beat shit out of 'em, and then we'll torch this place."

"Quit your stallin'!" the overseer boomed. "This is your last warnin'!"

Carrmak waved the others to the front wall, then called with a sneer in his voice. "You ayn't got the 'thority!" With that he stepped quickly to the side of the door.

He expected the overseer to enter first. He'd grab the man's shotgun and take it from him. But the overseer was cautious; he sent one of the others in, truncheon in hand. Carrmak's foot drove into the man's ribs from the side, sending him sideways to the floor, then the trooper was out the door headfirst, and landed rolling. The shotgun roared, sending a load of birdshot too high, and as the overseer jacked another shell into the chamber, Carrmak was on him, disabling him quickly and efficiently. One of the enforcers attacked with his truncheon, but the collapsing overseer was in the way, and Carrmak recovered the fallen shotgun. Meanwhile the crewmen, after initial hesitation, were pouring out of the barracks. The remaining enforcers fled toward the manor house, calling a warning ahead of them.

After they'd taken out their packsacks, the laborers touched off first the barracks, then other outbuildings, but left the stables alone, and sheds with livestock, and the cabins of the serfs. The hay barn began to blossom with flames. One of the crew suggested they grab some serfs' women and have a little fun. Carrmak said none of that; they had nothing against the serfs. Instead they looted the headquarters building. No one offered to loot or torch the manor house though; that would be suicide. One of them had backed a large truck from the equipment shed before they torched it. They piled into the back, most armed with pitchforks, some with axes. Most were flushed with excitement, though two or three looked as if they wished this wasn't happening. Carrmak, with the shotgun and a pocketful of shells from the overseer's desk, spoke to the driver.

"Where's another place around here as bad as this one? Or almost as bad. You know?"

"Lamskor Place," the driver answered, grinning.

"How far?"

"Six or eight miles."

"Let's go then. We'll fuckin' burn it too."

The driver waited for Carrmak to climb aboard. When he banged the cab roof with his hand, the man shifted gears and drove from the yard.

They'd only driven half a mile when the hay barn collapsed, sending a great puff of flame high into the air. The men cheered.

They trashed the Lamskor place too. The overseer had been warned—word had spread by phone—but Carrmak had faced him down, shotgun to shotgun, and told him to go in the house. With his enforcers, the man had retreated into the manor then. On the way, Carrmak had assigned teams to certain tasks, and they finished their destruction more quickly. By now it was clear to him that most of the managers here didn't know how to cope with violent rebellion; it was outside their training or reality, perhaps even their concepts. He sent two men in another truck with another shotgun, to recruit another crew and go wherever they thought best. He put Kusmar in charge. Kusmar was a dominant; they'd pretty much do what he said. He'd be less fastidious than Carrmak about what he did, what he burned, but that was part of insurrection.

It was late now, the sun nearly down and dusk near at hand. Carrmak told his driver to drive to the district seat. That's where the hiring hall was, no doubt with men waiting to be tabbed by brokers, maybe even crews waiting for transportation. They should be able to recruit a small army there, a platoon or more. Five miles short of town though, they saw an enclosed truck coming toward them. Even from a little distance they could see the sheriff's insignia on it.

Carrmak thumped the cab roof and yelled down, "Ram the sonofabitch!" The driver slowed a bit but kept going, while his riders crouched low, bracing themselves as best they could. The driver of the sheriff's truck realized too late what was about to happen. He hit his brakes, and a moment later the farm truck hit him head on at about twenty-five miles an hour. Metal tore, glass broke, and the farm crew piled out. The posse had locked their doors from the inside. A crewman hacked the sidewalls of the tires with his ax. Then they all stood looking at each other.

"There's a place half a mile up the road," Carrmak said. "We'll get another truck there—two or three of 'em. We won't stop to burn the place. Just get trucks and go on into town, like we planned!"

From the hiring hall, three truckloads of laborers spread into the countryside, each with someone more or less in charge, each with ideas of which estates to hit and which to pass by. Carrmak stayed at the hall to see what would happen. Sometime after midnight, soldiers arrived by rail and surrounded the hiring hall. The handful of men still there were arrested and handcuffed. They complained that they were innocent, that the men the soldiers wanted were out attacking estates.

"We'll get them too," the lieutenant said. Then the men arrested were hauled away to the provincial capital. The next day they were put on a railroad car, under armed guards, and taken to a military prison near Linnasteth.

Forty-nine

Major Rinly Molgren glowered first at the morning report, then at his master sergeant. "What's this shit about? Dumping civilian prisoners on us!"

The sergeant had learned patience years before. He'd also learned to recognize a hangover; the major had one, not too bad, but bad enough. What the officer wanted to know was all written in the report, but no doubt the pain in his forehead, and the queasy stomach, got in the way of reading it. "They're charged with rebellion," the sergeant answered, "assault, destruction of property, and a few counts of murder. The first few were jailed at Millinos, but more kept bein' brought in, and they considered 'em too dangerous to keep there."

The major sat back and exhaled audibly in exasperation. "Shit!" He looked up at the sergeant again. "Have you seen these new prisoners?"

"Yes, major."

"What do they look like?"

"Dirty, hungry, and worried, sir."

The major grunted. It was after ten o'clock; he should have been in two hours earlier, and knew it. He was going to have to cut down on this damned partying, unless he found a whiskey that didn't leave him feeling so wretched in the morning. "Assign them to cells, did you?"

"No, sir. We never had civilian prisoners before, so I left 'em in the holding pen till you could decide how you wanted 'em handled. I did have a couple removed for questioning though."

"Did you question them? Or did you leave that for me, too?"

"I questioned 'em. They're in a cell now; it didn't seem smart to put 'em back in with the others."

"Umh." Wincing, the major heaved himself to his feet. "Let's look at them, Sergeant. Blasinga can take care of things here for a few minutes. And bring the records on them."

They went downstairs to the ground level. In the holding pen, the prisoners looked as the sergeant had described them: handcuffed, slouched, and hangdog. Most of them didn't look dangerous at all. Molgren was willing to bet that if they were sent back to work on condition of good behavior, they'd be no trouble to anyone. But it was too late for that. Rebellion! They'd likely end up in the rock quarries, those who weren't executed.

One of them stood a little apart from the others, as if no one wanted to be too close to him. "Sergeant," the major said quietly, "who's the one by himself? The one standing straight?"

"The men we questioned say he's the instigator, sir, the one who started it. Seems he ran it like a military operation—gave orders and assignments. They say that in a fight, the man's a one-man army."

"Hmm!" The major was remembering a request that had come down lines from command a few deks ago. More than a year ago. "Have him brought to my office under guard, Sergeant. Right away. Leave the rest in holding for now." He turned and left then, thinking. If the prisoner seemed suitable, he just might be able to get a bounty for him. An extra hundred drona was always nice to have, and it never hurt to do a favor for a general.

Fifty

The Assembly of Lords was scheduled to meet again, and Fingas Kelromak was back in Linnasteth to attend. As usual, when he arrived, he came to the townhouse of Jorn Nufkarm, to be updated on the capital and the activities of the Crown. When he sat down, though, it was Nufkarm who asked the first question.

"How went the harvest?"

"Mine? Overall quite well. The potatoes went nearly two hundred bushels per acre."

"Indeed! I take it that's good."

"Surely you know the answer to that," Fingas said playfully. "Your estate grows potatoes."

Nufkarm gazed blandly at him. "I'm trying to raise a crop of reforms; I therefore cultivate politicians. My familiarity with potatoes ends at the table." He patted his impressive belly. "I leave the farming to my dear brother, who considers himself to have the best of the arrangement. Did you have any, um, troubles at your place?"

"None; I was fortunate. It was no doubt useful to have a reputation for decent quarters, good bedding, and good food."

"Any in your neighborhood then?"

Fingas's expression was a partial answer, his features tight, his face slightly pale, and he didn't answer at once. "Trouble?" he said at last. "Rather more than one might wish—certainly on Rorbarak. They burned the serfs' hamlet there, and violated some women. On most estates, though, serfs weren't molested. What have you been hearing?"

Nufkarm shrugged his shoulders. "You read the papers: *The Herald* at least. It's the worst outbreak of violence in a millennium."

."And what response from our peers?"

"Hmh! One proposal is to have the army discharge a large number of serfs. To get away from hiring so many casuals. Get them home, back into the fields."

Fingas's eyes sharpened. "Remarkable! Somehow overlooking the fact that by enlisting, they are no longer serfs."

"Not overlooking it at all. Arbendel has proposed that the manumission act be abrogated by royal decree. His argument is that practically all the unruly casuals are manumitted serfs, or rather their descendants. Ergo, free no more serfs."

"Good god!"

"Exactly. They think we have troubles now! That could produce not only uprisings in the provinces, but insurrection in the army. Which of course has something to recommend it from our point of view, but it's entirely too dangerous. As it happens, wiser heads recognized this and quashed the proposal. Not all conservatives are fools.

"Meanwhile, the war and Engwar have taken the blame again, though people don't say this publicly. And coming after that terrible fiasco recently, where our good general left some five thousand corpses along the roads in northern Smolen ... If he wasn't Engwar's cousin, he'd be fired by now, though the rumor is that he only did it under pressure from Engwar. And Engwar, of course, defends him. I'm afraid our good sovereign will definitely not get the special war tax renewed, unless something quite unforeseen happens.

"On the other hand—"

"Yes?"

Nufkarm waved at the radio on a table. "Just this morning

he announced a special sedition act. We'll need to tone down the _Bulletin_ substantially."

"He can't do that!"

"Of course he can. We're at war, and the Conservatives control the Assembly."

"But the Charter!"

"Indeed the Charter. But there is precedent, and I repeat, the Conservatives control the Assembly. Think about it. And I strongly advise you not to publish underground leaflets to fill the gap. Given your social inheritance, you'd be the first one Engwar would suspect. Be prudent, dear Fingas; hold your peace. Engwar is digging his own grave, or rather constructing his own political—shall we say castration?

"Do nothing rash. Stand ready. Take whatever _safe_ steps present themselves. When he makes a serious mistake, we'll make whatever use of it we can. With patience we will bring him down. If we are impatient, someone else will bring him down later, but we won't be privileged to see it."

Fifty-one

Subcolonel Jomar Viskon sat frowning at the papers he held: an invoice and a bill of particulars. "Who in Amber's name is Major Rinly Molgren?" he asked exasperatedly. With all he had on his desk today, he didn't need some off-the-wall crap like this.

The sergeant major resisted telling him it was there on the sheets he held. "He's the C.O. of the stockade in Linna Commune, sir."

"We haven't been looking for men like this for more than a year now."

The comment hardly rated an answer, so the sergeant major said nothing for several long seconds, waiting. Finally he broke the silence. "The prisoner's in the waitin' room, Colonel. Manacled and guarded."

"Well crap!" The colonel looked at nowhere, then focused and took a deep breath. "Have him brought in."

"Yessir."

The sergeant major left, and Viskon sat drumming his desk top. Ten seconds later a staff sergeant pushed the door open and held it. A rather large, hard-looking man stepped in, wearing manacles on his wrists, and followed by a corporal holding a pistol. Anyone who had to be guarded that closely wasn't going to be of use to anyone, Viskon told himself. When all three were inside, he spoke with exaggerated patience. "All right, Sergeant, seat your prisoner and close the door."

He looked the prisoner over, scanned the bill of particulars again, then glanced up and found himself matching eyeballs with the man for a moment. The fellow was genuinely unperturbed, and he'd swear there was excellent intelligence behind those eyes. "Your name is Coyn Makoor?"

"Yessir," Carrmak answered.

"It says here that you were arrested for inciting to riot, assault on authorities, arson, grand theft, assault with a vehicle, murder, and inciting to murder. Is that right?"

"I ayn't seen what you're readin', sir. So far's did I do those things; I dint murder no one, and I dint tell nor ask no one else to. The rest of it sounds about right."

"Murder or not, I suppose you know what's likely to happen to you. What your sentence will be."

"I can guess, sir."

"And what would you guess?"

"Likely they'll cut off my head."

"They will indeed." The prisoner still didn't seem perturbed. Interesting. Perhaps he was someone to whom the future is unreal until it's at hand. "The officer who sent you to us was under the misapprehension that we were still recruiting for a special fighting unit. We are not."

The man didn't respond. Viskon found himself wanting him to, and asked a question. "Why do you suppose Major Molgren thought you'd be suitable for such a unit?"

"Umm. Four reasons: One, I'm dangerous in a fight. Two, men gen'ly do what I tell 'em. Three, I'm gen'ly in control of myself. And four, I understand what I'm told, else'n I ask questions."

Viskon stared, then looked again at the invoice for the name. "Makoor," he asked thoughtfully, "were you ever in the army?"

"No, sir. But I was with the Red River Sheriff's Department for three years. Promoted to senior sergeant. Then three sheriff's men 'rested my dad; brawk his face and knocked out an eye. Dint knaw who he was; said he'd been spearin' horse pike in the spawnin' season. Not that him and me got on so good, but I half killed the one in charge. Off duty it was, but they had to fire me for it."

Viskon had never heard of the Red River District, didn't know where it was. But the training in sheriff's departments was partly military, and there was something about this man . . . He looked at the staff sergeant.

"Sergeant, keep him here for a few minutes. I'll be back." He left then, walking down the hall to the general's office. When he returned, he had the prisoner taken to the local stockade and confined, until he could instruct Lieutenant Hesslor, the commanding officer of the Commander's Special Unit. If the new man proved to be an unacceptable problem, or lacked sufficient training to function in the unit, they could always imprison or execute him then.

Part Three

WINTER WAR

Fifty-two

The leaves had mostly fallen in Linnasteth when the T'swa arrived. Their transport put down on Engwar's estate a few miles outside the city. Engwar wasn't there to meet it—it would have been unseemly—but he had the T'swa commander flown to the palace to a reception.

Colonel Ko-Dan arrived without an entourage, beyond Captain Ibang, his aide. The T'swa have no dress uniform, but even walking through the palace in field uniform, Ko-Dan was the nearest thing to true royalty it had seen, though his father was a farmer and his mother a blacksmith's daughter. The servants glimpsing him (they hardly dared to stare) were awed, even a little frightened.

Engwar's entourage included, beside attendants, his council and certain aides currently in his special favor. And Undsvin, who if not back in his cousin's good graces, was at least partly out of his doghouse. And as Commander of the Komarsi Army in Smolen, it was appropriate that he attend.

The greetings were formal, held in the smaller receiving room. Then the participants relaxed, more or less, though first conversation with the guests was reserved for the king.

215

The two T'swa unobtrusively ignored the canapes and drinks. Engwar noticed, but decided not to be offended. They were, after all, from a barbaric world, and presumably didn't do it to insult.

What troubled Engwar more was their youth. It was unseemly that a regimental commander be, apparently, in his early twenties, regardless of how formidable he might appear physically. But if he was as good as the T'swa reputation . . .

"You are not," Engwar commented, "the only mercenaries in this war, Colonel. We've been severely irritated, not to say injured, by the activities of a mercenary regiment employed by the Smoleni. My first job for you is to eliminate it. Wipe it out!"

Ko-Dan smiled slightly, his large T'swa eyes unreadable. "We were told they're here, Your Majesty, in the situation briefing we received before we left Tyss. In fact I know something of them. They were in training on our world when we graduated. And had earlier earned a reputation in combat on Terfreya, though they'd trained only a year at the time."

Ko-Dan's casual attitude irritated the king. "Yes? Well they're here now, and I want them gone! Killed, captured, driven out, whatever. But preferably dead. That is my first order to you: Get rid of them!"

"Ah," Ko-Dan answered gravely. "Has Your Majesty read the contract he signed with our lodge?"

"Read it? That's what I have a secretary for."

"Did he read it to you?"

Engwar's gesture expressed impatience. "I seem to recall that he did. Yes."

"I'm sure Your Majesty signs many documents and can hardly be expected to remember each of them. Let me make a suggestion. Captain Ibang and I need to leave quite soon to see to the proper disposition of our troops." That wasn't true. They could make camp quite well without their commander, but Ko-Dan foresaw an awkward situation developing if he stayed. "I'd like to meet with you late tomorrow afternoon, or evening if you prefer. After we've had a military briefing, perhaps from General Tarsteng or one of his staff." The T'swa commander paused, just for a moment. "Meanwhile you'll have had a chance to review our contract again, perhaps with the general.

"I should tell you now, however, that my regiment can be most effectively occupied in the demoralization of the Smoleni army. A regiment of mercenaries, even as capable a regiment as the Iryalans, will not defeat your army. If any force available to Smolen is able to do that, it is the Smoleni army itself."

He bowed then, slightly. "Captain Ibang and I are most honored to have been so royally received, but we must return to our men now. Let us know when, tomorrow, we may meet with you to discuss business. We will be ready for your transportation at any time after 0800." He turned to the officer who'd escorted them. "Lieutenant, please return us to our encampment."

His mouth slightly open, Engwar watched them leave the room, then turned to his secretary. "What's in that contract?"

"It's in my office, Your Majesty. Would you like to go over it now?" He flashed a hopeful glance at the general. "Perhaps Lord Undsvin could review it with us."

Engwar turned to his cousin. "By all means do, Undsvin." He turned again to look at the door the two T'swa had left by. "Those strange black men are damned inscrutable." *Or is it insolent?* he added silently. "I wonder if they realize how much I paid for them. They damned will ought to do what I tell them to! Especially isolated here, a very long way from their home world."

Undsvin had done his homework. "Cousin," he said mildly, "the T'swa are not only the best fighting men in human space, they are the smartest. At least half of their value to anyone is their military judgment. I might say their military wisdom."

He paused, assuming a more clearly respectful and subordinate attitude. "As for their isolation here— About four hundred years ago, I forget on what planet, some kingdom hired one of their regiments, and for whatever reason, the ruler there became angry with them. So he had them surrounded and shelled heavily and at length, then sent troops in to kill the survivors. Not the sort of thing we'd do, of course.

"About a year later, several T'swa regiments descended on the kingdom with Level Two weapons, and with cold ferocity destroyed the king's army. The king himself they delivered to his enemies, who, as I recall, executed him publicly."

Engwar looked at his cousin alarmed. "Really!" he said.

"It's described in a book I have, if you'd care to read it. They are not an offensive people, nor do they easily take offense. Their interest is only in fighting, never in cruelty, and they have no fear at all of death."

The king frowned, not angry now but a bit bewildered. "Remarkable! I will take your word for it." He turned to his secretary. "Let us look at that contract together. Bring it to my office now. Undsvin and I will be there momentarily." He looked around as the secretary left, and beckoned to the first butler, who was in charge. "Aljin, these others may stay as they please. Undsvin, I've decided I feel quite sanguine now, with the arrival of these T'swa. I believe my fortunes are about to turn."

Fifty-three

Sergeant Jak Fenssen was not your stereotypic informer. About five-feet ten, he was a brawny if somewhat overweight 230 pounds. His face showed the marks of fighting, mostly during his younger years. He seldom fought now. Not that he was unwilling, when it came down to it. Rather, over the years, while developing his fighting reputation, skills and insights, he'd also shed any hesitation to kill or maim. He was seldom challenged.

Nonetheless he informed; it was a duty assigned him by Colonel Viskon.

Fenssen was first sergeant of the Commander's Special Unit, which had been having particular difficulties since Gulthar Kro had left as its commanding officer. He therefore reported to Viskon, confidentially of course, on how things went there. Its current C.O., the third since Kro, was a Lieutenant Hesslor, arguably the strongest man in the unit. Hesslor had begun his command by having two men executed, which had established his willingness. The effect had worn off, however. Now the unit existed in a kind of tension bordering on murder.

If Viskon could have, he'd have disbanded the unit and had

most of its men imprisoned for various good reasons. Which would have ended the headache. But that wasn't an option Undsvin had given him. Actually, Undsvin had decided to do just that, more than once, but the basic idea of an elite unit at his personal call still held a strong attraction for him. He no longer had any illusion that this collection of men would work out, but he'd keep it, for the time at least, tinker with it, and perhaps learn from the experience.

From time to time Undsvin would have an idea, which he'd have Viskon translate into action. Viskon was a bright young man; the challenge and exasperation both would do him good. Viskon, in attempting to cope with the responsibility, occasionally proposed an idea of his own, such as the possibility that Coyn Makoor, already Sergeant Makoor, might be the kind of material from which a commander could be molded.

That week two things had happened in the unit, which was down to only forty-two men. Hesslor had killed a man with a table leg—a man who'd given him particular trouble—had smashed his skull. Later the same day, the man's two best friends had cornered Hesslor with knives, undoubtedly to kill him. Hesslor, however, had a small pistol in his pocket—perhaps he'd foreseen the confrontation—and had killed them both. It's impressive how deadly even a small caliber slug can be when fired at the breastbone at point-blank range.

Judging from Fenssen's comments, morale was at its lowest. Viskon and Undsvin had discussed the deteriorating situation, and Viskon had had a suggestion. Undsvin had told him to go ahead with it. Now Viskon looked at Fenssen appraisingly. Fenssen felt the gaze and sat unperturbed. He was a rock, exactly as the first sergeant had to be in a unit like his. "Anything new about Makoor?" Viskon asked.

"No, sir," Fenssen answered.

There was seldom anything anecdotal about Makoor. The man had no cronies and no enemies. He stood apart without seeming aloof, and for whatever reason, no one had seen fit to pick a fight with him. There was something about him. Fenssen had already told Viskon all those things. He'd also told him that, inexperienced or not, Makoor was the best soldier of the lot. An opinion which he, Fenssen, kept to

himself was that Makoor had been in the army before, and
deserted. Perhaps as an officer, despite his freedman dialect.

"The general has something different he wants you to do
for him."

Fenssen didn't reply, just sat stolidly, waiting.

"Incite Hesslor to fight Makoor. Do you think he'd do
that?"

"If he could catch him off guard, or had enough advantage." Fenssen grunted then, with a sort of grimace, as close
as he ever came to laughing. "Maybe another table leg."

"Who do you think would win?"

"It'd depend on Hesslor's advantage. He's bigger and
meaner, but in a straight fight, Makoor would prob'ly win."

"How might you go about getting Hesslor to attack him?"

Fenssen didn't hesitate. "I'd tell him Makoor said he was
going to be C.O. himself some day."

"That would do it?"

"Prob'ly."

"What sort of advantage do you think Hesslor would create for himself?"

"No way to know."

Viskon sat pondering. He preferred not to waste Makoor,
and felt uncomfortable with such a large degree of uncer-
tainty. Nor did it help that he didn't understand men like
these.

"Do it," he said.

Fenssen nodded. "Yessir."

"That's all for now, Sergeant."

Fenssen got to his feet, saluted, and left the room. Viskon
watched the door close behind him. It seemed to him that
the first sergeant would make a good C.O. for the unit, and
he'd suggested it to the general. Who'd refused to consider
it. That had been just before Hesslor. "Men like those," the
general had said, "need a good first sergeant more than they
do a good C.O. Any company does, and these men more
than most. But what they really need is both. We've got the
one now, and I'm depending on you to find me the other."

The subcolonel hadn't expected it to happen so soon. The
next afternoon, the report came that Hesslor had been killed

in a fight. His killer was in custody. Viskon called Fenssen in and asked him what had happened.

"I did what we agreed on: told the lieutenant that Makoor was after his job—that he'd told me so. The lieutenant went in his office and didn't come out for about an hour. When he did, he had a bat he'd took to carryin' sometimes, and ast me where Makoor was. I told him off duty, prob'ly in the barracks.

"Bisto came in about ten minutes later. He said Hesslor had gone in the barracks with the club in his hand and told Makoor to go outside with him. He motioned that Makoor should go out first, which meant Makoor had to turn his back on him. While they were going to the door, Hesslor raised his club to hit him from behind, and Makoor killed him."

The sergeant shrugged, and grunted again. "I questioned four different men, separate; they all said the same thing. 'Cept for how Makoor did it; nobody agrees on that. What Bisto said was, it was so quick, it took 'em by surprise."

"Surely someone must have said something. Warned Makoor what was happening."

Fenssen shrugged again. "I ast 'em that separate. They all said no one did."

"Do you think they were telling the truth?"

Fenssen shrugged again. "They all agreed. And they'd had no chance to talk to each other from the time I questioned the first one till I'd done with 'em."

"Umm. All right, Sergeant, you can go now. And thank you."

A written order from the general got Sergeant Makoor's prompt release, and Fenssen told him the colonel wanted to see him. Standing now before Viskon's desk, Carrmak seemed as calm and unruffled as when he'd first been questioned, weeks earlier. Viskon wondered if such calm might be a symptom of something pathological.

"None of the witnesses seem to agree on how, precisely, you killed Hesslor. How did you?"

"It was too quick to think abawt," Carrmak answered. "I din't trust him, so I give a little look back over my shoulder and seen him raise his club. I spun and moved inside the swing, and did whatever it was I did."

Viskon regarded him thoughtfully. It sounded reasonable. "That makes four men killed in the unit inside a week. You seem like an intelligent man, Makoor. What do you think is wrong?"

A slight smile curved Carrmak's mouth before he answered. "Colonel, a dozen or so of 'em are flat crazy, and some of the rest ayn't much better. Put 'em all together and you've got trouble."

"Hmm. What would you do about that? If it were up to you."

"Me? I'd cull the outfit. Keep maybe a dozen and a half. That's abawt how many's worth it."

"Interesting. Are you one we should keep?"

Carrmak definitely smiled then. "I think so."

"Given the list of charges against you, when you were brought here, I'd have said you were a violent psychotic. A troublemaker at the very least."

Carrmak pursed his lips thoughtfully. "At most farms I was their best worker. Where the food and the treatment was even halfway decent. At this one place though— After a few days there, we were all of us like gunpowder. And when the foreman hit this old gaffer in the face with his stick, that was it for me. It was like the gaffer was my dad again."

"Umm. I suppose you read and write?"

"Yessir."

"Sit down and make me a list of who you'd keep and who you'd let go."

Viskon shoved tablet and pen across his desk. Carrmak sat and wrote. When he was done, Viskon looked the sheet over and almost marveled. The man had not only made the lists; he'd done it alphabetically! "Thank you, Makoor. "Return to your barracks now. Stay there until I send for you."

When Carrmak had gone, Viskon phoned the unit's orderly room and told Fenssen to come over. He told the sergeant what Makoor had suggested, and asked him to provide a list of who he'd cull. Fenssen's list agreed quite closely with Carrmak's.

The next day, Makoor was promoted to warrant officer third class, and appointed unit commander. The unit, to be culled promptly, would henceforth be known as the Commander's Personal Guard.

Carrmak had a private room again, a place where he could meditate. He discovered that his body wasn't as flexible as it had been; a half-lotus would have to serve for the time being.

Instead of meditating, he contemplated his situation. Why was he here? What use could he make of his position? Kill the general? There'd be a new commander within a day or two. Listen and learn, and somehow get information to Burnt Woods? To do that, he'd have to make effective contacts. It might be possible. What seemed most feasible, though, was to desert and get back to the regiment. He was sure he could do that.

On the other hand, it seemed to him that here, he was in a position with potential. The question was, potential for what?

Relax, he told himself. *Don't push it. It'll come to you. It'll show itself.*

After that he did meditate.

Fifty-four

Colonel Ko-Dan and his aide stood by the railing of the excursion liner *Linna Princess*, watching the farmland of northern Komars passing on both shores of the Linna. They weren't alone; the railings were lined with T'swa troopers in a calm yet somehow festive mood. They were going to war. The contract allowed them two weeks for conditioning and acclimating, orientation and briefings. Ko-Dan had decided that one had been enough.

The sun was bright, the sky blue between scudding white clouds, but the wind was chill. The trees along the banks and roads and around the farmsteads were mostly bare. There were scattered evergreens, and some species of deciduous trees still bore remnant brown leaves, but overall, the aspect was one of impending winter.

Ko-Dan had just commented on a dubious Komarsi decision. "But you declined the general's request to advise him," Ibang observed.

Ko-Dan regarded the surface of the river. "Advice has purposely been omitted from the contracts," he replied. "And we are neither trained nor experienced in directing large units. As I pointed out."

Ibang's teeth flashed white. "He was disappointed none the less. Particularly since he knows that the Iryalans have been advising and training the Smoleni."

Ko-Dan's answer was serene as he watched the Maragoran version of a gull dip a small fish from the surface of the river. "We are T'swa, and therefore visibly quite strange. To the general, we are an enigma. As for the barbarous Engwar II Tarsteng, I shall give him everything the contract calls for, but little if anything more."

Ibang chuckled, then changed the subject. "The Iryalans are sure to challenge us."

"Very likely, sooner or later. It will be a pleasure to contest with them, especially after the inept drafts we face on Carjath." The colonel's gaze became remote then, as if contemplating some other realm, some other reality. "This war will be more than strenuous. I believe we will find it stimulating in various respects. There will be surprises, things one can hardly foresee."

Ibang nodded, his smile beatific now. Meanwhile, perhaps within ten days, they'd test the Smoleni and see what kind of fighting men they were.

Fifty-five

Tomm Grimswal stood by a tree in the darkness. Stood because orders said to; you weren't as likely to fall asleep on your feet.

Wintry temperatures had arrived on schedule in the Free Lands; nothing severe yet, but seasonable. Only the snow delayed. A cold night wind moaned through the treetops and rattled the leafless *roivan* branches. Tomm had been a high school student in Rumaros before the war. He didn't like the wind, and he'd decided too late that he didn't like the army. He especially didn't like picket duty at night.

For one thing it seemed unnecessary. The Komarsi weren't going to come in the night. In fact, they weren't going to move this far from their lines day or night. Besides, clouds hid the stars, and the moons if any of them were up now. You couldn't see ten feet, and all you could hear was the wind.

He was tired of holding his submachine gun, too. A rifle was long enough that you could lean on it, but on night duty you got SMGs because any fighting would be at short range, and you couldn't aim at night anyway.

He'd sit down and maybe catch twenty winks, except Marky

was on the other side of the tree, and he'd tell the sergeant. Marky Felkor was unreasonable about orders, even when the orders were obvious bullshit. He thought because he'd been in the fighting along the . . .

From just around the tree from him, Tomm was startled by a burst of submachine gun fire, and then another. His immediate thought was that Marky had fallen asleep and fired by accident, maybe from a dream. He heard Sergeant Tarrbon call out: "What post is that?"

"Fourteen!" Marky shouted back. It was the last thing Tomm Grimswal ever heard, because just then a large hard hand closed over his mouth, and a razor-sharp knife slit his throat nearly to the spine. It might have been soundless, except that when he'd felt the hand, the youth's thoracic muscles had spasmed, driving air from the severed trachea with a rude and liquid noise. His submachine gun fell to the frozen ground unfired, its safety catch still set, its only sound a thud.

Corporal Il-Dak realized at once that the soldier's comrade had heard the noise, and instead of lowering the body quietly, he dropped it and jumped sideways six feet, landing in a crouch. Overhead a flare popped, and another, flooding the forest with brilliant white light. Though he didn't look up at it, the brightness blinded him, blinded all of them for a moment. Then he spotted his partner, sprawled where the first shots had found him. He bounded forward like a night cat to find and shoot the other picket, but someone fired from behind another tree, a burst needlessly, wastefully long. Five slugs tore into Il-Dak's torso. And his own burst tore into frozen ground as he fell. All around, the T'swa slunk forward, avoiding the glare so far as possible, keeping to the inky shadows. More shots were fired.

From here and there came gunfire. *These aren't Komarsi,* thought Lieutenant Joran Bannsfor. Not deep in the forest in the dark of night, sixty miles north of the Eel. Which meant the T'swa had arrived! He peered hard and saw nothing.

The flares, on their parachutes, had been swept southeastward by the wind. Bannsfor fired another, off somewhat to his right, then glimpsed movement among the trees just ahead, coming toward him as he reloaded the flare pistol. Marsoni's rifle banged beside him. *T'swa or whatever,* he thought, *these people know how to move.*

And thought no more. Some of the T'swa had infiltrated unnoticed, and one of them fired a burst from behind him. Bannsfor fell dying. Private Marsoni spun even though hit, and fired a single round from his bolt action, the bullet finding nothing, before a T'swa round took him in the face.

Major Hober Steeg had wakened to a call of nature, and been standing beside a straddle trench when the first burst had ruptured the night. *T'swa,* he thought. Before he'd even buttoned his fly, there was firing from here, there, seemingly everywhere, and he dropped into a crouch. The first flares had almost blown away already, but more were being fired; the T'swa night vision, it seemed to him, wasn't an advantage to them any longer.

He held his pistol in a white-knuckled fist and peered around with no idea what to do next. Meanwhile the firing increased. "Shit!" He said aloud, and started for his nearby command tent. Then a different sound assaulted his ears as a grenade blasted the tent ahead of him. A bullet plucked his sleeve, and he threw himself onto the ground. He could see his on-duty radioman sprawled in the tent door, and wondered if he'd gotten a message off. A man in black ran past in a crouch, a submachine gun in his hands. The major, prostrate, twisted and fired. The man didn't pause, but before Steeg could shoot again, someone else had, and the man in black fell, half spinning. The face was black too, the eyes large in the flare light: a T'swi for sure! The black man rose to his knees and fired a burst at something, then dropped to his side, drawing another magazine from his belt, slamming it into his weapon. The major shot again, once, twice, and the T'swi went limp.

The major got to his feet and headed for the radio.

Artus Romlar sat in his winterized command tent at base camp. Morning lit it through the fabric roof. The T'swa were more than an intelligence report now. A force of them, probably a company, had hit 2nd Battalion, 5th Smoleni

Infantry, shot it up and withdrawn. Fairly standard T'swa procedure: When you arrive in a war zone, you engage the enemy in a small action to test his fighting quality and learn what you'll be dealing with. *Then* you plan.

A stocky, middle-aged Smoleni woman popped into the tent with breakfast. There were snowflakes on her shawl. She put the tray on his table and he thanked her. More bodies might be found later, he thought, and some of the wounded would no doubt die, but the initial count was encouraging: 42 T'swa bodies had been counted. The Smoleni Battalion had lost 96 killed and 152 wounded. The T'swa would be impressed and pleased with the quality of their opposition.

Where were they quartered? Or bivouacked? He should have something on that soon. Since the big Komarsi strike of Sevendek, Colonel Fossur had set up a field recon network of converted fur trappers, with iron rations and forestry maps. They ranged in threes through the forests in the zone north of the Eel, watching the roads. Each trio had a radio that would reach Shelf Falls.

This snow, if it stayed, would complicate things for the recon network, disclose its presence and force them to keep moving constantly. But it should make them more effective, too, because enemy movements would leave far more conspicuous tracks. The biggest danger was that the T'swa would hunt them down.

He had no doubt that as soon as the snow was deep enough, the T'swa would be out learning to snowshoe.

Fifty-six

By day's end there were four inches of snow on the frozen ground. The next morning the weather station at Burnt Woods registered eight below zero, and it had scarcely topped zero at noon. It was sixteen below the next morning, and colder still on the morning following. Test holes found the river ice up to eight inches thick.

Then the weather moderated. Marine air moved in from the southeast, and midday temperatures rose well above freezing. The next cold front moved in four days later, and before the sky cleared, what was left of the old snow was covered by twenty-five inches of new—an unusually heavy fall—and the temperature was near zero again. It wasn't truly winter yet, the locals assured Romlar, but with the solstice little more than six weeks away, a major thaw was unlikely.

Kelmer Faronya had ridden a freight sleigh thirty-five miles to Jump-Off. This fall no trapping parties had moved into the Great North Wild; most of the trappers were in the army. But several parties of old ex-trappers were preparing to trek north for something more important now than

231

furs. They would hunt meat—*erog* and *porso*—and send it back on sleighs. Kelmer was there to record their leaving. Such a hunt was a violation of the rules governing the Confederation reserve, but the meat was badly needed, and the game populations would recover quickly enough from a single year's heavy hunting, just as it recovered from the heavy die-offs of the occasional extreme winter.

So said his guide, the local fur broker, an old man called Hanni. And Kelmer had no reason to disbelieve; these people had lived intimately with the land and its creatures for generations.

Each party had a sleigh to haul its supplies and gear. Just now they were parked before the combined store and fur warehouse, loading supplies: flour, beans, and dried fruit mostly, and cartridges. Beyond that they'd live off the land. Most of the village was there: fifty or so besides the hunters.

What impressed Kelmer most about the hunting parties were the animals hitched to their sleighs: long-legged *erog* geldings, their heavy shoulders higher than a man's head, with long necks that raised their antlers ten feet above the ground, and prehensile noses to aid in browsing. He'd glimpsed them before, in the forest and along the roads farther south, and been awed. They were even more impressive up close.

"What's their advantage over horses?" Kelmer asked.

"Well, first off their legs are so much longer. Helps in deep snow. But mostly, horses need hay in winter; they can't make do on twigs, 'specially *jall* 'n *fex* twigs, which along with *kren* is what we mostly got up 'round here."

"Why don't the farmers use *erog?*"

"They ain't no farmers up here."

"I mean farther south. Around Burnt Woods, for example."

"Ah. *Erog* ain't no way tame as horses. These here was either took as foals or dropped by a penned mare. And gelded. Ain't nobody could harness an *erog* stallion; the geldings are bad enough. One of them big old hooves hits a *loper,* his head is broke right then, maybe 'long with his neck. They'd do the same to you. And they bites worser'n a horse. Horses'll bite, sure, but them boogers"—he gestured at an erog calmly chewing its cud—"can truly take a chunk outta you. You don't go up to *him* and stroke his nose."

"Do people ever ride them?"

Hanni crowed with laughter. "No how! Too mean!"

"Horses can be mean, but people ride them."

"Sure. But these long-neck critters could reach around 'n bite you in the saddle. Maybe take yer knee off!"

Kelmer nodded thoughtfully. "I don't suppose all the hunters will go to the same place."

"No no. They'll go up the river together 'bout thirty mile, then a party'll peel off every ten, twelve mile up different side branches to different trapping bounds. All told, they'll hunt over a big territory. They'll hunt *porso* a lot more 'n *erog*, 'cause *porso* runs in bands of twenty or thirty, sometimes more.

"One man in each party'll keep camp while three cast around till they come on tracks. Then one'll go back 'n fetch the gelding and sleigh, while the other two catches up to the *porso* and kills all they can of 'em—maybe five or six—'fore they scatter too bad. Then they'll leave the guts and heads for the jackwolves, use the gelding to drag the carcasses to the sleigh, and haul 'em to the river, where one man'll camp by 'em. Some fellers'll go up the river every couple weeks with big sleighs and teams, and bring back what's out."

The sleighs were ready, and the hunters. Men who seemed mostly to be in their sixties, tough old men with their earlappers up in the zero cold. They climbed together onto the sleighs, and the men at the reins slapped their geldings on the rump. The *erog* started off, mostly with a jerk, drawing the sleighs down the riverbank and onto the ice. Kelmer watched them through his visor, recording.

And wished he were going with them, to live and record a week in their life. He wasn't a warrior, he told himself, he was a photojournalist. He'd gotten into this job to record an interesting way of life—interesting and exciting scenes and events.

"And they'll hunt all winter?" he asked.

The old fur broker raised an eyebrow at the question. "Not likely. They'll come out when they ain't much *porso* or *erog* left 'round where they're huntin'. When what they ain't killed has scattered, maybe moved out of the district."

Kelmer lost himself in visualization for a moment. "They'll have killed a lot of animals."

"Son," Hanni said, "with all the folks down in them refugee camps, all we can kill won't begin to be enough. All we can do is help. Make a difference."

Fifty-seven

Colonel Ko-Dan and Captain Ibang walked into the reception room outside Undsvin's office. Both of them saw the guard standing beside his door, and knew him at once. He knew them, too, and knew he'd been recognized. They saw it in his aura, though he never twitched.

Twenty minutes later they'd finished their business, and started back to their billet in the GPV assigned to them by the general. "You noticed Undsvin's guard," Ibang said.

"Yes. Major Carrmak. I must say I was surprised."

"The Iryalans are remarkably resourceful. I take it you don't intend to tell the general who his guard is."

"We are contracted in a military role, not as a counter-espionage service. If his cousin was a different kind of man, and I thought better of their cause . . . As it is, we will give Engwar his money's worth of fighting—show him the value of a T'swa regiment—but provide him no bonuses." Ko-Dan chuckled. "Whatever Carrmak is doing, it's nothing he learned in the lodge. His commander had a reputation for imagination."

Ibang laughed aloud. "Imagination or not, none of us could masquerade as a local, here or on any world but Tyss."

* * *

The general's elite guard, now only a section with two ten-man squads, had been moved to a single large two-story house. Though twenty-two men shared it, Carrmak, as commanding officer, had a small, second-story room for himself.

He'd put together items that would be useful, when the time came, for escaping to Smoleni territory. They were in a pack which hung in his closet, with his greatcoat hanging over it. Tonight his web belt, with its holstered pistol, was also in the pack.

He hadn't known what to expect when the two T'swa walked past him into Undsvin's office. But he'd decided to stay, see what happened. By the time they'd walked out, twenty minutes later, he'd become optimistic. When his shift ended, twenty minutes after that, and nothing had happened, it seemed clear that they hadn't said anything. And if they hadn't then, they weren't likely to later.

Nonetheless he was prepared to go out the window, jump into the back yard, and run for it if anything seemed to threaten. For a while he waited ready. After an hour, he undressed and went to bed with his pistol in easy reach.

Fifty-eight

Undsvin had never intended to fight the Smoleni in the northern forests. From the beginning, his strategy had been to shut them off from effective supply sources and starve them out. That was the reason he'd allowed his troops to abuse the local populations as they captured one southern district after another. And why he'd allowed refugees to move north, even though they were an impediment to his advancing army: Stories of murders and rapes would spread with them, and many in the towns ahead would flee northward, putting much greater pressure on the limited Smoleni supplies.

Meanwhile the serfs who made up more than half the Komarsi army had broad competencies of their own. They'd worked with their hands from childhood, doing almost everything there was to do on the estates they'd been part of. Besides field work and barn chores, they'd built and repaired almost everything required, except the manors themselves and their furnishings. And there was no shortage of lumber in Smolen: the sawmills along the Rumar and other major rivers had had many stacks of it dried or drying when the war began. Thus by summer's end, the Komarsi army in Smolen was housed mostly in barracks it had built outside the towns. In-town billeting was limited largely to headquarters personnel; discipline and training were more readily maintained in units barracked in the countryside.

Now that winter had arrived, the troops stayed close to their camps. They were drilled enough that, along with camp chores, they were kept busy, but their main function now was to be there, to occupy southern Smolen. For one thing, they weren't equipped to operate in the northern winter. Their supply of snowshoes was limited, although that was being remedied, and skis were nonexistent. Units along the Eel-Strawstack border with the Free Lands skirmished rather frequently with Smoleni raiders—particularly rangers practicing their new, T'swa-style tactics—but they took no offensive actions.

Even the T'swa were not particularly aggressive now. On Tyss there'd been no opportunity to train in snow and cold. Here they'd been issued snowshoes, and were learning to use them. They were discovering the nature of the landscape in winter—what the operational problems and opportunities were in different landscape types. But T'swa learn fast, and even before the solstice they were out hunting and destroying Smoleni recon teams.

Fifty-nine

With the war essentially on hold, Undsvin had gone home for the first time since before the invasion began, to spend the solstice holidays with his family. His daughter had given birth to his first grandson, whom he hadn't yet seen, while his younger son, who'd turned sixteen, had grown what seemed like four inches.

Then, on his second week back at Rumaros, a royal order had come, to fly to the palace at once. It didn't say why. Undsvin felt ill at ease about it, but the king was the king; the general was in the air inside an hour.

It was sleeting that day in Linnasteth. Streets were glazed with ice, and traffic was nearly nonexistent when Undsvin's floater arrived at the palace. The guards who met him stood beneath large umbrellas, to whisk him up the cindered walk and through the ornate entrance.

The king didn't meet him in a reception hall or audience chamber. They met in Engwar's office, just the two of them. (Engwar's bodyguard didn't count; he was a necessary cipher.) Undsvin knew at once that Engwar was deeply agitated. The pouches and dark smudges beneath his eyes told of hours spent rehearsing and dramatizing his troubles instead of sleeping. Still, the king was clearly making an effort to control himself.

He gestured at the chair before his desk, the motion a nervous twitch. "Sit, cousin, sit!"

Undsvin sat.

"What are you doing to win the war?"

"I'm depriving the Smoleni of their farmlands and goods, forcing them to use up their limited supplies."

"They are getting supplies through Oselbent! Both food and munitions! By sleighs over the swamp country!"

"I'm aware of that, Your Majesty. But all that buys them is an extra dek. Two or three at most. They can't bring in enough to begin feeding their people."

Engwar sat heavily, contemplating what his cousin had said. Then, more calmly: "What are the T'swa doing? Why don't I hear of them attacking the Smoleni?"

"T'swa companies have begun harassing Smoleni units weekly now. And they've effectively eliminated the Smoleni surveillance system."

"I didn't hire them to harass, or to destroy surveillance systems. I hired them to destroy the Smoleni."

"Engwar," Undsvin said almost gently, "the T'swa are marvelous fighting men, but they are human. Their world has no snow or cold; they've had to learn to travel and fight in the northern winter. They are already damaging the Smoleni; in time they will demoralize them. And they may yet play a decisive role in shortening the war. But they cannot destroy them."

Engwar gnawed a lip. "The Assembly is complaining about the war. The treasury has shrunken badly, existing taxes are far from adequate, and the Assembly has refused to authorize new. Rich though they are, they have cried and complained at the inflation of currency. They care nothing about their king or country, only their own wealth! So I froze prices, and the merchants rose up screaming! Some have even publicly burned stacks of their goods in protest, while others have closed their doors. Supposedly withholding their goods from sale, though I have no doubt they are selling them on the black market and getting richer than ever."

He exhaled tiredly. "The freedmen have rioted in their disreputable townships, and that fool Nufkarm has publicly urged our royal assistance for them. While that greater fool, Arbendel, has stated that no one should receive assistance without signing an agreement of serfdom. The upshot of that was a wave of arson that resulted in merchants distributing food, a terrible precedent that will have who knows what long-term effects."

The king paused then and looked beseechingly at his older cousin. "Dear Undsvin, I need a victory. I truly need a victory. Something that will excite people, make them glad for the war."

My god, dear cousin, Undsvin thought. *What world do you live in?* "Your Majesty," he answered, "I will come up with something. Let me have a week, and I will let you know what my plan is. Though it may well require a dek or two to carry out."

He left the palace wondering how he could have said that. But by the time he landed again at Rumaros, he had the basic idea.

Sixty

Undsvin appreciated the potentials of enemy spies, especially in occupied territory. Potentials some of which were positive.

In Rumaros, about seventy percent of the people had stayed when the Komarsi took over. Their situation was poor. There was poverty and hunger. An important part of their income came from the taverns and girls who entertained the Komarsi soldiers, and from those who kept house and cooked and otherwise served the officers. Thus there were abundant opportunities for careless talk to reach the Smoleni intelligence lines that the general had no doubt existed.

So he told no one what he really had in mind, not even Viskon, who in most matters was his confidant as well as his aide. There'd be time enough later to let them know. Instead he called his staff together to give them orders, and false premises for those orders. The T'swa commander was requested to attend.

It was not a conference: opinions weren't asked for; joma wasn't even served. When they were all seated, he gaveled them needlessly to order in a way that was quite bizarre:

he rapped the table with the butt of his pistol. What, they wondered apprehensively, was going on with their commander?

"Gentlemen!" The room fell silent. "I've brought you here to tell you about the coming offensive!"

The groan was silent, a psychic protest. Every one of his officers agreed with Undsvin's so-called siege policy, of waiting and letting the Smoleni starve. And they all remembered the ill-fated strike northward in early Sevendek, that began so well and ended so terribly.

"By late winter the Smoleni will be hungry, their morale and their physical strength low, and their guard down. They won't expect us to move before the snow has melted and the roads dried out. Also, by the equinox, the severe cold will be past, and the days longer. But the roads will still be frozen, and the Eel will be locked beneath at least twenty inches of ice, more likely thirty or more. The rivers in the north perhaps fifty.

"We will move at the equinox, striking northward with perhaps five divisions, up every road between the Rumar and Road 45. Snowshoes for five divisions are being produced in Komars even as I speak, made of a cold-resistant plastic."

His officers glanced at one another out of the corners of their eyes. By then there might well be four feet or more of snow, on the roads as well as in the woods. To move and supply artillery—to supply large forces at all—would be a monstrous task. And even at the equinox, subzero weather could be expected—not thirty, forty, or fifty below, but bitter weather for large-scale operations. None of them had operational experience or training in such conditions. And if breakup came early, the snowpack melting before operations were complete . . .

"Other forces will follow," Undsvin continued, "to secure the territory taken. We will continue in this manner all the way to Burnt Woods, capturing the refugee camps on the way. The people will either submit to us, or be forced north past the last villages and camps, to freeze and starve in the snow. If the Smoleni government doesn't surrender then, a force, perhaps of brigade strength, can be sent north up the

Granite River, the north branch of the Rumar, to the hamlet of Jump-Off, to close the supply road from Oselbent."

He looked them over, his expression implacable, and they ceased exchanging glances, though none of them met his eyes.

"The planning and preparations for this offensive will be much more demanding than any to date. We'll need to build up major supply and ordnance depots on the Eel Valley Railroad, probably near the villages of Meadowgreen and Eel Fork."

His voice became more conversational now. "I realize there are problems inherent in this. We will develop plans to deal with them. Anoreth, you will prepare a basic operations analysis. Have a draft of it in my hands by next Twoday. On Fourday we will have another meeting to discuss that analysis. Between now and then, the rest of you will give thought to this. I expect you all to take a useful part in that discussion. Afterward I'll assign a planning mission to develop a complete operating plan, from which we'll go to logistical planning."

His voice became imperious again. "I'm going to demand the utmost in careful speed in the whole planning operation. And it requires speed! The equinox is less than a quarter away! You will work harder than you ever worked before. If anyone lags, obstructs progress in any way, I'll find other duties for him. Specifically he'll be leading a penal platoon in the offensive.

"Any questions?"

Faces had paled. Middle-aged staff officers grown fat and soft, leading penal platoons into combat? If the Smoleni didn't kill them, their own soldiers were liable to! Such a threat to noblemen was unprecedented.

Among the Komarsi staff officers, only Colonel Sharf, Undsvin's intelligence chief, seemed unflapped. "The Smoleni will learn of these depots," Sharf said, "and may very well deduce from them the basic features of our plans."

"It will be your responsibility to see that they deduce incorrectly," Undsvin answered, and looked them over. "Anything else?"

No one spoke.

"Very well. Sharf, Colonel Ko-Dan, please remain. The rest of you are dismissed."

When they'd gone, Undsvin said to Sharf: "Colonel, regardless of what I said before the others, I *do, do* want the Smoleni to learn of this. And I have no doubt that some of the gentlemen who just left will feel constrained to talk about it to their friends. Particularly stressed as they are by my threat of penal platoons. Word will spread. Let it. *Do you understand?*"

"Yes, sir."

"Good. You are dismissed."

He watched Sharf out the door. *You understand enough to follow orders. Beyond that you are utterly mystified, and burning with curiosity. Well. Enjoy!* He turned to Ko-Dan. "Colonel, what is the status of the Smoleni surveillance system?"

"It no longer exists, General. We tracked down and killed most of the men they had operating. A few escaped us; we lost their tracks in a snowstorm. However, the Smoleni may simply discontinue it temporarily, expecting us to withdraw our hunter teams."

"Exactly. I'm depending on it. When they do, I want you to leave them alone. Do not visit the north shore of the Eel. Raid northward along the Upper Rumar if you wish. Any questions?"

"None whatever, general."

Undsvin looked at the T'swi curiously. "Well then, I believe our business is over for the day."

When Ko-Dan had gone, Undsvin sat wondering. Did the T'swi have no questions because he wasn't curious? That seemed unlikely. Surely his orders regarding the Smoleni surveillance system must have seemed strange to him. Just what had he surmised?

In his own office, Ko-Dan had described the meeting to his aide. "You realize what he plans, of course."

Grinning, Ibang nodded. "The Smoleni will learn of the big depot at Meadowgreen, and with their supply problems will be greatly tempted to raid it. No doubt bringing a sleigh column down the road to carry away what they get. And presumably moving major elements of their army with them to protect the sleighs.

"This will, of course, require considerable effort on the part of the Smoleni, and the commitment of much energy and resources, of which they have little to spare. Once their columns are well underway, say past Shelf Falls, they'll be increasingly reluctant to discontinue, except for compelling reasons. Then I suspect the general will want us to clean out their surveillance teams again. After which he'll situate forces at the Eel to ambush their strike force and destroy their sleigh columns.

"That accomplished, he may or may not launch an offensive at the Equinox. I suspect he will not."

Ko-Dan nodded, smiling. "Anything further?"

"He will, of course, have to take certain commanders into his confidence, but that will be quite late in the sequence. His assumption will be that the Smoleni will not learn of the planned ambush." He reached for his cup and sipped the joma, grown tepid during their talk. "Through his Smoleni employers, Colonel Romlar will learn of the supposed offensive. And as deeply as he obviously perceives, will suspect that something is amiss, and send scouts to investigate. A probability our general may well overlook. It is quite possible then, even probable, that some of them will avoid our re-inserted hunter teams, discover the Komarsi ambush forces, and warn the Smoleni away."

Ko-Dan chuckled. "An apt analysis. But there is another possibility, let me say probability. Because the Smoleni truly need supplies, and I suspect they need successes to nourish their spirits. I visualize Romlar warning them in advance that they are being baited, and the Smoleni deciding to try the raid anyway. In which case they'll plan a surprise attack on the Komarsi ambush force."

He got to his feet and replenished his joma from the pot on his sheet-iron stove. "Consider that the Iryalans are training Smoleni woodsmen as what they term 'rangers.' In some numbers. From our own limited experience, there is no doubt that these so-called ranger units will prove much better than anything General Undsvin can field. Much more mobile and confident in the forest and the snow, much more energetic and responsive to situations, and more skillful with their weapons." He sat down again. "And of course, the Iryalans are likely to involve themselves. I would rather expect the Komarsi ambush force to be savaged."

"Ah!" Ibang's eyes brightened. "And we will prepare a counter-ambush of our own. Perhaps even engaging the Iryalans in a decisive fight!"

The colonel's upper lip dipped cautiously in the scalding drink. "Exactly. Of course, we've made a long and involved series of assumptions, any of which may be in error. But it feels right, as right as the T'sel gives me to feel about something that hasn't yet set up in the reality matrix."

Sixty-one

Kelmer Faronya took off his skis and leaned them against
the porch rail. Then he stepped up onto the porch, spoke
cheerfully to the guard, and rang the president's doorbell.
The butler answered.

"Good evening, Mr. Faronya. Step inside please." Kelmer
did, and the butler closed the door against the cold. "We
haven't seen you for a time. Shall I tell Miss Lanks you're
here?"

"If you would, please." He waited while the man left. A
minute later, Weldi came smiling down the stairs and put
her hand on Kelmer's arm. As always, the touch speeded
his pulse.

"Kelmer, dear," she said as she guided him toward the
guest parlor, "we've missed you. I've missed you." She
frowned. "And when I heard about the attack on the supply
train . . ." They sat down on the settee. "Were you in
danger?"

"*I* wasn't. Not really." He looked back at the experience.
He'd gone to Jump-Off again, this time to record a sleigh
train coming with supplies from Oselbent. "Hanni Distra
took me out the supply road in a cutter pulled by an *erog*.

We'd gone about twelve miles when we heard rifle fire about half a mile ahead. We stopped, of course; couldn't see what was going on. There was a stretch of tall reeds in the fen just ahead. After the shooting stopped, we waited for a few minutes, not knowing what to expect. Then there was more. This time it sounded like machine guns and rifles both. Soon after that was over, there was a big explosion, and after that two really big ones.

"We talked about whether to go back, or stay awhile and see what happened next. There was a radio with the train, and a company of infantry at Jump-Off, with skis. So we waited. When nothing more happened, I skied on ahead, listening hard. After a while I came to bodies in the snow—our own people and some T'swa. I didn't hunt around and count, but I saw more than half a dozen bodies, including two T'swa. None of them were moving. It looked like the train had had scouts ahead on skis, and the T'swa had ambushed them where the road passed near a stand of *fex*.

"The T'swa wore snowshoes instead of skis, and from their tracks, they'd gone on to attack the train. There were a lot of them, maybe a company. What I didn't know was, were they still there? Maybe waiting to hit any relief party that might come from Jump-Off?"

He stopped, his expression abstracted. After a moment, Weldi asked, "Then what?"

"Then I went ahead a few hundred yards, following the T'swa's snowshoe tracks, till I passed through a narrow neck of muskeg. There were several dead T'swa there, too, and I could see the train ahead, out on the open fen. And where the T'swa had spread out along the edge of the trees, as if they'd been firing from there. I found out afterward there'd been machine gunners with the train, and they'd started shooting when they saw the T'swa. Then the T'swa had taken cover and picked off the machine gunners before going on. They're marvelous marksmen.

"I couldn't see any activity at the train, so I kept going, and found a couple more dead T'swa before I came to it. They'd blown the tracks off the steam tractor, and blown up a couple of sleighs loaded with ammunition. Then they went on east along the road. There were a couple of guys with the train that weren't dead, just wounded. And suffering from exposure; they'd been lying in the snow too hurt to move much. They were lucky it wasn't cold; not a lot below freezing. So I hurried back and brought Hanni with the cutter, and we started west with the wounded.

"After a little while we met troops skiing out from Jump-Off. They'd heard the explosions from thirteen miles away! When we told them what happened, they went on east. They wanted to catch the T'swa before they hit another train.

"I'd recorded everything I saw and heard. Then today I got a real early start and skied back here. I met two more infantry companies on the way, headed for Jump-Off. I haven't heard what happened to the company that followed the T'swa."

Weldi took one of his hands in hers. "Oh, Kelmer," she murmured, "I worry about you so when you're gone. I'm never sure . . ." She stopped then, and kissed him. He put his arms around her, and they kissed some more. His breath labored as if he'd been running upstairs. After a minute she pushed him away. "Not here," she said.

"Where then?"

She didn't answer at once, her gaze troubled. "Not anywhere. I—I love you too much. I'm afraid we'd do something we shouldn't." They sat looking soberly at each other for another minute, then embraced again and kissed some more. Finally she pushed him away and got up. "I think— you should go." She fluttered her hands. "But don't stay away. I just need to, to think."

Kelmer nodded, backing away. "I'll come back tomorrow if I can."

His mind was spinning as he put on his skis and started back to camp. He thought how much he loved Weldi Lanks, how lovely she was, how desirable. _And she loved him!_ Halfway to camp he stopped, a decision made without even looking at it, and turned back to the village, kicking hard. He stepped out of his skis, bounded up the porch steps, and rang the bell again while the guard eyed him quizzically. The butler's eyebrows arched when he saw who it was.

"Mr. Faronya! Did you forget something?"

"I'll say! Something important," Kelmer answered as he went in. "I need to speak with Weldi again."

She met him in the hall, her expression troubled. "Is anything the matter?" she asked.

"Marry me!" he said. "Marry me and nothing will be the matter!"

She stared.

"Marry me and I'll try hard to make you happy. All our lives."

She stepped into his arms then, looking into his eyes. "Oh yes, Kelmer, yes, I'll marry you." She kissed him, then stepped back. "We'll have to talk with Daddy, though. I'm not of age."

He nodded, suddenly unsure of himself. She went upstairs while he waited. A few minutes later, a disheveled president followed his daughter down the stairs, wearing slippers, and with trousers pulled on over his nightshirt. He looked grave, as he often did.

"My daughter tells me you want to marry each other," he said.

"Yes, sir. Very much, sir."

"I presume then that you love her."

"Yes, sir."

He turned to Weldi. "And you love him, I take it."

"Yes, Daddy, very much."

"Hmm. Well. And when did you want this wedding to take place?"

They stared at each other, unsure what to say, then Kelmer looked at the president. "We haven't talked about that, sir, but ... soon. I could be in a firefight next week, and—that could be it for me."

Heber Lanks's long face grew even longer, and he turned to his daughter again. "When would you suggest?" he asked.

"Tomorrow," she said, without hesitation.

He pursed his lips, looking to Kelmer again. "How long have you been talking about this?"

"We, uh—just since this evening, sir," Kelmer said.

"Ah. Well. Let's set a tentative date for some day late next week. That will give you both time to think about it some more." He raised his hands defensively. "And to get a wedding dress fitted and made."

"Father!" Weldi said, "we're in a war! And this is Burnt Woods, not Cliffview! I don't need a gown; I'll wear my best dress. And I've known for deks that I want to marry Kelmer; *I'd* have asked *him* if he'd taken much longer." She shook her head. "Next week isn't soon enough. Colonel Romlar could send Kelmer to Shelf Falls tomorrow, and who knows . . ." She cut her sentence short.

The president's expression was rueful now. He looked at Kelmer. "I suppose you've been thinking about this for deks too."

"Yes, sir." Actually he hadn't. He'd been wanting for deks to take Weldi to bed, but he'd thought seriously about marriage only a couple of times. Now, though, he had no doubt. He did want to marry her, and be married to her forever.

"Well." The president stood regarding the carpet for an endless half minute. "Today is Twoday, the twentieth of Onedek. How would, um—Fiveday the twenty-third be?"

Weldi startled them both; she laughed. "Daddy, you're hopeless. Fourday!"

"Um." He waggled his head, clearly not in denial. Perhaps in self-commiseration. "Fourday afternoon then, if Colonel Romlar agrees. That will give you time to move things into the guest bedroom. The one you have now hasn't got room to add anyone else's things, not even a soldier's."

She threw her arms around her father's neck and kissed him, then hugged Kelmer and kissed him much differently. Her father looked more lugubrious than ever.

Kelmer skied back to camp almost without touching the snow.

Sixty-two

Surprisingly, the wedding hadn't much interfered with presidential duties. Because Weldi, to the president's surprise, had insisted there be no advance announcement and no guests. Colonel Fossur served in the semiformal position of groom's uncle, counseling Kelmer in advance on how to treat one's bride, particularly in bed. Idrel Fossur had served as the bride's aunt. At the ceremony, it was the president, of course, who solemnly reminded the bride that her marriage would have priority over the parental family. Colonel Fossur, in turn, reminded the groom that responsibility to his wife had precedence over his relationships with other friends. Colonel Romlar had stood beside the groom, suppressing his tendency to grin, while Mrs. Fossur had supported the bride. The mayor of Burnt Woods presided.

When the ceremony was over, the newlyweds, with their skis, some food, personal luggage and precious wine, had been loaded into a cutter drawn by the mayor's handsome harness horse, an animal which he loved and never allowed anyone else to drive. So it was the beaming mayor who'd taken the newlyweds and their skis to his getaway cabin on Owl Lake, and left them there.

*   *   *

Thus on Fiveday the twenty-third, the War Council met in the president's office almost as if nothing unusual had happened the day before. Colonel Fossur presented and evaluated information received on two large new supply depots the Komarsi were building: one at Meadowgreen, on the railroad three miles south of Mile 40 Bridge across the Eel, and the other near the village of Eel Fork, where the river flowed into the Rumar, some twenty-five miles north and west of Rumaros. He felt they might presage a spring offensive to deny the Smoleni the production of northern farming settlements.

The president examined the statement. "You say *might* presage a spring offensive. What are the other possibilities?"

"I was coming to that, sir. I've had a report from two agents in Rumaros that Undsvin plans an equinox offensive, a very large one, supposedly using six divisions plus followup forces. My agents found that hard to credit, too. The story is that Undsvin made heavy threats to ensure compliances from his staff."

"Why should they mount an offensive in spring or any other season?" Belser growled. "The smart thing to do is sit back and starve us out. It would cost a lot less, and save a lot of young men's lives."

"Most of those lives would be serf lives," the president pointed out. "And I doubt that Engwar worries about serf lives. Elyas, at our last meeting you reviewed Komarsi civil unrest and other economic and political problems caused by the war. Could it be that Engwar wants an offensive to take his people's minds off the problems at home?"

Fossur shook his head. "It's conceivable, but I've seen no evidence that things are that bad there. And considering how badly it went with their last bold stroke . . ."

Belser interrupted. "Have you heard what they're stockpiling in the new depots?"

Fossur looked surprised at the question. "As a matter of fact I have. About what you'd expect: Munitions ordinary to a campaign, plus fodder, barrels of hardtack, and cases of dried fruit. Presumably other foodstuffs will come later."

The president spoke thoughtfully. "An equinox offensive by a large army might make sense, if they're properly equipped. We'd have much more difficulty safeguarding our supplies. We'd have to disperse them, and they could follow the sleigh tracks. And if they drove us out of our villages and refugee camps—drove us all into the forest with three or four feet of snow still on the ground—for all intents and purposes the war would be over."

Vestur Marlim replied before the general could. "Mr. President, such an offensive would cost the Komarsi heavily in material and blood. I can't believe they'd do it when our condition will be critical by early next winter at the latest."

They all sat quiet then. It was Belser who broke free of it. "Let's raid the depot at Mile 40," he said. "We need the supplies worse than they do."

Marlim stared. *And this was a man who, last summer, lacked fight! But ...* "Eskoth!" he said. "You can't be serious!"

"Certainly I'm serious! If we pull it off, we'll not only ease our supply situation—particularly munitions—we may also dislocate the Komarsi plan, whatever it is."

The War Minister shook his head. "It's altogether too dangerous. We'd never get away with it."

Remarkably, Belser didn't get angry. "If your house starts to burn when you're sleeping on the second floor, it could be dangerous to run down the stairs or jump out the window. But it's absolutely fatal to stay in bed."

"What if your neighbor is on his way with a ladder?"

"And what if he's not? What if his brother-in-law borrowed it and didn't bring it back?"

"Gentlemen!" Lanks said, and they stopped. "Colonel Romlar, you haven't said anything yet."

Romlar smiled ruefully. "That's because I don't have anything to say yet."

Lanks looked at him, still with a question in his eyes, then turned to the others. "I'd like both of you—Elyas, Eskoth— to sit down and draft an analysis. By tomorrow. And for security reasons, minimize the staff involved. Then bring copies to Vestur and me. We'll discuss this further on Oneday."

Fossur completed his intelligence review then. One of the data he mentioned was that companies of Komarsi infantry had been observed practicing on snowshoes. Which fitted the rumor of an equinox offensive.

Romlar still said nothing. He wanted to let the ideas ferment awhile.

Sixty-three

On Oneday the War Council met again. They discussed Belser's idea at length—he'd provided a basic operating plan by then—and decided: As dangerous as it was, and as much as it would cost their limited and shrinking supplies, they would do it. It was time, said Heber Lanks, for daring.

It was a simple plan, as military plans go. An infantry brigade on skis would move down the 40-Mile Road, followed closely by a sleigh column—all the logging sleighs readily available. Details of troops would cobble together cargo boxes, spiking them to the log bunks.

The brigade would assemble in the forest near Shelf Falls, where presumably no one would see. Converting logging sleighs for package freight was not unheard of; these would be prepared wherever they happened to be, which would conceal their significance. They too would be brought together near Shelf Falls.

The brigade would suppress Komarsi troops protecting the Meadowgreen depot, and load the sleighs. The Iryalan mercenaries and two battalions of the newly trained rangers would scout ahead and on the flanks of the column, and would cover the withdrawal, once the sleighs were loaded. Speed, even haste, was emphasized.

Romlar then developed a plan of his own, compatible with theirs. But kept it secret even from the War Council; reviewing it only with his own battalion commanders. There'd be time enough to coordinate with others, especially with the commanders of the ranger battalions, when they approached the Eel.

Sixty-four

On his side of the road was forest. On the other side lay a field, and beyond it more forest, all deep in snow. Kelmer Faronya tromped a place for himself in forty inches of it, then released the toe-bindings of his skis and stood one of them upright. With the other he swept the snow from the leaning trunk of a blowndown *jall* and clambered onto it, steadying for balance against a stout branch stub. From there he had a view of the troops moving south along the road. The Smoleni wore army green. Rifles slung, one company after another skied by, as silently as an army ever moves. Occasionally Kelmer murmured to his camera, sometimes narrating, sometimes verbally switching it off or on. After several minutes he cut it off, and waited till he saw the guidon of Battery C, one of 7th Regiment's howitzer batteries, the last unit before the sleigh column. Then he switched the camera back on and watched them pass, their guns with the wheels mounted on broad flat runners.

The sleigh column came into view behind it. The horses were not in good condition, though better than they may have looked to most eyes. They were shaggy against the season's cold, and unkempt like the old men who drove them. And somewhat gaunt, which was particularly undesirable in winter; it had been most of a year since they'd tasted grain.

Fortunately for the horses, the weather was mild. Just then, in early afternoon, it was about twenty-five degrees, not a lot below freezing. Had the weather been severe, it would have been much harder on them than it was.

The sleighs they drew were mismatched and crude, their runners and bunks rough-sawn timbers, or in some cases ax-hewn. Their cargo boxes were partly of boards, but mostly of slabs with bark on one side. Just now the cargo on each was only a pile of hay bales. They'd started out with more, had eaten some and left others in piles along the road for the return trip—hopefully a return trip. The cargo boxes would hold other than hay then, if things went well.

He watched the whole long column pass, 114 logging sleighs drawn by 228 horses, with a small herd of spare horses trailing. When they were by, Kelmer jumped down and donned his skis again. All he had to do now was pass the entire sleigh column and most of the brigade, and catch what was temporarily his outfit—Headquarters Company of the Smoleni Army's 2nd Brigade. Before dark if he could.

The Iryalan 1st Battalion was along, but operating at a little distance. And with the brigadier's ready agreement, Romlar had detailed Kelmer to 2nd Brigade, had said it was more important to get cubeage of the column than of the troopers in this raid, at least until the sleighs were loaded and the return underway. Kelmer felt a certain resentment at this—to him it seemed rejection—but mostly he felt relief. Around regimental headquarters, he'd felt a deep current of excitement, as if they'd be going into some particular and unusual danger. Which it seemed to him could only mean they expected to fight the T'swa. And if, in the past, he'd felt a deep visceral fear of combat, he'd added to it now an intellectual fear. For he'd gained a wife, someone he very much wanted to return to.

And there was something more. At Blue Forest he'd trained for a year under T'swa cadre, and felt a strong affinity with them—with their whole species. An affinity which he couldn't reconcile with killing them or being killed by them.

*   *   *

The weather held unseasonably mild, which helped progress. Troop morale was stronger, too. The packed snow was slicker, and the sleighs, growing ever lighter as the hay was eaten or loaded off, pulled more easily and rapidly.

Second Ranger Battalion was the point force, scouting the route in advance of the brigade. The Iryalan 1st Battalion was ahead on the right, and the 1st Rangers ahead on the left. There'd been no sign of Komarsi, nor of T'swa patrols. There'd been no recent tracks of anyone, only traces of old snowshoe trails buried by later snow.

Finally, on the next to last day of the trek south, Romlar sent a courier to Brigadier Carnfor, saying he planned to visit him in camp that evening, needing to speak with him.

Wearing the regiment's white winter field uniform, something new to Maragor, he arrived after nightfall, after camp was made, and they hunkered on an area of tramped-down snow around a fire. There was no joma, not even war joma; grain was too precious now to scorch for drinking. There was hot tea though—melted snow boiled with *fex* buds to make a brew that was hot, bitter with tannin, and rich in vitamins. Very briefly they traded trivia and sipped. Then Romlar turned to business. "In the morning," he said, "the Third Ranger Battalion will take over the right flank. My battalion has something else to do."

The brigadier raised his eyebrows. "The Third? I thought they were at Shelf Falls."

"They've been following a mile or two behind the sleighs. My analysis is that the depot is bait for a trap. There are reasons to suspect there'll be concealed forces on the south side of the Eel, waiting to jump you after you've crossed. If so, the T'swa will be involved. If I'm right about this, they plan to chop you up badly. I'll take my battalion, along with the ranger battalions, and surprise their ambush, hit it from behind."

Carnfor stared. "A trap," he echoed. The brigadier had foreseen that as a possibility, but to have it set before him with such seeming confidence . . .

Romlar unfolded a forestry map of the area. The depot had been inked in on it. Contour lines showed a respectable ridge a mile west of the depot; a green wash showed it forested. "I expect they'll have artillery here," he continued, pointing, "along the ridge top. They'll probably let you cross the bridge, then knock it out. And besides the predictable units emplaced to guard the depot, they should have a strong infantry force hidden here." He pointed to the stretch of forest between the ridge and the open ground the depot was set in. "There's woods enough there for a brigade."

He pointed to the open country south of the depot. "This would be a logical place for their artillery, especially if they expect you to answer with some of your own. But I don't think that's where it will be. And odds are they'll have no forces north of the river. Our scouts would almost surely find them, and that would spoil their trap.

"Also, there'll probably be a freight train parked at the depot, a long one. If there is, it will no doubt be full of concealed troops, waiting to jump out when you've been cut off south of the river. Be ready for that."

The brigadier gazed into the flickering campfire, his drawn face ruddied by its flames. "How sure are you of this?" he asked.

Romlar shrugged. "I have no explicit evidence; I'm basing it on hints—peculiarities and anomalies in the situation. But I'm reasonably confident there'll be something of the sort. The reason I didn't bring this up in War Council was the danger of spies. You people need all the supplies you can get, and this is an opportunity. And if you're to get them, it's best the Komarsi don't know we suspect.

"If I'm wrong, well and good. You should get the supplies without too much fighting. If I'm right, you should get the supplies anyway, and we should be able to surprise and shoot up their ambush force."

"What makes you think you can do that? Especially if the T'swa are involved."

Romlar didn't elaborate on his plans. He simply said, "The Rangers will coordinate with us."

The brigadier gazed long at Romlar. *He looks so damned young,* Carnfor thought. *And it seems too pat! But so far he's pulled off everything he's tried. And if confidence means anything . . .* "Thank you, Colonel," he said. Grimly now. "We'll be ready."

They discussed coordination then, and Romlar left. *We do need supplies,* Carnfor thought, *munitions even more than food. But can we afford to risk so much for them?* He watched Romlar ski away, perhaps finding some slight assurance in the boy-colonel's broad white back and his easy skill on skis.

Romlar's battalion broke camp early and set out well before dawn. They crossed the ice early the next evening, more than eight miles upstream of the Mile 40 Bridge. South of the Eel much of the country was open farmland, but between it and the Welvarn Morain were areas of forest, some of it rather thin from long-time summer grazing. The troopers then moved eastward, mostly under cover of woods. After a bit they came to an abundance of ski tracks they took to be those of the 3rd Ranger Battalion, which had crossed before them, as intended. At a point just east of Road 45, the troopers camped that night in a stretch of ungrazed forest along the west slope of a little ridge.

Romlar traded his skis for the snowshoes he'd carried on his pack, and scouted cautiously ahead with two men. When he reached the ridgetop, the moonlight showed him the larger ridge a mile or so ahead, on which he expected the Komarsi artillery to be set up. Between the two was another ridge, smaller than either. If he was correct, the T'swa would be on the middle ridge. The map indicated that all three ridges and the ground between were wooded, and as far as he could see, that was right.

The 3rd Rangers should, he thought, be ahead and well to his left, waiting for morning, and for the sounds that would cue them into action, sending them up the higher ridge to attack the Komarsi artillery ambush. The T'swa, hearing the firefight, would hit them from behind, hopefully thinking they were his troopers. The 3rd, meanwhile, would be expecting them.

A lot of ifs—more than he liked. His genius as a commander was that his ifs almost always worked out; his attunement to the reality matrix was remarkably good. The trick was to get the necessary hard evidence as well, or as much as you could, and put it all together. But sometimes hard evidence was short when you wanted it.

Tomorrow would answer his questions, he told himself. As for wasting his regiment—his fear, any fear, was aberration. He'd do what he had to, what the situation called for.

Beckoning, he backed down below the crest, then followed a contour southward till he came to a brushy saddle. There he crossed the ridge, watching carefully ahead. Moonlight and starlight on the snow provided excellent visibility. In the near-level bottom between the two ridges, he saw ahead of him the broad, heavily tracked trail of many men on snowshoes. He gestured the other two to stop, and alone slipped ahead to where he could see the tracks better—close enough to see their direction. Northward; it fitted. Turning, he started back to camp, to brief Major Esenrok and his company commanders on what he'd found.

While they slept, an overcast developed, and at first dawn it was warmer than it had been the previous afternoon. When the officer of the guard made out the faint beginning of day, he woke Romlar, then sent men to waken the company commanders, who in turn had their men wakened. The troopers crushed heat capsules and dropped them in their canteens, that they might start their day with hot water instead of eating snow. Then they sat hunched in their sleeping bags, munching cold iron rations while the sky paled. One by one they stood, swinging their arms, running in place, bending, getting ready for the day. Somewhat before full daylight, they had their packs and snowshoes on, rifles ready. Romlar moved them to the top of the first ridge. It was the warmest dawn they'd seen since autumn.

There they waited—longer than they'd have preferred, but patiently, calmly. Anxiety was something they'd banished years before, primarily in Ostrak sessions. At 1007 hours, Romlar's radio brought him a code phrase that told him the brigade was in place, about to come out of the forest and start across the bridge.

Then nothing, and more nothing, then distant rifle fire that quickly increased. Machine gun fire followed, also distant, swelled briefly, then leveled off. Ahead, the 3rd Rangers would be slipping through the trees now, ready to begin their assault of the ridge. Romlar whistled, not shrilly, and gestured, then started forward on his snowshoes, white-painted skis and poles strapped on his pack. His whistle was echoed by others.

Abruptly there was nearer rifle fire that intensified; the 3rd Rangers had engaged the infantry protecting the Komarsi artillery ambush. Now the troopers moved quickly. From the main ridge ahead they heard the sound of light mortar bombs. Almost at once, howitzers began to thunder, and the troopers moved still more quickly, down the slope through deep soft snow, from time to time sliding sideways till they reached the bottom. There they began to trot. Quickly they reached the T'swa tracks, and still they trotted. The sound of firing was closer. Then scouts saw T'swa ahead, and knelt. The line of troopers drew even with them and moved forward; they hadn't yet been seen.

They opened fire before they were noticed, aimed fire, deadly fire, and at once the T'swa began returning it. But dressed in white and kneeling in the snow, the Iryalan troopers were not good targets. They pressed forward. Romlar visualized the 3rd Rangers dropping two companies back to hold off the T'swa, who had to press uphill against them, slow heavy work on snowshoes. The other two ranger companies should be pressing on to reach the artillery at the top. The howitzers continued to boom, but mortar bombs should still be dropping among them, reaping gunners.

Then, from the left, Romlar heard more rifle fire. The 2nd Rangers, he thought, or companies from it. His whistling now was loud and shrill, as he ordered his battalion to shift to the right, to flank the T'swa right if they could.

Kelmer had reached the timber bridge with the first elements of the 2nd Brigade. His stomach was nervous, his bowels knotting, but he felt no great fear. There was no hint of paralysis. He stood beside the north end of the bridge, recording the troops crossing, the depot visible in the distance. The first Smoleni platoons were across before there was any sign that the Komarsi knew they were there. From outposts came first the popping of rifle fire, then the crackling of machine guns. At first it was at long range and not heavy, so not many men fell. The Smoleni companies continued to cross. It was warm enough that, with the exertion of the march, they went with earlaps up and coats open, their mittens in their pockets.

Kelmer was almost the only one on skis. The Smoleni infantry had stacked skis, poles, and bedrolls along the road in the forest, to cross the bridge on snowshoes. Through his visor, Kelmer watched and recorded the first companies deploying and advancing under light fire. The Smoleni riflemen had the cover of deep snow, which, along with distance, made them poor targets. They were not returning fire themselves. They might have if their ammunition supply had been greater; as it was, they were holding off till they were nearer, and could aim their fire.

Thus there was no nearby gunfire to cover the sound when more intense fire began to the west. Kelmer guessed that the White T'swa were involved. That would be the action Romlar had left him out of.

The artillery commander listened nervously to the small arms fire on the slope behind him. He was protected by three rifle companies and four additional machine gun sections, which seemed like a lot, crouched as they were behind log parapets with cleared fields of fire. But the firefight hadn't slackened in what seemed to him five or six minutes of furious exchange. He didn't hear the Smoleni mortars thump, and the first bombs arrived without warning, some exploding in treetops, some on contact with the ground.

He panicked then. His orders were to begin fire on a radioed command, but fear froze his mind, fear that his crews would be decimated if he waited. He gave the firing command at once. The howitzers bellowed, sending a salvo toward their initial targets—a salvo very premature.

More mortar rounds exploded. A fragment bit him and he yelped, sat down abruptly in the snow and rolled backward, grabbing at his right arm.

Kelmer pulled his attention to what was happening in front of him. A battalion had crossed, and another, and the beginning of a third, almost as if drilling. Only the lead units were receiving enemy fire. It seemed to him too easy, that something was bound to happen.

He heard the first artillery salvo—first the booming of the

guns, then the sound of the shells in flight. The guns had been registered in advance, and their rounds hit on or near target, one striking the bridge span between the center and north-bank piers, the explosion throwing Kelmer bodily backward into the snow. Others landed on the far side. Two fell short and another long onto the thick river ice, throwing chunks of it into the air on geysers of water. More landed in the woods on the north, rending trees, flinging snow and frozen earth. Fragments of steel and wood whirred and warbled. Men screamed, shouted, fell shocked or bleeding or died.

Kelmer realized he wasn't hurt, and untangling his skis, struggled to his feet. For a moment then he hardly moved, not from fear but indecision. Cross the river on the ice? Or drop back along the road into the forest, to record what was happening there? He chose the forest.

More than a mile away, the howitzers roared again, this salvo with time fuses, targeting the troops who'd crossed.

A Komarsi intelligence agent had reported by radio, the day before, that Smoleni scouts had passed the Valar Road. Colonel Ko-Dan had led his regiment into position a few hours later. He'd assumed that the Iryalans would attack the artillery ambush, and planned to strike them against the anvil of the emplaced Komarsi defense. But now, the word passed to him was that the force engaging him from behind was dressed in white, and he realized at once that *they* were the Iryalans. He'd been outguessed and set up. The troops assaulting uphill ahead of him must be rangers.

He assumed that the entire White Regiment was behind him. He couldn't know that Romlar, hedging his intuition, had left the Iryalan 2nd Battalion at Burnt Woods, in case Ko-Dan had outguessed him and sent a force by some wide-swinging route to attack the Smoleni government there.

Neither confusion nor hesitation were any part of Ko-Dan. He ordered one company to strike hard against the new pressure on their left, and another at the Iryalans behind him. The rest would continue uphill. It was important that the batteries on the ridgetop not be overrun.

He knew the ranger units were good. He didn't realize how good.

* * *

Among Komarsi veterans, the Smoleni already had a reputation for marksmanship, but the Komarsi infantry protecting the artillery had never experienced the kind of accuracy these rangers showed them. To expose yourself enough to use your weapon was deadly dangerous. Nor was all the mortar fire directed at the batteries on the ridgetop. Rounds were detonating in the treetops above the infantry, and on the ground among and behind them. Thus the rangers were able to press on uphill despite casualties.

The Komarsi had built their parapet with trees cut from the field of fire, and in the process, trampled the snow heavily. Thus the leading ranger elements had removed their snowshoes. When they began to come over the Komarsi parapet, the Komarsi broke and tried to flee uphill. It turned into a slaughter.

The ranger battalion C.O. radioed to the mortar sections to discontinue their fire on the hilltop and direct it against the T'swa. It was too late. The mortars, protected by machine guns, had been set up in a glade where they wouldn't have to fire through a screen of treetops. Their machine guns were under heavy attack by the T'swa, whose accurate fire had decimated the gunners, and before the mortarmen could reset their sights, the T'swa were overrunning them.

When the rangers reached the ridgetop, most of the gun crews fled down the east side of the hill. The rangers took no prisoners; the gunners who didn't flee were shot down. The Komarsi wounded were left unmolested but untended; the ranger medics were busy looking after their own.

The first company commander to reach the top called for any men with experience in artillery. There were three in his company. He gave a fourth man a compass and sent him up a tree to give him azimuths and range estimates as needed. The three ex-artillerymen became instant gun commanders, showing others how to load, aim, and fire the 4.2-inch howitzers. Within a couple of minutes he had five guns manned, each with three instant crewmen. Most of the 3rd Rangers, though, manned the parapets lower on the slope, to hold the top against the T'swa pushing upward.

The captain's attention was on the man in the tree. "Can you see a train from up there?" he shouted.

"Yessir! A great long sonofabitch!"

"Gimme an azimuth on it!"

The man sat on a branch, holding himself in place with one arm, and sighting through the compass, gave the captain the reading. The captain decided the present range settings were good enough to start with, and had his novice gunners traverse their guns to the new azimuth. Then he ordered what he'd dubbed gun number one to fire for range. It boomed, stunning the gunners, who had no ear protection.

They waited. After a few seconds the observer called down, "She 'sploded in the air 'bout two degrees left of the train and 'bout even with the locomotive!"

Good, the captain thought. *They've got time fuses, and the range they're set at is good enough to start with.* "Add two degrees more azimuth," he called to the gunners. "Gun number one, add one degree to your elevation; number two add two degrees; number three add three . . ." He shook his head when he'd finished, not knowing if he'd made any sense at all. He didn't even know whether elevation was set in degrees. "All guns fire when ready."

Again the number one gunner pulled the lanyard, again the gun roared. After a few seconds, the others began echoing it raggedly. Briefly they waited again. Then, "Holy shit!" the observer shouted. "It blew 'bout fifty or a hundred feet above the train! Yoma! There's another, and—guys are jumpin' out like fleas!"

"Keep firin'!" the captain shouted. "And Ingols! Keep tellin' me what's goin' on!" He shook his head while the gunners reloaded. *We may not know what we're doin', but we're doin' it.*

The 2nd Royal Komarsi Grenadier Brigade was a show unit, yeomen drilled to the highest parade sharpness. Just now they stood on snowshoes in the woods east of the ridge, almost crowding them. Waiting, they listened nervously to the firing in the open fields ahead and on the wooded ridge behind. Their brigadier jumped at the sudden sound of the howitzers' first salvo. So soon! He barked a command to his trumpeter, who raised his long ornate horn and blew. His battalions surged out of the woods, into the field, well before the plan had called for.

* * *

When the artillery had stopped firing, Ko-Dan realized the Komarsi gunners had been overrun. And when, scarce minutes later, they began to roar again, he knew what that meant, too. Meanwhile he was taking casualties on all sides. His purpose in being here had been to trap the Iryalans; instead his own men were caught between forces, beset by what seemed to be three regiments, all of them dangerous. It was time to leave.

His right flank was taking the least fire; that was the side to break out on, before the Iryalans could get more men there. He gave the order, and almost at once his men moved, striking hard. Briefly the firing intensified, but the Iryalans in position were mostly riflemen. Some were overrun and killed, while others fell back out of the way, to fire on the T'swa as they poured past.

When the T'swa had gotten out, Romlar ordered his men not to pursue. They were outnumbered. If the T'swa became aware of that ... After a minute's breather, he ordered his men up the hill. They had artillery training; it seemed likely that the Smoleni on top hadn't. He'd leave gunners there. Then, along with the ranger battalions, he and the rest of his troopers could move down the east side of the ridge and hit the Komarsi infantry he assumed were still in the woods there.

By midday, the Komarsi defenders, though considerably more numerous, had been routed. They'd been hit by their own artillery, by the light Smoleni howitzers on the north bank, and by the Smoleni infantry, the mercenaries, and the rangers. Nor were they allowed to reform and harass the loading of the sleigh column.

The empty sleighs had crossed the river on the ice and been driven to the depot, Kelmer with them, camera busy. Men worked furiously loading them, while at the river, the brigade's engineers worked equally furiously rebuilding the broken bridge span. The horses could never pull the loaded sleighs up the river's considerable bank, not without at least triple-teaming them, which would slow things unacceptably.

A handcar had been parked on a siding. Brigadier Carnfor had sent scouts with a radio, pumping it eastward. They were to warn him of any Komarsi reinforcements approaching.

The brigade had approached the job of loading with priorities and a plan, but given the delay, their considerable casualties, and the obvious fact that the Komarsi had expected them, they'd loaded hastily. They took almost solely foodstuffs and munitions, but not as selectively as planned. When the handcar scouts radioed that another train was coming, the final sleighs were loaded almost at random. Then the sleigh column started for the river while artillery ranged on the tracks eastward, destroying them. The three ranger battalions and the mercenaries moved east on skis to meet and discourage the Komarsi reinforcements.

Some of the munitions sleighs were too heavily loaded for the horses to pull easily, and men had to throw off cases of ammunition or shells as they went. The first to reach the river had to wait briefly while the engineers finished decking the new, temporary span with corduroy, manhandling the logs into place. They tied them down with Komarsi detonating cord.

The sleighs began to cross, while engineers chopped holes at intervals into, but not through the river ice, and set charges of Komarsi explosives in them. In the distance eastward they heard gunfire, but it grew no nearer. When the last sleighs had crossed, the brigadier radioed the battalions under Romlar's command. The brigade artillery was remounted on its skis and pulled away, and its infantry regiments began to cross the bridge. The rangers and mercenaries would cross on the ice downstream of the destruction. When the entire brigade was across, an engineer lit the det cord, and with a vicious, cracking explosion, the decking fell to the ice below. After that they blew the ice.

As the brigade moved north into the forest, a drizzle began to fall, thick and cold.

Sixty-five

The column didn't make camp till after dark. The temperature was falling, and the drizzle, after wetting everyone and everything, had turned to snow that fell thick and silent onto the trees and the ground between.

On the march, Artus Romlar's headquarters tent was simply a larger shelter tent, made with six panels instead of three, providing room for three men to function with map books and radio. They banked it with snow for insulation.

Arms behind his head, Romlar lay awake, not anxious but depressed. Depression was foreign to him, but there it was: He'd been wasting his regiment.

The thought was irrational. The regiment had been formed to make war. Its troopers had been born warriors, who'd volunteered and trained to make war. And the usual end point of making war, certainly for T'swa, was dying in one. Other people died of other causes: mercenaries customarily died in or from combat.

Wasting his regiment. In the fighting south of the Eel, he'd lost just thirty-seven killed, and eighteen unaccounted for. They'd also been able to bring out twelve wounded and unfit for action, who now rode on sleighs assigned as ambulances, atop plundered Komarsi supplies. Even for so brief an action, those were moderate figures, considering they'd fought T'swa.

The T'swa! He had no doubt he'd see more of them on this campaign. They wouldn't miss the opportunity for a good fight on their own terms. They'd follow, and his troopers were the rear guard; he'd volunteered them. They'd hardly catch up this night, but in case they did, his troopers were sleeping fully clothed. And given the snow, the pickets he'd set out could see almost as well at night as the T'swa did.

Wasting his regiment! At least he hadn't held back from committing his men to combat, and they'd done very well. *He'd* done very well; his aberration hadn't affected his muse. His predictions had very largely been accurate, seemingly more accurate than the T'swa commander's, and the Komarsi had ended up badly bloodied.

Yet I'm lying here depressed. Kantros lay next to him, jackknifed in his half-zipped sleeping bag, his breathing soft and regular. Romlar sighed and sat up. The lotus posture was out of the question in a sleeping bag, so he knelt to meditate. It didn't last long; he fell asleep in just a few minutes.

When they broke camp at dawn, fifteen inches of new snow had buried the trail the sleighs had packed on the trip south. And still it snowed. It quit about midday, leaving a storm total of twenty-three inches atop the old. Units changed their order of march with every hourly break, so that the same men weren't breaking trail continually.

By the time they made camp again, some time after dark, the temperature had fallen well below zero. Kelmer Faronya, who'd been taking cubeage of the column on the move, joined the battalion again, attaching himself to Jerym Alsnor and A Company, as before.

The brigade chief surgeon carried a standard Weather Office thermometer, and when they broke camp next morning, the temperature was −48 degrees. The horses walked through a cloud of their own freezing breath, whitening their bony sides with rime. Men wore ice on their week-old beards, and rime thick on their eyebrows and collars. Their eyelashes threaded delicate frost beads, and their noses and cheeks were waxy gray with frostbite.

An hour after the column hit the road, the T'swa caught up with the rear guard, Romlar's White T'swa. The T'swa, on snowshoes, could fire with only a momentary stop. The Iryalans, on skis, had to turn and put their poles aside to fire; fighting on the move wasn't practical for them. So they stopped, and knelt behind such cover as the trees provided there, removing their skis and donning snowshoes. It was a drill they knew well.

They were considerably outnumbered, and the T'swa, fighting on the move, seemed likely to flank and surround them, so when it seemed to Romlar that everyone but his couriers would be on snowshoes, he ordered a flank retreat westward. If the T'swa chose to pursue them, well and good. If they chose instead to continue pursuit of the Smoleni and their supply train, the Smoleni were well warned by the shooting. The rangers would already be moving to cover the rear, and his troopers could then attack the T'swa flank.

Ko-Dan chose to pursue the White T'swa, who stayed ahead of him. There was not a lot of shooting, but the T'swa did most of it, for they didn't have to stop and turn to find targets. Their targets were always in front of them; they needed only to pause to fire. And gradually, despite their white uniforms, the troopers accrued casualties.

It seemed to Romlar that his men had an advantage though. They'd undoubtedly gotten more rest, more sleep. The T'swa, on snowshoes, must have pressed hard well into the night to catch the column traveling on skis.

They climbed a low ridge and made a brief stand there, taking advantage of the terrain cover while shooting downhill at the T'swa in brown Komarsi winter uniforms. But they stayed only briefly, enough to give the T'swa some casualties, then turned again and hurried on. For several minutes there was no firing, and Romlar wondered if the T'swa had, in fact, broken off. He'd wanted to draw them farther from the column if he could. Then he heard a shot, and another, and more, and knew that the T'swa were still coming.

He knew where he was going, had chosen it on his map. He'd give them a bloody nose there, and escape.

Toward noon they crossed another ridge, this one little more than a wrinkle in the earth, just big enough to show on his map book. Now the critical terrain was less than a mile farther. He sent orders to two machine gun platoons to move ahead.

The two platoons came to the miles-long stretch of open fen, a mortal danger but also a near-perfect opportunity. The difference lay in sacrifice—their sacrifice. Their shrill whistled signals, passed on, told Romlar they'd arrived. In the fen, knee-high sedge-like graminoids and clumps of dwarf shrubs had prevented the snow from settling normally. Snowshoeing into it, they sank knee-deep, which slowed them markedly. Forty yards out they stopped, turned, and dug themselves into the snow, where they waited, catching their breath.

At the whistled signals, the rest of the battalion had speeded up to disengage. It took the T'swa a minute to realize what was happening, and to speed up themselves. The troopers bypassed the machine gunners, galloping past them as fast as they could. The men in the lead, breaking trail, had heavy going in the deep fluffy snow. When they fagged out, they slowed, and others moved ahead to take their place.

When the T'swa reached the fen, they'd have clear shots at the fleeing troopers, all the way to the other side. It was nearly five hundred yards across to the forest, and the first troopers made it in about two minutes, sweating heavily at the violent exertion, despite the arctic cold. They stopped within the screen of trees, and formed a firing line.

By that time the rest of the battalion was halfway across; all but the machine gunners, who'd already begun to fire at the T'swa arriving at the fen's edge. Their fire allowed much of the battalion to get across before the T'swa could direct appreciable fire at them, and at such long range, in their white uniforms, not many were hit. The T'swa, who'd also been running, were breathing hard; thus their aim wasn't up to standard, and at any rate much of their fire was aimed at the machine gunners.

It took the T'swa about half a minute to silence the

machine guns. By that time, for them to start across the fen would have been suicidal, and suicide would serve no function for them there. They stayed back within the forest's edge.

Meanwhile, on the far side, the battalion donned skis again, and all but a small rear guard moved on. A few minutes later, when the T'swa showed no sign of following farther, the rear guard left too. But as far as the T'swa could tell, they might still be waiting in their white uniforms.

At their next break, the platoon leaders checked their men to see who was still with them, then informed their company commanders. Jerym Alsnor, now Captain Alsnor, looked around, tight mouthed. "None of you see Faronya then?" he asked.

No one had since before they'd crossed the fen.

"Shit!" Kelmer wasn't a combatant, though T'swa riflemen could hardly know that, certainly not at a distance. And it was inappropriate that non-combatants die in combat. On Terfreya they'd lost Kelmer's journalist sister, Tain. Now here they'd lost Kelmer. Hopefully he was still alive.

He carried the word to Romlar himself. Not that there was anything to be done about it.

The fallen T'swi still had an aura, but it was shrunken and faint. The man could not live long. "Can you hear me?" Ibang asked. His pistol was in his hand.

"Yes." The answer was faint, little more than a hiss. The eyes had not opened.

"Do you wish to let death find its own time? Or shall I bring it to you?" Ibang had bent near the man's lips, that he might get the answer.

"I will wait, and contemplate."

That was the customary response. Today it seemed invariant among both T'swa and Iryalans; he hadn't heard one pistol shot. Mortally wounded T'swa normally preferred to have the complete experience of death, pain and all, rather than have it truncated. But when time and circumstance allowed, it was customary to offer the death stroke. And on a mission of this sort, any wound that disabled a man from traveling on his own feet was a mortal wound.

Ibang straightened. "Captain," someone called, and he turned to see a corporal looking at him. "Here is an Iryalan who does not seem badly hurt. His aura is not a warrior's aura. You may wish to deal with this one."

Ibang went over to them. The Iryalan wore skis, and lay sprawled sideways, legs twisted. His helmet was specialized for some purpose not immediately apparent. It was not protective, and had a hole in the back, near the top. *A spent round,* Ibang told himself, *probably a ricochet. Otherwise he'd be dead, or near it.* He removed the visored helmet and the thick woolen liner to examine the wound. The Iryalan groaned, stirred, and tried to raise himself. The soft snow made it impossible without more effort than he was ready to make. The bullet had scored the man's scalp, and his hair on one side was clotted with blood. It seemed evident to Ibang now that the helmet was a camera of some sort. The man wore a pistol with its holster snapped shut, but there was no rifle by him. Clearly then a noncombatant, a journalist of some sort. Given his stunned condition and the deep snow, the man would have serious difficulty getting up, with skis and pack on and his legs twisted as they were. Ibang unclipped the man's pack from his harness, unbuckled the ski bindings, then put a hand on the man's shoulder and shook it gently.

"My friend," he said, speaking Standard, "you must get up if you can. Otherwise you will freeze here."

There was no visible response for several seconds, then the head turned, producing a wince. The blue eyes were open, the expression confused. Ibang took the man's hand. "I will help you stand," he said.

The Iryalan groaned, turned his body, and made the effort; Ibang raised him to his feet. It was obvious from the grimace that his head had hurt when he'd gotten up. Meanwhile he was up to his buttocks in snow. Whether from the pain or an awareness of something missing, his hands went to his head and found dried blood instead of his camera helmet. Ibang shook snow from the torn and blood-caked woolen liner, and handed it to him.

"Put this on," he said, "or your ears will freeze."

Kelmer stared at it blankly for a moment, then comprehension dawned. He took the liner and put it on. Ibang turned to the corporal and handed the T'swi the camera helmet. "Keep this and stay with him. I will bring Ko-Dan."

Ibang left. When he'd found his colonel, they went together to the Iryalan, who was alert enough now to look worried. Ko-Dan removed the liner and examined the wound. "Corporal," he said, speaking Standard, "he carries an aid kit. Use it to bandage his wound." While the corporal bandaged, Ko-Dan questioned Kelmer. His answers verified what observation indicated.

"Can I have my helmet back?" Kelmer asked when they were done.

"Certainly," Ko-Dan said, and Ibang handed it to Kelmer, who wiped the visor and lenses, then adjusted the helmet's suspension to allow for the bandage. Clearly he was able to think. When he'd put it on, he activated it by voice, and found it still functional. He looked around, recording.

"I suggest you put your snowshoes on, instead of skis," Ko-Dan said. "Your injury may affect your balance for a time, and snowshoes will be easier to use."

Kelmer squatted and awkwardly strapped the snowshoes on, then stood on them. The pain in standing had been slight this time, and he had not dizzied. Ko-Dan had watched him. "You are not one of Romlar's White T'swa," he said. "They were chosen as warriors, and your aura is not a warrior's aura. Yet you are able to keep up with them physically. How is that?"

Aura? Kelmer didn't know the term. "I did the basic year of training with the Sixth Iryalan Mercenaries. Then the government sent me here with the First, to record the war."

"Ah! Then you have come to know some T'swa intimately, in their role as training cadre. That explains your ease with us. So. You are indeed a noncombatant. I am going to let you go, to follow your people. Assuming you feel able to travel alone. Do you?"

"Yes, sir."

"Good." Ko-Dan took off his own pack and removed two rations from it. "I suspect you can make good use of these. In cold such as this, it is well to have all you need to eat." He watched Kelmer tuck the rations in the inside pocket of his coat. By feel, keeping his lens focused on the colonel. "In turn," the T'swi continued, "I will ask favor of you. I am

Colonel Ko-Dan. Please tell Colonel Romlar for me and my men that he has a very fine regiment, and his leadership has been outstanding. It has been a pleasure to contest with them. I also suspect he has had more than a little to do with preparing the Smoleni troops we fought on the ridge. They are truly exceptional for troops which, unlike his and mine, lack the T'sel."

He stripped off a mitten then, and extended a large black hand. Kelmer shook it, and Ko-Dan grinned. "Yes," the colonel said, "you are T'swa-trained; you have the calluses and strength."

He began to turn away.

"Colonel?" said Kelmer.

"Yes?"

"May I record your troopers before I leave?"

"Certainly. We shall not do anything very interesting though. We shall eat, and return the way we came."

The T'swa commander turned away then, ignoring Kelmer utterly, as did the others. Kelmer knew that odd T'swa trait, from the training cadre at Blue Forest, and was neither offended nor puzzled. He recorded them eating and talking—laughing despite the dead around them—and wished he understood Tyspi. Then they got up, slung their packs, and snowshoed off southeastward.

He turned and started off northward across the fen. On the far side, he saw where the troopers had changed from snowshoes to skis. He switched too—he felt steady enough, and on snowshoes he'd fall farther behind instead of catching up. Then he set out following them.

Sixty-six

Briefly the troopers continued northwestward till they hit Road 45, which they followed north till after dark, taking advantage of its freedom from obstacles. Then Romlar had them dig into the snow again and pitch their shelter tents, after posting pickets of course. He'd let them sleep till daylight, assuming that nothing happened, and it seemed to him that nothing would. It was his intuition that the T'swa no longer followed him, and this was supported by several facts or apparent facts: The T'swa must have traveled much of the night before; they'd snowshoed very hard for several hours during the day, in pursuit; and to catch up again, they'd have to snowshoe much of the night without sleep, for their snowshoes were slower than skis.

No, it seemed highly unlikely that the T'swa still followed.

He had every reason to be pleased with 1st Battalion, his leadership, and the performance of the Smoleni rangers. But he found no joy in it, which was irrational. With today's casualties, notably the two machine gun platoons, he'd lost 189 troopers on this operation alone. And his White T'swa now numbered fewer than nine hundred.

Call it wastage or something else, his regiment was

shrinking, and rational or not, that troubled him. It didn't keep him awake though; not this night. He was too thoroughly tired. He ate a high-fat ration, stretched out in his sleeping bag, and fell asleep at once.

To dream. He was in a spaceship, not as a passenger, but as commander. Colonel Voker was with him, looking as he had at graduation, old and wiry and tough. And Varlik Lormagen, as young as he'd been in the old cubeage from the Kettle War. And Dao, his platoon sergeant from basic training, big and hard and black. They all looked serious except Dao, whose mouth and wise T'swa eyes smiled slightly.

We all have the T'sel now, Romlar thought, *but Dao more than the rest of us. Maybe it's something in the T'swa genotype.*

"We are different," Dao answered. "We are the T'swa, the true T'swa. We differ genetically, and especially culturally. But you are as deep in the T'sel as I." He eyed Romlar knowingly, and chuckled. "Though yours has slipped a little lately. That sometimes happens."

It seemed to Romlar that the others hadn't heard any of this conversation. Voker said, "Artus, the Imperials are out there. You hear them, don't you?"

He did. They were knocking on the door. He looked out the window, and the front porch was full of imperial marines.

"I want you to take your regiment and drive them away," Voker ordered.

"I'm sorry, Colonel, but my regiment is all dead."

"All dead! What did you do to them?"

"I got them all killed on Maragor, Colonel."

The knocking had loudened to booming. *In a moment,* Romlar thought, *the door will burst open, the air will rush out, and we'll all have to recycle as new-born slaves. Not just Voker and Lormagen and I, but everyone in the Confederation.*

There was a gunshot in the dream then, and Romlar jerked awake. To realize immediately what had happened: a tree had split from the intense cold. He'd heard them do that before, here and once at Blue Forest, and in training in the Terfreyan austral taiga after the war.

He'd been dreaming something unpleasant, and the dregs

remained in his subconscious. Something about—Voker. And Dao. He lay silently trying to pull those slight threads and bring the rest to view, but fell asleep again before he'd made any progress.

The sun went down. Dusk faded to twilight, and twilight to dark, and still Kelmer hadn't caught up with the troopers. He was bushed by then, but had only a single shelter panel, not enough for a tent. And as cold as it was . . .

He pushed on. He'd never felt so alone, so abandoned. After a bit he was wobbling, knees weak, and finally he fell. It seemed to him he could go no farther—that he would die there of the cold. He thought of Weldi. Tears filled his eyes, and he was gripped by a sudden fear that they'd freeze there, perhaps blinding him, so he covered them for a minute with his mittens, blinking furiously.

Then he forced himself to his feet and pushed onward. The battalion might be camped just ahead; a hundred yards on, he might be challenged by a sentry. He wasn't. At Blue Forest, he reminded himself, they'd spent a night in the snow without any panels at all. They'd dug depressions and lay down in them in their sleeping bags, covering each other with snow. But the last men down were covered by sentries, who were covered in turn by their relief. Here he didn't even have someone to bury him. And that night at Blue Forest hadn't been this cold; not nearly.

He'd skied only half an hour more when he collapsed again. After lying in the snow for a minute, he unsnapped his pack, and with one of the snowshoes strapped to it, dug himself a narrow hole in the snow, deep into the old base. He lay the panel in it then and sat down on it, wondering what the temperature was. He'd eaten both the T'swa rations already, and it seemed too much work to open one of his own. Instead he took out his sleeping bag and crawled in, leaving one arm free to pull snow over himself. When he was covered, he pulled his arm in and lay there, afraid to go to sleep.

Nonetheless, within two minutes he slept.

He awoke having to urinate. Faint daylight penetrated the snow. He undertook to sit up, and found himself held.

Warmth from his breath had melted a small space around his head, and the cold penetrating from outside had frozen the moisture into a shell of ice. For a moment, fear swelled in his heart, then subsided. He moved his legs; they were free. So was his torso below the chest. He worked his bag open, got his arms out, and with mittened hands broke the ice around his head, then sat up.

It was another bitter arctic morning, colder, he thought, than the morning before. He broke off a piece of his ice mask and put it in his mouth to melt, surprised that he was no colder than he was. *Actually*, he thought, *I've slept colder when the temperature wasn't nearly this low.* Then he dug a ration from his pack, and sitting up in his bag, ate it. Exposed to the air, he was quickly colder than he'd been in the night. He put the rest of his rations inside his coat, crawled out of his bag, put his boots on, and relieved himself against a tree, watching the urine form a mound of amber ice on the bark.

Finally, working clumsily in mittens, he donned pack, skis, and helmet, then continued on the trail of the battalion. With a remarkably light heart. Not only had he not frozen to death. He'd discovered that the danger was not so great as he'd thought. Half an hour later, he found where the battalion had camped. And decided it was just as well he'd stopped when he had. Otherwise he wouldn't have learned what he had, wouldn't have discovered that he could survive alone.

Sixty-seven

First Battalion left Road 45 that morning, angling north-eastward toward Road 40 and the Smoleni column. The weather remained brutal. Even near noon, when Romlar spat at a tree, the saliva hit like a pebble, frozen. The cold sucked the heat from them, and the high-fat rations they gnawed from time to time weren't adequate, pressing as they were. By early afternoon they'd eaten the last of them. Such a speed march itself would burn more than ten thousand calories a day, and their bodies carried no fat to draw on.

More than the virgin snow made travel slow. Instead of roads, they found tangles of blowdown, occasional swamps of bull brush to push through, soft-snowed fens and bogs to cross. Twice they came upon old logging roads, but never in a suitable direction.

The impulse was to press, press, press, to reach the column and the captured Komarsi rations. Yet they needed to rest from time to time, and no one grumbled when Romlar called a five-minute break each half hour. Five minutes wasn't enough to cool down seriously.

They reached Road 40 near sundown, and followed the

tracks of the column. It did not gladden them to find the bodies of several horses along the way, frozen rock-hard. They kept going until, soon after dark, a sentry challenged them. Minutes later they saw campfires.

Night held the forest in an arctic fist when Kelmer reached the road. He'd slowed the last hours, his reserves exhausted, and was weary almost to the point of collapse. He might have laid down in the snow an hour earlier, but his confidence had slipped, replaced again by anxiety and thoughts of Weldi. The road gave him new life, and briefly he speeded up, but it was only surface charge, and within the next hour he twice fell to the snow, to struggle up tight-jawed and push on.

Finally a ranger sentry challenged him. The Smoleni directed him to where the Iryalans had made camp, and trooper sentries directed him to the colonel's buried tent. The camp seemed dead, its fires cold and dark.

Kelmer stood his skis up by Romlar's and Kantro's, set his pack beside them, then opened the entrance flaps. Romlar wakened when he crawled inside. "Who's that?"

"Kelmer Faronya reporting, sir."

"Great Tunis!" A moment later a battery lamp lit the tent. "What happened to you?"

Kelmer took his helmet off. "I got hit. It was superficial. Enough to knock me out though."

There was a moment's silence. "Who bandaged you?"

"The T'swa. They found me unconscious, and recognized me as a noncombatant, so they let me go. Colonel Ko-Dan asked me to congratulate you for him. He said—" Suddenly Kelmer found himself thick-witted again, from exhaustion. "It's all on cube. He said fighting you had been a pleasure."

Romlar chuckled. "He would." Then, "You're bushed. Drag in your pack and bed down with us."

Kelmer found it a heavy effort to crawl back out and get it. When he'd laid his sleeping bag out, he saw the colonel's boots standing by the end wall, and took off his own. Romlar watched. "Here," he said when Kelmer had crawled half into his bag, and handed him a ration. Kelmer stared. He was so tired, he was asleep before he'd finished eating it.

Sixty-eight

They suffered two more days of arctic cold, though that second day was the worst. Almost a third of their horses died from the combination of cold and exhaustion, contributed to by the total lack of grain. Brigadier Carnfor did not press for speed, but he kept the pace steady.

At first, when a horse died, it was hastily cut up before it froze solid, but that slowed the column. After that, when a horse went down, it was simply dragged out of the way and gutted; it could be salvaged later. Horses from the replacement herd replaced them, and when there were no more replacements, sleighs without a team were left by the road. They too could be picked up later, in weather less severe, with fresher horses.

The constant brutal cold numbed the minds of some men, and there were suicides, none of them troopers and none rangers. Frostbitten noses and cheeks were general. The medics cursed men who froze their fingers, for they'd been given procedures to avoid the problem. They cut off fingertips, even whole fingers, so they wouldn't become gangrenous when they thawed.

A few men, discovering their fingers frozen, hid the fact

286

to avoid the knife, keeping them secret till they began to rot and stink. As a result, several hands had to be cut off.

Even before the weather eased, though, morale was improving. Jokes could be heard, coarser than usual. Fires were made at night, and horse meat stewed. It was tough and stringy, and lacked fat, but it was edible, and the broth was hot.

The regiment stayed with the column for those two days, the easier pace resting them. Then they left it behind, speed-marching to Burnt Woods. Enroute they passed horses being driven south to begin the recovery of abandoned carcasses and sleighs. Nothing was to be wasted.

Although the supply situation, critical in the long run, was not so severe as earlier forecast. Once The Archipelago had committed itself and began to send supplies, it had been relatively easy to send more of them than originally planned. Thus long trains of sleighs arrived at Jump-Off fairly frequently. Not enough to cover needs, but enough to stave off, somewhat, the time of serious hunger.

The Krentorfi ambassador would be leaving for Faersteth in three days, and the president asked Romlar that Kelmer be allowed to accompany the ambassador in his floater, taking video cubes and an audio report of the depot raid to the queen and her court. After that they'd be made available to theaters in a number of countries.

Kelmer asked that Weldi go with him; the ambassador said it was an excellent idea. Kelmer spent the three days editing and narrating. But he worked only till eight in the evening. He would not neglect his bride.

Sixty-nine

Despite the cold of northern Smolen, the troopers wore their hair short. Thus when Kelmer sat at his keyboard, and Weldi came into the one-time storeroom assigned him to edit in, she would eye the broad, still-livid scar that parted his scalp from the right rear almost to his forehead. She'd been that close to widowhood! She didn't consciously intend to interrupt his work, but on one occasion she allowed her finger to trace gently the path across his crown.

He turned and smiled, then stood and kissed her. She looked at him thoughtfully. "You're a very brave man, Kelmer," she said, "and I'm proud of you."

He kissed her again, partly to cover his discomfort at her words.

First Battalion was on light duty for a few days, resting from their mission, and that evening after supper, Kelmer took time to ski to the Iryalan camp and visit Jerym Alsnor. The evening was balmy, about 20 degrees, with a very few snowflakes drifting down lazily. Jerym put aside the tattered book he was reading—he was perhaps the thirtieth to read it—and grinned at Kelmer when he came into the winterized squad tent that housed A Company's six officers.

"Just couldn't stand it, eh? Had to get back to bachelor quarters."

Kelmer smiled back, then glanced around at the four other officers there at the time, two reading, two meditating. "Actually I came to talk to you," he said. "Is there somewhere we can go?"

Jerym stood up and took his garrison jacket from its peg. "Yeah. We can go for a walk." They left the tent, with its snowbanked outer walls of small logs, to saunter the well-packed snow between the rows. When, after a minute or two, Kelmer had said nothing, Jerym took the initiative. "What can I do for you?" he asked. "I warn you though, all I know about married life is what I saw growing up."

Though your sister and I discussed it seriously enough. But I'm not going to talk to you about that.

"You know how I used to wonder how I'd react to combat, to the danger of getting killed."

"Yeah. It seems to me you've done pretty well."

Kelmer grunted. "Jerym, it scared the shit out of me. One time literally, when a dud grenade landed almost at my feet. And I still get scared. Really scared."

The White T'swi shrugged. "There's nothing wrong with that. You've been in combat a number of times, and did what you were there to do." Jerym looked him over. Tain had been the warrior in the family, he had no doubt, though when he'd known her, he didn't see auras, except perhaps subliminally. "You weren't born to be a warrior," he went on. "Your aura shows it. And you haven't had the Ostrak Procedures or Ka-Shok training." He paused. "Why do you doubt your bravery?"

"Because I feel so damned afraid sometimes."

"Okay. Could it be that bravery has to do with action, with behavior, instead of with feelings?"

They continued walking, the photojournalist thoughtful now. "How do you feel," Kelmer asked, "when you're in combat? Or getting ready to go into combat."

"Differently than I did on Terfreya. On Terfreya, getting ready, I'd get excited. I lost that doing Ka-Shok meditation. In general, in combat, I feel highly alert, very quick and responsive, very vital and alive. But that's a consequence of

having been born a warrior, and six years of learning how
to handle it and do it right."

From a mile or more off to the west came the howl of a
loper, the Maragorn great wolf. The sound was a high-
pitched keening, as sharp-edged as the ringing of a wine
glass tapped by a spoon, belying the long-legged, thick-
necked, two-hundred-pound predator that voiced it. It was
answered by another almost at the edge of hearing. The two
men stopped to listen. The reclusive gray predators were
uncommon, perhaps had always been. When the brief duet
was over, their listeners walked on in silence for a bit.

It was Jerym who broke it. "So you came out here to talk
about bravery and fearfulness?"

Kelmer nodded.

"What specifically brought it up?"

"Weldi told me I'm a very brave man. It made me feel
like a phony."

Jerym grinned, and suddenly hugged Tain's brother.
"She's right, Kelmer! She's right!" He thumped the journalist's shoulder. "It's okay not to believe her, but she's right!"
He looked around. "Come on to the messhall with me.
There's always a kettle of hot water on the stove, and cannis-
ters of *fex* buds. We'll have a cup of tea and talk about
other stuff. Then you can go find someone prettier than me
to be around."

That night after Weldi had fallen asleep, Kelmer lay
thinking for a while. He'd come to the conclusion that he
was, if not actually brave, at least no coward. Jerym had
been right: men differed, and the proper criterion was
behavior, not emotion.

Part Four

T'SWA VICTORY

Seventy

The latter part of the winter alternated between further extreme cold and unseasonably mild weather. Neither of the combatants showed any interest even in minor harrassments, let alone substantial operations. Fossur's spy network had little to report, nor did Undsvin's, though Fossur continued to get political information via the Krentorfi ambassador.

The word was that General Lord Undsvin Tarsteng was in disgrace again, but that Engwar had left him in command, perhaps because of political agitation for his replacement. At any rate, Undsvin was his cousin, and no one else had demonstrated particular promise in a command role.

The equinox brought thawing temperatures, and the snow began to settle, but there was a great deal of it to melt, and the ice was massive on lakes and rivers. Spring would not arrive overnight. It would be weeks before the supply road from Oselbent would become impassable to sleigh trains.

The White T'swa continued training: running and marching on skis and snowshoes, practicing their tumbling and jokanru on the packed snow of their exercise areas. The Smoleni army, on the other hand, aside from the ranger battalions, pretty much laid up. Men with families in the north, in villages or refugee camps, were furloughed to be with them. Even in the ranger battalions, a third of their men were on leave at any one time. It was a season of rest and renewal, as it had always been in Smolen's north country.

By the end of Threedek, the spring thaw was at its peak. Snowmelt ran gurgling downstream over the river ice, and formed a foot-deep layer of icy water atop the frozen lakes. The remaining snow, hardly crotch-deep now and shrinking, was wet as water, except that usually a crust froze at night. The rawhide thongs of snowshoes soaked it up like blotters, and became thick and soft. It was time to hang them up. Used much in that season, they'd require restringing.

Security fell slack; it seemed needless. Conditions were obviously impossible for military operations, even by the seasoned backwoodsmen of the Smoleni rangers.

A long line of armed, white-clad men alternately walked and trotted through a forest, their gait seemingly tireless. Their snowshoes were of tough white plastic, and when the snow had shrunken enough, they would abandon them. Their packs too were white. Their mortars, machine guns, and supplies were in white bags that rode on white tobaggons. Their route took them up the eastern side of Smolen, where settlements were absent over large areas. The region was predominantly shallow-soiled rock-outcrop terrain, with peatlands and numerous lakes.

They followed a predetermined map course, crossing lakes on rubber boats, paddling through shallow water that lay atop three to four feet of rotting ice. Thirty to sixty percent of the drainage lengths consisted of lakes, so it was rarely necessary to cross the swollen and often dangerous streams. Near the end of their march, they were able to abandon their snowshoes, but it became necessary to detour around peatlands, where the remaining snow was underlain with a foot or so of icewater. Their trek was mostly over by then.

These men were black, not white. After the Battle at the Depot, Engwar himself had seen to it that white field uniforms and gear were provided them; he considered them his own special regiment, even if they did not take his orders. They appealed to the romantic in him, and surely they were more interested than anyone else in actually fighting. Besides, when he'd been under pressure to replace his cousin as commander of the army, it had been Colonel Ko-Dan who'd spoken up for the general.

Neither Engwar nor Undsvin knew where the T'swa were now, though; Engwar didn't even know they were gone. Ko-Dan was taking a big risk, and secrecy was vital.

Seventy-one

Gulthar Kro had settled into the Smoleni 3rd Ranger Battalion more comfortably than in any family or group he'd ever been part of. For a day and a half, the battalion had hiked the graveled road from Shelf Falls, where they'd been replaced by the 1st. Where there were fields along the road, the ground was mostly bare. In the forest, there was still a foot or so of granular snow. Flocks of spring birds wheeled and whirred. About midday the forest ended on their right, and some distance ahead, Kro could see the village of Burnt Woods, its houses flecks of color in the spring sun, red and blue, yellow and white.

The battalion turned off the main road a mile or so before they reached the Almar, and hiked a half-mile east to the army encampment, halting in ranks on the drill field. There the battalion C.O. turned it over to its company commanders. Kro turned his company over to his 1st sergeant—he had business of his own—and began walking alone toward town.

During the company's period of intensive training, and during the Great Raid, he'd been occupied, physically and mentally. After resting briefly at Shelf Falls, the 3rd had gone south again, patrolling the district along the north side of the Eel for several weeks.

But since the equinox they'd loafed a lot, and Kro had always had a problem with loafing: it made him brood. He'd looked again at his reason for coming north, the challenge he'd set himself. He felt no loyalty to Komars, nor to Undsvin any longer—in fact, he'd admitted to himself that he liked the Smoleni better than his own people—but he did not easily abandon a challenge.

So he'd left camp with a purpose in mind: to find and kill the merc colonel, whom he now knew by name if not on sight.

Kro had great confidence in his own physical strength, which might well exceed the merc commander's. He was a truly formidable street fighter, too—had exceptional natural talent and savagery to go with his strength and quickness, and had learned some valuable techniques over the years. But he had no illusion that he could beat the Iryalan colonel in a hand-to-hand fight or with knives.

On the other hand, his face and form were familiar to a number of the mercs, and as an officer of a merc-trained outfit, he might gain access to their colonel. The first trick would be to kill him, the second would be to escape. But if he could cultivate him, he could catch him alone some time, perhaps even sleeping. And with surprise and his service pistol, or his knife if possible, kill him. Then escape into the forest. They'd have to catch him, and tracking would slow them.

Those were some of the thoughts that ran through his mind as he trotted easily north on Road 40. He crossed the Almar, normally thirty to forty feet wide. Just now it was bank-full and more, a hundred feet wide in places, all of it squeezing forcefully between two bridge piers only twenty-five feet apart. A short distance to his right lay the millpond, roofed gray with massive rotting ice. At the junction with the river road, he turned west toward the merc camp.

Patience was the key, he told himself. Don't grab at the first opportunity unless it's a very good one. The mercs at Shelf Falls had relaxed their security during breakup, and spent more time in camp—had slept till after sunup, took long noon breaks, and didn't run field exercises that took

them far from camp. It was probably the same here. If
their colonel wasn't in camp today, there would still be this
evening, and tomorrow, and the next day. Meanwhile he
knew approximately what he'd say.

The snow had melted in the merc camp, except for
shrunken piles where it had been banked along the tent
walls. The ground was trampled mud. Kro looked into one
of the squad tents. "Afternoon," he said. "I'm lookin' for
yer colonel. Where'll I find his tent?"

One of the mercs was sitting in a strange cross-legged
sort of posture on a little rug, and didn't look up. A couple
were napping. One of those who were reading got to his
feet. He was a small man—five-six and a hundred and fifty,
Kro guessed—but in a fight, could have destroyed any of
Undsvin's brawlers, he had no doubt.

"I'll take you there, Captain," said the merc. "It's simpler
than telling you."

A row of muddy boots stood at the entrance, and the man
paused to put on a pair of them, tying the laces around his
ankles. "It'll be nice when this mud dries," he commented.
Pleasantly, as if it didn't really matter to him. Kro had
repeatedly been struck by how good-natured the mercs were.

"Yeah. I just come up from Shelf Falls. It's even worse
down there, seems like. What kind of man is yer colonel?"

"Smart. Artus is smart. You should have seen what he's
brought us through, here and on Terfreya."

"Tough?"

"Where it counts. Easy to get along with though. There;
that's his tent: his, his exec's, and his aide's. If he's not
there, his command tent is right through there."

The trooper pointed, then left. Kro went to the tent and
looked in. Its furnishings were similar to the one he'd looked
in a minute before, except there were only three cots. Only
one man was inside, a large man, napping. Kro's heart
jumped; he could see a small colonel's sun sewn on one
sleeve. He could cut his throat right now, and no one the
wiser, for a few minutes anyway.

The colonel turned over. His open eyes were on Kro, and
for a moment it seemed to the Komarsi that the man had
read his thoughts. He sat up then. "How can I help you,
Captain?"

Despite the moment just past, the answer came easily. "Sir, my name is Gull Kro. I've come to make an offer. You took some casualties down below the Eel, and a bunch more, I heard, when you led the T'swa away, comin' up Road 40. I'd like to be a replacement."

Romlar raised an eyebrow. "What would your C.O. think of that?"

"I think I could talk him into it. I can learn more from servin' with you. And maybe you could teach me things about command. Then, when you leave, I could help train others."

The merc colonel smiled. "Maybe you could at that. But it's at odds with T'swa tradition to take replacements. Besides, we all started out together, my men and I. We were recruits together as teen-aged kids. We trained for six years together, and fought two wars together. We're closer than brothers; we think alike. I don't have to tell them much, mainly just what our objectives are. They take it from there; they know how to get it done."

Kro shifted gears. "Well then," he said, "last summer when I got here from down south, I watched you guys train in hand-to-hand. I never seen nothin' like it before. Could you teach me that? So I could teach my men?"

"Hmm. I'll tell you. It took us . . ."

Sudden rifle fire to the north cut him off in mid-sentence, and from his sitting position, the colonel seemed to pounce to the door. In five seconds his boots were on, the laces wrapped and knotted 'round his ankles. He snatched his ammunition belt with pistol attached, buckled it and grabbed a rifle, then was out the door before Kro fully grasped that it was the flurry of distant shots which had so galvanized this man. Somewhere in his burst of activity, the colonel had also put a helmet on.

Kro found himself running behind him as if on a tether. To his astonishment, the camp was full of running men, a few barefoot or shirtless, all of them armed, most galloping northward between the rows of tents. As they fanned out of the tent area, Kro saw men in white running from the forest some 300 yards ahead. With no order given, the foremost troopers dropped to kneeling positions and squeezed off aimed shots. Others ran between them, and in perhaps fifteen yards these too knelt and fired. All had grabbed weapons—rifles or the twenty-pound, one-man machine guns they used.

It was as if the whole regiment had realized instantly what was happening and what needed to be done.

Meanwhile the men in white were firing back, and mercs too were falling. The current first wave of troopers had reached the ditch on the south side of the road, and lay on the side of it, legs in the water, squeezing off round after round, while the rest ran up and hit the ground among them. Kro found himself lying beside the colonel, pistol in hand. It didn't seem like the time to shoot him though, despite the noise and battle focus. Somehow it wouldn't be right.

The damned water was ice cold.

The attackers, those in the open, lay prone now too, returning the fire. Others, he couldn't tell how many, were firing from the edge of the woods. Those in the open were easy to see, white against the wet ground; he was willing to bet they'd all be casualties quickly. Those in the woods, on the other hand, he couldn't distinguish from the background.

The fire from the woods was shockingly accurate. With only heads for targets, the enemy had killed a number of troopers in just a minute or so of fighting. Then mortar bombs began to crash along the forest's edge, some as air bursts detonated by branches. The mortar men hadn't run out into the field; they'd set up back among the tents. Bombs began to fall along the road, too, in and behind the ditch. For a moment Kro thought they were short rounds fired by the mercs in camp, then realized they came from the forest ahead. It seemed to him that he and the colonel would both die today, side by side, comrades at arms.

The T'swa—they had to be T'swa—seemed uninterested in pressing the attack, as if they were satisfied to chew the mercs up from where they were. After another minute, he wondered how many there were of them, because merc mortar rounds continued to burst along the edge of the woods and in the treetops, but no more seemed to be coming from the forest. He became aware then that other mercs had run not out to the ditch, but west from camp, into the woods that crossed the road nearby. Those mercs were flanking the T'swa now. The merc mortars stopped firing, and their colonel whistled several shrill shrieks. The men in the ditch jumped up and charged, their colonel with them, across the road and toward the woods. Willy nilly Kro charged too, wondering if the colonel knew what he was doing.

More mercs fell, crossing that last hundred and fifty yards. Most, though, plunged into the edge of the trees. A grenade hurtled toward him, and Kro's gut spasmed. He snatched the thing in mid-air, and side-armed it back. It exploded no more than twenty feet away, and he felt a fragment strike his chest, burn across his ribs and take a nick out of his upper arm. It seemed to him trivial, made him feel somehow invincible. A T'swi in front of them showed enough of himself to aim his rifle, and Kro pulled his pistol trigger, felt the recoil through his wrist, once, twice, a third time. The first shot bit, the other two knocked bark from the side of the tree. He was aware that the colonel was down, and looked around for someone more to shoot, someone wearing white. Instead, someone shot him through the face, from the side. Kro went down as if clubbed.

Two ugly grenade fragments had hit Romlar, one in the right thigh, the other high on the chest, knocking him down. The wounds were nasty but not severe, and he got up again in seconds. By that time the fight was all but over, and the surviving T'swa were pulling out.

That told him something—that and what he'd already seen and heard. Even before they'd left the ditch, Romlar had been aware by the sound that there was fighting in the village. But by the time he'd limped back out of the trees, the shooting had all but ended there too. The major T'swa force, he realized, had occupied Burnt Woods, with the intention of capturing the Smoleni government. Only a small force—perhaps just a single company and not more than two—had engaged him here, as if they were more than they were. Their function had been to prevent his intervening in the village, in case it was seriously contested.

Clearly the T'swa had traveled overland during breakup, probably taking an easterly route to minimize the risk of detection. They'd have crossed the Granite south of Jump-Off, and swung around to strike from the north, the side from which certainly no one would attack.

There was no point in further action. The T'swa would have captured the president and his people already, unless they'd died in the fighting. Either way, the war was effectively over.

The way it felt to him, though, Heber Lanks was alive, alive and a prisoner. He shouted orders. At least he had the opportunity to salvage the wounded for a change, his and the T'swa's.

Seventy-two

A squad of T'swa, well-spaced, sprinted across the back yard of the president's house. From a window, someone fired bursts from a submachine gun, and one, then another of the T'swa fell. They did not shoot back. From the porch, a guard's rifle banged, just once, then he fell dead. The first T'swi to reach the house bounded onto the porch, shooting the glass out of a window, and jumped through. Another followed. A third crashed through a door. Others had run to the back of the house. They could have thrown grenades in but didn't, as if they wanted to take the occupants alive.

Kelmer Faronya had been in his editing room when he first heard shots. He'd gone to his window then, concerned, wondering what was going on, and had seen T'swa dash around the corner of the barn on the next property north. Without taking time to consider, he ran up the stairs to the room where he hoped Weldi would be. She wasn't there. Then where? He ran back out and went down the whole flight of stairs in three bounds, wheeled and ran for her father's office—to run bodily into a T'swi coming out of the study. They went down together, Kelmer trying for a throat

303

block, but fingers dug his carotids, and he blacked out almost at once.

The president had come out of his bedroom, pistol in hand. For a moment he'd hesitated: It was him they'd come for, had to be. If he gave himself up, it might save lives. So he tossed the gun on the floor, walked to the stairs and started down, hands raised to shoulder level, palms forward. A T'swi darted into the foyer, they saw each other, and the T'swi lowered his submachine gun. The president didn't hesitate; he continued down. He'd never seen a T'swi before, except in Kelmer's videos. The face was the color of a gun barrel, the large eyes calm. The T'swi met him at the foot of the stairs and took his arm, firmly but not hard.

The voice was deep and had no edge. "Mr. President," said the T'swi, "you are a prisoner. Please lie down on the floor, in case there is more shooting."

When General Eskoth Belser heard the first shots, he was examining a map. He turned in his chair. "Arkof! What is that shooting?"

"I'll find out, General."

He didn't turn back to his map though, because the shooting continued, now from more than one direction. For a moment he simply sat upright, looking out his office door, frowning and waiting for Arkof to learn something.

There was shooting nearby then, and getting abruptly up, he stepped to a rack and took out a submachine gun. A magazine was already seated, and he jacked a round into the chamber as he strode out into his reception room. The sergeant major had been outside and was just coming back in, a submachine gun in his hands. "It's T'swa, sir. Arkof's lying shot in the street. Best you keep low." He turned then and hurried back out.

Belser paused for a moment. There was gunfire in every direction. Then he realized; they'd come for the president. He strode out the door.

The house was set behind a small front yard with a waist-high picket fence, shrubs, and last year's dead flower patches. A massive *kren* stood in each front corner, remnant snow in their shade. He'd started for the gate when four soldiers ran down the street. A submachine gun clattered harshly, a long burst, and all four fell to the gravel. Belser ran to one of the *kren*, his gun held chest high. A man in white uniform ran from behind the house across the street, and for just a moment Belser thought it was one of the Iryalans. Then the black face registered. He stepped out far enough to fire a short burst, but failed to hit the T'swi. Before he could curse, bark and splinters burst from the side of the tree, head high. Just enough of him had been exposed. The general fell dead, reddening the snow.

Ko-Dan sat in the president's office. The president was there, and Fossur, and Weldi and Kelmer. And the Krentorfi ambassador, standing white-faced. A sergeant, the president's secretary, sat at the shortwave radio.

"Call the commanding officer of your local military forces," Ko-Dan ordered. "I will speak with them."

The sergeant looked questioningly to the president. "Do as the colonel asks," Lanks said calmly, then turned to Ko-Dan. "Let me speak with them first. They'll be more receptive."

The T'swi nodded. The sergeant pressed the microphone switch. "NC-1, NC-1, this is the Cottage, this is the Cottage. Over."

"This is NC-1. Over."

"The president wants to speak with Brigadier Carnfor. Over."

They waited for a long five seconds. "This is Carnfor. Over."

The sergeant handed the microphone to Lanks. "Elvar," said the president, "I am under military arrest, in the custody of Colonel Ko-Dan of the Black Serpent Regiment. T'swa. My cabinet is also under arrest, and General Belser is reported dead. I hereby appoint you commanding officer of the Army of Smolen until otherwise notified. Colonel Ko-Dan wants to talk with you. Please oblige him. I am giving the microphone to him now. Over."

Again there was a lag. "All right," Carnfor said. "I'll talk to him. Over."

"Brigadier Carnfor," Ko-Dan said, "I have your President Lanks, his cabinet, daughter, and son-in-law in custody, along with Colonel Fossur and other key persons. We see no purpose in shedding further blood, and propose a cessation of hostilities. Over."

"Colonel," Carnfor said, "you may have the government, but we've got you, and you're a long way from the Eel. You should know us well enough to realize that if we choose, we can wipe you out. It may cost us, but we can do it. Over."

"Indeed, Brigadier Carnfor. But if you attack us with any effective force, you will quite probably kill our captives. I'm sure you do not wish that. Over."

"We're a free people, Colonel. We can always elect a new president, and he can appoint new officials. This may sound strange to you, but we can. I'll make a deal, though: You let your hostages go, and I will personally give you a safe conduct out of the country. You'll be free to leave, and take your weapons with you. Over."

"Brigadier, that is not the kind of agreement that the Lodge of Kootosh-Lan allows me to make. And if you know anything about us, you know we do not object to dying. I can guarantee, however, that the president and his people will not be harmed, unless by yourselves. Over."

"I don't doubt you, Colonel. But when you get them to Rumaros, you and I both know what'll happen to them. That sonofabitch Engwar will either execute them publicly or parade them around Komars in chains and rags, on exhibition. No, I can't do that. Over."

Ko-Dan's thick eyebrows arched. He wasn't that familiar with the historical behavior of some Komarsi royalty. "If we arrive safely out of the present de facto boundaries of Smolen," Ko-Dan replied, "I guarantee their safety, and reasonable conditions of captivity. Over."

"That's a guarantee you can't make good on. You people are tough, but not that tough. Over."

Ko-Dan pursed his lips for just a moment, then answered. "I suggest you call Colonel Romlar of the Iryalan Regiment. He and his men know my people and my lodge better than anyone on Maragor except ourselves. Ask him what force my guarantee carries. Over."

The company mess tents in the Iryalan camp had been replaced, the previous autumn, with low log buildings. Two of these were being used as de facto hospitals, with tables for beds. That's where the runner found Romlar, not as a patient but as a commander checking the wounded. His own wounds had been dressed, and he was walking.

At a rapid limp, he followed the runner to the command tent, and sat down at the radio. "This is Romlar. Over."

"Artus, this is Elvar. We've got a situation." Carnfor reviewed what it was. "How good is the T'swa guarantee? Over."

Romlar knew what the brigadier hadn't said—couldn't say, under the circumstances: If they lost the president, their cause was basically lost. In Komars, unhappiness with the war would subside, and that was a key factor in Smoleni hopes. Also, while they could elect a new president and persist for a time, they'd have lost their credibility with the rest of Maragor, and without increased support from abroad, they could not long survive, as a nation, or ultimately as a people.

"Elvar, it's as good a guarantee as you'll find. If the Komarsi try to take the president away from the T'swa, there'll be a bloodbath. They'll have to wipe the T'swa out, which will bring every regiment the lodge can round up, and with Level Two weapons. And the Confederation won't say a thing. The Komarsi government will be out, and the reparations will make their nobility weep bitter tears. Engwar will either end up dead in combat, or a suicide, or they'll deliver him to you for trial. There's precedent for all this. Over."

There was silence for several seconds, as Carnfor assimilated Romlar's words. "Thank you, Artus," he said simply. "NC-1 out."

"White T'swa out." Romlar sat back and let his eyes close. He had no surgeon; the Smoleni had several. He'd call them back in a few minutes, and see if he could borrow one or more of them.

In the president's office, Ko-Dan had had the radio tuned to the White T'swa's frequency, and everyone there had heard what Romlar said. Heber Lanks couldn't help but think that, were it not for his daughter, he'd wish the Komarsi *would* try to take them from the T'swa. Seemingly

it would guarantee the long-range restoration of Smoleni
territory and independence, and reparations as well. But he
doubted it would happen. Engwar wasn't that insane; surely
Undsvin wasn't.

"The Cottage, the Cottage, this is NC-1. Over."

Ko-Dan thumbed the microphone switch. "This is Colonel Ko-Dan. Over."

"Colonel, I will accept your guarantee if the president
approves. Let me speak with him. Over."

Ko-Dan handed the microphone to Heber Lanks.
"Elvar," the president said, "we overheard what Colonel
Romlar told you, and you have my approval to accept Colonel Ko-Dan's offer. See that he has free passage. If the
new government wishes to renew hostilities with the T'swa
afterwards, it will be free to do so, of course. Meanwhile,
Ambassador Fordail of Krentorf is here, witnessing all of
this. We must hope he can influence the international com-
munity to continue their support. Over."

"Your message received, Mr. President. If you'll sit tight
for a bit, I'll get messages to every unit I can contact. My
love and best wishes go with you, sir. NC-1, out."

Ko-Dan waited half an hour, then radioed NC-1 again to
arrange truck transportation for his regiment. The reply was
that the Smoleni had insufficient trucks and fewer power
slugs. A large carryall and several trucks could be provided,
however, along with a section of engineers to repair culverts
and bridges washed out by breakup. Agreements were come
to.

The T'swa waited till daylight the next morning, then left
for Rumaros, most of them on foot and heavily loaded. Their
captives rode in the carryall.

Part Five

CLOSURE

Seventy-three

The regiment's medics had administered synthblood, opiates, and antibiotics, had sutured wounds and splinted limbs—pretty much the limit of their skills. Instead of sending a surgeon, Carnfor had sent ambulances to take men in emergency need to his field hospital, and to the small district hospital in Burnt Woods. They also took the ranger with the badly damaged face, Gull Kro. Kro's wound wasn't life-threatening, but he was one of Carnfor's own officers.

Covered trucks picked up the T'swa wounded who were fit for the ride to Rumaros.

Romlar had left those matters to his executive officer, Jorrie Renhaus, and gone to bed in his tent. He'd lost Fritek Kantros to a T'swa bullet. Eldren Esenrok had lost most of a leg and too much of his blood to a T'swa mortar round; his survival was uncertain.

With Fritek dead and Jorrie spending the night in the command tent, Artus was alone, which was how he preferred it just then. He'd declined to take anything for his pain. It wasn't that bad, and he preferred not to dull his mind if it wasn't necessary.

He allowed lassitude and depression to settle in though.

How many men do you have now? he asked himself. The question was rhetorical. He knew how many: 733, including wounded whom he judged could return to combat effectiveness after proper treatment. Or 773, if he could salvage all of the men he'd sent into Komars as agitators. Depending on how you defined "waste," he'd gone a long way toward wasting his regiment.

That was the sort of thoughts he fell asleep to.

On Iryala, Lotta Alsnor sat in a lotus in the *ghao* at Lake Loreen, in deep meditation. She was preparing to monitor Tain Faronya, riding through hyperspace in the imperial flagship, accompanied by an invasion fleet. Before she reached, though, an image, a being, appeared to her. Eldren Esenrok: she knew him at once. Her immediate thought was that he'd died.

Nope, he told her. *Maybe later tonight. Maybe tomorrow. Just now, the body's still hanging on, what's left of it. It's close enough to gone; I seem to be sort of in-between. I suppose that's why I could come here like this.*

Is there something you want me to do?

For Artus. He's pulled in a bunch of shit; something the Ostrak Procedures didn't reach. It's gotten to him. We've had a couple of big bouts with the T'swa, and he's lost quite a lot of us. No fault of his; he's done a helluva job. You might want to help him out.

He was gone as abruptly as he'd arrived. Briefly Lotta adjusted her focus and perception, then projected. . . .

Romlar awoke as he would have if someone had come into the tent. And found that someone had: Lotta. When she'd come to him before in the spirit, she'd always seemed just that, a spirit. This evening she looked physical, except for the aura. Ordinarily he had to make a certain effort to see auras, but not hers this evening. She stood clad in a glow of auroral blue that sheathed her thinly below the chest, expanding upward, flaring around and above her head like the flame of a bunsen burner. It seemed to him it would have been visible to anyone.

But it illuminated nothing. He could see no sign of it on the tent walls or ceiling.

Then it struck him. "I'm dreaming." He said it aloud. "No, I'm here all right."

"I didn't know you could travel—like that. In a form that looks physical. I'll bet anyone could see you."

"I didn't know I could, either. Eldren told me you could use some help."

Eldren. Another gone; this one a close friend. Closer in his way than Fritek. "He's lost his body then," he said.

"No, it's still alive; it might still make it."

Tears threatened, growing out of some undefined emotion. Relief perhaps. He grinned through them. "You don't have any clothes on."

She laughed. He wondered if anyone but himself could hear it. "So I don't," she said. "But in this form there's only one way I can help. Regardless of appearances. Shall I?"

"Let's do it."

"Are you comfortable?"

"Not bad, considering I took two grenade fragments today."

"Warm enough? It's cold in here."

That surprised him. How could she tell? "Yep."

"Need to go to the bathroom?"

"The latrine, you mean. Nope. I was there just before I came to bed."

"Good. I've sat in on some of your dreams, so I've got a starting place. All right to begin?"

"Go ahead." He closed his eyes. For him, sometimes the Ostrak Procedures worked better that way.

"Okay, here goes. Is *wasting* a good subject to start with?"

He chuckled ruefully. "A very good subject."

His aura had verified it for her before he'd answered; it had thinned and darkened. "Good," she said, and her mind settled into a psychic posture from which she could monitor and support him. "So say the words 'to waste,' and keep saying them until something happens."

This was a procedure he hadn't done before, something new perhaps. "To waste. To waste . . ." He said it several times, then got an image of the open fen he'd used to break the T'swa pursuit, and the machine gun platoons fighting their bloody rear-guard action. She watched his recall with him, like a holograph, heard the gunfire, even felt the iron

cold. "There was no other way," he said, as if he knew that
she watched too. "It was that or take a lot more casualties.
I had to sacrifice . . ."

He stopped. Cold waves of gooseflesh washed over him,
intense, electrifying, and he abandoned "to waste." "To saci-
fice," he murmured, "to sacrifice," repeating this until he
got another image: Tain Faronya aboard an imperial warship, being questioned. A gate stood before her, the teleport
the imperials had captured without knowing what they had.
An officer—he felt like an intelligence officer—held an
instrument in his hand. He pointed it at Tain, and though
there was no sound with these images, Romlar saw her
scream with pain, recoiling. *Where did this come from?* he
wondered. *How can I be seeing this? I wasn't there!*

The image dissolved. "Keep saying it," Lotta told him.

"To sacrifice. To sacrifice . . ." It returned. This time he
heard Tain scream, and heard the officer speak to her. The
words, in Standard, seemed not to come from his lips but
from a computer vocator. They exchanged words, while
seven years later in his tent on Maragor, Romlar watched
and listened. Then some uniformed men tried to push her
into the teleport gate. Abruptly she wrenched loose from
them, lunged forward into it—*and went berserk, bounding
from the platform with a wild and guttural howl, crashed
blindly into one of the uniformed men, knocking him sprawling, then charged into a table with men sitting behind it,
rebounded, still howling, staggered, lunged, and fell over a
chair onto the deck, where she lay thrashing and kicking.*

The image snapped out of existence, leaving Romlar staring at nothing, his hair on end. After a long moment he
spoke: "Where did that come from?" he breathed.

"You're doing fine," Lotta answered. "Keep saying it."

"To sacrifice. To sacrifice." He paused. "You know what?"

"Tell me."

"She did sacrifice herself. For us. For all of us: the regiment, the worlds as she knew them. . . . She assumed it
would kill her to enter the gate, or at least leave her mindless. And if she was dead or mindless, she couldn't tell them
what it was."

His aura had cleared, but it hadn't flared. "Right," Lotta
said. "Keep saying it."

"Sacrifice. Huh!" He saw himself talking with Lotta, not a three-dimensional image of her, here in his tent in Smolen, but the flesh-and-blood Lotta in his command tent in the Terfreyan jungle. And repeated the words he'd spoken then: "I wouldn't bring in more gunships; I don't want air superiority that way. I want to drive them off with inferior numbers and inferior weapons. That will stamp us with the mystique we want them to remember the Confederation by."

He shook his head. Lotta had watched the images with him, he knew, images colored by the events that grew out of that decision. The events and the casualties. Half of all the casualties he'd had on Terfreya.

But it didn't affect him now; he looked at it as if it was just what it was: a decision intended to produce the best result with the least cost over the long run.

"Keep saying it," Lotta ordered.

"To sacrifice. To sacrifice. To sac—un-n-nh!" He saw people, men and women, on the bridge of a spaceship. And shuddered. Lotta saw his aura flare, then collapse, and the image dissolved. He continued without prompting: "To sacrifice. To sacrifice . . ." Gradually, as he repeated, the image formed again, unmoving, like a still photo or a freeze-frame. It was a large bridge, ringed with instrument and monitor stations, while above them screens showed space, ships, a world—Home World!

"To sacrifice. To sacrifice." The image took life, became a sequence. There was no sound. One of the people on the bridge, tall, aristocratic-looking, was clearly the commander, and it seemed to Romlar that he'd been that man. It also seemed to him he'd seen these people, this bridge, in a dream. Perhaps only in a dream? Was that all it was? Another sat facing him, sat on an AG chair, wrapped archaically in a blanket, looking as if in the final stage of some degenerative disease. The man's gaze was powerful though, powerful, gentle—and compelling. He was pointing at the monitor that showed Home World, and his lips parted. Though Romlar didn't hear the words, he knew them. "Destroy it!"

He saw himself, the figure that seemed to be him, step to a console and touch a series of keys. In the present, in his winterized tent near Burnt Woods, his eyes were squinched tight. His aura had contracted almost to nothing, as if it were his skin that glowed murky yellow. Then the picture he watched flew apart in a blinding flash, and chills rushed through him more intense than any orgasm. His aura flared and contracted in a sort of irregular pulsing, as the chills continued. He writhed on his cot as if trying to escape.

This went on for nearly twenty seconds, then faded. His aura swelled, clear gold again with flecks and sparkles of red. His eyes opened and he laughed. "Speaking of sacrifice," he said, "I had a crew of nearly seven thousand on *Retributor*, and blew them all up. With the emperor and myself. He'd ordered me to destroy our Home World." He shook his head ruefully. "No wonder the ancients developed the Sacrament. There were *weapons* in those days."

"Okay. How do you feel about sacrifice?"

He shook his head again, but the grin was still there. "We'll come up with something better before we're done. Better than sacrifice, better than sacraments. We'll call it sanity."

"Okay," she said. "You're looking good. Are we done?"

There was no hesitancy in his answer. "Yep." His aura glowed pure and steady.

"Good. We're done then."

"And you're leaving now?"

"I need to. This isn't easy for me."

"I love you. I haven't told you that for a long time."

"I'll remember. I love you too."

She faded then and disappeared, to find herself back in the *ghao* with moonlight shining through the window. *We didn't get it all*, she told herself. *We may have taken care of "wasting" and "sacrifice," but there's something still there that we haven't touched. He's not ready yet, and I'm not either.*

When she'd rested—moved around and swung her arms a bit—she tranced, then reached to Eldren Esenrok. The ravaged body had stabilized; Eldren had returned to it, and slept. It seemed to her he'd live, but she stayed with him awhile, helping him communicate with his stump, with its nerves and blood vessels. They could look into other matters later.

Seventy-four

In Linnasteth, spring was far more advanced. A fragrance wafted in through open balcony doors, the sweetness of *Syringa vulgaris*, the lilac, which had accompanied man to many worlds in his ancient expansions.

Engwar didn't notice. His round face turned grim as he listened to his justice minister. "The entire Reform Party is in outcry at Fingas's arrest," the minister was saying. He held out a copy of that day's *Bulletin*. "They insist that the offending issue does not constitute sedition, and—"

"Yes?"

"Several of the Conservative Party have publicly agreed with them."

"*What?! Who . . . ?*" Engwar stopped, got hold of himself. "Never mind," he said petulantly. "I can name them without help." He paused to blow gustily through his narrow, full-lipped mouth. "We're at war! I'll give them something to chew on! Arrest his editor as an accessory, and then . . ." He scowled at the worried-looking minister. "Then find some further crimes he's guilty of. Create evidence if necessary. We will have a great trial before the nation, and I want . . ."

His commset buzzed, and he slapped its flashing button angrily. "Yes?"

"Your Majesty, General Undsvin is calling. He . . ."

"I told you I did not want to be interrupted!"

"That's what I told the general, Your Majesty. He said you'd want to hear this. He said it's what you've been waiting to hear."

For just a moment, Engwar's face went slack, then, "Connect us!" he said, rapped the privacy switch and picked up the receiver. "What is it, Undsvin?"

He listened open-mouthed. "Really? Really? Great Amberus, Undsvin, this is marvelous! Truly marvelous! Where are they now? . . . This afternoon! Look, sweet cousin, I want to be there. I'll fly up today. . . . Yes, I insist. Have suitable quarters prepared. I'll have you called later with anything further you need to know."

He turned, a man transformed, beaming excitedly at his justice minister. "The T'swa have made a raid—*and captured Lanks!* Isn't that marvelous? He'll arrive in Rumaros later today! I told people! I said the T'swa were worth the money! Now they have proven me right!

"Do not arrest Fingas's editor. I may even release Fingas himself when I get back, as an act of magnanimity and celebration.

"Go now! Go! I have things to see to!"

Seventy-five

Undsvin gnawed his lip and paced; he wasn't thrilled with
Engwar's resolve to come to Rumaros. For several reasons.
Most compelling, there was an element of risk. Rumaros
was an occupied town, still with more than twelve thousand
Smoleni, some of them undoubtedly having weapons hidden
away. But the risk was something he could take steps to
counter. More unpleasant and far more certain was
Engwar's anger when he learned that Lanks had been taken
five days earlier and he hadn't been informed.

Of course, Undsvin hadn't been informed himself till this
morning. Ko-Dan had explained calmly that he hadn't
reported it because he'd guaranteed the hostages' personal
well-being—it had been requisite to the arrest. And because
the Crown would wish to take Lanks from him if it knew,
and Lanks was his safe conduct through Smoleni territory.
Also, his regiment had needed to cover most of the distance
on foot—the Smoleni lacked adequate motor transport.

Ko-Dan had finally called when he'd reached the Rumar
River Highway. The colonel had gotten Smoleni approval to
arrange convoyed truck transport from Rumaros, to pick up
his regiment there.

More troublesome was Ko-Dan's insistence on sharing custody. Clearly he was serious about the hostages' well-being. *Well-being.* A term subject to interpretation.

At least Engwar's displeasure would be directed at Ko-Dan, though he'd be impossible to get along with afterward. He'd be angrier at Ko-Dan's guarantee to Lanks than at the delay, for there was no doubt that Engwar would want to humiliate the president publicly, while causing him pain and anguish privately. He'd probably be rehearsing his plans for that on the flight north.

The general sighed, a sound unusual from him. He'd taken steps to ensure—or nearly so—that the capture would not be leaked by his people, and hopefully the prisoners' arrival would go unnoticed. That should avoid public demonstrations. He'd taken comparable precautions to keep Engwar's arrival secret. The safest place to put him up would be in his personal apartment, on the upper floor of the building, which was well fenced and well guarded. But suppose word did leak? Certainly Smoleni intelligence was active in Rumaros. Suppose one of them had a mortar secreted in the city, or several of them!

Undsvin had done all he could. Now only the waiting remained. Lanks and his people, with their T'swa escort, had been landed on the roof, and taken by lift to cells in the cellar. Ko-Dan's arrogance had been an aggravation. He'd gone down with the prisoners, examined their quarters, and insisted they be made more comfortable. At least he hadn't objected to the heavy guard there, but he'd left men of his own to supervise, to see to the prisoners' "well-being."

Engwar, of course, would never consent to be landed on the roof. He'd be landed on the lawn, and received as properly as secrecy allowed. The staff had been told that Lord Cheldring was arriving to inspect headquarters, a believable lie. Cheldring, uncle to both of them, had been more than simply regent during Engwar's childhood. He'd also been Engwar's guardian, and still served him occasionally in special capacities.

Undsvin had considered posting snipers on the roof, but decided against it. It would be noticed, would draw attention and curiosity, and so far it wasn't necessary. If evidence of a leak developed, he could order it then.

The general glanced at the clock. Engwar had said he'd arrive at 2000 hours, and Undsvin had thought that, as eager as his cousin had sounded, he'd be on time for once. But it was 2007 now. He fidgeted, then took a report from his pending basket and tried unsuccessfully to read. Which irritated him: He was one of the senior nobles of Komars and the ranking general of the army, yet here he was dithering like a debutante.

At 2051, the general's command radio broke the suspense. It came on the air with: "Commander in Chief Komarsi Military Forces in Smolen, this is His Majesty's Floater. This is His Majesty's floater. His Majesty will land in your courtyard at approximately 2100 hours."

Undsvin put hand to forehead in dismay. After his efforts for secrecy! Now he could only hope that no one was monitoring the command frequency. He sat like a stone for several minutes, then stood, turning to his two guards. "Lord Cheldring will soon be landing. We'll wait outside for him."

The king was coming here! Into his hands! It seemed to Coyn Carrmak that his face had surely betrayed him, had anyone been looking. But Innelmo, sharing the shift with him, showed his surprise at least as much. And clearly Undsvin had been unnerved by the call; as if he really had expected Cheldring, rather than the king. Carrmak took a slow breath, moderately deep, and then another, calming mind and body, counting the seconds of inhalation, the seconds of holding, the seconds of letting it back out.

He wondered if the king's arrival had anything to do with Burgold's behavior earlier. Ordinarily Burgold had at least something to say about his shift. Today he'd said nothing, and Carrmak had wondered then if something confidential had happened.

Undsvin led them outside. It was dusk and getting chilly, and they were dressed for indoors. Carrmak didn't crane his head around watching for the aircraft; that wouldn't have been acceptable to the general. He did glance around the courtyard though. Sixty yards away, the "open" end had been closed by a privacy wall about ten feet tall, with a bored guard at its gate, a submachine gun slung over a shoulder. Beyond that, the only people he could see were Undsvin, Innelmo, and himself. But Engwar would surely travel with bodyguards.

Undsvin was looking upward, waiting. More minutes passed. His head began to move, as if he watched something coming from south to north. Carrmak waited stolidly. He judged the craft's approach by watching Undsvin, until it was in his own range of vision. It wasn't as large as he'd expected; there couldn't be a lot of people on board. Given the size of the magazine in his pistol, even half a dozen would stretch things if they were armed, because he'd have to deal with Undsvin and Innelmo as well. He'd see.

It landed some eighty feet away. After a few seconds, steps extruded, and the door slid aside. A large man in uniform appeared, a bodyguard perhaps, came down the several steps and stationed himself at their foot. Then a boy emerged, in cape and tapered trousers, to stand at the other side. The king came next; Carrmak knew him at once by the richness of his cape, evident even in evening light. He was followed by another burly man in uniform—carrying baggage in each hand!

They were all on the ground, their attention on the king, whose attention was on Undsvin. One more man appeared in the door then and started down—the pilot, Carrmak decided. Then the king and Undsvin walked toward each other, Innelmo and himself a stride behind the general.

"Your Majesty!" Undsvin said.

"Dear cousin!" said the king.

Carrmak had his pistol in his hand with no one aware of it. His first shot struck Undsvin in the back, through the heart; the second took Engwar through the breastbone. The third struck Innelmo through the chest as he began to turn. Two more felled the bodyguards, one of whom got off a shot of his own, hitting Carrmak in the guts as he dropped into a squat, striking only soft tissue but burning like a red-hot poker. The pilot had started back up the steps. Carrmak shot him too; with a cry, the man fell backward. Carrmak was running then, jumping bodies. He dashed up the stairs and inside before the guard at the gate had gathered his wits enough to shoot.

He moved quickly to the pilot's compartment and sat down. Except for customized add-ons, he found it standard—almost everything made in the Confederation was standardized. Flying it was simple, and he'd been given basic flight training in their last year on Terfreya. The gate guard was shooting now; Carrmak heard slugs strike the floater. He touched the switch which closed the door and retracted the steps, then raised the floater vertically and abruptly to sixty feet and swept away across the roof in a course that curved northward. He was beginning to feel his wound.

His hair began to bristle, and he turned. Hardly five feet behind him was the boy in the cape, pointing a submachine gun at him. Carrmak heard the firing mechanism click, and saw the look of shock on the boy's face; there had been no round in the chamber. By that time Carrmak was half out of his seat, his pistol drawn. In the split second available, he decided not to kill him. His shot struck the thin shoulder, knocking the boy backward into the cabin, the submachine gun clattering onto the deck.

Carrmak gave his attention to the floater again, setting a course in a northerly direction and locking the controls. He took a moment to partition off the pain, then turned on the ceiling lights and stepped into the passengers' cabin. On the wall separating the two compartments were a medical chest, a fire extinguisher, and a rack that hung open, no doubt where the submachine gun had come from. Carrmak picked through the medical chest, then knelt to tend the boy he'd shot. Young, about thirteen he thought. And conscious, though dazed. As he bandaged, the boy jerked.

"Hold still," Carrmak said. The boy's eyes were large, and vague with shock. The pain hadn't really hit him yet.

"You—shot the king!" he said.

"Right. What's your name?"

"Jemi Kelisson Arkenvess." With that he seemed to gather his senses somewhat. "You're a traitor! A regicide!"

"I'm a regicide, right enough, but I ayn't no traitor. I'm not Komarsi."

"What are you then?"

Carrmak realized he'd been using the freedman dialect, and switched to Iryalan. "I'm a mercenary. Like the ones who blew up the munitions ship at Linnasteth last summer, and did other things like that." He finished his bandaging and began to tape the boy's wrists together. "What are you? A squire?"

The boy ignored the question. "You'll never get away with it!" His voice was weak but fierce. "They'll hunt you down and shoot you like a dog!"

"Let's hope not." As he lifted Jemi Arkenvess to put him on a seat, the pain broke through the partition he'd set up between his mind and his ravaged gut and damaged back. His knees gave with it, and he half dropped the boy onto the seat. For a moment, everything went black, and he kept from falling by clutching the back of the seat. When the pang had passed, he taped the boy in so he couldn't fall out or get out. Then he turned toward the pilot's compartment, intending to see what sort of navigational aids he had. "It won't do you any good, because we've caught the Smoleni president! We've got him locked in a cell in Rumaros! And Lord Cheldring will be regent again."

Lanks a prisoner? Could that have been what Burgold wasn't talking about? Could it be why Engwar had flown there? He paused, composed himself against the pain, then began to pump the boy for more. "Do you expect me to believe a lie like that?" he asked.

"He is! His Majesty flew to Rumaros to see him!"

"Nah! They wouldn't keep something like that secret. They'd tell the whole planet."

Carrmak's ploy had played out: The boy's mouth pinched shut, angry that this murderer didn't believe him. It occurred to Carrmak that, if it was true, maybe the Komarsi *would* keep it secret for a while. Who knew what considerations might apply from their point of view.

He returned to the pilot's seat and called a map onto the screen. It provided little detail north of Rumaros, but it did show villages. One of them was Burnt Woods. It also showed his present flight course, with his existing location. He read the bearing he needed, and reset his flight controls.

Pain brought beads of sweat to his upper lip. Bent over by it, he went into the cabin again and explored the medical kit further. The only powerful painkiller there was also sleep inducing. The tablets were scored. Judging that Jemi

Arkenvess weighed a little more than a hundred pounds, he broke one in two and gave a half to the boy, with a cup of water. Jemi could afford to sleep.

He watched while Jemi washed down the pill, then said, "The reason I know you're lying is that President Lanks is way up north, where your people could never get their hands on him."

"That shows how much you know! The T'swa caught him! They went up there through the wilderness and caught him in his palace—his house! I heard His Majesty tell Lord Cheldring!"

"Really! Hmm! Maybe I believe you after all."

The T'swa! He wasn't sure if there was a precedent for their capturing a head of state, outside of retribution for treachery. And that couldn't apply here; Lanks wasn't the contractor.

The T'swa looked for ways to cut wars short, though, and capturing Lanks would no doubt shorten this one. Just as shooting Engwar . . . Another pang hit Carrmak's guts, and he turned away so Jemi Arkenvess wouldn't see. When it passed, the level of pain left behind was worse than before.

The boy was already sleeping, he realized, and Carrmak wobbled back to the pilot's seat. He'd see what they knew in Burnt Woods. Another pang struck, and he ground his teeth against it. This one left him less than clearheaded. He hoped he wouldn't vomit; that would be bad. *Maybe the president's in his office right now*, he told himself, *or in bed. Maybe the kid's lying after all. Maybe*— He grimaced, then managed a chuckle. *Maybe I'll pass out before I get to Burnt Woods.*

Seventy-six

The Komarsi corporal was heavy-bodied from overeating and little physical activity. But he was also conspicuously strong—a freedman who'd followed the harvests for several years. Just now he was peering through the bars at Weldi Faronya, and smirking. "Yer a pretty thing, ya knaw?"

She darkened. Kelmer was on his feet at once; the corporal pretended not to notice. "I likes them long legs, too. But what I like best is that fuzzy thing up atween 'em."

Kelmer strode to the bars and gripped them, face tight with anger. "I'll report this," he said.

The corporal snorted. "You? Yer a prisoner! Report all ya likes." He looked at Weldi again. "You knaw what's gawnta happen to ya when His Majesty's done with ya? He's gonna give ya to us to play with. And I'll be first, 'cause I got the biggest one in the army."

He guffawed then, hooted with laughter, as Kelmer began to shout curses at him. When his prisoner had run out of curses, the smirking corporal opened his mouth to taunt him some more. The words never got out, because Kelmer spat in his face. The Komarsi stepped back, wiped the spit from his cheek and looked unbelievingly at it on his fingers.

With a sudden oath he reached to his holster, ripped open the flap and drew his sidearm.

He'd been unaware of the T'swa sergeant coming up behind him. He'd entered the cell area in time to see and hear the entire performance. As the corporal's weapon cleared its holster, hands gripped his wrist from behind and jerked across and up. He squealed, almost screamed. The pressure threatened to rupture the ligaments in his shoulder, and the pistol clopped onto the concrete floor. Then a hand gripped the corporal's collar from behind. Grimacing and white-faced with pain, he was jerked around and frog-marched out into the corridor. Sergeant Ka-Mao eased the pressure only a little on their way to the lieutenant's office.

The Komarsi lieutenant was tall and rawboned, a surly, lantern-jawed man with a nose broken in a tavern fight years earlier. A yeoman farmer's son, he was proud of his commission and jealous of his authority. He'd been a shift officer at the military prison in Rumaros, and the provost marshal had commended him in inspection reports. That had resulted in a transfer to Command Headquarters as a shift officer in the headquarters security company.

General Undsvin had had the cells installed for civilian prisoners, but they'd been empty for more than a dek. When he'd learned of the Smoleni government's capture, he'd thought of them at once, and the provost marshal had put the lieutenant in charge. From the beginning, the man had resented the presence of T'swa on his turf, outsiders with loosely defined but seemingly absolute oversight authority. He considered it a deep personal insult. It would have been bad enough if the T'swa interlopers, one on each shift, had been commissioned officers. But these were enlisted men, and rejects at that, men to some degree disabled, unfit for combat.

When Ka-Mao shoved the corporal in through the open door, the lieutenant stood so abruptly, he knocked his chair over. *"What in Yomal's name is going on here?"*

The T'swi released the man, thrusting him sharply aside, and recited calmly what had happened. When he was done, the lieutenant stepped around his desk and slapped the corporal's face, backhand and forehand, the sounds like shots.

Then he turned to the T'swi, scowling. "You can go now, Sergeant. I'll take care of this piece of shit."

"Thank you, Lieutenant." The T'swa veteran was completely matter of fact. "This man was nearly the cause of at least three deaths. Including yours as the officer in charge. He must not be returned to the cell area." Ka-Mao saluted then and left, closing the door behind himself. The lieutenant stared after him, then turned and slugged the corporal in the mouth, knocking him down, splitting his lips. "Yomal *damn* your ass!" he snarled. "If this ends up on my personnel record, you stupid horse turd, you'll wish you were never born." Without sitting, he rapped keys on his commset, calling the provost marshal's office, and arranged to have the corporal taken away under guard.

Ka-Mao, of course, included the affair in his shift report, a copy of which went to the general's office. Since Undsvin's murder, headquarters had been in near chaos, and Colonel Viskon, as acting commander, was overloaded with demands from Linnasteth. When he'd worked his way to Ka-Mao's report, the next day, he swore vividly. He too phoned the provost marshal's office. Afterward he called the lieutenant, questioning him, then told him to expect his replacement in an hour. He'd hardly hung up when Colonel Ko-Dan radioed him.

"When will the security apartment be ready for the president and his family?" Ko-Dan asked.

Viskon hadn't checked since ordering it. "Tomorrow," he said. *And it damned well would be; he'd check out progress as soon as this call was finished; skin some asses if need be.*

"In the interim, what privacy has been provided for the president's daughter?"

"A portable screen has been provided for the sanitary facility in each of the occupied cells, as you requested. Required."

"You have, of course, seen the report of yesterday's extreme insults to her, and of the threat to her husband's life."

"Yes. The offending corporal has been replaced. He's being held in the stockade pending a court martial. The officer in charge of the prisoners has also been replaced."

"Thank you. I have confidence in both your intentions and your competence, Colonel Viskon, but it was necessary that I call to ensure that the situation has been fully corrected. That was a very close thing for Komars. Please inform me when the president and his family have been moved into their apartment."

After the call from Colonel Viskon, the security lieutenant was so angry, he didn't trust himself to leave his office for a few minutes. Basically he didn't blame the corporal for what he considered his humiliation, nor even the T'swi. It was that aristocratic *pig* he blamed. When he'd regained some composure, he went to the cell area. Ka-Mao wasn't there. Walking to the bars of the Faronyas's cell, the Komarsi glared in at Weldi. He said nothing, but as she stared back white-faced, he made a movement with his right fist as if disemboweling her with a short sword. Then he turned and stalked away.

Breath frozen in their chests, Weldi and Kelmer watched him leave, not knowing what had caused such hatred. This man seemed to them more dangerous than the corporal, and they were left with their imaginings. Weldi's were sick with fear. Kelmer's were a mixture of fear and violent intentions.

Seventy-seven

General Lord Heklos Erlinsson Brant was a small man with a spine like a steel rod, a learned posture reflecting neither rigidity nor any special toughness. In fact, he was a pliant man, within limits, bending readily with shifts in policy and power, always heedful of politics. The youngest general in the Army of Komars, he'd been commander of the Infantry Training Center at Long Ridge until, øn the second day after Undsvin's death, the new regent had appointed him Commander of the Army of Occupation, and he'd been flown at once to Rumaros.

Heklos was, in fact, a competent organizer and administrator. But his appointment had resulted at least as much from his pliancy, and from the fact that Lord Regent Cheldring Tarsteng Brant was his paternal uncle. Cheldring had been regent for and guardian of Crown Prince Engwar while Engwar was growing up, and at Engwar's death had declared himself regent again. The Komarsi Council of Ministers and the Assembly of Lords had ratified Cheldring's self-appointment by a slim majority. Under the circumstances, his supporters insisted, a strong man was needed quickly on the throne, and Engwar had died without acknowledged offspring.

Despite Hecklos's new appointment, which was also a promotion, he was not fond of Cheldring. He remembered his uncle from childhood as generally disapproving and sometimes caustic. So in this the second week on his new post, he was less than happy at Cheldring's unexpected arrival in Rumaros. Cheldring had left his bodyguard in reception, outside Heklos's office, and invited/ordered Heklos to send his own guard out. Then they sat alone together over joma, and talked.

"You are wondering why I came," Cheldring said.

"Indeed, Uncle."

"I have come to end the war." He dipped his upper lip in his cup and frowned, not at the joma but at his thoughts. "The kingdom is in serious trouble. It was in trouble before, and the malcontents are taking advantage of Engwar's death. The Assembly of Lords is being notably uncooperative, and as regent I lack the leverage to coerce them. They approved me, they said, because they needed a strong man to lead the kingdom. But now they do not want me strong. The merchants and many of the industrialists rail because of inflation and shortages. The reformers try to destroy the country. The freedmen are more rebellious than ever, as if a fire had been built under them and they were stirred with a spoon. The serfs are insubordinate. And I, as mere regent, cannot declare martial law without approval by the Assembly.

"Meanwhile the capture of the Smoleni government has not had the result one might have expected. They have appointed an acting president, and he a cabinet of shit-boot farmers. Who have stated their determination to continue—*and win!*—the war. Empty bravado, of course. But by humiliating that bungler Undsvin, and through him the army, they have gained a certain credibility, in Linnasteth as well as abroad."

He scowled down at his bony hands, studying them as if to learn something. "So I will discuss possible peace terms with President Lanks. This will tend to undermine the authority of their acting president, and a man in prison is likely to be more reasonable than one who is not."

Heklos hadn't looked forward to directing the war. To cover his relief, he asked, "What sort of terms do you have in mind?"

Cheldring grunted. "I will offer him independence and a treaty of peace, with a new boundary along the Welvarn Morain. That will give us most of the Leas—the more fertile eighty percent of them."

"What if he declines?"

"I will point out the hopelessness of the Smoleni supply situation. And tell him we have an agreement with the Lodge of Kootosh-Lan for another regiment of T'swa; he'll have no reason to doubt me. And if it comes to it, I'll offer to return the coastal strip to him.

"In either case, it will leave them in a weak and irreparable economic situation: They'll be dependent on imports for most of their food, which will badly tilt their export-import balance. And along with their lack of resources for industrial development, they'll discover the taste of real poverty." He sat back, looking self-satisfied, pleased with the images. "They will develop severe internal stresses, and before long, internal strife. I will not be surprised to become their master in economic fact, if not in name."

Heklos poked at the idea with his mind and wondered. He could imagine the obstinate Smoleni clearing more plowland in the north and feeding themselves despite the loss of the Leas.

Cheldring wasn't troubled with such thoughts. He dovetailed arthritic knuckles over his brocade vest. "Once the peace is signed, I will use the Leas to heal our internal wounds. I'll offer small yeoman holdings there to serfs who've earned sergeancies, and small estates to yeomen's sons who've become officers. That will end the demonstrations and quiet the reformers. The rest of the Leas I will claim for the Crown, then offer it as land grants to the younger sons of Conservative nobles, estates large enough to qualify them as Assembly candidates. That will strengthen my position substantially."

And allow you to claim the Crown as well as the Throne, Heklos thought wryly. *Shrewdly planned, Uncle!*

"I will meet with Lanks after dinner," Cheldring went on,

"and feel him out. What sort of conditions do you keep him in?"

"He shares a small—apartment, you might call it—with his daughter and son-in-law; three rooms on the ground floor in back. His government occupies cells in the basement. The T'swa commander insisted that he have better quarters than our cells provide, so I had bars installed. . . ."

Cheldring interrupted. *"The T'swa insisted?!"*

"One of the conditions of his surrender was that he be treated respectfully."

The regent's grimace gradually relaxed to a thoughtful frown. He'd been briefed on the T'swa guarantee, and it seemed to him they'd carried it too far, but still . . . He grunted. "Perhaps it's just as well, given my purpose for being here. Anything else about their living conditions?"

"A basement room has been provided with mats on the floor, and dumbbells. They're taken there once a day for exercise and recreation, which also allows those in different quarters to see each other for an hour. This was at the insistence of the T'swa commander, who's appointed sergeants to supervise the prisoners' treatment. As a matter of fact, he's had two guards removed for showing disrespect to the prisoners."

"Hmh! Well. Let us eat. I will meet with Lanks afterward."

Accompanied by a private, a Komarsi lieutenant strode down the corridor, a tall, rawboned security officer with a lantern jaw and a scowl. On their way, they'd been joined by a thick-shouldered T'swi with a limp. The door they stopped at was different than those they'd passed; it had a small, unglazed window with bars, and instead of a knob, a handle and a heavy deadbolt. The lieutenant looked sourly at the T'swi, then knocked firmly on the door and called through the barred window. "This is Lieutenant Walls! I'm comin' in!" With key in one hand and pistol in the other, he unlocked the door and pushed it open. The private too held a gun in his hand. The T'swi stood relaxed, his pistol in his holster but with the flap loose.

There were three prisoners in the room. All had been reading. Without rising from his chair, Heber Lanks put his book aside. He recognized the man. "What may I do for you, Lieutenant?" His tone was correct but cold.

"General Heklos has sent me to take you to his office."

"Indeed? To what purpose?"

The lieutenant bit back what he wanted to say. "Lord Regent Cheldring will speak with you there."

"Ah! That is kind of the lord regent. But I am President of the Republic of Smolen, and this is my country. If the Lord Regent wishes to speak with me, let him come here to my home. I'll be happy to give him an audience."

The lieutenant turned away red-faced and angry, and gestured the private out ahead of him. His pistol still in his hand, he turned to the prisoners. His eyes swept them with a look of cold hate, ending on Weldi. Then he followed the private out. The T'swi left last. He'd have stepped in front of the lieutenant, had it come down to it, and drawn his own gun, but the Komarsi, he knew, hadn't intended to shoot.

When the door closed behind the T'swi, Weldi began to shake violently. Kelmer knelt by her and wrapped her in his arms. "I'm all right," she whispered. "I'm all right. I'm all right." But still she shook.

Her father had left the room, feeling helpless. It seemed to him that Kelmer was the one to comfort her, and that for him to stay might constrain them.

Kelmer held her, stroking her shoulders, her neck. "He can't do anything to you," he murmured. "He can't do anything to you."

After a minute the shaking stopped, but he continued to hold her.

The two Komarsi walked quickly to Heklos's office, one floor up in a corner suite; the T'swi had stopped at his own desk, in what had been a room service alcove when the building had been a hotel. At Heklos's office, the lieutenant, stony-faced, told the general what Lanks had said, being careful not to look at the lord regent.

Heklos, on the other hand, had little choice; he had to look. "What is your wish, Lord Regent?"

Cheldring's wide mouth was a slash. "I will go to this

insolent Smoleni." He got up. "Stay, nephew," he added. "Lieutenant, take me to him."

The lieutenant retraced his steps, the lord regent following, his bodyguard and the private two strides behind. As they came to the alcove, the T'swa sergeant got up and followed them. This time the lieutenant did not call through the barred window. He simply unlocked the door, pushed it open and walked in, pistol in hand. Cheldring followed, and the lieutenant stepped aside. The bodyguard and the private entered behind them, followed by the T'swi.

Heber Lanks got up from his chair. "Lord Regent," he said, and stepping forward, shook Cheldring's hand with cold formality. "Welcome to my temporary headquarters." He stepped back and gestured. "My daughter, Weldi." She stood up, still pale, her eyes dark smudges. "And her husband, Mr. Kelmer Faronya."

Kelmer's face was without expression. He stepped forward as if to shake hands. Suddenly he ducked, and pistoned his left leg sideways with all the power of a strongly muscled thigh. The lieutenant was standing obliquely sideways to him, and Kelmer's heel took the man explosively beneath the ribs, smashing the liver, bursting the peritoneum, rupturing the intestine. Air whooped hoarsely from the lieutenant's lungs as he flew sideways, flaccid. For Kelmer, time slowed abruptly as he watched the pistol fly from nerveless fingers. He dove for it, heard the roar of a gunshot but felt no bullet. His fingers closed on the pistol's grip before it struck the floor, and he rolled onto his side, firing upward, once at Cheldring, then at the bodyguard whose shot had missed him, then at the private, who'd broken and was turning to run.

Cheldring was dying when he hit the floor, his aorta torn. Kelmer almost missed the bodyguard, who'd been moving; the bullet smashed through the right elbow, and the man's gun thudded to the floor as he howled. The private he lungshot, sending him sprawling. Finally he shot the lieutenant, just to be sure he was dead.

The young journalist lay panting. The entire action had taken about three seconds. The T'swa sergeant stood with eyebrows raised, his pistol in one large black hand.

Kelmer became aware of shouts from down the corridor. Getting to his hands and knees, he vomited.

Seventy-eight

Heklos had taken over the situation with unhappy efficiency, first safeguarding the prisoners. Colonel Ko-Dan had made clear to him at the beginning what T'swa protection meant. Now Ko-Dan's sergeant also pointed out that the two nations being at war, the lord regent was not a murder victim but a war casualty. Heklos gave orders to suspend exercise privileges, and the T'swi did not object. The two off-duty T'swa guards now posted themselves on either side of the president's door, with submachine guns.

Ka-Mao reported the sequence of events to Ko-Dan. Heklos, he said, seemed intent on containing the situation, to avoid confrontation with the T'swa.

Heklos was concerned that some elements of the army would try to exact revenge. He'd notified Linnasteth of Cheldring's death, and what had led to it. While he waited for instructions, which he was prepared to ignore if necessary, two T'swa companies double-timed into Rumaros and took positions around the Komarsi headquarters.

In Linnasteth, Cheldring's death leaked at once, and before nightfall, embassy row had spread the news across Maragor, including to Burnt Woods via Krentorf. From

336

Azure Bay, Pitter Movrik's agent sent off an official summary of events, so far as he knew them, to Splenn, via pod. With a copy, of course, to the Confederation Ministry, also located in Azure Bay. Then, unofficially, he went into his supply room, stepped through the gate, and reported personally to Pitter Movrik, who did much the same thing to inform Lord Kristal on Iryala.

Over the next ten days, a lot happened. Engwar's queen claimed the throne. The Council of Ministers rejected her out of hand. Lord Nufkarm proposed that Fingas Marnsson Kelromak be crowned. Fingas was descended on his mother's side from King Ferant II Blundell, who'd been deposed a century and a half earlier, giving rise to the Tarsteng Dynasty. The relationship was thought close enough to satisfy the less extreme formalists. While the matter was under debate, the sedition charges against Fingas were thrown out as invalid; Cheldring had already released him from prison. A rumor spread that if Fingas was crowned, a convention would be called to write a constitution. Meanwhile, large and surprisingly orderly freedman demonstrations were taking place in Linnasteth and other major towns. (Carrmak felt reasonably sure who'd provided the leadership.) It was also reported that some units in the Army of Occupation were refusing to drill.

The Council of Ministers, deeply worried by all this and seeking to relieve its intensity at least, appointed Lord Nufkarm regent. He in turn ordered a schedule drawn up for the return of army units to Komars, a de factor abandonment of the war. Smoleni farmer refugees had already begun to move back into the districts abandoned by the Komarsi the summer before, to begin their spring plowing.

The Archipelago requested permission to ship relief supplies up the Rumar when the river was free of ice—the lower reaches were already—and Nufkarm approved it. Through the Krentorfi government, he then proposed a truce, with representatives of the two warring nations to meet in Faersteth and discuss armistice terms. Although he could hardly say so, Nufkarm intended to offer a favorable trade agreement.

Both governments agreed to release their offworld

mercenaries. Movrik's agent in Azure Bay, representing the Lodge of Kootosh-Lan as well as the Iryalan Office of Special Projects, sent a pod to Splenn with notification. Romlar began work on getting his infiltrators out of Komars.

The next day, Heber Lanks, with his daughter and son-in-law, arrived back at Burnt Woods in a Komarsi floater.

When the troopship arrived from Splenn to remove the regiment, Romlar still hadn't accounted for all his infiltrators. Brossling had flown to Komars to sift through the jails there, and question leaders among the freedmen. Carrmak would have been sent, but he was still recovering from abdominal surgery.

Over the several weeks since his last fight with the T'swa, Romlar had visited the little hospital in Burnt Woods from time to time, and the army's field hospital, talking to the wounded, both troopers and T'swa. And Gulthar Kro. Kro's face had been substantially disfigured. The bullet had torn through his upper jaw, palate, and cheekbone. His speech was somewhat impaired.

By the time that Brossling had returned with the last infiltrators, Kro was in reconditioning camp. Romlar visited him there. "Gull," he said, "I owe you for grabbing that grenade."

Kro snorted a harsh laugh, and in his awkward speech said, "Colonel, you owe me nothin'." He peered hard at Romlar. "You know what I went to you for?"

Romlar shook his head. "What?"

"Undsvin sent me up here last summer to kill you. Then I kind of forgot about that. Finally I decided I better do it, so I went to your camp."

Romlar half grinned. "Really?! Well I'll be damned! Hmm. But you didn't—kill me that is. And out in the woods, you may have saved my life. You saved me getting wounded a lot worse than I was, anyway. And you were out there fighting alongside the rest of us. So I still owe you."

Kro clamped his jaw as best he could. The fit wasn't very good. The merc commander was beyond understanding.

"How'd you like your face fixed?" Romlar asked.

"Whadya mean?"

"We've got doctors on Iryala that can remake your face."

Kro's gaze was intense now. "How'd I get there?"

"I'll load you aboard with my men. After we get you there ... I've got pull. I'll tell you what. It seems to me—it seems to me we've known each other before. Long ago."

Kro looked at him more puzzled then ever.

"Do you want to go?"

"Sure I wanna go."

"Okay. I'll go to your C.O. and get you released. We're leaving tomorrow."

Seventy-nine

The regiment arrived at Splenn by ship. There Romlar arranged with the Confederation Ministry for Gulthar Kro's passage to Iryala. Kelmer Faronya and his wife would ride home in a courier. The regiment gated home, arriving at a security area of the Landfall Military Reservation. They were quartered overnight there, and given a reception next day by the OSP, with the king himself attending briefly. *Interesting*, Romlar thought. *Why the king?* Colonel Voker had flown down from Blue Forest, which was a lot easier to understand, and Varlik Lormagen, the original "White T'swi," from the school he and his wife operated on the coast.

The next day the troopers were given new paycards that accessed the credits they'd accrued, and they dispersed for a dek, most to visit their families.

Romlar, however, was taken by limousine to Lord Kristal's handsome home on the royal estate. Lotta Alsnor met him at the horseshoe drive, and they faced off, holding hands between them, looking at each other. He grinned broadly. "How come I get to have such a pretty girl?" he asked.

She laughed. "Bullshit, Artus; I'm a scrawny little minx.

Wiry anyway. But say it again; I like it." She paused for a moment, squeezing his thick hands. "I suppose you're wondering why you were brought here. And what I'm doing here."

"It has crossed my mind."

"Well then, let me take you to Emry and we'll uncross it."

She led him inside and through halls, his attention not on what he might or might not learn there, but on the beauty and harmony of the art and other furnishings he passed. He'd never imagined a home like this before.

It was more than a home. One wing held Kristal's staff—offices with people sitting at monitors, dictating to computers, talking with each other. Kristal's receptionist didn't seat them. "Just a moment," she said, then spoke quietly to a commset and disconnected. Smiling, she motioned toward a door to one side. "Go right in."

The old man was on his feet to greet them. He took Romlar's thick hard hand in both of his slender ones, and shook it. "Artus, it's good to have you back. It's spring where you've come from, right?"

"Spring going on summer."

"Well. And here you find summer half used up." His deep bright eyes examined Romlar's. "I have a new assignment for you. To start when you've had your leave." He paused. "And when I say a new assignment, I mean a *new* assignment.

"I take it your regiment came home in good mental and spiritual condition?"

"Absolutely. Most of them better than I did."

Kristal nodded as if he knew what Romlar alluded to. "Good," he said. "Good.

"Your regiment will not be contracted out again. The Confederation has its own need for it. An imperial invasion fleet is on its way, little more than two years distant. I want you to be part of a secret royal commission to develop strategies and tactics to counter it. Defuse it if possible. This will mean turning over regimental command to someone else—whoever you consider best suited to the job."

Romlar wasn't smiling now, but his face was relaxed, his answer casual. "Coyn Carrmak," he said. "He's my best battalion commander, and the smartest man I've got. Men tend naturally to listen to him and do what he says, and beyond that, he's the luckiest person I know." He glanced at Lotta then. "With the exception of your brother. Jerym's come through more than anyone else in the outfit, and unscratched."

He turned back to Kristal then. "You said the regiment isn't going to be contracted out again. What are you going to do with it?"

"Train it. That's partly where you come in. Over a period of time the commission will develop strategies and tactics, as I said. Your regiment will learn and train in tactics and techniques no one's invented yet.

"Are you willing to have the job?"

Romlar grinned. "I'm your man. It sounds interesting."

"Fine. It's yours. To begin with, you'll work here at the capital. Part of the time just down the hall."

Romlar put a hand on Lotta's arm. "And where does Lotta fit in?"

The king's personal aide laughed. "She'll take you to lunch and tell you about that. Meanwhile, I have a great deal to do here." His gesture took in not only his desk and monitor, but the whole wing. "We'll talk again, very soon. Perhaps over dinner this week."

Lotta led Romlar to his lordship's conservatory, and the small staff dining room there. They sat in a private corner beside a bank of Iryalan tropical flowering ferns, their fronds soft green. A waiter came over, described the menu and took their orders, then left.

"So what hat do you wear in all this?" Romlar asked.

"I'm Emry's psychic resource and special intelligence section."

"Then we'll both be working here."

"That's right."

"If you'll marry me, we can take an apartment together and save on rent."

"I'm afraid I can't share an apartment with you."

His eyebrows raised. "Why not?"

She laughed. "Because Emry has assigned me a small house on the hill, as free from psychic disturbances as you can get near the capital. Free official housing for his special assistant; I'm one of a kind, he tells me. To be more exact, he said: 'Lotta, you're like Artus. You're one of a kind.' "

Her smile softened. "There's lots of room for two, if you'd like to share it with me. Our schedules won't always match, but we'll be together a lot more than once every few years."

Romlar chuckled. "I love you, Lotta. Very much. I'm sure I've told you that before."

"I seem to recall something like that. Would you like to see the house? Before we fill out the marriage application?"

He laughed aloud, then leaned across the table and they kissed.

THE END

special interest. I'm not a kind, he tells her. To be more exact, he said. Come, said she. Alice, you're not a kind.

The smile widened. I have a sense of an for two minutes. We're alone a while ear. Our schedules won't always mingle, but we'll be together belong those time every few years. We're all tangled. They were little. Very simple. I never told you that before.

Want to travel round the flat. Would you like to come? Perhaps he lit and the marriage parliament. He laughed aloud, then turned toward the fire, and they stood.

THE END

Appendix

The following brief background of the Confederation and the planet Tyss, home of the T'swa, is excerpted from "The Story of the Confederation," by Brother Banh Dys-T'saben in The Young Person's Library of Knowing About *(revised edition).*

You have already heard, my friend, of the Confederation of Worlds. But as yet you do not know very much about it. The Confederation of Worlds is an organization of 27 planets on which humans live. The primaries of some of the 27 can be seen from here on Tyss. Ask your master or your lector to go outside with you some night soon and point out to you those which are visible.

Those 27 are not all of the worlds on which people are known to live in our region of the galaxy. They are simply most of those which have spaceships, and with spaceships, the Confederation worlds can usually control the others and cause them to do certain things they want them to. Our own world of Tyss is not one of the 27, of course, and we do not have spaceships. We have the T'sel, and that which grows out of it.

The story of the Confederation of Worlds is quite interesting, and until recent centuries it was known only on Tyss. Even today, most people in the Confederation do not know it.

The first part of it is also the story of how we came to live on Tyss. Very long ago, many thousands of years ago, people came to this region of space from another region very far away. They came across space in eight very large ships, at a speed much swifter than light, and the distance was so great that it took years to cross it. If you decide to follow the Way of Wisdom and Knowledge, or possibly if you do not, you will be able to visit that time and see that long journey for yourself.

They left their homes to escape a great war. The people who began that war, and who commanded it, were willing to force their wishes on others. They were willing to kill great numbers of people for that, although few of those killed had chosen for themselves the Way of War.

It was not like any war fought in this region, for they used weapons so powerful that they could kill all the people on a planet in one attack. And that is what they did—they killed all of the people on certain planets, as a warning and threat to others.

On one planet, the government on one great populous island nation bought eight ships, old but large, for they believed that their world would be chosen for destruction. And besides that, they were a people who despised and rejected war, because of the kind of war, called "megawar,"* which they had in that region. Hurriedly they prepared the ships for a very long voyage. Each ship would take several thousand people, and also things they would need when they settled to live on some far world, including seeds and certain animals. For there would be no towns or manufactories*[1] waiting, or even people, but only the native planet in its wild state. Then each sept on the island selected 1 in 200 of its people to go, and when all had boarded, the great ships left, never to return.

---

1. Words marked with an asterisk are defined and talked about in a glossary volume not provided with this book. The asterisks have been included here, however, as they give some notion of what concepts are unfamiliar to six-year-old T'swa children, and by extension, what words *are* familiar to them.

*   *   *

They traveled together on a set course, not stopping anywhere at all until they were far outside the region they knew about. They wanted to be very far away from the war before they chose a new home. After that they continued on the same general course, but deviated* to one side and another to inspect star systems along the way for a planet on which they could live.

In this way they discovered the garthid peoples, who look quite different from humans. The garthids live on planets mostly too hot, and with gravity mostly too strong, for humans. Indeed, our own world of Tyss would seem cold to the garthids, although most humans find Tyss much too hot. Nonetheless, the garthids did not want humans to settle in their sector. So the people of the ships got from them the boundary coordinates* of the garthid sector and went on, not visiting any more worlds until they were well away. Our ancestors did not want anything to do with wars, because the wars they knew had been so indiscriminate* and unethical.

At last the little fleet of ships came to systems far enough away that again they paused here and there to explore for a world they could live on. Soon they found one. It was our own Tyss.

But meanwhile, certain things had happened on the ships. By that time they had been gone from their home planet for more than four of our years. And what did they do, enclosed in a crowded ship for more than four years? The crews were busy, of course, operating the ships and taking care of them. The other people had certain things to do too, such as taking care of children and cleaning. But still, much of the time they had nothing needful to do, and they were quite crowded. So they sat about and talked a great deal. And having nothing like the T'sel, soon they were bickering.* Before long, some of them came to dislike others quite strongly.

Factions arose. A faction is a set of people who feel very strongly in favor of some one thing or set of things, or against some one thing or set of things. It is a group of people who disagree with others, and it exists only in reaction to its polar* opposites. Factions are a major cause of destructive war, which is to say, the kind of war that does not respect the different Ways.

So before they had been very long on their journey, the rulers of that fleet recognized that they carried with them the seed of the very kind of war they had fled! For given time, the factions would surely start to fight among themselves! Therefore the rulers began to counsel together about what they might do to avoid war. But they did not have the T'sel: they could not see how such wars could be avoided.

They did know, however, that the destructiveness of indiscriminate war is proportional* to the destructiveness of the weapons used. Also, the human mind is prone to explore the operating rules of the physical universe. You already know something about that. When done in a particular systematic* way, following certain rules and limitations, this exploration was known then by the names "science"* and "research."* Certain operating rules of the physical universe, or approximations* of them, which science discovered and described, could be used to do things with, or to make things with. And the doing and making were known as "technology."* The weapons of their huge destructive war had been crafted by technology, using the knowledge from science.

The rulers recognized all that.

Now, on the ships, not all of the people together had the knowledge to make those hugely destructive weapons. For theirs had not been a world which emphasized science. And indeed, not even their ships' computers,* in which they stored their knowledge, had any great part of the knowledge needed to make those weapons. But the rulers believed that the human mind, free to do research, would in time redevelop that knowledge and once again make those weapons. And this worried them greatly.

Yet they did not want to give up the machines which enabled them to live the way they had been used to. And to continue to make those machines and keep them operating required technology. So they believed they could not do without the technology.

Thus they decided to abolish* research if they could. Without research, without science, they could not redevelop the knowledge with which to reinvent those great weapons.

Reactive wars they still might have, but they would not be nearly as destructive as the war they had fled. They would still be able to kill large numbers of non-warriors—those who had not chosen the Way of War—but they would hardly be able to destroy whole populations or render planets unlivable.

To abolish science was the only thing they could think of to do about it, and they did not at first see how they could accomplish that. All they could do was to erase certain knowledge within their computers. So they erased all knowledge which they thought might be dangerous.

But they believed that that would not be enough, for it seemed to them that in time, the knowledge would be rediscovered.

Now, they knew that some of the people with them, called "mentechs," had worked in primitive technologies of the mind, which they regarded entirely as an electrochemical* system. So they sent to the mentechs and asked them if they could suggest anything.

And they could. They thought it might be possible to treat everyone who was on the ships, and their children forever, so that they would never follow the way of science. They could still follow freely the way of technology, but research—the activity of science, the exploration of the rules of the universe—would become impossible. Hopefully, even the possibility of science—the thought that there could be such a thing—would no longer occur to them.

The rulers decided to try it.

But, you may be thinking to yourself, that is going about it in a strange and illogical way. Why not simply decide not to make such weapons? Why not simply respect the different Ways? But they did not have the T'sel. So they did the best they could think of.

Soon the mentechs had developed a sequence* of actions, a treatment. This treatment caused the person to not look for understanding beyond that which people already had. It would not even occur to them that there was any further understanding to be had, and they would dislike and fear and reject any idea of it.

And secret tests showed that it was successful. People

treated and then tested thought exactly the way the men-techs had predicted.

Here is how the treatment worked. The person was given a certain special substance which, to put it briefly, made him very susceptible to obeying commands. Whatever the command might be. The commands given were, in summa-tion,* that the understanding of nature was already as com-plete as possible; nothing further was knowable. And these commands were enforced by brief shocks of great pain. It did not take long to do this, and numerous people could be treated each day on each ship.

Now, people of different septs had been put to live in different compartments of the ships, so far as possible. And when the mental treatment had been tested and proven, the rulers approached the sept leaders. They told them only that they had a mental treatment which would make it impossible to develop great weapons. They did not tell them how it was done, or what the commands were. And they asked them to prepare their people to accept treatment.

And because they feared and hated the great war so much, many agreed to accept the treatment. Some accepted because their leaders told them to; other septs voted, and accepted because the majority agreed. But five septs refused the treatment. They voted, and most of their members said they should not accept. They said that while they abhorred* the great weapons, they did not trust anything which tam-pered with the mind and would make them less able in any way.

The rulers then discussed whether they should force the treatment on those five septs. But they could not bring themselves to do that, because they had at least some respect for different ways. On the other hand, they could not make up their minds, at first, on what else to do. So for the time being, the five septs were kept locked up, totally apart from everyone else, and the rest of the people were treated—even the rulers. Even the mentechs. And by so doing, they denied themselves the satisfaction of playing or working at science. In fact, there appears to have been some loss of the willingness to question authority on anything.

What that meant was that they became a little less willing to decide each for himself, and thus tended more than before to follow orders and usual ways in directing their lives.

Soon after that, something happened that helped the rulers make up their minds about the five septs. They were by then far outside the garthid sector, and they found a planet where people could live. It was not a planet where any of them would want to live, for it was too hot there for the people of that time, and the gravity* was stronger than they were used to. But people might survive there. And because the conditions seemed so severe, it was considered that anyone living there would never be able to make great weapons. So they put three of the five septs there, with certain animals and the seeds of certain plants, which they thought might be able to live there.

That planet was Tyss, our home, and those three septs were our ancestors. And here we have lived for a very long time. Now we think the heat natural, and no more than proper, and the gravity seems just right.

Then the ships went on.

In far later times we learned what happened to the rest of the people. After Tyss, they found other planets on which people could live. Rather soon they found another that was too hot except in the coolest part, and they put there the other two septs that had refused the treatment. And after looking at several more planets, they found one which they liked very much. They called it Iryala, and made it their home.

In time they became very numerous on Iryala, and sent ships out to select other planets where some of them could go to live. Some people on Iryala wanted to follow ways that were not welcome there, and some wanted to adventure, and some, wanting to acquire wealth* and power,* thought it would be easier to do so elsewhere. After thousands of years, they occupy many worlds in this region of space. But Iryala held to itself alone the right to have manufactories to make spaceships, so Iryala was predominant.

Now, when the people of the ships landed on Iryala, they still had the machines used to prevent people from doing scientific research, and they could easily make more of them. So it was arranged that each child would also be treated when it was old enough to survive the treatment.

For thousands of years they did this, and only with our help have recently regained the concepts* of science and research. The most they could do was to recombine information they already knew into new configurations* and test them, which, of course, was very useful in colonizing Iryala and doing the many things needful to establish a self-sustaining* technology there.

But after several centuries, even making new configurations became disapproved of. So they created the concept of Standard Technology. This assumed that the existing technology was complete and perfect. Any changes in it, they believed, would degrade it from that perfection.

Meanwhile, because of the treatment, they could not know what the treatment was intended to suppress. Except of course at the deepest, least available subconscious level, the commands were no longer understood by the technicians who chanted them. The treatment, which they had named "the Sacrament," was thought of as simply a formula which would protect the people from great wars.

And after 20,000 years, knowledge of their origins faded to legends among those people because of certain things that happened. . . .

Author's Note

The T'swa, the White T'swa, and a number of the people in this book also are written about in three earlier novels from Baen Books: *The Regiment*, *The White Regiment*, and *The Kalif's War*.

JOHN DALMAS

He's done it all!

*John Dalmas has just about done it all—parachute
infantryman, army medic, stevedore, merchant
seaman, logger, smokejumper, administrative
forester, farm worker, creamery worker, technical writer, free-lance editor—and his experience is reflected in his writing. His marvelous
sense of nature and wilderness combined with
his high-tech world view involves the reader
with his very real characters. For lovers of fast-
paced action-adventures!*

THE REGIMENT

The planet Tyss is so poor that it has only one
resource: its fighting men. Each year three regiments
are sent forth into the galaxy. And once a regiment is
constituted, it never recruits again: as casualties mount
the regiment becomes a battalion ... a company ...
a platoon ... a squad ... and then there are none.
But after the last man of *this* regiment has flung
himself into battle, the Federation of Worlds will
never be the same!

THE WHITE REGIMENT

All the Confederation of Worlds wanted was a little
peace. So they applied their personnel selection technology to war and picked the greatest potential warriors out of their planets-wide database of psych
profiles. And they hired the finest mercenaries in the
galaxy to train the first test regiment—they hired the
legendary black warriors of Tyss to create the first
ever White Regiment.

THE KALIF'S WAR

The White Regiment had driven back the soldiers of
the Kharganik empire, but the Kalif was certain that

he could succeed in bringing the true faith of the Prophet of Kargh to the Confederation—even if he had to bombard the infidels' planets with nuclear weapons to do it! But first he would have to thwart a conspiracy in his own ranks that was planning to replace him with a more tractable figurehead ...

FANGLITH
Fanglith was a near-mythical world to which criminals and misfits had been exiled long ago. The planet becomes all too real to Larn and Deneen when they track their parents there, and find themselves in the middle of the Age of Chivalry on a world that will one day be known as Earth.

RETURN TO FANGLITH
The oppressive Empire of Human Worlds, temporarily filed in *Fanglith*, has struck back and resubjugated its colony planets. Larn and Deneen must again flee their home. Their final object is to reach a rebel base—but the first stop is Fanglith!

THE LIZARD WAR
A thousand years after World War III and Earth lies supine beneath the heel of a gang of alien sociopaths who like to torture whole populations for sport. But while the 16th century level of technology the aliens found was relatively easy to squelch, the mystic warrior sects that had evolved in the meantime weren't....

THE LANTERN OF GOD
They were pleasure droids, designed for maximum esthetic sensibility and appeal, abandoned on a deserted planet after catastrophic systems failure on their transport ship. After 2000 years undisturbed, "real" humans arrive on the scene—and 2000 thousand years of droid freedom is about to come to a sharp and bloody end.

THE REALITY MATRIX

Is the existence we call life on Earth for real, or is it a game? Might Earth be an artificial construct designed by a group of higher beings? Is everything an illusion? Everything is—except the Reality Matrix. And what if self-appointed "Lords of Chaos" place a chaos generator in the matrix, just to see what will happen? Answer: The slow destruction of our world.

THE GENERAL'S PRESIDENT

The stock market crash of 1994 makes Black Monday of 1929 look like a minor market adjustment—and the fabric of society is torn beyond repair. The Vice President resigns under a cloud of scandal—and when the military hints that they may let the lynch mobs through anyway, the President resigns as well. So the Generals get to pick a President. But the man they choose turns out to be more of a leader than they bargained for. . . .

Available at your local bookstore. Or you can order any or all of John Dalmas' books with this order form. Just check your choice(s) below and send the combined cover price to: Baen Books, Dept. BA, P.O. Box 1403, Riverdale, NY 10471.

PRAISE FOR
LOIS MCMASTER BUJOLD

What the critics say:

The Warrior's Apprentice: "Now here's a fun romp through the spaceways—not so much a space opera as space ballet.... it has all the 'right stuff.' A lot of thought and thoughtfulness stand behind the all-too-human characters. Enjoy this one, and look forward to the next." —Dean Lambe, *SF Reviews*

"The pace is breathless, the characterization thoughtful and emotionally powerful, and the author's narrative technique and command of language compelling. Highly recommended." —*Booklist*

Brothers in Arms: "... she gives it a geniune depth of character, while reveling in the wild turnings of her tale. ... Bujold is as audacious as her favorite hero, and as brilliantly (if sneakily) successful." —*Locus*

"Miles Vorkosigan is such a great character that I'll read anything Lois wants to write about him. ... a book to re-read on cold rainy days." —Robert Coulson, *Comics Buyer's Guide*

Borders of Infinity: "Bujold's series hero Miles Vorkosigan may be a lord by birth and an admiral by rank, but a bone disease that has left him hobbled and in frequent pain has sensitized him to the suffering of outcasts in his very hierarchical era.... Playing off Miles's reserve and cleverness, Bujold draws outrageous and outlandish foils to color her high-minded adventures." —*Publishers Weekly*

Falling Free: "In *Falling Free* Lois McMaster Bujold has written her fourth straight superb novel. ... How to break down a talent like Bujold's into analyzable components? Best not to try. Best to say 'Read, or you will be missing something extraordinary.'" —Roland Green, *Chicago Sun-Times*

The Vor Game: "The chronicles of Miles Vorkosigan are far too witty to be literary junk food, but they rouse the kind of craving that makes popcorn magically vanish during a double feature." —Faren Miller, *Locus*

MORE PRAISE FOR
LOIS MCMASTER BUJOLD

What the readers say:

"My copy of *Shards of Honor* is falling apart I've reread it so often.... I'll read whatever you write. You've certainly proved yourself a grand storyteller."
—Liesl Kolbe, Colorado Springs, CO

"I experience the stories of Miles Vorkosigan as almost viscerally uplifting.... But certainly, even the weightiest theme would have less impact than a cinder on snow were it not for a rousing good story, and good storytelling with it. This is the second thing I want to thank you for.... I suppose if you boiled down all I've said to its simplest expression, it would be that I immensely enjoy and admire your work. I submit that, as literature, your work raises the overall level of the science fiction genre, and spiritually, your work cannot avoid positively influencing all who read it."
—Glen Stonebraker, Gaithersburg, MD

" 'The Mountains of Mourning' [in *Borders of Infinity*] was one of the best-crafted, and simply best, works I'd ever read. When I finished it, I immediately turned back to the beginning and read it again, and I can't remember the last time I did that."   —Betsy Bizot, Lisle, IL

"I can only hope that you will continue to write, so that I can continue to read (and of course buy) your books, for they make me laugh and cry and think ... rare indeed."   —Steven Knott, Major, USAF

What do you say?

Send me these books!

Shards of Honor • 72087-2 • $4.99 ____
The Warrior's Apprentice • 72066-X • $4.50 ____
Ethan of Athos • 65604-X • $4.99 ____
Falling Free • 65398-9 • $4.99 ____
Brothers in Arms • 69799-4 • $4.99 ____
Borders of Infinity • 69841-9 • $4.99 ____
The Vor Game • 72014-7 • $4.99 ____
Barrayar • 72083-X • $4.99 ____

Lois McMaster Bujold: Only from Baen Books

If these books are not available at your local bookstore, just check your choices above, fill out this coupon and send a check or money order for the cover price to Baen Books, Dept. BA, P.O. Box 1403, Riverdale, NY 10471.

NAME: _____

ADDRESS: _____

_____

I have enclosed a check or money order in the amount of $ _____.